The Gravedigger's Guild

Susan E. Farris

For James & Eleanor Campbell,
Ray & Arlayne Atkinson,
and Kitty Martin.

And her children shall rise up and call her blessed.

-Prov. 31:28

CONTENTS

PROLOGUE: TWILIGHT FALLS

The magnolias and oaks groaned and stretched their deep green branches wide overhead, like an old man rising creakily from a stiff chair. In the morose twilight of early evening, the portly Mr. Roy Mullone struggled to light the torches along the walk to the Chapel of the Cross. A fickle breeze had sprung up but was doing nothing to dispel the late-May humidity of Madison, Mississippi. Or the mosquitos. He swatted at one blood-sucking devil already attacking his elbow. Branches swayed sullenly over the ancient graveyard, emitting timbrous moans the less lively occupants of the Gothic Revival's yard would have been jealous to hear. He wholly commiserated, muttering under his breath.

"One more of these ordeals then I hand it off to a younger man. Two more at most. Three." A string of unholy expletives followed as the Bic lighter nipped his finger. He had forgotten to soak the wicks. But Roy Mullone was nothing if not an innovator. He had gotten everyone, everyone, to show up for tonight's grave digging, hadn't he? Alice Matins deserved nothing less.

He massaged the swollen joints of his hand, then dug out his backup bottle of butane and carefully dribbled it on the bright cotton. With a flinch, he flicked the Bic again, but the fickle wick caught with a burst. He sighed, relieved, and trotted to the next in the long line of torches.

Twilight was slipping softly past the trees when the cars began arriving. They crunched down the gravel drive and discreetly lined the back-parking lot, leaving the spaces next to the historic Episcopalian church empty. The soft crunch of their tires resounded off the soaring river-bottom brick walls in a swelling clatter.

With a small wave towards the windshields, he turned back to his work as one by one the engines cut off and peace was restored to the clearing. The men would wait for him, one final breath of rest before their long evening of toil. A service of love for the departed. And Alice, with her years of tireless service and kindly-meant advice to each and all, was more beloved than the usual subject of interment. At least Roy thought so.

Roy had dribbled the last of his butane on the last wick when Collins Streisand popped out of his well-worn Ford truck and strolled up, looking fresh from the shower. Unsurprised at Collins' impatient appearance at his mother-in-law's wake, Roy shook out his throbbing hand while watching Collins approach.

"Evenin', Roy!" he said. He plucked the Bic from Roy's palm and spryly lit the last torch.

"Collins," Roy intoned, rubbing at his inflamed hand, "We save the last torch for the Father's prayer." Collins waved away his words, the muscles of his bicep straining against his shirtsleeve. However, he glanced towards the church, and even though the long building lay dark, Roy watched Collins' eyes swiftly scan its tall, narrow windows with their arched tops. Roy knew who he was looking for, but Maggy Matins, Collins' sister-in-law, had not yet arrived. Having spotted no one, Collins looked up at the heaven-pointed bell tower and let out a small sigh of relief.

Roy stared at him, waiting for a response. Catching his look, Collins shrugged. "Oh—it'll be a'ight. He'll understand we forgot this one time. 'Sides, it's not like anyone but us ever sees that part anyway." He glanced at his watch and back at the drive.

"These things matter—"

"Say, shouldn't he be here about now?" Collins interjected, looking over his shoulder, clearly distracted. "The undertaker will be here soon, and we should go ahead and do our bit." He shoved his hands in his pockets and hunched his shoulders. "With the weather forecast the way it is, I want everything to go as smoothly as possible this evening for my family." Roy grumbled to himself but agreed, feeling the stress behind the younger man's words. He pulled out his cell phone to check for missed messages, his arthritic fingers protesting.

"He's on his way. Just a couple minutes late. Let's go ahead and show the boys the plot so we'll be ready when he gets here." Roy flipped his phone closed and waved at the cars. Doors swung open and legs swung out. In the gloom, the Gravedigger's Guild shuffled up the path, men of all ages, races, and walks of life slapping backs and shaking hands as they came.

Behind them, their wives helloed at each other and trickled into the church's fellowship hall to prepare for the reading of the Psalms, the other half of that evening's wake. He caught delicious whiffs from the Crock-Pots and towel-wrapped casserole dishes they hefted, and his mouth watered at the thought of the potluck later. As Roy watched the couples kiss each other fondly on the cheek before drifting to their separate tasks, loneliness licked at his heart. Collins waved at his mother, Mrs. Streisand, who emerged from her car alone, as she hurried inside with a Crock-Pot full of what was sure to be her barbecued meatballs. Inside the fellowship hall, lights flicked on, oddly cheerful in the gathering gloom.

With a glance at Collins' tanned face, blank and unreadable in the lowering twilight, he asked, "Will your father be joining us tonight? We've missed him at the last couple of openings."

Collins shook his head, a grimace flickering across his tan face. "He's away on business in Nashville—trying to work out some partnership with a hot yoga chain or something." He shrugged, muttering, "Probably buy them outright, knowing him."

Roy clapped him on the shoulder, his brows furrowing in sympathy. He had heard Mr. Streisand rant at his son many times for Collins' "soft" business tactics.

"You're a good businessman in your own way. When you're not being a hard-ass like your ole' man." Collins looked at him with a purse-lipped smile and arched eyebrows. Roy looked back, eyes narrowed slyly. His stubborn nature as president combined with Collins' explosive temper as treasurer had made for a legendary and long-standing feud within the Gravedigger's Guild. But at the end of the day, they were practically family. Because of Alice. Roy's gaze drifted wistfully into the trees she'd loved so much. Collins' voice snapped him back.

"Thanks, Roy. Hopefully, things don't fall apart at the gym worse than they already have while my hard-ass is gone this weekend." Collins tilted his head from side to side, cracking his neck. "Right now, I just want to get through this evening without anything blowing up." His brow furrowed, and he pressed his lips together, uncharacteristically anxious. "I don't think Quinn can take any more stress."

Roy nodded. "Don't worry. We'll get through this with a minimum of pyrotechnics." Collins chuckled as Roy turned to greet the men who strode up around them. He looked over their jeans and sturdy shoes and nodded, a faint smile drifting across the Guild president's face. They had come dressed to work.

The men had gathered in a half-moon around him and Collins. Richard "Rick" Seymour elbowed Collins good-naturedly while Charlie Plath fiddled with a torch, knocking it askew. Roy cast his eyes at the clouds above them, praying for patience with the meddlesome man, then clasped his hands.

"Well," he said, drawling the word out sociably, "Let's go take a look at Mrs. Matins' plot, shall we?" They tramped off through the moss-covered headstones, leaving footprints in the dampening grass.

Collins lingered. Irritated, Roy turned to urge him along and saw worry pinch his usually placid brow. A dark BMW pulled up the drive and parked next to the church. Maggy had come early.

DAY ONE: CLOUDS GATHER

CHAPTER ONE

Despite the overcast sky, the red folder glared up at Maggy from the passenger seat in the watery light of early afternoon. She had no idea why she had left it there to torment her instead of tucking it into her briefcase on the backseat with her long-neglected sketchbook filled with old drawings of magnolia blossoms and cabins covered in kudzu. Or why she'd bothered to bring the briefcase—it wasn't like she needed it after her last conversation with Heather.

Briefly, she considered pulling over and putting the folder away, but shook her head and shot a glare at the dash as the radio spewed static. After nearly two days in the car driving from New York City, she would be at her older sister Quinn's house in a few minutes and would be able to slide the folder deep inside a dark inner pocket and not think about any of it for a while.

She didn't know what had possessed her to stop by the lawyer's office on the way through Jackson, anyway. At the time she had reasoned it was a chance to stretch her cramping legs, but now she found herself mentally backpedaling. Mr. Leonard would be happy to talk to her and Quinn together after the funeral. Even if Maggy was technically the estate executor, no need to go rogue dealing with this, right?

The butter yellow, Craftsman-style house with its many

gabled windows appeared through the trees, ancient pecans lining the drive. Even in the gloomy weather, the small house looked cheerful and bright, bikes and soccer balls and other toys littering the yard—a homey contrast to the pull-out couch of Olivia's six-floor walk-up where she was currently crashing after her breakup with Marcus last month. Mama had been impressed by his good looks, fancy degree, and quick rise through the law firm, and so had Maggy, but now... She cut off the thought before it could spiral further into the roiling darkness that seemed to continuously lodge behind her breastbone these days, curling up her throat like the kudzu creeping along the road to constrict her breath and choke her voice to a whisper.

She blinked hard and wiped at her eyes. She had worse things to deal with now than boyfriend problems. Rolling her tired shoulders as she stared at the house in the distance, Maggy thought of the travel set of watercolors she had left in New York. Quinn's house would have been the perfect little vignette to paint.

As the house loomed, the paint's brightness grew almost obnoxious. An empty Pampers box sat on the curb next to the trash, and guilt twisted uneasily in Maggy's stomach. This would be her first time meeting her four-month-old niece, Clara. Maggy remembered the flatness of Quinn's voice, how vaguely she'd answered when Maggy had called at her mother's urging to suggest she come down from NYC to help out as she had done for the other babies, back in February a few days before Clara was born. Her sister's noncommittal answer hadn't inspired much desire to hazard her boss Heather's ire, infamous even in the fashion industry, so she had let the matter die.

Maggy plucked at a loose thread on the wheel as she studied the yard, weeds growing up around the neon pink azaleas and deep blush roses that should have been trimmed last season. If Maggy were honest with herself, worsening deadlines at work and a long drive could only account for so much neglect on her part.

The folder glowed up at her from the passenger seat. Quinn had dealt with so much on her own with Mama's sudden illness and the funeral, on top of a cranky newborn—it couldn't hurt if Maggy took care of executing the estate, right? Frustrated, Maggy drummed her thumbs on the wheel. So decisive at work, when it came to her family, she became bogged down in frustration and indecision. Irritated, she slapped off the radio, its static mumblings and blips finally overwhelming her taut nerves.

She turned into the drive, pecans snapping and popping under her tires over the familiar crunch of gravel. Every time she turned down a country drive, she missed the deep and steady rumble of her truck's engine, the proud gleam of the hood in the afternoon sunlight. But Mama had been right. With its gas-guzzling mileage and unwieldy length, it wasn't practical for city driving. Now, there was more than the truck to miss.

She parked and sat, an ache in her heart and knuckles white on the steering wheel, staring up at the house. In the sunlight, the wide windows winked at her as if letting her in on some private joke. An abandoned scooter leaned against the front porch steps, already deep in a breezy shadow. Geraniums bobbed cheerfully in their pots between the latticed porch rails. Modest compared to most of the other area homes, the tidy little Craftsman was positively palatial to Maggy. Before this trip, she had always stayed at Mama's, a cozy, faux-log ranch a few miles west. Despite her visits over here before, and Collins' many snaps of her nieces and nephews running rampant through it, this house still felt foreign and a bit off-limits without Mama's chaperoning, or rather refereeing, presence.

Quinn's call inviting her to stay had surprised her, almost more than the other call, the one about Mama. She pushed back the memory, anger curdling in her stomach and turning her mouth sour. She released her white-knuckled grip, then pulled her bright hair loose from the messy topknot she had tossed it in for the drive. She shook away the rising heat as she shook out her hair.

The screen door of the open-air carport swung open with a creaking slap, errant children spilling out the side of the house. Collins and Mrs. Hernandez, the babysitter, followed a few steps behind, hollering. A raucous chorus of "Aunt Mags!" and "I told you it was her!" drifted through the car and she grinned, waving.

Outside her window, a matching pair of sunshine-bright mops and excited blue eyes greeted her, and four hands left lots of sticky prints. She cracked the door.

"Back up, boys! I don't want to whack you!" Laughter answered her as the ten-year-old twins, Davy and Liam, scuffled away. As soon as she stepped out of the car she was tackled backward as strong, young arms wrapped around her waist mercilessly in anaconda hugs. Collins stood back, grinning with arms crossed as he watched his brood attack their aunt. The spry Mrs. Hernandez made clucking sounds and told them not to strangle their aunt, but she was smiling as she spoke and waved at Maggy.

"Oof! When did you get so tall!" Maggy laughed and hugged her nephews, stooping to wrap them in her arms. They smelled of funky boy sweat and peanut butter, which was smeared all over their faces. She bopped Liam on the nose, his telltale freckles giving him away.

"Hey, you're supposed to eat your food, not wear it!" Mouth still full of said sandwich, he grinned at her and stuck out his tongue.

"Why just eat it when I can wear it too?" He waved the PB&J and took another big bite before Davy pushed him aside and shoved a dinosaur figurine towards Maggy.

"Look what Dad got me! It even roars!" Davy's curly hair bounced as he jumped up and down to emphasize each word. He punctuated the sentence by roaring along with the dinosaur. Widening her eyes, Maggy oohed along appropriately. Mrs. Hernandez shooed the rascals back towards the house with warnings to go finish their lunch for-gods-sake or no dessert tonight, and they shot off, pushing and shoving each other. A small hand tugged at hers and Maggy looked down to find four-year-old Kylie—with her straight, dark hair so like Collins and big, blue eyes like Quinn—looking up at her shyly.

Maggy picked her up and squeezed her in a big hug. "Hello! How's my little sunshine?" Kylie smiled and put her face down on Maggy's shoulder, wrapping her arms around her neck. "Ok,

I'm going to take that as a 'good!' Are you doing good?" A small nod into her shoulder and a wiggle answered her.

Collins strode up with Allie trailing behind him. With a jolt, Maggy noted that he was in gym clothes. Surely her brother-in-law wasn't about to go to work this afternoon? They had the wake tonight, and she couldn't imagine Quinn would be happy if he disappeared.

"She's going through a shy phase right now." He tickled Kylie's ribs. She giggled. He leaned over and side-hugged Maggy. Kylie wriggled from her arms to follow her brothers in a mad dash towards the house. "You must be tired from the drive—New York is a long ways. I'll take your stuff upstairs for you if you like."

She nodded gratefully and handed him the keys before turning to gush over her oldest niece. Sixteen and now taller than either of her parents, it seemed Allie—named Alice after her grandmother and affectionately nicknamed "Allie"—had sprung up overnight. With dark brunette hair and dark eyes, Maggy was stunned to find her Star Wars-loving, mad-backyard-scientist niece wearing makeup. Looked like there had been some developments since she had visited at Christmas.

With a grin, Maggy bear-hugged her, then motioned for her to spin. Allie rolled her eyes but complied. Her days spent running cross-country were paying off too. She had a stunning tan and all the baby fat had melted away and was replaced with the trim runner's physique that was hard to miss. Maggy nodded approvingly, crossing her arms and tapping a forefinger on her elbow.

Behind her, Collins hauled her overstuffed bag into the house. A minute later, he toted out what looked to be an enormous cooler and put it into her trunk. Maybe being a gym rat was good for something if it gave you muscles that could handle that without breaking a sweat. Maggy was puffing to make it up to Olivia's apartment.

She refocused on Allie. "Well, it looks like some of the Matins-family fashion sense has rubbed off on you after all," she said, surveying the nerd-chic look Allie had going on with her

Vans and ripped jeans. Allie smiled and flipped her hair back.

"I tried. Do you like it?"

"You look fabulous!" She wrapped an arm around the girl's shoulders, which she had to stretch up a bit to do, and they strolled towards the house. "And I hear you've been doing well with track, even won a few medals. Enjoying it?"

"It's all right. I don't know if I'll run next year; it takes a lot of time and I have to go to practice during the summer. Thinking about taking art instead now that Gran won't be coming to all the meets."

Quinn was going to flip when she heard that. Maggy nodded, trying to play it cool. "If that's what you want to do. But tell me about life! I need all the gossip!" Biting her lip, Allie looked towards the windows.

"Can you stay? For a while, I mean." Maggy paused and drew Allie to a stop to listen. The girl glanced at the windows again nervously. "Things have been… tense. Since Clara was born. I've been trying to help, but it's been really hard the last few days since Gran died. I'm…" Tears gathered at the corners of her eyes and she blinked hard. "I'm worried about Mom. She hasn't been herself."

Maggy rubbed Allie's arms and pulled her in for a hug, reaching for the best words. "I'll stay for as long as I can, sweetie." She stepped back and looked at her. "What do you mean by tense?"

Allie gulped. "Mom's been so snappish the last few days. Hollerin' at us and randomly exploding. I know we're a handful, but she's usually so patient and takes time to explain things. Now, she's just going, 'Do it 'cuz I say so' and storming off." She rubbed at her arms. "She loves having music playing on the radio and it's been silent." Alarm bells went off in Maggy's mind with aching familiarity. "And I keep finding her alone, just crying. The littlest things seem to set her off."

Maggy worried at her lip. "Things will be different with Grandma gone. People—well, people who are grieving aren't themselves. Try to remember that." A loud clatter echoed from inside the house, and she could hear Collins hollering at Davy and Liam. "I'll see what I can do to help your mom." As they strolled towards the house, she thought about the contents of her luggage. If she was going to stay past the weekend, she might need to borrow some clothes from Quinn. All her clothes were on the formal side. Not that she had many casual clothes to begin with, in her line of work. Maybe now was a good time to invest in some comfier clothes. She swung the screen door open with a creak and reminded herself that clothes of any kind would have to wait until her bank account wasn't screaming at her.

It was calmer inside than she had expected. And eerily silent, just as Allie had said. Through the window over the sink, Maggy could see Mrs. Hernandez surveying the twins and Kylie from her perch on a lawn chair as they ran in dizzying loops around the backyard. Collins leaned on the island sipping a glass of water, staring up the stairs to his left, a gym bag at his feet. He set the water down and took a step as if about to climb the stairs, but halted, brow creased. On the marble counter of the island stood eight dark jugs of sweet tea and several bright tubs of sliced lemons. Maggy blinked, then chuckled. The cooler Collins put into her trunk earlier suddenly made more sense.

"I take it, Quinn went a little overboard in prepping drinks for tonight?" she asked. He shot her a scowl and shrugged but remained silent. Taken aback, she wondered what was eating him. Allie shrugged, palms up, and mouthed, "Good luck," before scurrying upstairs. Parched from the car, Maggy set her purse down and grabbed a glass from the cabinet.

As she filled it at the tap, she watched Collins from the corner of her eye, his jaw clenching and unclenching. Allie had been right about the tension. Impudently, she decided to test it.

"Are you about to head to one of the gyms?" she asked. She kept her voice even and neutral.

"Oh, don't you start on me too!" He snapped and turned to face her. She looked at him, eyebrows raised. She motioned at his sweatpants and branded shirt.

"Saw the clothes and thought I'd ask. It's just a question."

He rubbed at his forehead and leaned back on the island.

"You Matins women and your 'questions.' Yes, I've got to

go sign some new-hire paperwork over at the Lefleur gym—the one that we opened right before Clara was born—and there's a piece of equipment that's acting up I need to check on. It shouldn't take long." Maggy shrugged and *hmmed* in her throat. His voice ticked up, defensive. "Jesus, you're just like your mama with the side-eyes and all that. If I don't go do it now, I won't be able to until Sunday afternoon at the earliest and the dang thing's too expensive to get torn up."

Stung, she clacked the glass down. She fought to keep her voice even. "I understand work pressure, Collins." She leaned her hip on the island across from him. She was achy from the long drive and didn't want to sit at one of the new-looking, country-chic barstools. Quinn must be on a redecorating streak.

"How could you? You don't own a business. Or multiple in my case. My dad co-signed the loan for Lefleur and he's on my back because membership isn't where it needs to be. And with the new baby always crying, I haven't had the energy to tackle it…" As the words tumbled out of him, he trailed off and rubbed at the back of his neck, flushing. "Sorry, I shouldn't lay all of that on you. Forget it." She chewed her lip, wondering if she should tell him.

"I just got fired." His head shot up.

"What? You love that job!"

If only he knew what it was like. "We were on a deadline. When I told my boss I was leaving for the funeral, she said that was job abandonment and fired me on the spot."

His mouth fell open. "Is she crazy?"

"Kinda. Yeah." They looked at each other for a moment and then laughed, rocking back and forth at the absurdity of something so stupid.

"You could sue, ya' know."

"That's what Olivia told me. But I don't even know if HR will let it go through. Or if I'd want to sue. Or if I want to go back. There's a lot of 'ifs' right now. I just want to get through this weekend." She leaned her elbows on the counter and sipped at her water, considering how thoroughly her life had fallen apart in the last few weeks.

He rubbed at his face. "Shit." He glanced up the stairs again. "This is really bad timing. But look, I saw the folder."

Maggy held a poker face even as her heart flipped. Shoot, she had forgotten to put it away. So, he was so pissy about that? As he put down his glass, she decided a good offense was the best defense.

"You had no business looking through my things." She set her glass down as well, clasped her hands, and pinned him with her stoniest "I am the boss here" stare, perfected from years of working in the cut-throat fashion editing industry. Forget that her career was going up in flames right now, she at least had some skills to show from it.

He waved a hand dismissively, not put off by her glare. "How long have you known?"

"Known what, exactly?"

He put his hand on the counter and stared her down. "Known that you were estate executor!"

She relaxed a little, forcing her shoulders to ease down from where they had taken residence up by her ears. So, he hadn't read any farther than she had.

"For your information, I only found out yesterday—Mr. Leonard called. He said I should come sign the paperwork." She twisted her earring. "So, I swung by on my way through Jackson. I haven't even read the will yet… haven't been able to make myself." He scoffed, and she raised her eyebrows. "I swear I didn't know. Mama never said anything to me about it."

Shoving his hands in his pockets, Collins stood up straighter. "You need to tell her. Soon."

"I will." Maggy took another sip of her water.

"Quinn doesn't like when things are kept from her."

With a long exhale, Maggy stood too. "I know. Believe me, I know."

"Then why don't you go tell her now?!"

She huffed, hating how their interactions always devolved. Collins was such a hot head she could never take him seriously. How had they ever dated? "There's no need…"

"There's plenty of need!" His volume rose and a flush began

creeping up his neck.

"If you've forgotten, you married my sister, not me, so stop trying to order me around! It won't work." At her reminder, he colored tomato red, his fists clenching on the counter. Inhaling slowly and letting it settle, she rubbed at her eyes, sore from staring at the road. She had too much angst in her own life right now to deal with his.

At his continued silence, she offered a token explanation—not that she owed him one. "Look, I'm waiting to talk to Quinn about it until we can both go to Mr. Leonard. He knows all the details of the will and how executing an estate even works. It just makes sense!" She held up a hand as Collins opened his mouth to retort. "I'm not going to drop a bomb on her. But I have NO answers right now, so I think it's best if we don't worry about it right this second. Maybe tonight. Maybe tomorrow after the funeral."

He took a step back, crossed his arms, and took a deep breath, letting it out slowly.

"Fine. But it's on you when she reacts badly when she finds out you waited." With that he grabbed his gym bag and stormed out the garage door behind her, letting it fall to with a bang. She listened as he cranked his truck with a loud rev and backed down the drive, spraying rocks.

Before she could move, her phone dinged for the first time in hours. She dove for her purse by the sink and emerged with the glowing device. Thumbing it open, she scanned her messages hopefully. She had already sent her resume and cover letter around to a half dozen other publications. She didn't know how she felt about staying in fashion; it had been more Mama's passion than hers, a way "to put Maggy's artistic talents to good use." But with her bank account dwindling fast, now was not the time to consider a career change. The thought of gas money for the drive back to New York made her cringe; she'd probably have to sleep in the car.

Her eyes dimmed when she read the text from her temporary "roommate" and best friend from art college Olivia. She was the only one of her friends from school who hadn't told her she'd sold out when she'd taken her first job in fashion editing, and she'd been there the day Olivia's first show had tanked and overnight she'd had to figure out how to rebuild her career.

Hey sweetie! Thinking of you. Heather called. I had to tell her like 5 times that you'll pick up your stuff when you get back. She tried to get me to come get it. I guess you blocked her number? (Good for you) She said you weren't answering.

Maggy tapped out a quick reply.

Yeah, I blocked her after she cussed me out when I told her I couldn't turn around & drive 10 hrs back to pick up 1 box of things. Told her to leave it with security. #nothankyou #dramafreeforme

More drama from Heather when she desperately needed a break. For the last six months, Heather had thrown tighter and tighter deadlines and ridiculous demands at Maggy. By the grace of God, she'd met them all. She didn't know if Heather were trying to make her quit or testing her to see how she would handle a promotion. What she had not expected was being fired on the spot when she had told her boss that she needed to take two weeks of bereavement leave. With that, she supposed she had her answer. Nervously, she wondered if Heather had blacklisted her.

A string of hearts and party crackers finally answered her text. With a smile, Maggy silenced her phone and went to find Quinn and hopefully, her newest niece.

They were upstairs in Kylie's sunlit room, Quinn drowsing in the overstuffed armchair she always used when nursing, a little swaddled bundle held to her breast. Worried, Maggy noted the dark circles under her eyes and new lines sneaking across her forehead. She wondered if she should send her a care package of the eye cream and retinol moisturizer she used or if Quinn would be insulted by it. With a shrug, she filed it away as a question for Collins. Maggy gently shook her shoulder.

"Hey! I'm here," she whispered. Guilt snaked around her throat and squeezed, and she took a step back, swallowing hard.

Quinn stirred, pulling her shirt back in place. Honey-bright hair the same shade as Maggy's fell in her eyes and she pushed it behind her ear, smiling wanly.

"How was the drive?" Quinn asked in a whisper as she shifted Clara. The tiny baby stirred and hiccupped out a cry and Maggy watched as Quinn visibly held her breath until she settled.

"It was long," Maggy answered. "Same as always. But I'm very excited to see this little one! How are you holding up?" She spoke softly, sensitive to how tense Quinn was with this baby; she had never seen her look quite this on edge before. Quinn didn't answer, distractedly swaddling the blanket a little tighter. Touching her older sister's shoulder gently, Maggy repeated her question. Even as a new mother at nineteen, Quinn had been such a confident mom, always two steps ahead of Allie's shenanigans and chuckling indulgently at her antics while seeming to continue effortlessly navigating her college classes—with a hefty dose of help from Mama. It wasn't like her to look out of sorts and anxious.

"Hmm? Oh, we're making it." Quinn sat back, settling the baby gently into the crook of her arm. "It's been pretty rough the last couple of days with everything, but we're making it," she repeated. With a big yawn, she leaned her head back. "Is Mrs. Hernandez here?"

Maggy nodded. "I left her in the backyard corralling the boys and Kylie."

"Good. Good. Maybe we can get a proper nap in before tonight." She rubbed at her face and groaned, the air whistling out. "I take it Collins has already left for *Lefleur*?" The word drawled sarcastically. "I could hear y'all a bit downstairs."

"Yes. Sorry if we disturbed you." Maggy watched as Quinn closed her eyes for a moment, frowned deeply, and rolled her shoulders. She stood up, handling Clara as carefully as a live grenade.

"Well, at least I can always tell when you're here because you get Collins good and riled up. The way you two bicker. What was it this time?"

The red folder flashed in Maggy's mind and she bit at her lip. "I asked Collins why he was in gym clothes. He got a little bit defensive about it." It was half of the truth. Quinn glanced at her and nodded.

"Not surprised. I kinda gave him heck over that earlier."

Quinn laid Clara down in the crib before flicking on the baby monitor. Maggy hesitated, then stepped up beside her and gazed down at her sleeping niece, with her dark wisps of hair, button nose, and puckered lips. Her chubby little cheeks shot a pang of envy through Maggy as she gently traced a finger across her sleeping niece's palm.

"She is such a pretty baby, Quinn." She put her hand on her sister's shoulder. Quinn covered it with her own.

"She is. I don't get to see her peaceful like this very often, but she is a pretty baby." Quinn conceded. "My little surprise baby." Maggy squeezed her hand. "And it's about dang time you came to see her!" Quinn said, a lighter note in her voice as they turned to leave the room.

As they went down the stairs and sat in the surprisingly tidy living room together, Maggy filled her in on what had been happening: her increasing workload at the magazine and unexpected dismissal, the fights and breakup with Marcus. She tried to keep it light, seeing Quinn's growing fatigue.

"Oh honey, I'm so sorry about all of that. It sounds awful," Quinn murmured. Picking at the lint on the couch, Maggy looked to where her sister was curled up around one of her many handmade throw pillows. The room was filled to bursting with framed inspirational artwork, snuggly blankets, and cozy throw pillows—even more so than Maggy's last visit. Over the monitor, the baby bleated then quieted, causing Quinn's shoulders to shoot up to her ears. Allie's words echoed in Maggy's head. She studied her sister as she spoke, knowing Quinn got crafty when she was feeling cooped up at home.

"It was. It still is. I need to find a new apartment and now a job. It's a lot to deal with." Maggy watched as Quinn glanced at the baby monitor again, then buried it underneath the pillow. Maggy looked down, plucking at the couch, stomach churning. "How have things been here? I was so worried about you and Collins dealing with everything—" Quinn cut her off.

"We've got everything arranged and Catherine has been wonderful, marshaling the ladies to get the house clean and drop off enough casseroles for the entire summer. All we have to do is bring drinks tonight for the wake and open the front door tomorrow for the reception." Quinn spoke crisply but wouldn't meet her eye; her lips paled. Maggy's heart pinched at the mention of Quinn's best friend Catherine and she licked her lips.

"I meant with Mama passing... and how you're feeling."

Quinn fiddled with the pillow's fringe. "I'm ok. Or at least ok for the circumstances. I mean, we just lost our mom." She sniffled and reached for a crochet-covered tissue box. Maggy pulled the lint out from under her nail. It still didn't feel real to her, Mama being gone. She had even started dialing her number on the drive down, habit kicking into gear with the car. She looked at Quinn's reddened eyes, so bleary and pleading for understanding.

Quinn continued, "I just don't know what to do without her. Think about it: we're orphans now." The thought landed like a sucker punch, and Maggy struggled to inhale, pressing a hand to her diaphragm and willing the muscle to move. Quinn spewed on, "Like how am I supposed to deal with that? I don't feel like I'll ever be whole again, ya' know?" Tears streamed down Quinn's face and she blew her nose loudly, turning the tissue and blowing even louder. She looked at Maggy, waiting.

Maggy blinked at her, mind stuttering as it struggled to process that she was truly alone in the world. She shoved her fist further into her abdomen, willing herself to breathe. Finally, air whooshed back into Maggy's empty lungs, cold and shocking.

"Yeah, I know," she lied, feeling numb. "I know what you mean."

CHAPTER TWO

In a rush to get the children bathed and into pajamas for the evening, Quinn had forgotten to tell Allie that wakes were not a place for cleavage. She was always forgetting things these days.

Now, her sixteen-year-old daughter stood before her in a bright red, plunging V-neck dress and thick, wingtip eyeliner that would make her grandmother roll over in her grave, or casket, as the case may be. Where in the world had that flimsy bit of clothing even come from? Foggily, Quinn considered upping her Wi-Fi security game and maybe getting one of those debit cards that lets you approve every single purchase as well. Her scattered musings were brought back to earth by her daughter's rage.

"It's just a dress! You're not being fair!" Allie stormed about the living room, waving her arms, picking pillows up off the couch and tossing them back down at key points. Four-year-old Kylie stood wrapped in her froggy bathrobe, hugging Quinn's leg, thumb securely in her mouth. Her eyes widened as she studied her sister. Doing her best to shake herself out of the funk she had been in all day, Quinn watched Allie dispassionately from the kitchen, which was open to the family room. When Allie was in one of these moods, it was best to let the storm rage itself out. Allie got her temper honestly from her mother.

"We are going to honor your grandmother's life. Not flaunt your body for that boy." That one was met with a particularly hostile glare. After catching Allie and her childhood friend, Harry, making out a few weeks ago, Quinn had been sworn to secrecy. On the condition that Allie tell her father—and soon. With her tattle-tale brothers so close by, Quinn was risking spilling the beans, and she knew it. She watched as an idea lit up her daughter's face, her contoured eyebrows shooting up. Allie picked up a pillow. In hindsight, the ridiculous number of pillows had been a good investment, even if Quinn had protested the cost with Mama at the time. They gave Allie something safe on which to take out her moods.

Allie began, "I could put a sweater on…"

Quinn cut in. "And the next thing I know, you'll have taken it off because you're 'too hot' and be scandalizing the entire church. I was once a teenager myself."

"But…" she tried to rejoin. Quinn held up her hands, having had enough. She had four other children to take care of and herself to get ready, and they were already running short on time, even with Mrs. Hernandez and Maggy helping.

"Tonight is not the night for this. If you want to come, go change into something that will not make you the gossip of the church for the next month. Or keep that on and stay here. Your choice."

"Grandma's dead. She's not going to care what I wear." Allie's mouth formed a perfect O. Her eyes went wide in shock as she realized how horrible the words sounded out loud.

Pressing her hands together in front of her mouth, Quinn muttered, "Jesus help me," then replied, voice shaking and quiet, "I'm going to pretend you didn't say that, for your sake."

Danger averted and anger already back in full force, Allie threw down the pillow with particular vigor and stomped up the stairs. Quinn rubbed at her temples as she listened to the thud of her steps. Allie's outbursts the last few days had been violent enough to rival her own. Her thoughts drifted towards family grief counseling but were interrupted.

"What if I put a cami on under it?" drifted back towards her.

"Absolutely not!" Quinn yelled up the stairs. A door slammed so hard the plates in the cabinet rattled. With a sigh, she wiped at her face and turned back to Kylie, who still stood beside her, thumb in mouth. Distracted, she pulled the thumb out with a pop. She could really use Collins' help tonight getting the kids settled, but he was gone again.

Swallowing her irritation at her MIA partner, she tugged at her rumpled shirt and picked up her phone from the marble counter where she had abandoned it when Allie walked in. As she turned the device over in her hand, she realized despite the annoying number of committees she was on, her phone had been startlingly quiet in the days since Mama had died. She tried to push the thought aside and run down her mental to-do list instead. She took a sip of her cold coffee and added "research grief counseling" to her notes app. Outside, the clouds looked awful; she needed to check the weather, then feed the baby, then get dressed herself...

Kylie tugged at her hand. "Mama, I'm getting cold," she whimpered. Quinn's stomach plummeted into her feet. She had forgotten the child standing right in front of her.

"Oh baby, I'm sorry." Quinn scooped her up, phone still in hand with the unread weather report queued up, and plodded upstairs. Kylie's damp head nestled on her shoulder, her weight hanging uncomfortably from her neck. Exhaustion was already beginning to wear on Quinn. Her nerves were as frayed as a rope pulled to the snapping point. At the top of the stairs, she tripped over an invisible toy, its sharp ridges telling her it was probably one of the twins' dinosaur figures.

She bit her lip to keep from cursing as she stumbled into the wall, clumsily turning so as not to crush Kylie. A wedding picture, glass already broken out, was not so lucky and crashed to the floor. As Quinn shakily set down Kylie and bent to replace the picture, the door to the old nursery swung open.

Maggy stepped out in a high-waisted dress with box pleats, concern on her face and a couple of books in one arm. She tripped over the same dinosaur toy and it roared at her in protest. The books flew as Maggy windmilled her arms to keep from falling as well. They landed, pages splayed, at Quinn's feet to reveal a worn Bible and a dog-eared romance novel. Ever dramatic, Maggy recovered with a flourish that would have made an Olympic gymnast proud. Kylie giggled. Quinn rolled her eyes. She didn't have time for this.

Without missing a beat, Maggy hollered over her shoulder towards a lit doorway down the hall, "Davy! I told you to pick up your brontosaurus earlier. Come get it, now, before it kills someone!"

"Sorry, Aunt Mags!" Davy bounded down the hall in dinosaur pajamas, his light hair a mirror to his aunt's—and scooped up his toy. *When will Davy and Liam's dinosaur phase end?* Quinn thought. He flashed a grin that revealed a missing tooth and loped back down the hall, roaring.

Quinn stared, irritated, as Maggy bent and retrieved the books, turning the cover in an attempt to hide the busting-out blonde of the smutty romance from Kylie's view. Without looking, she tossed the paperback over her shoulder into the darkened room.

"A bit of light reading?" Quinn asked, voice brittle. Since she had stopped "helping" Collins with the accounting at the gym when she was pregnant with the twins, she couldn't remember the last time she'd had a chance to read uninterrupted, even on the toilet. In the last week, Quinn had realized just how much Mama had *done* around here in her many impromptu visits. From straightening pillows on the couch to folding loads of laundry and picking up the never-ending trail of toys, there just seemed to be so much more to do without her constant presence popping in and out from breakfast to bedtime. Maggy looked up, her fingers smoothing the onion skin pages of her Bible. She looked back down, continuing to undo all the folds and creases.

"Olivia's been lending them to me. They help to take my mind off things." Finished, she turned and set the Bible on the nightstand inside the door, then knelt and grabbed a pair of shoes before shutting the door. A pair of Louis Vuitton heels that cost more than Quinn's mortgage dangled from Maggy's hand. Quinn chewed at her nail.

"And what sort of things would you need your mind taken off of?" She tried to make her tone light, but even to her it sounded acidic. She looked down and tugged at the tufted carpet with her toes—she needed to run a vacuum up here. Maybe she should get one of those habit tracking apps or post a chore chart on the fridge as Mama had suggested...

"Besides a dead mother?" Maggy's tone was that of a socialite, poised and calm but with icy warning underneath. Belatedly, Quinn foggily remembered something about a breakup and her boss not being happy about her coming down for the funeral. Maggy fiddled with a buckle on the stilettos, waiting for an answer. Down the hall, Clara began crying, and she rubbed at her forehead, needing to wrap this up.

"I'm sorry, Mags. This whole situation—," Quinn waved a hand vaguely at the house and a spit-up stain on her T-shirt, "—just has me so tired. I'm half out of my mind. Forgive me?"

Maggy, who had glanced over her shoulder towards the crying as well, nodded tightly before softening. "Of course. I know things haven't been easy." She paused and inhaled. "And *I'm* sorry I didn't make it down to help out. Things have been complicated."

She took a step and set the shoes down by the top of the stairs. With surprising speed and an alarming amount of bobby pins that appeared as if by magic, Maggy twisted her hair into a swirly updo worthy of a magazine cover while managing to avoid Quinn's deepening frown. Who had time to do hair when a baby was crying? Mama's always put-together appearance flashed before her, eternally cool and unwrinkled in her sundresses, and Quinn grimaced as she watched her sister's flashing fingers.

Unable to help herself, Quinn asked, "I thought you were helping Mrs. Hernandez get the twins bathed?" Maggy looked at her as she slipped the last pin in place, smooth face betraying no twinge of anger or irritation. Quinn gripped her phone tighter.

Annoyingly calm, Maggy, of course, had an answer. "I took

Liam, and she took Davy. They're both bathed, already in their pajamas—which are adorable by the way—and have brushed their teeth. I was taking a minute to get dressed and unpacked. Want me to get Kylie into her pajamas while you get ready?" Her voice ticked up in a query. Quinn looked down at her bathrobed toddler. Kylie, eyes big and round in adoration, stood staring up at Maggy. Kylie had been glued to Quinn all week, the change in the atmosphere making her usually sunshiny personality anxious and dim. She had brightened up considerably since Maggy walked in that afternoon which, Quinn reminded herself, was a good thing. But it still stung.

"Alright," Quinn huffed, and Maggy bent to pick up the now grinning and wiggling little girl as Quinn took a step toward Clara's wails. Feeling frumpy in her frayed jeans and soiled shirt, Quinn ran her fingers through her short, frizzy hair, trying to work out the worst tangles. When was the last time she had brushed her hair out? March? Her thoughts drifted as she headed towards Clara's room. Maggy's voice interrupted her, and she turned to see Maggy with Kylie on her hip and perfectly groomed brows quirked.

"Oh, I meant to ask. Do you have Mama's pearls? She was always wearing them, so I thought she might have given them to you for safekeeping when she went to the hospital. And well… she promised them to me. I was kinda wanting to wear them tonight if I could."

With an audible plop, Quinn let her hands drop. She groaned. "Yeah, I'm sure I put them in the safe somewhere, but it's buried under a mountain of laundry right now—" Maggy waved her free hand vigorously, cutting her off.

"Forget I mentioned it. It's not worth stressing over right now." She smiled and turned to head down the hall. Quinn looked at the time on her phone and called after her.

"Oh hey! We were supposed to meet the ladies at the church like ten minutes ago with the drinks." She held up the glowing screen to show Maggy. "But I still need to feed the baby. The cooler with water for the Guild is already in your car. Once you get Kylie dressed, would you mind heading on without me?" She paused and did some quick mental gymnastics—if feeding Clara didn't take too long and she threw on whatever… "I'll only be, like, five minutes behind you."

She finished, an optimistic smile plastered on her face. When had a basic conversation with her little sister gotten so strained? An uncomfortable flutter answered in her stomach, but she pressed a hand to her waist and willed away the rising heartburn.

Shifting Kylie to her other hip, Maggy nodded, her head cocked slightly. "Do you want me to take Allie on with me as well?" They both winced as they heard the bathroom door slam.

"We're having a bit of a wardrobe crisis at the moment. Let me handle her," Quinn said as she rolled her eyes. They both suppressed grins—a flash of their old selves back for a second. Then Maggy turned her shoulders ever so slightly and the veil fell back over. An all too familiar heat flared under Quinn's breastbone at the calm look on her sister's face as she turned fully back to Quinn. She should look as pale, red-eyed, and heartsick as Quinn knew she did herself. Instead, Maggy stood there looking like a fashion plate in a pleated and tucked dress with a sweetheart neckline. She pressed at the thick pad of flesh between her thumb and forefinger, wondering what Maggy was about to say.

She watched Maggy inhale, "By the way, thank you. For inviting me to stay here. I know it's crowding y'all with y'all redoing the nursery and everything, but it's homey and… well… it would have been weird staying at Mama's without… Mama."

Quinn teared up, the drops shimmering at the edge of her lashes. She brushed them away and fanned at her face with both hands.

"You're my sister. Of course, I want you here." She couldn't make herself add that for the last fifteen years that was all she had wanted from Maggy.

Maggy nodded, biting her lip, and turned away again, murmuring to Kylie. As she watched her sister's back recede, Quinn's phone buzzed under her hand with a text from Collins.

Running late at Lefleur. Had to fix the stair stepper again. Going to clean up here and head straight to the church. See you there ❤

Her shoulders sagged. He was there, and she was here, again. Another wail drew her down the hall towards Clara.

Settling her shoulders, she stepped into Kylie's room, functioning as the nursery for now. Suns and rainbows that Maggy had painted smiled cheerily all over the walls even in the lowered lighting, just like Kylie's personality. Kylie was sharing with the twins as Collins redid the nursery in his ever-decreasing spare time; Maggy had said she was unbothered by sleeping on an air mattress in the bare-bones nursery-in-process.

She picked up her tiny daughter and shuffled quietly over to the fluffy armchair she had used for nursing all five children. As she settled into its pillowy folds, she blinked away the memory of Mama pointing to it decisively in the store, insisting on it as the very first gift for her pregnant teenager and unborn grandchild.

Gently, Quinn laid her little girl across her lap and rubbed her back until Clara's crying died down to soft whimpers. Clara having colic hadn't been fun for anyone in the family, but from the pitch of her crying, Quinn could only assume she was suffering the worst. Absentmindedly, she worried at the worn corduroy of the chair with her other hand, picking at loose threads and running her fingers back-and-forth along its ridges.

As she continued to rub Clara's back, she looked out the window and watched the clouds swirl. This dim room was so different from the life she had imagined for herself in boardrooms and skyscrapers; it was better in some ways, but when she saw Maggy all dolled up, looking so effortlessly beautiful and chic, she couldn't help wishing. The clouds coiled up then rolled away faster than she could follow in the waning twilight, and she imagined herself whipping along their furious currents anywhere but here. Guiltily, she refocused on Clara.

She unbuttoned her shirt and leaned back into the dusty smell of the soft chair, trying to relax enough to encourage Clara to latch in the few minutes she wasn't crying. Despite his text, a small, silly part of her hoped to see Collins' car come sweeping up the gravel drive anyway, to hear his booming voice ask her what he could do to make her load lighter like he did every night, to feel his stubbly kiss on her cheek. Instead, she heard her sons giggling with Mrs. Hernandez in the next room, thumping into the wall as they bounced in their beds, and Allie stomping back and forth still in a tizzy as she slung her closet door open and closed. Distracted by the noise, she gasped in relief as Clara nuzzled into her greedily. It was a small victory, but today she would take it.

CHAPTER THREE

Collins could feel the blood pulsing in his temples. There was a root. There was a big-ass root right through the middle of his mother-in-law's grave plot, directly across the top of the soil. How in tarnation do you miss something like that? They stood around Truman and Alice Matins' plot—or rather, just Truman's now. While Truman's plot was still a smooth expanse of lawn, somehow his wife's was riddled with oak roots, the largest of which ran straight through the middle of the plot. He turned to Roy, about to demand an explanation.

In unison, all the men of the Guild turned and also stared at Roy, who stood relaxed, his wrists crossed over the handle of his shovel, and looked placidly at his sixteen-year-old nephew Harry. The boy was tall and good-looking, with dark eyes and hair and a patchy beard barely starting to sprout in a misguided show of maturity. Having been Allie's friend and in Roy's guardianship since they were toddlers, Collins knew Harry was overall a good-natured and pleasant boy, but once he got an idea stuck in his head, he was stubborn as a mule, much like his uncle.

Roy pursed his lips and narrowed his eyes at the boy and Collins shuddered, recognizing Harry was already in the eye of the storm. Collins had received that look once or twice himself, and it had not gone well. The teenager stood with his hands shoved in his pockets, avoiding his uncle's gaze.

In the lowering twilight, a mockingbird shrieked in an uncanny imitation of a siren and Roy rolled his shoulders. "Harry, care to explain," with a dramatic pause he waved at the root that ran directly to a gigantic old oak tree, "This?"

The boy shrugged but didn't answer.

"Harry, you told me everything was fine!"

Collins looked at the waning light; he needed to salvage this situation quickly. He cut in. "You didn't inspect it yourself?" Roy side-eyed him, but kept dressing down Harry, his tone scarily calm.

"I gave you a simple task to do. Did you even come out here like I asked?"

"It looks fine! There's plenty of space and we have saws in the groundskeeper shed. I don't see why we can't just cut it out of the way," Harry grumbled, "Or get a backhoe and have the whole thing dug in five minutes." A collective groan went up from the circle. Collins rubbed his eyes, resisting the urge to punch the child. He had enough problems to solve right now at the gyms without a mouthy teenager making his mother-in-law's funeral go to hell in a handbasket as well.

Roy stood with a hand over his mouth for a moment. He reached out and plucked some matted grass from the foot of the gravestone, then swept his hand over the face of Truman's headstone, Alice's long-deceased husband. He lifted his palm to reveal a dark layer of grime and pollen.

"You didn't come out here at all, did you?" Mullone rubbed his fingers together, examining the grit. His eyes were wide with suppressed anger, his mouth a thin line. Looking at his nephew, he demanded, "Harry? Answer me!"

"I didn't see the point!" Harry thrust out his hands exasperatedly. "We were just out here a week ago mowing and weed-eating and everything looked good enough then. It's just a root! And why does a headstone need to be spit-shined, anyway?"

Collins muttered, "That's it," and stepped forward to give Harry a tongue-lashing he'd really remember, but Roy held up his hand to hold him off. Behind him, Charlie had a coughing fit, his eyes watering with suppressed laughter. Rick punched his arm, hard, to quiet him. Ego bruised, Collins seethed. How dare Roy screw up his mother-in-law's burial?

Roy's words were icy. "I'm disappointed in you, Harry. Because of you, our whole plan for Mrs. Matins is done for." He looked at him scathingly. "This is not how we do things, and you know it." The boy opened his mouth to protest, but Roy made a cutting motion with his hand. "We are *not* going to discuss it right now." He dug in his pocket and pulled out a ring of keys, with some that were wrought iron and looked like they were out of a storybook. He flipped through them with a clatter. "Now, prove to me that those ears are good for something and go get the maps that are on my desk in the vestry office. All of them. I thought we wouldn't need them tonight, but because of your foolishness, it looks like we're in for a rough evening." He found the one he was looking for, a modern enough deadbolt key, and handed it over.

Harry turned, shoulders slumped, to head towards the administrative building behind the chapel, dragging his feet audibly over the grass. Roy called after him, "All of them! And don't crease them up either!" Harry waved half-heartedly in acknowledgment over his shoulder and plodded off.

With a groan, Roy leaned his shovel against a headstone and pulled a bandana from his pocket to wipe at his face. The men shuffled uneasily, knowing what came next. Collins lifted both of his arms and let them drop in exasperation and the old man shot him another side-eye.

"There's no need for theatrics, Collins. The boy is learning." He tucked the bandana back into his pocket and grabbed the handle of his shovel before turning to look at Collins with a level gaze.

"He's a teenager. And a mule-headed one at that. Why didn't you double-check him? It's basic management skills." Collins placed his hands on his hips. The older man continued to eye him, sucking in a corner of his lip.

"I had things to do, Collins. Sometimes, I have to call in

reinforcements to get it all done."

Collins groaned, "Reinforcements? Really, Roy? You're retired. How much do you have to do? You had two days to come out here and check it yourself. Why didn't you?"

"Helping Quinn make the arrangements for her mama, for a start. You know as well as I do that Alice had trusted me with a lot of her... preferences." Roy coughed and looked at Truman's headstone. He frowned and pushed his glasses back up the bridge of his nose.

Collins pushed past Roy's obvious discomfort. "That wouldn't have taken all of your time. Alice had most of her arrangements planned out, bought, and paid for almost twenty years ago, practically the day after Truman was killed in that horrible accident. What is it really, Roy?"

Charlie piped up, "This is just like the Pearson burial all over again." Collins shot him a withering look. He had not asked for commentary from the peanut gallery, especially not Charlie.

Rick rolled his eyes. "I hardly think we'll have to call in a favor for a ground-reading sonar like we did for Mr. Pearson, Charlie. We'll figure something out." Charlie shrugged and muttered something sarcastic under his breath.

Ignoring him, Collins shifted on the balls of his feet and crossed his arms, refocusing on Mr. Mullone, not ready to let it go. "Roy. What's going on with you?"

Roy stared into the trees, blinking. After a second, he shrugged. "Sometimes, I like to believe in the best of people, especially my own family. And sometimes, I'm just tired. Take your pick. But that isn't going to solve our problem now." Before Collins could retort, he pointed the handle of his shovel towards the root and raised his voice slightly addressing the group. "So, we've got a minute before Father Fry gets here. Why don't we solve it?" Collins crossed his arms but knew when he was outmaneuvered.

The men gathered around and added their murmurings to the wind that had picked up speed. Fingers jabbed in various directions and Mr. Mullone and Collins nodded or shook their heads in turn.

After a lengthy debate, Rick reluctantly gestured to the flower bed behind Roy. As the spearhead of the Garden Guild, Mrs. Streisand's infamously beautiful flower beds wound through the plots, overflowing with the starry blooms of Japanese dogwood, bright pink splashes of native azaleas, intoxicatingly perfumed miniature gardenias, and a low-growing, ornamental purple cane they were forever trimming back from the lawn. Collins never ceased to wonder at what his mother could create with a few wisps of plants. He'd often found her out here with Alice, soil smudged all over their faces, grinning and sweating as they put out tender new sprouts. With a wince, he thought of telling her of their trespassing and looked at Roy to see a similar grimace on his face.

They looked at each other. "I mean, it makes sense. We know there are no big roots at least." Roy spoke what everyone was already thinking. Collins rubbed at the sudden tension in his neck.

"Yeah… but I'd rather not have to tell my mom we ripped up half of her flower bed."

"Why are we discussing ripping up flower beds?" Father Derek Fry stood behind the group in the darkening twilight, an amused expression on the young pastor's face. As an athletic trainer and gym owner, Collins admired the man's build. Even though he had been out of the Welsh military for years, he was still thin and clean-cut, and he looked like he could judo chop someone into behaving in a heartbeat. He made a mental note to ask the good Father sometime if he did bodyweight exercises and for some pointers if he did.

Roy pointed at the offending root. "We've run into a bit of a roadblock with the spot I'd originally intended for Alice." Collins' ears perked up at the familiar use of his mother-in-law's first name. "And we were discussing what might be the easiest way to solve the problem."

Father Fry nodded. "Why don't we consider the Yellowley family plot? She was a Yellowley by birth, yes? That might be preferable to starting a feud with the good Mrs. Streisand and her brigade." He winked at Collins, and Collins smiled in return at the affable preacher. "I'm pretty sure Collins will thank you for not upsetting his mother by killing the plants she works so hard to keep beautiful for us."

Roy nodded vigorously. "That's a great idea. I was *not* looking forward to that conversation."

Father Fry clapped him on the shoulder. "Good, that's settled." He waved towards the church, "And, the undertaker is here." Roy nodded his head forcefully, looking like a bobblehead on a bumpy ride.

"Then we'll take a look at the Yellowley plot after the greeting." Roy bent his head towards Collins in mute acknowledgment, and with a small wave, Collins motioned the rest of the men forward.

As they tromped back through the grass towards the church, the air went still, and Collins plucked at his shirt, the fabric clinging to him in sticky splotches. Needing to vent about Roy's latest irritation, Collins hung towards the back of the group, ambling alongside Rick Seymour, a family doctor infamous for his weekend barbecues and one of his best friends. Collins and Quinn had enjoyed many sun-drenched afternoons gossiping over the grill with Rick and his wife, Catherine, a divorce attorney to some of Jackson's wealthiest families, while the kids played in the pool. Glancing over his shoulder at where Charlie trailed hopefully out of earshot, Collins turned to him now and gestured to where Roy and Father Fry led the way.

"So, what do you think of all this?" he asked, trying not to work himself up.

Rick glanced at him, amused. Collins bit the inside of his cheek, thinking of his well-known blowups with Roy.

"We've dealt with worse," Rick answered neutrally. He looked at Collins with raised brows.

Collins nodded and studied the dark stonework of the chapel through the trees. "True. Unfortunate that it had to be at my mother-in-law's funeral. And with how," he paused, searching for a word, "fond he was of Alice. I would have thought our *Guild president*," he drawled the title out, letting the syllables roll off his tongue like heavy coins, "would have double-checked everything to make sure it would be perfect for *her*, ya' know?" He pursed his lips.

Rick furrowed his brow as they walked, considering. "You know we vote for Guild president largely for formality. But I hear ya'. It bothers me a bit too that he didn't double-check." He paused and Collins rushed in.

"You don't think he's slipping, do you? Getting too tired to handle all of this?"

Rick glanced at him, scoffing. "What? Nah." He chuckled. "Roy's plenty solid. This graveyard is harder than most to work with, between the two-hundred-year-old maps and unmarked graves and the ancient trees we're trying not to kill. I'm surprised we haven't had more mistakes."

"But Harry?" Collins groaned.

"Don't get me wrong, the kid is going through his know-it-all teenager phase real hard. But if Roy wants to try to teach him some responsibility, that's his business. That doesn't mean he'll be the next president or anything." With a clap on the shoulder, Rick reassured him. "Just try not to let it bother you too much."

"Hard not to, when it's my family."

The undertaker's night-black car came into view through the trees, and up ahead, Mr. Mullone and Father Fry stepped onto the pavement towards it.

Rick murmured, "I'm sure he couldn't agree more."

CHAPTER FOUR

Mr. Mullone found the nightingale's melancholy song breaking through the twilight a bittersweet relief as he watched Alice's casket disappear through the fellowship hall doors behind the chapel. He rubbed his hands together, cold and stiff, even in the summer's heat. He longed for the late winter evenings discussing the Romantic poets with Alice Matins in front of the fire until it was so late he was forced to go home. Alone. Always alone. His head drooped and even Collins left him to his reflections under the whispering trees.

The swishing crunch of grass pulled him from his reverie, and he looked up to see Father Fry standing next to him, gazing up at the steeple, hands in his pockets.

The young pastor spoke, his Welsh brogue softly rolling through the thick air, "Do you think it's time to have the bell restored? Mrs. Alice suggested it last quarter, so we could stop using recordings, but we tabled it." The young pastor glanced over at Mr. Mullone, who stared at him, hands clenched.

"Of course, it's time to have the bell restored! Why else would she have suggested it?" Roy sputtered under his breath about the foolishness of youth and the nonsense of putting things off until tomorrow. Father Fry patted him on the shoulder with a sad smile.

"I really came over here to see how you were doing, Mr. Mullone. Mrs. Alice was a special lady—and I know she was especially important to you."

Mr. Mullone swallowed.

"Darn humidity. Making my glasses fog up." He took his glasses off and polished them, coughing roughly. "I'm alright. I…" He sighed, deciding there was no point in pretending. "I loved her—that's no secret. I asked her to marry me at least a dozen times. And these last few months. Well, I thought she had changed her mind."

He blinked up at the bell owlishly and exhaled in defeat. "I thought she hinted at it, at least. Alice was always so proud of her health, never needing to take pills, her long walks, I thought I'd have years yet with her. It was all such a shock. Even to her, I think." He put his sparkling glasses back on and looked at Father Fry. "Anyway, guess we'll never know now what she meant to do."

With a nod, Father Fry agreed, his face clouding over as he looked back up at the silent bell.

Mrs. Matins had taken a liking to the young preacher, often debating with him over their big "family lunch" on Sundays. Mr. Mullone glanced at him again and was surprised to see Father Fry surreptitiously pull his phone out of his pocket. He looked to be checking for missed messages. A thought occurred to Mr. Mullone, a memory from earlier. "Say, why were you late? You're always on time…" He trailed off musingly. He was surprised the conscientiously punctual man would be tardy to her services.

Realizing he had been noticed, Father Fry slipped the phone back into his pocket quickly.

Awkwardly clearing his throat, Father Fry looked around at the men retrieving shovels and spades from their cars. "I got caught on a call I had to take." Mr. Mullone nodded, still curious.

"It must have been some call to be late to Alice's wake. She was like a mother to you!"

Father Fry turned and faced Mr. Mullone.

He laughed as he spoke, the sound light and lilting in the evening breeze, but his eyes were earnest. "Believe me, it was."

CHAPTER FIVE

Quinn was running late. As always. Maggy scratched resentfully at a tender mosquito bite as she meditated on her older sister's many deficiencies. She added a lack of punctuality to the list. She had arrived just as the men tramped off through the darkening yard so she could help the ladies put linens on the refreshment table—which they had refused to let her do—and to bring in the ice chest full of bottled water. She had discovered it was much too big to handle on her own, so here she stood observing and waiting for Quinn to arrive. She had *promised* she was five minutes behind her. That was an hour-and-a-half ago.

Through the wavering glass of the narrow window at which she stood vigil, she watched the lights bobbing back and forth in the distance. One remained steadfast on the ground at the foot of her mother's grave. Or what would be her mother's grave. Earlier she had watched the men lined up far down both sides of the walk to silently welcome her casket to the Chapel of the Cross, her mother's last big entrance.

Torches had flickered and crazed in the evening breeze as the hearse pulled up, but as the doors opened, a reverent hush fell among the trees and the flames stood tall and still. As she watched Father Fry's lips move silently in prayer from her vantage point, she realized the last torch was already ablaze, so the lighting symbolizing the passing of a legacy from one generation to the next did not happen as they carried the casket inside the hall. Resentfully, she wondered if it was a subtle dig at her by Collins for their earlier fight or an oversight by the new pastor. An acidic bubble rose up her throat, coppery and clinging. How many other tiny traditions would be brushed over without her mother to guard them? She swallowed against the searing knot and pressed a hand to her stomach, willing down the rising anxiety.

Behind her, the ladies flitted along the table laying out linen and casseroles, eternally tutting and fussing over details only they could see. Unsteadily, she now used the toe of one foot to rub the ankle of the other, a treacherous balancing act in her patent stilettos. Three steps from her car to the arch of the door and the bloodsuckers had swarmed.

The ladies of the church had ushered her into the vestibule in a cloud of perfume and pearls that threw her back into her cloistered childhood with such tornadic force she nearly vomited on the heart of pine floors. For thirty minutes "Miss Margaret" had deflected their ministrations and polite prying into her "big city life" as best she could. Their volleys were hard to return while directing the undertaker's men to arrange the flower sprays that had pink peonies—her mother's favorite—next to the casket, and any with peace lilies—the "most morbid flower, so waxlike," as far away as possible.

After the blue hairs clucked their approval of her flower arranging ability, she had stationed herself at the window where she stood now in what she hoped looked like a meditative and melancholy retreat. So far, they had let her be, except for the occasional proffering of water or plate of finger sandwiches.

She kept expecting to hear her mother's piping voice amongst the twittering. The dim fellowship hall yawned, vacuous and empty without it. It was hard to come to grips with—she glanced at the sprays of flowers and the closed casket—all this when she had talked to her mother just two weeks ago. Earlier, only Mr. Mullone's sad gaze, as the coffin had been born into the echoing room, convinced her that her mother's remains were inside the gleaming ebony casket. The gnawing itch at her ankle pulled her from the fresh memory.

Exhausted from the drive, she plunked herself on a nearby kneeler, ignoring the Trinitarian weave she used to trace with love on the upholstery, and petulantly picked at a growing welt on her ankle. A weight, like a heavy book, pressed on her chest and her head pulsated, causing colors to flash and fade. As the colors strobed across her eyes, she twined her fingers into the Gothically carved struts along the side, trying not to thunk her head into the sloped shelf above. How many times had Mama plunked her down on one of these and told her to confess her sins after one of her and Quinn's escapades? She pushed the thought away; she should have brought her sketchbook to distract herself. At least she could have passed the time drawing. Mama wouldn't have approved of her getting graphite and ink smeared all over the sides of her hands, but she could hardly object now.

Maggy scratched at the welt even more fiercely. A pink bottle floated into her eye-line. The tiny bottle was cupped in a plump hand.

"Put some calamine on it, sugar. It'll keep you from turning it into a nasty scar," said Mrs. Greaves. The grey hair of her perfect perm quivered with mirth. She eased carefully onto the kneeler beside her and tapped her cane gently on Maggy's knee.

"And your skin is too beautiful to go wasting on scars, Maggy," she added, looking slyly at her out of the side of her eye. Maggy couldn't help but smile. She gratefully dabbed the pungent lotion in bright, pox-pink spots across her legs and arms—appearances be hanged.

"You're the only one 'round here who still calls me that, Mrs. Greaves." Maggy nodded towards the dark-clothed ladies clustered around the refreshment table with its Crock-Pots and insulated carry bags. Some slowly drifted down into the chairs ringed around the casket like magnolia petals onto dark water. "It's been all 'Miss Margaret' this and 'ma'am' that. Some even call me Alice Matins' child or Quinn's sister. It's like they forgot I grew up here, that I'm blood."

"They haven't forgotten, child. But it's been so long they don't quite know what to do with this act you've got going on." Mrs. Greaves turned and looked at her, cupping Maggy's chin in her hand and turning her head back and forth to take in the diamond earrings and the slash of scarlet lipstick. She nodded appreciatively and continued, "You slip in and you slip out at the holidays, and most of us never even know you're in town 'til you're gone. They don't know Margaret Matins, city sophisticate and fashion editor; they remember Maggy, country rascal and stealer of communion wafers." She huffed, her lips vibrating gently. "Think of it this way: the only way they know to identify you right now is by your family, your 'blood.' So, you are Alice's child and Quinn's sister for the time being."

Tears pricked at Maggy's eyes at the thought of all those useless years in New York, but she commanded them back, knowing that if she gave into weeping for any reason that she could not stop. She must maintain some sort of decorum.

Mrs. Greaves patted her back like she had so many times before as her godmother and confidante, the touch familiar and soothing.

"What's really on your mind, darling?" She settled back to listen.

Maggy rested her hand on the upholstery, gently drawing a fingertip along the Trinity knot, before she looked back at her godmother.

"Is all of this necessary? The dig and the wake with the Psalms and then the funeral and reception? We're so tired. Me with…" She searched for words, choking on fifteen years of failure. She couldn't bear to repeat the whole meltdown of her life right now, even to such a sympathetic listener. "…the drive, and Quinn with the baby and dealing with all the arrangements." She rested her head on her knees, feeling small. "Even thinking of Mama being gone is exhausting. Why do we have to go through all of it just to get her in the ground?"

Mrs. Greaves inhaled slowly through her nose. "If we were just 'getting her in the ground,' then yes, it is a lot." She nudged Maggy with her elbow. "But as someone who's planted my share of people, life likes to distract us, even from grieving. So, think of this as a time dedicated to remembering all the things your mother did, all she meant to us. It's more than honoring her; it's celebrating her." She fiddled with her pearls, lips trembling. "And selfishly, it's a time to grieve who we were with her and the future we had planned with her in it. And that's the first step to letting it go so we can keep living ourselves. At least until the day we see her again in heaven." She dropped the pearls and peered at Maggy, smiling sadly. "And for that, I think it's just about right. Don't you?"

"Well, when you put it that way…" Maggy trailed off, her smile wavering. She rubbed at her stinging nose. Her heart constricted at the thought of ever letting Mama go. Mrs. Greaves chuckled and swung her cane to her other hand.

"Help an old lady up, would you, sugar?" Maggy sprang up and offered her an arm. Mrs. Greaves rose, a slow process combining hauling on Maggy's arm and pushing on her cane with some unladylike grunts. Mid-way up her knees popped like soda tops and Maggy winced in sympathy.

"That sounded painful."

Placing a hand on her back as she straightened, Mrs. Greaves shrugged good-naturedly. "My body cracks like a glow stick. One of the charms of growing old. I don't complain though—my mind is still sharp as a tack!" Finally upright, Mrs. Greaves clung onto Maggy's arm and moved determinedly towards Father Fry, dragging Maggy in her wake. The well-worn vestry Bible flipped itself open to the Psalms under his hand as the ladies each grabbed a match and lit long tapers in burnished silver candlesticks spaced around the hall and on top of the casket. Shadows danced, fairylike, in the bowls of the flowers. Even to Maggy's critical eye, the effect in the dimmed space was otherworldly.

Father Fry took her hand warmly, his green eyes soft and crinkling at the edges.

"Miss Matins! A pleasure to meet you at last." His voice rumbled with warmth and sincerity. "I love your family—Collins and Quinn and the children are a delight and of course your mother, I… Well, she was always more than a match for me discussing theology. And your escapades are legendary! I should love to hear about them from the source."

The man's innocent enthusiasm made Maggy smile in return. Even though she had glimpsed him earlier through the window, his relative youth finally registered. Where she had been expecting a white-haired, Episcopalian minister, she was shocked to see a handsome, young pastor. He couldn't be a day over thirty-five. She studied his smooth skin and dark hair and wondered if he had modeled in another life; she could imagine finding him in one of the menswear spreads of her magazine. The accent added to the charm. She tried to place it—Scottish maybe, or Welsh?

"Maggy, please," she said, already knowing she was a goner, "And I'd be happy to tell you a few of the tamer stories sometime. I'm assuming you'll be at the reception after the service tomorrow?"

"Yes, yes, it's at your sister's, isn't it? Where is she? I thought you two might arrive together after your long drive from New York." How much did these people know about everyone else's business, she wondered? The women were bemusedly watching their pastor fawn over her. She noticed he was still holding her hand and, smelling matchmaking, withdrew it gently. But not her smile.

"I left her at home with the babysitter trying to get the littlest down for the night. I thought she was just behind me with the sweet tea and about a store's worth of lemons," she said, glancing at the refreshment table and its empty drink dispensers in elegant black-wire stands. Mrs. Streisand already held a cup. She caught Maggy's look.

"Oh! We were wondering what to do about drinks. The men must be getting thirsty by now. We were debating if it would be possible to fill up some cups for them from the water fountain." She fluttered her heavily ringed hands against the plastic cup and pursed her lips. Maggy and Father Fry responded at the same time.

"That's a good idea. Why don't we…"

"There is ice and bottled water in my…"

They all jumped as the door in the vestibule flew open with a bang, and a sweaty Collins trotted in, flushed and scowling. Spotting Maggy's purse where she had left it in a chair, he snatched it up and began rifling through it without a word.

Maggy stared, slack-jawed, then snapped her mouth shut. Lord have mercy, he wanted to die today, didn't he? "Collins! What do you think you're doing?!"

He went still, the purse dangling from his hands. He blinked, taking in all the ladies staring at him. He glanced down at the purse, Adam's apple bobbing.

"I've been sent to retrieve drinks. We're gettin' awfully thirsty out there." He forced a wide smile. Mrs. Greaves planted her cane firmly on the floor while Mrs. Streisand pulled herself up to the full effect of her six foot, three inches tall plus kitten heels and stared at her son. Father Fry lowered his eyes and rubbed at the back of his neck.

"Say, Maggy, how do you find anything in here anyway?" Collins asked drolly, then added softly, "I need your keys." His mother shook her head almost imperceptibly at him, eyes wide, but he missed it as he craned his neck scanning the group.

"It might have something to do with *not* rummaging through other peoples' things," Maggy fixed him with a stony stare. "Again." He swallowed a second time and shot a nervous look at her.

"Is Quinn alright? I thought y'all were coming together," Collins asked, voice low, as he continued to look for his wife. Much too slowly for her liking, he finally handed the purse over.

"Had trouble getting the baby down," Maggy murmured, plucking the purse from his moist hand and returning it to the chair. Her eyes were tight at the edges.

She crossed her arms and continued to glare at him. The sheer gall. And after what he'd said to her this afternoon too. "Hopefully, she gets here soon. Her purse is even bigger. You can have a lot of fun rummaging through it." Mrs. Greaves snorted.

Collins closed his eyes and let out a long exhale through his nose. It whistled in the silence. Maggy waited for a snarky reply but he remained quiet. Father Fry tapped his thumb loudly on the Bible for a second then asked, "So how is the digging going? No more irregularities?"

"Irregularities?" Maggy asked.

Collins glanced out the window at the torches along the walk. "Well, the first site turned out to be a no-go—"

"You mean Mama's spot? Next to Dad?" Maggy's mouth hung open. And no one had bothered to tell her why?

Collins cleared his throat and nodded, flushing. "Correct. So we're digging deep in the historic section now. And we hit a bit of another snag." He cleared his throat again. Maggy groaned and Collins hastened to add. "Roy's in charge. He'll figure it out— probably scooch it over a bit so we don't end up double-bunking."

Through barely parted lips Maggy said, "Yes, that would be preferable." They all stared at the flickering tapers for a moment. They guttered with a snap.

"Well, Roy always figures these things out in the end. He's never led y'all wrong yet," Mrs. Greaves said, a twinkle in her eye. Mrs. Streisand pressed a hand to her mouth to cover a smile, and Collins shot her a reproachful look. As civil as the two men were at Sunday lunch, Maggy recalled her mother's stories of Mr. Mullone and Collins' clashes over Guild business on their weekly phone call.

Collins cut his eyes over at Maggy who primly smoothed the box pleats at her waist, chin lifted.

"That's a nice dress. Marcus buy it for you?" he asked, eyes narrowed. Maggy wasn't in the mood for his pettiness.

"I buy my own things. And you know very well we broke up last month if that's what you are so crudely alluding to," she shot back. "I sent you and Quinn a snap of me moving out." Mrs. Streisand had a sudden fit of coughing. Collins scratched a mosquito bite on his elbow.

"I guess that's so." He fell quiet.

The inimitable Mrs. Greaves volleyed into the silence, "How is Allie, Collins? She's sixteen now isn't she—and so smart, just like our Alice was at her age. Quinn named her well. Will she be coming tonight?"

Collins crossed his arms. "I believe so. She's old enough for these things now." Silence fell, a heavy blanket covering the group. Mama would have known how to smooth over this situation just so, had everyone laughing in an instant. Maggy coughed, trying to clear the sudden catch in her throat, the sound echoing through the hall like a pistol shot.

Seeing that no one else wanted to hold up their side of social niceties, Mrs. Greaves returned to the breach. "Maggy, we missed you at the anniversary party in March. Quinn was rather hoping you'd make it down for it." Smiling awkwardly, Maggy remembered only an RSVP card and silence. "It was a big one, wasn't it, Collins? Y'all's fifteenth? How lovely to have your anniversary and Allie's birthday on the same day!" Maggy wanted to kiss Mrs. Greaves for her cheekiness as she watched Father Fry's ears blush, and Collins shove his hand in his pockets. She interceded before she had a full-on snub fest going down at her mother's funeral. That *would* be the gossip of the summer.

"Yes… I would have loved to be here, but we added some new sections to the magazine this year without hiring any extra staff, so deadlines have been so tight that I couldn't make it for the baby being born or the party." She clasped her hands. "Collins, you came for the cooler in my car, right?" Her heels clicked authoritatively on the wooden floor as she turned smartly, one of her signature moves at the magazine—or it had been. She dug out the keys from her purse containing her depressingly quiet cell phone and handed them to Father Fry. "Father Fry, would you help him take the water to the guys then bring the ice in here so it will be ready when the rest of the drinks arrive?"

Collins strode out, back taut and footsteps thunderous. Father Fry smiled gratefully at her and hurried after him. She had a feeling he had a few things to say to his parishioner. She glanced at her phone—still no replies to her applications—and slipped it back into her purse. Dabbing the corner of her eye, she took a deep breath. Mama may have been pushy, but she had been incredible at sending her solid job leads. Her heart sank at searching on her own.

She plastered on a smile and turned back to the ladies. A few were eying her appreciatively. But more were eying her shoes. Mrs. Streisand breathed, "Are those… Louis Vuittons, Maggy?" Mrs. Greaves winked at Maggy.

"Come on, Judith. You know Maggy is a fashion editor. She isn't exactly going to be wearing Naturalizers from Shoe Barn." She turned to Maggy. With a grin, she said, "Well then, sugar. Come on and tell us about the scandalous world of New York fashion." Maggy chuckled and pulled out her phone, relieved to have a distraction from the family-awkwardness. And a delay from the grief now boiling up in her stomach.

"You will not believe these ridiculous outfits from Fall Fashion Week," she began, her mother's casket sparkling darkly in the corner of her eye.

CHAPTER SIX

Quinn needed a break. Pandemonium had broken out the moment Maggy left, the twins charging downstairs roaring like dinosaurs and Kylie bursting into tears. The sound of their combined cacophony had woken Clara from her fitful snoozing and her screams had joined the fray. While Mrs. Hernandez and Allie, in her slip, had chased the younger ones back into some semblance of order, Quinn had begun the long process of rocking and soothing the baby back to sleep.

Now in the dim light from the lamp, the overhead having burned out earlier that week and no time to change it, Quinn surveyed the contents of her closet dismally. A few bright, silk blouses from her brief days as a CPA four babies ago hung, rumpled and crooked on old velvet hangers. A weight, as of two heavy hands, descended on her shoulders as she thought of those days in the gym office, Allie coloring on the floor behind her. That room didn't seem stuffy and cramped anymore but warm and unconfined. Golden. Until Ralph, Collins' "real accountant," came along and wrecked it all. She brushed a hand over her face to refocus. Her phone rang and she tapped at the speaker icon. Catherine Seymour's voice crackled over the line, staticky from her car's speakerphone.

"Hey hon! Just letting you know I'm going to be running a

bit late tonight—one of my clients insisted they could only meet after hours. Rich people for you. Need me to pick up anything on the way? More tea? Kleenexes? Xanax? A hip flask?"

Distracted, Quinn dug through her "clean" clothes pile. Did she have so few clothes? She was eternally washing and folding—surely not. The baby wailed again upstairs, and she heard the thud of footsteps as Mrs. Hernandez hurried to comfort her.

"Quinn! You there? Normally, I'd get a groan out of you with that kind of joke."

"I'm sorry, sugar. I'm so scattered right now. No, thanks. I think we're covered unless you want to magic up a new wardrobe for me."

"Done! I can stop by my house and grab a dress for you."

A hand over her mouth, Quinn surveyed the rest of the room, with the rumpled bed and mountain of clothes spilling from Collins' closet, and spied a dark lump on the floor next to her nightstand. Snatching it up, she grimaced tiredly as she saw her navy dress from last Sunday, only worn once since washing. It would have to do.

"I think I just found what I need, but you are an angel for offering."

"Alright, sweetie. I'm just a text away if you need anything. And I do mean anything. Down to the hip flask."

Quinn laughed and dropped her phone on the bed. As she was zipping up, Allie burst in without knocking. With a dramatic groan, she threw herself face down on the bed. Quinn strained to zip the dress to the top, her shoulders stiff and sore from holding Clara so much. She glanced at her reflection in the dusty dresser mirror; it was only slightly wrinkled. As she picked up her deodorant to freshen up, she glanced at her daughter, lolling back and forth in what she assumed was supposed to be anguish. Mama would have left her to her melodrama, but she was not her mother.

She turned back to the mirror. "Care to share with the class?" she asked her daughter's reflection as she swiped at her underarms, careful not to leave white stripes on the dark dress.

There was no backup outfit if she got crud all over this one.

A scowl popped up to meet her gaze in the mirror, and Allie sat up with a huff. While she still had on the wingtip eyeliner and overdone contouring, Quinn noted approvingly that she had changed to a dark eggplant dress with a ruffled hem that fell at the knee, much more appropriate than her earlier Roxanne recreation.

"I look like a hideous old lady! Harry's going to hate me." With a wail, Allie flopped back down on the bed. With a clatter, Quinn abandoned the tinted moisturizer she had been about to swipe on. Remembering what it was like to be young and in love, she sank onto the mattress next to her daughter, pushing Allie's hair back from where she had tossed it in an arc across the bedspread.

"*I think* you look elegant and sophisticated. Very grown-up. And if he doesn't think that too, he's an idiot." She stared at the ceiling, shaking her head. Had she been this much of a diva as a teenager? Cringing, she remembered a similar tantrum before her senior prom over impossibly frizzy hair. But it hadn't been Mama who'd calmed her down. She had rolled her eyes and left her to cry it out. No, it'd been Maggy that had sat her up and, in a stinging cloud of Aqua Net, whipped her misbehaving hair into a gorgeous updo. Even back then, Maggy had a talent for creating beautiful things from the impossible.

With a sniff, Allie sat up. "Do you think so?"

Quinn nodded. "I do. And honestly, sweetie, at your age even the nice guys can be complete doofuses. You're beautiful— and more importantly smart and talented. Be confident in yourself."

Allie chuckled and wiped at her nose. "Thanks. But I still don't feel *elegant and sophisticated.* And none of my jewelry matches this dress." She chewed at her berry-glossed lip and shot a look at Collins' closet. "Would it... would it be all right if I wore Grandma's pearls tonight?"

Swallowing, Quinn looked at the teetering pile of laundry hiding the safe in Collins' closet. "I don't know, sweetie... That's a big thing to be responsible for. And..." She waved at the mess.

Jumping up, Allie piled clothes to the side, chattering excitedly. "I'll be so careful! I promise! And I'll move all of this for you, you won't have to touch a thing…" The gushing continued as Quinn picked at the corner of her chapped lips, worrying about Maggy's reaction. Surely, she would be ok with Allie wearing the pearls tonight if she explained the crisis?

"All right, you can have them—"

"Thank you! Thank you!" More chattering erupted and Quinn tried to cut in.

"Just for tonight!" A vehement nod in the ceaseless stream of babble answered her, and Quinn stooped, back cracking, to tap the code into the glowing panel on the safe, relieved. Maybe she could finally get them out the door.

CHAPTER SEVEN

It was like walking through soup outside, even in the cooler evening air. Collins was thankful for the breathable fabric of his "fancy golf shirt" although Quinn always complained about the price. Father Fry labored through the humidity in his Polo, beads of sweat on his upper lip. Maggy's shiny BMW keys dangled from the other man's hand.

"Here," Collins said, snatching them from him. "There's a trick with these fancy European car fobs." He clicked the trunk open quickly, easily, and shoved the keys into his pocket. Father Fry looked at him, eyebrows quirked sardonically. He investigated the trunk and whistled.

"I always expect women's cars to be messy, with clothes and stuff, but this is pristine. Is it new?" he asked.

Collins shook his head. "She's had this about ten years," he replied. It had been eight; Maggy had bought this car with her share of Truman's first trust payout. The same payout that had let Collins open the fourth gym right when the business' growth had plateaued. Suddenly uneasy thinking about trust funds and financing, he swallowed and refocused on Maggy's car, his hand on the upraised trunk.

He drummed his fingers on the polished paint. "Saw pictures of this on Facebook when she got it. She had a classic Chevy truck before. Such a shame. It was a beaut." This car only accounted for a fraction of Maggy's payout money though; he wondered what she'd done with the rest. Clothes? Traveling? Making all those high-maintenance boyfriends happy? He doubted she'd had the sense to invest it like he'd told her to. Even the memory of her nonplussed look when he'd given her his financial advisor's number made him feel disgruntled and he swiped at his forehead, already collecting droplets of sweat in the heat. Maggy had taken the business card like he'd handed her a dead toad. Alice had just shaken her head and looked away.

Father Fry pulled him back down to earth. "I would imagine a truck would not be great for city driving though, between gas and parking," he said as he grabbed one of the red cooler's handles and slid it forward with an *oof*. "Get that other handle, would you? This is pretty heavy all filled up."

Father Fry grunted as they heaved it out of the car and onto the gravel lot, Collins barely straining. Collins couldn't help but retort, as they toted the overfilled cooler across the firefly swarmed grass towards the distant lights.

"Yeah, but it didn't seem like Maggy, you know? When you've known someone so well and then you see them change so much. Something got to her." Or someone.

"I've found that people have an astonishing capacity for change given the right circumstances."

"Yeah, but Maggy? She was always such a country girl. Gritty, but proper. I mean, she'd always liked to draw and sing, sure, but suddenly she's off to some fancy New York art school without a word of warning? Gotten herself a scholarship too." Collins stopped suddenly. Father Fry set his side of the cooler down with a sigh of relief. He eased himself onto the lid and rubbed at his shoulder awkwardly.

The weight of it all was getting to him, building like pressure in a dam. Collins needed to get this knot out of his chest before he exploded. He paced, chafing his hands together.

"I know this is an odd question, but… have you ever failed? Like, there is no coming back from this kind of fail?"

Without blinking, Father Fry replied, "Yes."

Collins paused in his pacing, astonished. "What did you do?"

Father Fry sat still, returning his gaze evenly. "I ran away from it."

Collins blinked. He hadn't expected that kind of response. Father Fry was a veteran and a man of God; he seemed to have it all together. If he couldn't handle failure, what was he going to do? Collins folded his arms, then unfolded them and brushed his hands through his hair. He began pacing back and forth. Father Fry sat still.

"Collins." He looked at Father Fry, who was staring at him, brow knit. "I was wrong." He took a deep breath and repeated himself. "I was wrong. I shouldn't have run away. Things would be very different for me if I had faced my problems. If I had acted with more character. You don't have to make the same mistake."

He stood and placed his hands on Collins' shoulders. "But just know that even when you do fail, you're not alone." Collins blinked hard at the sudden moisture in his eyes.

"Thanks," he whispered. Father Fry dropped his hands. Collins sighed. "I think… failure I can deal with. I mean, everyone fails, right?" He grimaced, remembering Maggy's face on his and Quinn's wedding day. This was going to be so much worse. Maggy had eventually forgiven him. He didn't know if Quinn could. "I just wish the past could be past, forget and forgive, you know?" he said.

"I get that," murmured Father Fry. He gazed back at the church, and Collins followed his look to see the ladies' shadows moving back and forth across the softly glowing windows.

"Can I ask *you* a question?" Father Fry asked with a crooked grin after a short pause.

"Sure." Collins had a sneaking suspicion he knew what was coming.

"Why did you think it was a good idea to sleep with two women at the same time? And sisters at that?" He laughed. "That seems like a spectacularly bad idea even for an seventeen-year-old."

Collins chuckled to hear the question that was usually

whispered, put so plainly. He leaned back and looked at the restless trees overhead. "That's the thing." He shoved his hands in his pockets. "I never slept with Maggy. Everyone just fucking assumes I did. Sorry for swearing," he said quickly, straightening up with a worried look. Father Fry spread his hands.

"No need to apologize. I'm the one being nosey."

Collins glanced towards the lights in the church, heat creeping up his neck. "I know everyone blames me for Maggy leaving, but Maggy and I were never good together. God, I told her it was over like three times, and she thought I was joking." He sighed, scratching at his arm. "And then it was like Quinn and I just *saw* each other for the first time. And I just knew. *This* is the one. And sure, we were young and dumb—"

Father Fry held a hand up. "You don't have to justify yourself to me."

Collins' thoughts trailed back to the gyms and their flattening cash flow, the loans coming due, Ralph swimming in paperwork. Dread clutched his heart. His voice flattened, weary. "I guess I should let all the gossip about that stop bothering me. Focus on getting my own house in order instead. Lord knows I've let things get out of hand."

"You could… talk to Quinn about it. To them both," Father Fry said quietly, not understanding. But how could he? He'd told no one, besides the slip to Maggy. Collins shivered involuntarily, thankful Father Fry couldn't see him clearly in the twilight. "Straighten up what you can. Without Alice around to keep it tamped down, it's up to you now."

Collins pursed his lips and nodded. "Maybe." His moment of reckoning was bearing down on him with all the force of a steam engine, but, dear God, he did not want it to be tonight.

Father Fry shrugged, a pinched look on his face. "This is Mississippi. I've only been here two years and I've already seen feuds that go back to the Civil War or further over smaller things. Don't want to let it get out of hand right when you have a chance to lay it to rest for good."

Collins rubbed at the back of his knuckles, thinking. It would be good to get some things out into the light while he had a chance—and a halfway forgiving wife. Collins nodded to himself. "You're right. It's just so…hard."

"It always is with family."

Collins nodded and dropped his hands before shoving them into his pockets. "Thanks for listening. It's nice to have somebody who gets it." Father Fry waved agreeably.

They remained in companionable silence for a few seconds before Father Fry sprang up.

"Let's take this on to the others, shall we?"

As they neared the glow of the lights, Collins heard raised voices, tense and defensive. Roy Mullone stood hunched over a granite monument, a pencil tucked behind one ear and wide, yellowed sheets spread before him. He swiped at his face with an old blue bandana. Collins and Father Fry drew up short as they saw not one but two open holes, men laboring to refill each. Careful squares of sod were stacked to the side. As the men sweated and swore, they shot disgruntled glares at the older man.

"Hold the light still, Charlie! I've got to get these other two sketched on here. We have got to make some better maps…" Mr. Mullone clutched a protractor and muttered calculations under his breath as he lightly drew pencil across the paper. Ice sloshed loudly in the cooler as Collins and Father Fry plunked it down at Roy's feet and he glanced up, frustration etched into the lines of his face. They began passing out water bottles to the flushed and sweating men, Collins studying the scene.

Charlie hovered beside Mr. Mullone and Harry, doing a poor job of holding up a lantern to light the maps they were studying in a show of being useful. Collins noted how clean his hands and shoes were in comparison to everyone else. He caught Rick's look and rolled his eyes.

"Harry!" Roy barked. "Take a good look where there are blank areas and *think* about the lay of the land. Where do you think we are least likely to run into any more surprises?" He jerked his head towards the men now dragging the sod back into place at the first gap.

Harry bit his lip, his barely-there beard bushing out in wild patches. His eyes scanned randomly back and forth across the paper. He pointed to a spot next to the rectory.

"Maybe there?" he said. The young man shoved his hand in his pocket and shrugged. Mr. Mullone groaned.

"We're fairly sure that's where the Johnstones' slaves were buried. Remember the debacles from the '90s I told you about?" he asked.

Harry nodded. "Oh, yeah."

Charlie muttered. "We really should get the ground-reading sonar out here again and get that area scanned so we can map it for good." Distracted, Mr. Mullone nodded and lightly drew a box around the area on the map.

Father Fry trotted back over and handed Mr. Mullone and Harry bottles of water. Collins drifted into the flashlight circle beside Mr. Mullone.

"What's going on?" Father Fry asked. "I thought we had started a new grave. Why are we closing a second one as well?"

"We found previous occupants in both," Mr. Mullone said dryly, swiping at his face again. He took the lantern from Charlie and handed it to Collins. Charlie scowled.

"Thank you, Charlie. Harry, why don't you help them get sod back on the other one? And fetch two cross markers as well!" Harry hustled away, looking relieved to be excused from his uncle's presence. Mr. Mullone turned back to the map.

"I know that boy is my nephew, but he—bless his heart—he is denser than a brick sometimes," Mr. Mullone said. Father Fry chuckled.

"Your metaphors are so colorful down here," he explained at their confused looks.

"Anyway…" Mr. Mullone continued, nonplussed, "I'm calling it for this section. This is the second unmarked grave, so we'll need to move to another spot. But I've got to figure out which one, and we're already tired out from two openings."

Collins studied the map. He'd spent a couple of summers working for a landscaper as a teenager before his father dictated that he start working at the gym, so the markings made sense to him.

"What about over here next to the ladies' rose garden? Not

a lot of trees, a natural progression from the 1950s section of the yard, no known burials." He swept his finger across the yellowed page.

Mr. Mullone put his hand on his chin, thinking. "We'll keep that in mind for the future, Collins. Not a bad spot. But it's awfully far from any of the Matins or Yellowley family."

"Awfully far," Charlie echoed. They blinked at him, having forgotten he was there. He slunk off, kicking at dirt clods.

Mr. Mullone shook his head and pointed to two spots on the map, indicating where they were at the very edge of the Yellowley family plot. Collins stared, bewildered. Those areas were surrounded by historic sections and centuries-old trees; they would be nearly impossible to work in without destroying monuments. A crunch of tires on gravel echoed up the drive and lights swept across the lot. The men stiffened.

"That must be Quinn," said Collins, spinning back to the maps, heart hammering.

"Haven't we dealt with smaller tree roots before?" he asked, pointing to an unmarked area surrounded by a stand of magnolia. It had enough distance from the trees that it might work. Mr. Mullone thumped the map.

"Beautiful spot. Right next to the first Matins family. Come on, boys! Time to go dig some test holes." Collins hustled away first to intercept Quinn. He was not about to let his wife be upset over her mother's burial if he had to dig the grave by himself with a teaspoon.

CHAPTER EIGHT

Allie sprang ahead of Quinn up the dark walk towards light and voices. As she disappeared into the fellowship hall, Quinn called after her, "Tell your aunt I'll be right there!"

They had finally made it to the church, over an hour late. She did not want to imagine how miffed Maggy would be, but Quinn knew her sister wouldn't let on around Allie. Fatigue already sapping her, Quinn trudged, tucking the unruly strap of her nursing bra under her dress. She paused to hastily smooth her hair and search for lip balm and a ponytail holder in her overflowing purse. She was lucky she had remembered to bring it; she was so scattered with their "unexpected blessing" baby these days. Behind her, the gate to the cemetery clanged. She sluggishly turned to see Father Fry and Collins emerge from the ornate fencing with its iron foliage and flowers twisting lushly upwards into an arch.

Collins jogged over to her, the smell of his cologne meeting her a few steps before he did; she loved that smell. He hugged her with arms damp from working hard and swept a strand of hair she had missed behind her ear before kissing her. His tenderness brought tears to her eyes. More tears. Always more tears these last few days.

"How are you? Did Clara go down alright?" he asked. She

kneaded at her shoulder.

"She fought way longer than I thought she would. Ms. Hernandez insisted that I come on—said she's handled colicky babies before. Maggy must be so mad with me."

He shook his head. "Don't worry about Maggy. You do what you want to say goodbye to your mom then go get some rest. Tomorrow will take care of itself; the Father and I'll take care of tonight." She finally took notice of Father Fry standing a couple of steps away and extended a hand to him.

"Thank you for being with us and Mom during her last moments. It meant the world to us," she said. Again, tearing up. She sniffled and began hunting through her purse, this time for tissues. Father Fry stepped forward with a handkerchief.

"You can keep it. I find them useful and a little bit longer-lasting," he said, smiling gently. They walked into the chapel to find Allie, almost as tall as her aunt, with her arm around Maggy's waist as the ladies cooed over her first set of pearls. Allie blushed.

"Thank you," she said. "They were Grandma's. Mom told me I could have them." Maggy hugged her niece and kissed her cheek but shot her sister a glare that could curdle milk. The ladies looked at each other nervously, settling shoulder pads and fiddling with rings. Quinn's stomach twisted. Of course, Allie would blurt it out that way; add that to the list of family dramas she would have to deal with sooner or later.

While Quinn sent Collins out to fetch the tea and lemons, Mrs. Greaves pressed a plate of finger sandwiches stolen from one of the covered dishes into her hands, distracting her, and Mrs. Vanderwahl with her trembling hair slipped a glass of water into her other hand with a gentle squeeze and hug.

As Quinn surveyed the room for Catherine, Mrs. Greaves gently bullied her into a soft chair. Her stomach sank as she realized her friend hadn't made it yet.

"Oh sweetie, let's get you settled over here." Mrs. Greaves pulled Quinn down next to her and laid her cane to the side. Quinn noted approvingly the softly glowing candles and perfectly circled chairs with the kneeler at the front.

She made a mental note to rearrange the flower sprays according to height in the morning before the visitation began. For some reason, the undertaker's men had placed them with all the showy pink peonies concentrated next to the casket. With the less vibrant arrangements fading into the ones made with white lilies, it created an oddly modern starburst effect in the otherwise historic, and demure, setting.

A soft hand on her cheek startled her out of her reverie. Mrs. Greaves sat studying her. "You're quite pale, Quinn. Have you been able to sleep at all?"

She shook her head, clutching at the glass of water. Between Clara and Mama, sleep had been elusive lately. Mrs. Greaves looked at her untouched plate and tapped the edge. "You should eat something, dearie." Obediently, Quinn nibbled the edge of a cucumber sandwich and set it back down, absentmindedly picking at the bread. Mrs. Greaves harrumphed and shook her head.

"Stubborn. All you Matins women are stubborn—trying to waste yourselves away from grief. It's one of the things that makes you special, but bless it, it makes me want to throttle you sometimes!"

Quinn chuckled and picked the sandwich back up and took a heartier bite. Mrs. Greaves side-eyed her and nodded approvingly.

To the side, she saw Collins hand Maggy a set of keys. Maggy's shoulders tensed then eased as he spoke. He turned away, waved at Quinn, and headed back outside. Relieved, she sat back in her chair and took another bite of her sandwich. Maybe whatever spat they had when Maggy arrived at the house earlier that afternoon was over.

Mrs. Greaves continued. "It does me so much good to see you girls together again at church. Do you know how long Maggy will be staying?"

"Hmm?"

Mrs. Greaves cocked her head. "I asked if you knew how long Maggy plans to stay?"

Quinn laid her plate aside and brushed her hands together,

stalling. It hadn't even occurred to her to ask earlier that day.

"At least the weekend. Maybe a day or two longer to sign some paperwork for the will? I haven't talked to her about it."

"She's staying with you, isn't she? You should ask her—maybe try to convince her to stay." Quinn's stomach fluttered hopefully at the thought, but she shoved it down. "We'd love to have her around for a little while if possible."

Quinn smiled tightly. This was Maggy, after all. She never stayed in one spot very long.

"Maybe. I'll ask." Mrs. Greaves nodded and prattled on about all the ladies bringing dishes tomorrow while Quinn sat silently, studying the back of Maggy's head.

Soon enough, everyone settled into chairs as the chitchat wound down. Quinn and Maggy sat stiffly next to each other. She saw Mrs. Greaves look pointedly at Maggy; Maggy stared steadfastly at her hands clasped in her lap, ignoring everything around her. Next, she turned her gaze on Quinn, eyebrow arched and imperious. Apparently, she would be dealing with the pearl issue sooner. Quinn rolled her eyes but obeyed the silent decree. She leaned towards her sister.

"I'm sorry about the pearls," Quinn said in a whispered rush. Father Fry took a sip of water and asked them to turn to Psalm One. "I didn't mean anything by it. I just needed to get Allie calmed down and out of the house. I should have been clearer with her about them or asked you first—"

Maggy held up her hands, stopping her. In solemn tones, Father Fry asked them to bow their heads in prayer.

"It's ok; we're all tired and on edge right now. Let's just get through tonight and we'll straighten it out, ok?" she said, a blush high in her cheeks and her eyes much too bright. With that, Maggy grabbed a pew Bible, thunked it open, and bowed her head.

Quinn could barely breathe. She tried to calm herself down, told herself to let it go, but her heart beat faster and heat rose in her cheeks. Her mind spun. The first five Psalms the Father read passed in a blur until his lilting Welsh accent changed to Mrs. Streisand's sharper tones as she took her turn at the kneeler.

Quinn glanced out the window to where the men's lights bounced back and forth, trying to find a point to focus on, before slipping back into the torrent of her thoughts. Whatever was bothering her, Maggy still hadn't let it go after all these years, to be so upset over a strand of pearls. Every little thing was a slight to her now.

Then it was Quinn's turn, Mrs. Streisand's nudge interrupting her thoughts. As she took her place at the kneeler, she knew she should begin at Psalm 11—her fingertip was already dutifully pressed there. In her mind, though, her mother stood with a far-away look in her prematurely aging eyes at the kitchen sink. The last rays of sunset gilding her long hair, Mama slowly scrubbed the dishes in scalding hot water, the words of another Psalm floating above the water's rush. It was just after their father died and the house was so quiet without his booming voice. Except for when Mama sang this Psalm. She flipped to Psalm 116.

"I love the Lord because he has heard my voice and my pleas for mercy." Maggy lifted stricken eyes to her. By verse nine she was weeping silently, but Quinn didn't stop, continuing, "I will walk before the Lord in the land of the living." Maggy covered her face with her hands, her magenta polished nails dark in the light. "I will pay my vows to the Lord in the presence of all his people. Precious in the sight of the Lord is the death of his saints. I will offer to you the sacrifice of thanksgiving and all in the name of the Lord." Maggy's shoulders heaved. She got up and rushed into the vestibule, hands still over her face. They listened to her heels echo on the planks.

The ladies stared at Quinn, who sat stone-faced, and nervously darted looks at one another. Quinn watched from the corner of her eye as Mrs. Streisand pursed her lips at Mrs. Greaves. In her gut, guilt coiled, small and cold. Vulnerable. She shivered and drew the familiar heat of her anger to her with the memory of sitting in the stale hospital room with their mother, alone.

"That's the first time she's cried," Quinn said quietly. The tapers in their silver candlesticks guttered and dimmed on top of the closed casket.

"Well then. Mrs. Greaves, why don't you carry on with Psalm 11?" asked Father Fry. They all bent back over their Bibles, continuing with the reading. Sometime later, Maggy slipped back into her seat, makeup fixed and eyes red. She did not take a turn.

Around ten p.m., Quinn sent up a little prayer of thanks for her aching behind when Father Fry inserted a lace bookmark into the vestry Bible and took one last sip from his water glass. He popped his knuckles.

"Let us bless the food," he said. A few minutes later, they all trooped out, with a heaped Hefty plate in each hand. Allie led the procession with a flashlight in one hand and a box of plastic cutlery in the other.

At the bobbing of the approaching flashlight, a round of tired *huzzahs* rose from the men working at the graveside. A clang of dropped shovels followed. They passed the plates and ate, standing and silent, only the trees creaking overhead in the breeze that had decided to return.

Collins hustled over and kissed Quinn on the cheek. She leaned into him, not caring about the sweat he was coated in. The children were so often covered in worse. Dispirited, she rubbed at the dark circles under her eyes and wondered what eye cream Maggy used to look so fresh. They were only a year and a half apart, but Quinn knew she looked a decade older. Collins said softly, "Why don't you go home after this? Mrs. Hernandez will stay the whole night, anyway. You can get some real rest."

Quinn shook her head, determined to stay until the end of the reading, and he wrapped an arm around her. Hopeful that Catherine had finally been able to slip away from her meeting, she scanned the crowd for her friend's headlamp smile but didn't find it. Instead, she noted Mr. Mullone's glance from her to Maggy standing behind them at the edge of the light. She placed a hand over her stomach, trying to quiet its protests as she turned away. Better to leave things be for now; she'd poked the hornets' nest enough for tonight.

She looked around at all the familiar faces of her church family, softly beaming in the lantern light, and swiped at her stinging eyes—Mama would have loved having such a captive audience. Behind Mr. Mullone, Mrs. Greaves tapped his ankle with her cane and nodded. Quinn chuckled. That old biddy was as subtle as an ostrich feather on a Sunday hat. Waving Mrs. Streisand's barbecued meatballs on his fork like a conductor, Mr. Mullone launched into the first telling.

"I remember the day I met Alice," he said. He brushed a hand across his forehead, leaving a streak of dirt before returning to his meatballs and story. "She was newlywed to Truman, and I was new to the county, but she marched straight up to me that first day in church and looked me over and said, 'You'll do.' And she put these very maps in my hands." He reverentially touched the maps with his pointer finger, weighed down on top of a granite crypt next to him. "She had a gift, knowing exactly what a person could do as soon as she clapped eyes on them." Everyone nodded and smiled fondly, having had similar experiences.

Father Fry chuckled, "After my trial sermon here, she called me up—how she got my number I've no idea—and without preamble told me, 'Son, you're going to have to do better than that if you're going to be my preacher.'" Quinn laughed, imagining her tiny mother smarting off to the handsome new preacher-man. She could see it easily. Maggy guffawed, clearly struck with his charm. She was always a sucker for an accent.

The telling continued, stories being shared long after plates had emptied. As both sexton and president of the Gravedigger's Guild, Mr. Mullone had some of the best.

"Oh, and how Alice loved music! She was always making up tunes," he said. He hugged Quinn, and she hugged her "second father" back. He waved Maggy into the light and wrapped an arm around her too. He looked at her then Maggy, and suddenly Quinn's stomach churned. "And she loved hearing the duets you girls sang, said you sounded like angels."

Mrs. Greaves piped up.

"Sing us something, darlings!" Quinn looked around nervously while Maggy demurred, glancing at Quinn, lips pale and cheeks flushed. More voices chimed in demanding a song.

"I've got baby brain so bad these days, I can't remember the words of anything," Quinn said anxiously. She'd already pushed Maggy far enough tonight; she didn't need to put her on the spot now.

"That's all right, sugar. Just sing what you can remember. We only want to hear a bit of your voices. The words are unimportant." Agreement echoed around the circle.

Quinn looked to her sister who was studying her with a worried expression, biting her lip. Maggy shrugged.

"Up to you, sis," Maggy whispered, a hand pressed to her stomach. She reached over and squeezed Quinn's hand. "We don't have to if it's too much for you. I'll handle them." She nodded to the circle of eager faces. A pang shot through Quinn at her sister's protectiveness. She clenched and unclenched her fists, swallowing, knowing she didn't deserve it. Her chest warmed with gratefulness at having Maggy on her side once again, and she released a breath she didn't even realize she'd been holding. She shook her head, a smile tugging her lips upward for the first time in days.

"It's alright, but you gotta lead, Mags."

Maggy grinned. A memory came flooding back, and Quinn saw Maggy radiant as she had been on her fourteenth birthday. Her happiness wasn't because of the cake and party—although Mama's cakes were legendary, it was because that following Sunday she would receive her royal blue robe and take her place in the choir. Maggy handed her a water bottle she had magicked from somewhere and cleared her throat. Quinn nearly laughed when she heard the familiar words of the old folk ballad in her sister's mouth. Maggy's voice wavered nervously then filled as she found the notes.

"Dogwood, cypress, magnolia, and pine—Come walk the woods with me tonight. Hear the mockingbird's lonely song, Dance in a circle of new moonlight." As the melody drove on, Quinn joined in, her soprano harmony soaring.

"Can you hear it calling, riding on the wind? Place your hand in mine. Destiny is rising tonight."

As their voices cracked with emotion, the others joined in as they knew the words, their voices echoing like morning bells in the trees.

CHAPTER NINE

Maggy was convinced that Southern ladies' purses were magic. That was the only explanation. In the lantern light, she leaned against a headstone, her hip digging into the gritty rock, as she swiped at the sweat working its way into her eyes. In front of her, everyone lined up neatly to toss their plates into the black garbage bags she and Father Fry held outstretched.

Earlier, Mrs. Streisand had drawn the bags from the enfolding depths of her adorable hobo bag and laid them primly in Maggy and Father Fry's hands with a wink. "Thought we might need a few things tonight, so I grabbed them on my way out," she'd said before sauntering back towards the chapel, content as a fat house cat that Maggy and Father Fry were well on their way down the aisle.

And earlier still, Mrs. Greaves had pulled a can of bug spray from her saddlebag purse and startled Maggy by enveloping her in a DEET-saturated cloud. She was smelly but thankful not to have to subject herself to any more calamine pox. When Maggy asked her, choking amid the noxious cloud, where she got such an accessory, Mrs. Greaves patted her shoulder and said, "Walmart, darling, Walmart." She'd leaned in and whispered with an all-too-knowing nod towards the knot of men with which Father Fry was animatedly talking, dark hair glimmering,

"A lady must always be prepared to look her best, don't you agree?" Matchmaking Southern-style: via purses and garbage bags and bug spray. Like the old biddies had even *known* to prepare for this.

The garbage bag grew heavier, and slowly people dispersed back to their tasks, including the crowd in front of Maggy and Father Fry. Maggy whisked her long, honey hair over her shoulder as they gathered up a few plates stranded on top of gravestones in companionable silence. In the lamplight to their left, men kicked thick, red-clay mud off shovel blades and kneaded knots out of their shoulders. One group began scooping loose dirt back into an open site under Harry's direction while another split off to continue another opening. She spotted Allie and was about to wave the girl over to help when Harry stepped over to her niece and took her plate from her hand with a flirtatious grin and a tickle to her ribs. She blushed and batted at him, but laughed and smiled adoringly. How long had that been going on? Maggy shook her head and glanced to see if Quinn or Collins had noticed the exchange, but they were in their own bubble as usual.

She picked up another abandoned plate and watched curiously as Collins gave Quinn one last kiss on the forehead before sauntering over to the men filling the grave. The world wobbled a bit and tilted. Her sister's marriage was one she had never understood or felt welcomed to even observe. As she smashed one more soggy paper plate down into the bulging bag, she sighed. She should stop being surprised by this fact. As close as she and Quinn had been, that had all ended the day Quinn decided to screw Collins and got knocked up. Mama had done her best to smooth it over, hush it up, including hushing Maggy. So Quinn got the love of her life, and Maggy got a fresh start in New York. To the rest of the world, it was ancient history. But to her, it still stung—a scab that would never quite heal.

She blinked, swallowed, and the world righted itself. Inevitably, her eyes dragged themselves back towards Collins and Quinn.

An oblivious Collins leaned on a shovel, cracking jokes to an appreciative audience. Quinn had caught sight of the flirting teenagers and paused to shoot what looked like a warning glance at Allie before heading into the gloom under the trees back towards the church. Her eyes snagged on Maggy's as she turned, and she shook her head with a wry smile.

Several steps behind Maggy and Father Fry, a cluster of women lingered, gathering up empty water bottles. Their voices rustled in the breeze. Suddenly, Maggy realized what they were talking about.

"I'd slap someone if they gave away my mother's pearls, niece or not."

"Hush now! No one wants to be the one to start the drama at their mama's wake."

Heat crept up Maggy's chest and neck, embarrassed for whoever this was that they'd make such a big deal out of one basement bargain strand of pearls. She glanced at Father Fry. In the dim light, she thought she saw the tips of his ears blushed up. He steadfastly knotted up his bag and reached for hers.

"Still. You'd think she'd do something. I'd throw a hissy fit—snatch those pearls right off her."

"You would *not!*"

Another voice cut in, "Can't say I'm surprised. She always was such a pushover, following big sis around." A pushover? Maggy recoiled. She knew she wasn't a pushover. But her mind flitted to the string of demanding boyfriends, dissatisfied bosses. No matter how high she jumped or how low she scraped, she couldn't please them. She winced.

A sharp whisper cut in. "Maggy always did everything Quinn told her to. All the pranks and the troublemaking? Quinn put her up to most of it. I heard Maggy was even set to go to the same college before all that stuff with Collins. And then," the voice dropped lower, "Alice was the one who arranged to get Maggy out-of-state before…" the voice trailed off suggestively.

Something broke loose in Maggy's chest, like an iceberg from an Arctic shelf. No, more like the freak tornado that swept Dorothy away. She choked on an angry swarm of words.

The inevitable *tutts* and "Bless her hearts" had ensued when

Father Fry turned around. The women startled and looked sheepishly at Maggy as Father Fry rumbled in his brogue, "Ladies, might I get those bottles from you?"

She didn't care how the rest played out. Maggy spun and strode across the close-cropped grass, careless of the Louis Vuittons.

The grass turned to gravel, then paving stones as she marched towards the church. She was done playing nice. She was going to have it out with Quinn once and for all. No more unanswered questions; no more being shushed into awkward silences at holidays. No more "Would you pass the potatoes, please?" when she'd rather hurl the dish at Quinn's head. She was tired of being Emily Post-proper and still being branded the runaway and the troublemaker simply for wanting an apology. Hell, for wanting to be acknowledged at all. Mama could very well rise up in her coffin and stop her if she didn't like it. The wind picked up, and a long, low branch scraped over the backbone of the church with a shingle-breaking clatter.

In her pocket, her phone played the Imperial March from Star Wars. She froze, hoping it would go to voicemail. It kept playing. A tightening in her chest caused her to wheeze, and she rubbed at her shoulder, her old self-soothing tick.

She didn't have to answer. No one would blame her. She was at her mama's wake, after all. But Mama would have urged her to try to work things out. She took a shuddering breath through her nose and hit the glowing button.

"Hey, Marcus!" Her voice chirped.

"Maggy, why did Heather just demand that I come pick up your stuff from work? She said you wouldn't answer. What the hell is going on?" Maggy rubbed at her shoulder again, the tightening in her chest worsening. She really didn't want to get into it with Marcus right now. She breathed in through her nose, out through her mouth, trying to ground herself.

"Yeah… Sorry. I've been screening her calls—I forgot to change you as my emergency contact, so she must have decided to call you." She rolled her eyes; they had only broken up a month ago, and she was understaffed with hellish deadlines, but that wouldn't matter to him. He didn't let stuff "linger" and he hated it when she did. "I'll pick it up when I get back. It's one box, right?"

He ignored her question, launching the interrogation. "From the way Heather was talking—God, that woman never stops screeching, you don't have a job now? And you sound all nasally. Have you been crying? What do you mean 'come back'? Are you out of town?" His words clipped together, fueled by coffee and years of cramming cases into his brain.

"I'm at my mom's wake. I've stepped out for a minute." She tried to focus on her surroundings as her therapist instructed.

"Oh God, Maggy… I'm sorry. I didn't know… I should have left it until Monday…" Marcus lapsed into an awkward silence.

Crickets. All Maggy could hear was literally the crickets and cicadas clogging the night air with their noise. And still, Marcus wouldn't hang up. She needed to get him off the phone, but in a way that wouldn't blow up this situation any further. Their breakup had been fairly amicable, for him basically throwing her out of her own apartment. And he had all her work files now, all her sketches and ideas for future shoots and editorials. She would need those.

"Marcus, it's late. Why are you calling at this time of night? You are so particular about your eight hours. I'm sorry that Heather called you—she didn't call you just now, did she?"

"No, no! It's not that." He trailed off, accentuated by a little puff of air. On top of it all, he was even smoking! Taking his time as usual.

Aggravation finally eased the panic trying to work its way up her throat. Maggy clenched her fist and asked, "Did I leave anything else at the apartment? I could have sworn I got everything into storage. If something's in your way, I could have Olivia swing by to get it." Olivia had been champing at the bit for a chance to chew him out.

"Oh, no! Nothing like that." Another little puff and a deep inhale. She heard a slurp as he took a sip of something, at this time of night, most likely scotch. She plucked at the top of her dress, trying to fan it for any bit of coolness in the clinging humidity.

Overwhelmed, Maggy snapped. "Marcus! I am at my mother's wake. Please. Get. To. The Point." She covered her eyes with her other hand and made herself count to ten as she exhaled. Apparently, she did it out loud.

"No need to get angry! I wanted to check on you after the call from Heather. I didn't know things had gotten to that point."

"Yeeesss," Maggy drawled, letting the Southern twang he always cringed at creep into her voice, "You dump me, and I come apart at the seams, the weak, little woman that I am." Maggy bent over, breathing deeply. The trees whirled overhead, but she couldn't tell if it was from wind or if she was about to faint from the surrealness of it all.

She heard footsteps running up behind her and glanced over her shoulder, alarmed, not wanting to be seen like this. Father Fry jogged up and paused at her upheld hand. He backed up a few steps, clearly not wanting to intrude on her conversation, but also not wanting to leave her distraught and alone.

Silence crackled over the line. Marcus exhaled. "I guess I deserved that one. I'm sorry. I would like to… help. To be there for you as a friend. What happened?"

Maggy's lips trembled, and she pressed a hand to her mouth for a second before she spoke quietly, "Apparently, my mother's death does not count as a family emergency but does count as job abandonment. She fired me on the spot when I said I was taking a few days to put her affairs in order."

"I am so sorry. Would you like me to sue?" That was Marcus. Always leaping to action whether she needed it or not. Mama had loved how driven and ambitious he'd been—said he'd been real marriage material. The thought made her want to lie down.

She thought about it for a second and shook her head.

"Maggy?"

Realizing he couldn't see her over the phone, she laughed, the sound crackling back to her over the line. Voice confident, but hands shaking, she continued, "Sorry, I was thinking to myself. Don't do anything. Heather never did think things through. The paperwork isn't even filed yet from what I know and when HR finds out… everything… they might back the whole thing out. I'll let you know."

"Say the word, cupcake," he said.

"Don't call me that anymore," she said softly. The band around her chest squeezed painfully. At least she wouldn't have to tell Mama that Marcus was gone now. She hadn't had the heart to tell her on the phone, even after a month had gone by. She rubbed her forehead and sighed.

"I guess that part of us is over." Marcus sounded regretful, almost. Maybe wistful was the word. She'd never known him to get sentimental. His straightforwardness had been one of the things she'd liked. It unsettled her, hearing him get misty.

"Yes, we're over."

She heard another long, sucking puff.

"Can you tell me about your mom, or is it still all too fresh?" he asked.

Maggy's face went numb. Her shoulders slumped.

"It was pneumonia," she said flatly. In her stomach Mrs. Streisand's meatballs roiled, giving her heartburn. "Came out of nowhere and for whatever reason, she couldn't shake it. Some sort of heart defect we didn't know she had."

"She was fairly young, right? Only fifty-seven?"

"Yes… Marcus, I need to go now. I'll talk to you later. When I head back to New York."

"Oh—ok," he seemed taken aback. "Well, call me if you need…"

"Ok, bye."

She cut off the call, not able to bear hearing the promise he always made and never kept. The years of sleep deprivation, endless coffee, ridiculous diets, and little blue pills washed down with God only knows how much alcohol to cope and to keep up with and be "worthy of" him. She was cutting it all off.

Maggy stared at the phone, the screen still glowing. She thought about chucking it into the nearest tree. Instead, she tucked it as carefully into her pocket as she would tuck Kylie into bed. Clenching and unclenching her fingers, she glanced at

Father Fry, hands shoved deep in his pockets. Shadows wavered on the windows of the church behind him.

Light slashed across the lawn from the vestibule door but did not reach them, no doubt from Mrs. Streisand looking to restart the reading of the Psalms. She spotted them with a bounce of recognition but spun and pretended to scan the darkness in the other direction. Maggy motioned vaguely at the fellowship hall, but he cut her off.

"Are you alright?"

"I'm fine," she snapped, "Sorry, I'd just… I'd rather you hadn't seen that." She waved towards the church.

"Go on. I think they're looking for you. I need to find Qui…" she trailed off, realizing Quinn would be inside but wanting to be anywhere but a gossiping crowd. Her arm sank. She was so, so tired of pretending to be ok.

He stared worriedly at her, chin down, before stepping closer. His hand fluttered at her cheek, not quite touching her. Her vision blurred, and she realized her cheeks were hot and wet.

The door leading to her mother's body banged shut and with it the light. A sob escaped her lips.

"I don't know what…. How could this… She's gone!" She was sure she stuttered through a lot more than that, but she was blubbering too hard to tell. With a pathetic little plunk, she dropped her forehead onto Father Fry's chest, overwhelmed. He shifted, startled, but didn't step back. After a few seconds, he wrapped his arms around her and patted her back slowly with light, little taps.

She sobbed for a long time. Long enough to realize that his cologne smelled good, something ocean water-esque. Long enough to realize her makeup was done for and to feel vain for worrying about makeup at her mother's wake. And long enough to realize how much like a romance novel it was to sob into the arms of the pastor with the sexy accent that she had just met— and how presumptuous it was in real life. How long *had* they been standing there? She hiccupped, shaking herself fully out of her stupor.

Taking a small step back, she could barely drag her eyes up to meet his. She wiped at her nose with the back of her wrist, horrified to see snot go everywhere. Father Fry performed a miracle by pulling a clean handkerchief out of his pocket and not watching her mop up her face. Somewhere an owl hooted at her awkwardness.

"Well, I feel childish," she said as she wiped the last of the tears away, "Crying all over you like that. What would Mama say?"

"Knowing her, she'd probably be all gaggled up with the rest of the women at the window right now offering to make popcorn," he responded with a shrug. She looked over to see a bunch of faces pressed up, staring at them. They scattered at their glance.

"There are no secrets in Mississippi," she said, laughing.

"That's for sure."

She offered the smudged handkerchief back, and he waved it away with a rueful smile.

"You keep it."

"Thank you, Father Fry."

"Please, Derek is fine."

She nodded sheepishly, hoping they were far enough into the shadows of the trees that he couldn't see how puffy her face was. "I suppose we're on a first-name basis now. Maggy." He pulled a hand through his hair and studied her. She noticed a tattoo peeking out from under his shirt sleeve, a fierce swirl of red and green ink.

"Speaking of secrets…" She pointed at it.

"Oh, this? This isn't a secret so much as a… youthful indiscretion… I'd rather not display."

"Looks like a dragon tattoo to me." She hiccupped again and swiped at a stray tear.

He chuckled, the corner of his mouth inching up. "It's the insignia of the Royal Welsh Infantry—from my time in the British army. Did two tours in Iraq before I 'took up the cloth'," he responded.

"I don't know if I'd call military service something to not

display," she responded, tilting her head to the side.

He grimaced. "My reasons for going into the army weren't noble. I was angry and full of pride—let's say God and a very persistent chaplain worked me over in the nick of time."

She nodded. "I get being angry. It's why I went to New York." They stood in silence for a moment. The humid air pulsed with cicadas.

"What are you going to do now?" he asked. She glanced up at him and he pursed his lips. "I mean, it kinda sounds like you don't have to go back to New York now unless you want to?"

She stared at the church and the shadows moving inside it. She thought of the lit tapers in the fellowship hall, the Tree of Life sculpture twisting and clinging up the far wall, glowing and mythological in its size. In the darkened sanctuary were the pews she had raced under as a child, sliding on her belly, and the drops of water she flicked at Quinn from the baptismal font when she thought no was watching. Of Mrs. Greaves patting her back like she always did, and Mrs. Streisand's Boy Scout ways and determination to fix everything with food.

"I don't know. I have a lot to figure out… with job stuff… And Quinn… I don't know if Mama told you…" she glanced up at him and paused, embarrassed, kneading at her forearm. She wanted any bit of tension to leave her body.

Derek spread his hands and filled in for her, "Between her hints and Collins, I know plenty. No need to tell me anything you don't want." She heaved a heavy breath, letting it escape slowly, relieved.

"So, you get that with Quinn, well, I don't know if she will even want to talk to me after… after everything. All this time." She waved at the church and the casket inside.

He studied her, finger over his mouth. "What do you want?"

She tucked a long piece of hair back into her now helplessly messy bun. "I don't know what to do now that everything's fallen apart." She scraped her foot over the grass, thinking. "I miss home. And my sister. But Quinn doesn't make things easy. One minute we're good and the next we're fighting like cats 'n dogs." After fifteen years of trying to stamp out her accent in

New York, she could already feel the edges of it creeping back into her voice after less than a day back home. It happened after every visit. "I just want to feel welcome here again, ya' know?"

"I get that more than you know." He scuffed his toe through the dirt. "Look, for what it's worth coming from me, family is always worth fighting for. If there's any way to set yourselves aside and fight together for a relationship." His voice soothed her with its melodic rise and fall, and the ache in her chest eased a bit.

She rubbed at her nose again with the handkerchief. "That's a pretty big 'if' in this case."

He nodded, his intense green eyes holding hers. "A risk worth taking, I think." She nodded. From him, reconnecting with Quinn sounded almost possible.

He looked at the church. "I should really get back in there. You coming?"

She shook her head quickly. "I need a few minutes to… gather myself." She fluttered the bedraggled handkerchief.

He smiled understandingly. "Take all the time you need. We'll be waiting for you." He patted her shoulders reassuringly once more before stepping towards the chapel. "See you inside." His Welsh brogue made her heart lurch a little, even in her addled state.

Maggy bit her lip and bobbed her head. "See ya' inside." She watched as he walked away. He was slim and straight, not gym-built like Collins, and she found his easy gait pleasant to watch. As he closed the door of the chapel with a little wave to her, the owl hooted again.

"Oh, *shut up!*" she said and turned towards a familiar path disappearing into the softly rustling trees. She needed a moment to breathe.

CHAPTER TEN

Massaging the knot that had crept steadily up her neck throughout the evening, Quinn glanced around the dimmed hall from where she lounged in a cushioned chair resting her feet as they waited on the stragglers from dinner. She glanced at her phone for any missed messages from Catherine. Just then a hand clasped her shoulder, and she looked up into her friend's sparkling eyes.

Quinn shot to her feet, wrapping her arms around Catherine's neck.

Laughter rang in her ears. "Hello to you, too!" Catherine drew back a little. "You didn't seriously think I wouldn't show up, did you?"

Quinn sank back down into the chair. "The way this night has been going, I wouldn't bet on anything happening."

Catherine winked. "Eh, funerals have a way of bringing out the unexpected in people. Next to weddings and divorces. I should know."

Quinn chuckled. "How comforting that we are so normal in our weirdness."

At the window, something had caught the interest of the ladies. Quinn and Catherine watched them speculatively while making bets on a tree falling and hitting the church or Allie and

Harry doing something inappropriate in the parking lot. Though Quinn supposed if it were the latter, Mrs. Streisand would alert her to it soon enough—or haul her granddaughter in here by the ear herself. All at once, the ladies broke away from the window and began to mill around the refreshment table or settle into chairs. Their low chatter reached them in a pleasant burbling of noise.

"Caught in their snooping." Catherine grinned. She began digging in her purse. "By the way, I brought you something." Quinn watched her curiously. She snorted when Catherine pulled out a silver flask, the candlelight gleaming in the polished metal.

"You didn't!" she whispered as Catherine snuck it to her.

"Couldn't let you go through this evening without a little liquid courage, now could I?" She jerked her chin towards the window. "Besides, it's not like every man out there doesn't have one."

Holding the cool metal flask down by her side out of eye-line, Quinn turned it over in her palm, studying the fine filigree on it. "This looks similar to Mama's."

"It is your mother's." Quinn glanced up and saw Catherine's small, sad smile. "She gave me a key, remember?" She paused and laughed quietly. "Also, it was really easy to find. She keeps it next to her Bible."

Quinn's fingers tightened around the flask. "That sounds about right. Mama and her bourbon." She touched her friend's arm. "Thank you."

Catherine patted her hand, then Quinn looked around and surreptitiously snuck a sip. She tried to cover a cough as Fireball burned its way down her throat. Catherine tittered.

"Really?"

"Serves you right for drinking at church."

"Bitch." She said it with a grin.

Catherine held out her hand. "Don't hog the booze."

In the small space of the fellowship hall, the smell of hot wax, powdery perfumes, and DEET-filled bug spray wafted through the air in alternating waves as they sat chatting and slipping the flask back and forth. Despite Catherine's calming presence, a vein in her temple pulsed in response, threatening a migraine, and she dug to the bottom of her candy-wrapper-filled purse in search of her emergency medicine. Before she could find anything, the door creaked open, making the candles flicker, and Father Fry entered alone. Hadn't Maggy been helping him gather trash?

Like meerkats on the Discovery Channel, all the ladies' heads turned towards him, an expectant hush falling. His eyes widened and with a small, awkward wave and a chuckle, he closed the door.

"Continue on, ladies! We'll get started back with the reading here in a bit." With a swivel, the ladies returned to their conversations, the burbling louder than before. Quinn noted the speculative glances of Mrs. Greaves and Mrs. Streisand and their posse towards the reverend as he approached her and Catherine. She wondered what plans they were hatching. If she had to guess, she'd say matrimonial, and of the variety involving her recently single sister. No doubt they'd try to involve her soon enough.

Father Fry slid into a chair next to her. His face was open and inviting, but his eyes pinched up in concern at the corners. It was a look Quinn was becoming all too familiar with these days.

"I'm sure you're taking a moment to yourself and I don't want to disturb you. But I wanted to come check on you real quick. Is there anything I can get you? A glass of water? Some coffee?"

She shook her head with a small smile.

"Thank you, Father, but no. I'm good for the moment. Catherine's got me taken care of." Catherine patted her knee with a sly grin.

He nodded and tapped his thumbs on the back of the pew. "Let me know if you do or if you want to talk. You know I'm always here for you and your family." Quinn shot a look at the plotting and planning ladies. If only he knew.

She bobbed her head and looked over his shoulder at the

door as she tried to stifle a yawn.

"I will. Right now, I would like to go ahead and get the reading started back if we could. Where's Maggy? Wasn't she with you?"

Clearing his throat, he looked down and clasped his hands. "She had to take a call…" Quinn shot up out of her seat towards the door, Catherine rising with her.

"How could she be working at our mother's…"

He grabbed her wrist, cutting her off.

"Not like that! It was Marcus?" His voice ticked up in query, but his smooth face showed that he'd already put the pieces together.

Quinn snatched her wrist back and plopped down, Catherine hovering over her.

"Why was Marcus calling her? I thought they broke up." Father Fry shrugged.

"They did, from what I could gather. But her boss—ex-boss?—called him when Maggy didn't answer about getting her stuff from work. I guess she left some things there when she was fired."

Quinn rubbed at her temples, the hazy memories from that afternoon clicking together. "I don't think she was expecting to get fired for coming to her mom's funeral. It's kind of illegal." Father Fry quirked an eyebrow at her.

"Kinda. Yeah."

Catherine interjected, "That still doesn't answer where she is now."

With a puzzled look, he motioned outside. "She was upset. I told her to take all the time she needed."

Quinn shook her head. Great. They could be here all night now. Maggy's outbursts were famously long-lived if no one interceded; Mama had always been too indulgent with her. She pushed herself back up.

"Where are you going?" Father Fry asked.

"To go find my sister! So we can do our mama's wake." Quinn flapped a hand at the casket with its brightly gleaming candles.

He shook his head. "Why don't you give her some time? She'll come in when she's ready. We can get the reading started without her."

Quinn was already shaking her head. "It's not right to start without Maggy. I'll just go get her." She muttered, "Pretty sure I know where she'll be too." She waved off Catherine from coming with her. "Would you make sure everyone is ready to start when we get back?" Frowning, Catherine nodded reluctantly.

Father Fry looked up at her and rubbed at his chin. "I suppose I can't stop you. But go easy on her alright? She's grieving too—a little differently from you. But she is."

Quinn blinked. Grieve differently? That made no sense. Grief was grief. She stepped around him. Sarcastically she drawled, "I'll keep that in mind." Her tongue curled around the taste of copper pennies and she glanced back over her shoulder to where he sat, leaned forward in the chair, forearms on the back of the plush seat in front of him. Catherine stared after her, a worried look etching her face. But this was something Quinn needed to do on her own. She was the only one who had ever been able to handle Maggy. The shrill of cicadas and creaking of trees surrounded her as she eased closed the heavy wooden door and stepped out into the restless night alone.

CHAPTER ELEVEN

Maggy was so thankful for the miracle of DEET. As allergic as she was to mosquitos, she would be marvelously welted up sitting underneath these pecan trees without the cloud of the obnoxious bug spray Mrs. Greaves had enveloped her in earlier. She could hear the whine of the blood-sucking little creatures as they cut through the thick air, but they didn't dare approach.

She sat on a picturesque stone bench at the tree line of the church's property, intermittently crying and taking the deep, calming breaths her therapist had taught her. Far to her left stood one streetlamp, marking the entrance to the drive and casting a somber glow across the street into Farmer Book's quiet field. Away from the hubbub of the wake, it was quiet. Or country quiet. Frogs croaked in the drainage ditch in front of her, cicadas and crickets competed to see who could thrum the loudest, the trees rustled and shook, and somewhere an owl hooted throatily.

It was almost perfect. Or it would have been perfect if she hadn't heard Quinn stomping across the grass behind her. Only Quinn would know to find her here. She shoved herself up a little straighter, bracing herself for the onslaught. So much for taking a minute or two. She could not stop her chin from wobbling.

She heard Quinn sigh, her breath half groan, half rasp. She came around the end of the bench and slouched onto the worn stone with Maggy. Maggy eyed her suspiciously, noting the pucker in her jaw. Had Collins told her about the folder?

"I came out here to be alone, you know," Maggy said, hoping that would fend her off.

Quinn pursed her lips and nodded. "I figured. Why else risk the Vuittons?" she quipped.

Maggy chuckled, then sniffled, relaxing microscopically.

"Oh, look at you." Quinn sounded exasperated, her breath coming out in huffs. She pointed at her own puffy face and red eyes, then waved a hand at Maggy's streaked mascara, muddy stilettos, and now wrinkled dress. "You're more of a mess than I am. I mean, at least I know I'm a mess. You're still wearing Prada and full makeup in the middle of Mississippi heat. Trying to act like you have it all together." She paused, waiting for a response.

Maggy settled her shoulders, stubborn even with mascara running down her face. Not everyone *wanted* to look like a hot mess all the time. At least she had started out trying.

When Quinn didn't receive an answer, she burst forth, "You *do* know that we have our *mama's* wake to get back to, right?" So that was what she wanted, to get this night over as quickly as possible. Maggy bit her lip. Quinn pressed some more. "You know I had to come get you because you refused to come in with Father Fry. I thought you liked him."

"That's not what happened."

"Then what?"

"With the casket and the candles and all the stories about Mama and the gossiping and Marcus calling… an… I… I just couldn't take anymore. I had to get away for a minute." Maggy rushed the words, hoping it would hide the tremble in her tear-ragged voice.

"You had to get away for a minute." Quinn's words hung in the air, sharp and sarcastic, fraught with fifteen years of meaning.

Maggy jabbed a finger at her, "You were over an hour late! Can't I have just a few minutes, *please*, to compose myself!"

Maggy slumped back, eyes brimming with tears. Snorting them back, she saw that Quinn clutched a handkerchief suspiciously similar to the one Father Fry had given her earlier. A pang of jealousy shot through Maggy, icy hot in her veins, but she tried to ball it up as small as the wad of cloth in her own hands. Quinn eyed her, imperious, and Maggy slumped further.

"I know we've been fighting for, like, the last sixteen years, but I could use my sister right now, so can we call a truce?" Maggy's words came out in a gush.

She was met with silence, and she looked up, hopeful. Quinn had turned her body fully towards her, her eyes widened in hurt. The stone dug into her back as Maggy pressed deeper into the bench.

Quinn sputtered, words spinning out like loose pea gravel from underneath tires. "I never stopped being your sister! You stopped being mine running off the way you did, all these years of the silent treatment, rolling your eyes every time you see me and Collins together." A bit of spit disappeared into the dark. "So, by all means, let's have a truce but don't for a second pretend like you're some innocent, put-upon victim who still has a thing for my husband."

As she watched Quinn's chest heave with the force of her breath, the words swept over Maggy like angry storm surge. She stared, bewildered, as her normally low-simmering sister crossed her arms, sat back on the bench, and glared across the road. Her gaze held so much heat, Maggy was sure the field would catch fire any second.

She realized her mouth was hanging open and snapped it shut with a strangled laugh.

"A thing for your husband? Really? You think I have 'a thing' for Collins?"

Quinn shifted uncomfortably but nodded tersely.

Maggy stared at her for a few seconds, expecting more after sixteen years. "That's it? That's all you have to say?"

Quinn nodded, still not meeting her eye. Maggy had had

more satisfying showdowns over teleconferences; at least the person on the other end of the line had the decency to have a full-on meltdown. This was just cold.

"You are *such* a bitch!" Maggy spat.

"And you're a spoiled brat." High and nasally, Quinn's old insult still stung.

Silence trickled uncomfortably down their backs along with the humid heat. As the minutes ticked by, Maggy dug her nails into the stonework, French tips forgotten, and jogged her knee, lost for what to say. Lost for what to do. Just lost. She'd been homesick in New York for so long, but deep down had always thought that, no matter how bad things got between her and her family, she could come home. That's what Mama had always said. But the way Quinn was looking at her now, disgusted and spiteful, said otherwise. The thought of Mama cold in that casket wrung all the fight out of her.

Maggy stood. There was no point staying where she wasn't wanted. "I guess I… I'll leave, so you won't have to deal with me making things awkward anymore tonight. Give my apologies to Father Fry."

"Go ahead. Leave. It's what you're good at."

Maggy lifted her arms, then dropped them helplessly. There was no pleasing her. She turned towards the trees and began to make her way back down the path to the chapel parking lot. "See you in the morning," she called sarcastically over her shoulder. Quinn nodded slowly but still pointedly not looking at her, reminding her of all the fights they had as teenagers.

She stopped at the first tree and put her hand on the rough, familiar bark to steady herself. There was one thing she had to know. If nothing else, she had to ask, "Why did you never apologize? You slept with my boyfriend and never even apologized. Why?" Quinn spun around, her arm dangling over the top of the bench but fist clenched.

Now her mouth hung open and her brow knit. "What are you talking about?"

Maggy's brow creased. "Collins? This whole thing we're fighting over." She repeated it more slowly. "You. Sleeping with *my* boyfriend."

Quinn went white. She pressed her fingertips to her temples. "But y'all weren't…" she trailed off "… together?"

Maggy shook her head. "We were still dating…"

"Oh my God…" Quinn bent over and groaned. Maggy flew back to her and grasped her shoulders.

"Breathe. Just breathe. You're ok. In for three and out for four, remember?" She held her steady, keeping her from tilting off the bench, as Quinn rocked side to side.

"I'm sorry. I swear I didn't know—How did I not know?" Quinn kept muttering over and over.

Maggy thought back to that blur of a day when Quinn had told her and Mama she was pregnant with Collins' baby and they were going to get married. How she had been so stunned that it hadn't even registered when Quinn asked her if "this" was ok. Now it was all clicking.

Chest still on her legs, Quinn looked up at her, lips pale. "So you and Collins were still dating when we were…?" Maggy shook her head.

"No." And Quinn's mouth popped open, confused. Maggy held up her hands. "Let me explain. Remember how he always cracked jokes with me? About everything?" Quinn nodded slowly, swiping at her face and sitting up, still breathing hard.

"Well, one of them was 'We should break up' over, like, stupid stuff. If I said I didn't like black pepper: 'Oh, we should break up; I love pepper.' And it was a joke at first, so I never thought he was serious. But eventually, he got tired of all the squabbling we did—which I thought was fun—and he started to mean it. But he never told me that. So, I still thought he was joking. But, in his mind, we were broken up. And in my mind, I was dating a crappy boyfriend."

Maggy could see Quinn's brows knit as she tried to process. "But he told me y'all had been broken up for, like, six months."

Shooting her a withering glare, Maggy retorted, "How does that apply at all to the *friends don't date friends' exes* rule? I'm your sister—I shouldn't be having to explain this to you!" Quinn hung her head and nodded. Maggy brushed at her eyes, studying the mascara smeared onto her hand.

She continued. "We were still hanging out and stuff. And sure, he didn't kiss me as much. Or at all, really. But it didn't matter that much to me. I mean, I had myself fooled into believing a lot of stupid things about first loves." Maggy slid her bra strap back up from where it had snaked its way down her arm in the humidity. "I thought it was just a rough patch."'

Quinn looked up and asked, "So when I came home at Christmas and he came over while you were gone—"

Maggy held up her hands, stopping her. "I do *not* want to know about the first time y'all hooked up. Spare me the details." Quinn put her hand on Maggy's arm, tears welling up.

"I'm so sorry! I really am. It makes more sense now why he didn't want to tell anyone and why he always came up to see me at Ole Miss."

Maggy bit her lip. She knew there had to have been a lot of sneaking around, but she didn't know how much. She brushed back her hair again and sniffed.

"Well, it doesn't matter now, does it? What's done is done."

Quinn whispered, "But I broke your heart."

Maggy listened to the nightingales and whippoorwills twittering in the dark, her heart beating slow and sure in her chest. She reached down and squeezed her sister's hand.

"Yeah. You did. And it really sucked."

CHAPTER TWELVE

Underneath the old magnolias, the digging was not going well—again. Mr. Mullone flicked on his flashlight for a clearer look and stared morosely at the humongous root they had already discovered in this new spot in the old Matins plot. A foot wide and as thick as his Bible, the blasted thing had brought them to a grinding halt. There was no help for it but to fill the hole in, shift a bit, and test a new area. Around them, mottled red patches of ground attested to how much shifting and testing they had already done.

Beside him, Collins glared at the root, following its twists and turns up to the mossy trunk of the offending tree. He rolled his shoulders and moaned, seeming to resign himself to the inevitability of nature. "We really can't cut through that one, can we?" he asked glumly, a hand gesturing wearily at the clay-wrapped root.

"Afraid not. Would probably kill the tree. Then we really would have an uproar on our hands," replied Mr. Mullone. He patted the younger man on the back. "Don't worry. We'll get your mother-in-law's grave dug before morning, and your wife will be none the wiser to all the fuss."

"Roy…" Collins' usually assured voice wavered, and he

flushed, embarrassed. Mr. Mullone eyed him speculatively.

"Roy, what if we were to… do something a bit unorthodox?" Collins rushed the words, and Mr. Mullone's gut twisted with what he suspected his muscly counterpart was about to suggest. His shoulders tensed, forming a knot under his left shoulder blade. Collins continued. "I know you've never been fond of this idea, but if Quinn and Maggy are ok with it, why not put Alice in Truman's grave with him? We know the spot is good and we don't have to worry about flooding or wild animals in this area. There's still space for two tombstones, so I don't see why not."

Mr. Mullone was already shaking his head, white hair glowing in the dark. "We are not bothering them with questions about where to put their mother or if they'll be ok with opening their father's grave. Alice made it clear that she trusted us to put her in the best spot possible with the family, and that is what we'll do. We'll not break with tradition now by… by double-bunking!" His stomach twisted at the thought of Alice being that close to Truman for all eternity. Although he had no right to think that, he supposed. She had always been a loyal woman. Collins' huff drew him back.

"Oh, come off your high horse! It's not breaking tradition; they do it up North and in Virginia and such all the time," he retorted.

"I don't care what Yankees and Virginians do. I care what we do. And we run a dignified graveyard, not a helter-skelter mausoleum," Mr. Mullone's raised voice made a few of the other men twitch their heads towards them. They looked away dismissively when they saw Roy and Collins at it like usual. Mr. Mullone ran his hands through his hair and flicked away the drops of sweat he collected on his palms. He wiped it absentmindedly on his pants leg as he glared at Collins.

"Well, it's not very dignified right now, is it, with half the graveyard torn up from all this damned digging!" Collins threw his shovel down and leaned against a nearby headstone marked Hinton. He stared towards the chapel, scowling. In the lamplight, Mr. Mullone noticed the dark circles under his eyes and the abnormally wrinkled shirt.

Wiping his stinging hands on his pants, he relented a little. "How's the new baby getting along, Collins? Sleeping through the night yet?"

Collins shot him a sharp look. "She's colicky as hell. None of us are getting any sleep. And poor Quinn's been having to deal with her non-stop through all of this."

Mr. Mullone sighed, something he found himself doing a lot recently, and looked up at the magnolia branches stretching overhead. They were magnificent. Alice had loved these trees, protected them fiercely. He studied their twisting patterns and how they wove back and forth around each other. A few blooms had opened early and filled the air with a tart, spicy scent. He hadn't lived as long as this tree they stood in front of, but he did have enough time on him to know that you couldn't get through life by always insisting on your way.

"Look, I don't want to be unreasonable. Let's do a couple more test holes, say three at most. If we find a spot, it won't take the boys long to finish. *If* we don't find a spot, *then* we will ask the girls what they think of your idea. What they say goes."

Collins slapped a mosquito away from his elbow, nodding. "Deal," he said, holding out his hand. He grimaced as they shook, and Mr. Mullone belatedly remembered his damp palms.

They turned back to the maps Mr. Mullone had spread out, Collins picking up his abandoned shovel. Mr. Mullone bent over the drawings and huffed in exasperation. "Now see, these maps, the oldest ones we've been working from? They have the groves generally outlined." He drew his finger across the paper to demonstrate. "I need Minister Gordon's sketches from the 1950s. He made detailed layouts of all the historic trees, roots his teams had run into, and suspected unmarked plots. I really should get around to making a compiled map…."

Collins leafed through the papers. "I thought you asked Harry to get all the maps? This only looks like half of them."

Roy nodded in agreement, his eyes scanning over the leaves. "I had them spread out over both sides of my desk. If he didn't flick the light on when he walked in, he might not have seen all of them. But I told him twice…"

Mr. Mullone trailed off, pulling the old set of keys from his pocket... "Harry! Blast that boy. Where is he when I need him?"

CHAPTER THIRTEEN

The two sisters sat side-by-side in the dim light from the far streetlamp, surveying Farmer Book's peaceful field and trying to figure out how to continue the uncomfortable conversation. Occasionally, one or the other sniffled and swiped at nose or eyes in the silence.

A gentle lowing echoed across the road. "Remember that time I nearly died trying to ride one of Farmer Books' cows?" Maggy asked, grasping for anything to talk about. Slowly, she slid her hand out from Quinn's and scratched at her itching nose.

"He had to punch that mean old cow right in the nose to keep you from getting trampled," Quinn replied, laughing. "Gosh, I've never heard you scream so loud." She quieted. "I dared you to do that. And I would never have forgiven myself if you had gotten hurt. I'm so sorry I was always getting you into trouble."

"Quinn, I know everyone thinks I got into so much trouble as a kid because of you…" Quinn shot a questioning look at her, but Maggy continued, "But really, I was enough of a hellion that I would have gotten into plenty of trouble on my own. I was fortunate enough to have a partner in crime. It's why Mama always whooped us both."

"She did that," Quinn said, rolling her eyes, "The worst was having to pick our own switches. I hated pussy willow season."

"We always deserved it though." Mama had never forced them to do anything they didn't want, but she did enforce consequences for their decisions. Maggy winced, remembering a particular incident when they had hidden Mrs. Vanderwahl's yard gnomes like Easter eggs. And then couldn't find them all again.

Quinn chuckled, her shoulders easing down from beside her ears. "True. Mama never did anything that wasn't fair." They sat quietly for another minute. Quinn shifted to face Maggy and leaned forward to place a hand on her knee. "Why did you never tell me? About Collins?"

Maggy shrugged uncomfortably and rubbed at her shoulder, kneading at the tension building behind her collarbone. Before Quinn's announcement, Mama had been pressuring her for months to break things off for good with Collins and focus on enjoying her senior year of high school without the drama. Even if he was her best friend's son, Mama hadn't liked the on-again, off-again treatment. Her heart hammered at the memory and her tongue clung to the top of her mouth.

An image of a broken glass and one particularly heated discussion at Mama's little log cabin leaped to mind, peonies in full bloom around them, vibrant and glowing—alive. She had blindly sworn she loved Collins and stormed off. A few days later, Quinn had broken the news. She shoved the memory down and pressed a hand to her mouth, considering what to say. In hindsight, Mama must have known something was going on, or suspected it at least.

Quinn swiped at her nose, waiting, expectant. The wind picked up, pulling stray pieces of hair from Maggy's French swirl and into her eyes. She tucked them away impatiently.

"Mama thought—" Maggy began, about to explain everything—her suspicions, her promises of silence to Mama, her continuous fights with Collins over it, the call from Mr. Leonard—when Mrs. Streisand strode up, looking perturbed.

"There you two are! We've been waiting on you to get the Psalm reading started again for the last fifteen minutes. My meatballs can only keep people happy for so long before they turn dyspeptic. Come along, people are starting to wander off." Her tone brooked no objection.

"Dyspeptic?" Quinn mouthed at Maggy. Maggy shrugged and giggled. Mrs. Streisand shot a look at them but smiled shrewdly when she saw them bump shoulders.

"Come along, girls, and be sharp about it. Don't want to keep your mother waiting too long now do we?" she said with a wink. Maggy looked at her, stunned, then at Quinn, who was turning red trying not to laugh at this bizarre night. Giggles bubbled up her throat at the baffling turn, as Maggy looped her arm through Quinn's, relieved for the momentary reprieve. She would work out what to say later. They followed their willowy old piano teacher and Quinn's mother-in-law back up the path to the chapel, supporting each other as they wept through gales of laughter.

CHAPTER FOURTEEN

That blasted boy was nowhere to be found. Glancing at his watch, Mr. Mullone blinked in surprise to see that it was nearly midnight. They needed to get a move on. He hallooed for Harry again and shot him yet another text. Mr. Mullone swore not so quietly under his breath as he searched around the lamplit area for his nephew. With a huff, he peered behind monuments to see if the thickheaded teenager had decided to doze off for a few minutes.

True to Mississippi weather's fickle nature, a stiff breeze had picked up a few minutes ago. Now it had worked itself into a full gale, shaking the trees back and forth. With a crack, a widow-maker crashed down from a nearby oak, chipping a marble headstone. He shuddered, thinking of Truman and his unfortunate accident. Worry made him throw out dignity.

"Harry!" he bellowed. The only sound that returned was the wind and scraping of branches. "Harry!" he bellowed, and this time he saw Collins glance up at him from where he was trying to weigh down the maps with rocks and note Mullone's creased brow. Collins folded the whole set up without paying any attention to the historic maps' creases and tucked it in his back pocket, then jogged over.

"What's wrong?" he asked, grabbing Mullone's arm, his

fingers digging in through the thin fabric.

With a gesture around the yard, Mr. Mullone replied, "Harry's disappeared." He pointed at the nearby fallen branch. "In the middle of a windstorm." Collins' eyebrows shot up in alarm. He knew Truman's story too. He looked at Mr. Mullone.

"I'll get the men and the flashlights."

CHAPTER FIFTEEN

The girls blew into the hall with a gust of wind, still laughing and trying to catch their breath. In the flickering candlelight, Maggy could see Mrs. Greaves tottering back-and-forth along the potluck table without her cane, shifting casseroles and Crock-Pots, and trying to make sure everything was covered up, plugged in, and with serving spoons balanced carefully on the lids just in case. Anxiously, Maggy eyed her as she worked her way up and down the row of dishes, setting things right, one hand skimming the tabletop to steady herself. Her breath hitched as she watched her strain to reach a pot just out of reach with an unwieldy Stoneware lid.

Her thoughts were dragged back by a pat on her hand. "Talk later?" Quinn asked with a smile. Maggy nodded back with her own smile. Maggy's stomach was so full she couldn't imagine wanting to eat more, but Quinn peeled off immediately from her arm and headed to the table.

As she watched Quinn smile at Catherine Seymour, her smile faded. In the fifteen years she'd been gone, it only made sense that Quinn would have found a replacement for her. And Catherine, as an attorney with all the fun gossip about Jackson's high-profile divorces and unrivaled good taste in fashion and husband, was an unparalleled choice of best friends indeed. With three kids of her own, they'd be on a half-dozen church committees and the PTA together for sure. Maggy wilted to think that she had been so easily replaced. She rubbed at her shoulder absentmindedly.

On spotting the sisters enter, arms wrapped around each other, Father Fry—Derek—had smiled broadly. Now, he clapped his hands and pitched his voice up. "Alright ladies, everyone grab your last bite of food and refill your drinks. Hit up the loos as well if needed. Let's get the readings restarted in, say, five minutes?" The ladies nodded and buzzed about, grabbing plates of snacks and drinks. Everyone looked flushed and reverent, saintly, in the glow of the candles.

As she watched her sister eagerly take the full plate Catherine handed her, Maggy remembered tossing Quinn's barely touched plate into the garbage bag earlier without much care. She winced at her thoughtlessness. Her chest tightened as she thought that maybe she deserved to be replaced after all. Mrs. Greaves clanged a lid onto a Crock-Pot, and Maggy hurried over to see if she could use any help at the far end of the table, glad for the distraction from her thoughts.

The old lady was patting irritatedly at a marinara splotch on the white tablecloth. She glanced up at Maggy with a wide smile.

"There you are. Hand me my purse, will you, dear?" Mrs. Greaves was all business when it came to linens.

Maggy complied, retrieving the magical object from a nearby chair and handing it over. Without any rummaging, Mrs. Greaves pulled a tiny Tide-To-Go pen from the very bottom and began blotting at the offending stain.

Curious, Maggy peered into the tangled contents. She spotted a hairbrush, lint roller, various balms, ointments, medications, pins and pens of all kinds, toys and candies, and what she was pretty sure was a tiny potted plant among other less easy to identify paraphernalia.

"You're quite the Mary Poppins, aren't you?" she asked, still peering in. A smack landed on the back of her head.

"It's rude to look in a lady's purse without permission! I

thought I taught you better," Mrs. Greaves said. The ghost of a smirk lingered about her lips though, telling Maggy that her comparison was rather apt. Maggy put the purse back down.

"Anything else you need help with?" she asked, eyeing her tottering steps skeptically.

Mrs. Greaves finished her blotting, tossed her napkin into a nearby trash can, and wiped her hands on her skirt distractedly as she surveyed the groaning table. Quinn stood at the other end, chatting with Mrs. Streisand and a few other ladies, finally eating what looked like alternating bites of pea salad and poppyseed chicken.

Keeping one hand on the table for balance, Mrs. Greaves moved towards one casserole that was not covered.

"There's one left," she said, "Will you hand me the tinfoil?"

Maggy hurried to bring both the tin foil and Mrs. Greaves' cane before the old woman's stubbornness got the best of them.

"I could have gotten that, Mrs. Greaves, really!" Her voice rose a little more than she meant it to, and she caught the ladies glancing at them as she grabbed Mrs. Greaves' elbow. Mrs. Greaves' eyebrows shot up, and she harrumphed. Gently, she moved her elbow back as she took her cane and hooked it into the crook of her arm.

"I'm a little firmer than you think, Maggy. Don't worry so much." She took the tinfoil from her too. "Besides, this is my casserole, so it wouldn't do to have just anyone cover it." Maggy smiled a bit, still unsettled. Her godmother had bustled about their kitchen so much when they were younger, it unnerved her to see Mrs. Greaves with a cane now. Everything had changed so much in the time she had been away. She looked down at the dish, trying to steady herself, even as the band tightened around her chest. The dish looked familiar.

Maggy swallowed. "Is this the chicken cacciatore you made for us all the time when we were little?"

"It is. You ate so much of it one time I thought you were going to throw up." Mrs. Greaves patted her arm. "Would you like the recipe? It's super simple in a cast-iron skillet."

Maggy's breath hitched at the reminder of just how much of

a failure she was, and she blinked rapidly. She wiped at her nose, trying to make the panic go away. "That's alright. I don't need it. My apartment is so small I end up eating takeout more often than not." She waved a hand airily and forced herself not to babble.

"Oh, but this is the perfect recipe for a night when you do feel like cooking. And you don't need a lot of space or fancy ingredients for it. Let me get a card..." Mrs. Greaves rummaged in her purse.

Maggy grabbed her arm. Too hard, much too hard.

From the corner of her eye, she saw Quinn put down her plate hastily and step around Catherine and Mrs. Streisand towards her, eyes widened in alarm. All she could focus on was her breath and the brown speck in Mrs. Greaves' right pupil.

"Just... don't. It's... I mean... I'd never have a chance to use... What I mean... He left me because... There's no sense in wasting any effort on me."

Mrs. Greaves clutched Maggy's elbow and patted her back reassuringly. Maggy hiccupped, and a removed part of her mind speculated the old bat had seen her fair share of breakdowns, and hers didn't even rate on the melodrama scale.

The patting continued. "Child, calm yourself." Maggy gulped. "That's it." Quinn appeared at her other elbow.

With an arch of her eyebrow, Mrs. Greaves said, "Now, take a deep breath." With some effort, Maggy relaxed her grip on Mrs. Greaves' arm and took a few slow, full breaths, forcing the air down to the bottom of her lungs. She smiled shakily at her godmother and sister.

"That's better." A reassuring smile beamed up at her.

"Christ, Maggy, what was that?" Mrs. Greaves glared at Quinn, and Catherine whacked her shoulder. Chagrined, she muttered, "Sorry."

Maggy watched this exchange with a sense of detachment, still breathing slow and purposefully. Suddenly, her neck flushed as she saw Derek lean back in a chair from where he had been canted forward, watching her worriedly across the room. A beatific smile spread like syrup over pancakes across Mrs.

Greaves' face as she followed Maggy's glance. She took Maggy's arm again, gently.

"Now, dear, why don't you tell us, what brought on this little spell? I won't force any recipes on you against your will, but if it's something we can help with, why, we're all family here."

Belatedly, Maggy realized most of the women were arrayed behind her across the table, worried and sympathetic expressions on their faces. Mrs. Streisand leaned across and patted her shoulder.

"We've all had meltdowns, sweetie. I went into a funk so dark when my first baby was born my Jordan came home and picked me up off the bathroom floor most days for three months."

Quinn nodded emphatically. "You've seen what a mess I am. I've had three breakdowns this week. Thank God for Collins." She rubbed Maggy's back. "We shouldn't have to do hard things alone. And you've got family here."

With a swipe at her eyes, Maggy looked away, still feeling foggy. She studied the Tree of Life, stretching up the wall with its sturdy roots and twisting branches and vine before ducking her head. She tucked a wisp of hair behind her ear. With alarm, she noted that she'd need to clean her Vuittons later, or they'd be ruined from the grass and mud. A throat cleared.

"Mags?" Quinn asked gently, refocusing her.

Scanning their concerned faces, Maggy realized she couldn't dither her way out of an explanation. Or rather, didn't want to. She was tired of hiding everything. The tapers on the coffin sputtered brightly, and she closed her eyes.

"Marcus broke up with me because I couldn't cook." The ladies gasped and various epithets passed around. "Well, that's one of the reasons. There were others. We both worked a lot. He didn't like paying for a maid—why couldn't I clean like his mom…"

"Why couldn't he get off his ass and clean…" a little lady with way too much eyeliner and a bottle-blonde dye job broke in. Snickers broke out all around. Maggy snickered too.

"Look, I get no relationship is perfect. Stress happens." She looked at Quinn. "I'm sure you and Collins get that better than anyone with the gyms not doing so well right now." Quinn blinked, then nodded slowly, her face strangely blank. Mrs. Greaves and Mrs. Streisand shot a look at each other. The sudden tension in the air was palpable. Maggy twisted her hands together, wondering if she had inadvertently stuck her nose where it didn't belong. She picked at a nail, gambling that if she acted like it wasn't a big deal, it wouldn't become one. Quinn crossed her arms, and Catherine put a hand on her elbow. She kept talking, trying to keep from drawing attention to whatever was going on with her sister.

"I tried. I tried so hard with Marcus. Tried cleaning on my own. And cooking a little." She shrugged, babbling. "Mostly frozen meals because what else did I have time for?"

With another shrug and a swipe at her nose, she glanced around, self-conscious. "Nothing pleased him. So... after I burned a Stouffer's lasagna rather badly one night because I got stuck on a call with my boss—he wouldn't stop fussing. And I just couldn't be the only one trying anymore. And I told him I would no longer be cooking, and what was he going to do about it? So, he... ended things." The women nodded silently.

"Would you like to learn? To cook? For yourself?" The blonde lady asked. Maggy vaguely remembered her name being something like Vicks. Vans? Something with a V.

Maggy thought for a second. "I think so. It seems like it would be nice."

Mrs. Vanderwahl—Maggy at last remembered, the lady with the gnomes—nodded contentedly. "We'll start with an easy vegetable then. Something like mac-and-cheese?" As she turned to confer with Catherine and the other ladies on the best order in which to teach Maggy, Quinn's brow furrowed.

"I thought you knew how to cook? We used to help Mama in the kitchen growing up." Her skeptical look told Maggy that she had more golden memories than she did.

"We chopped vegetables and labeled jars, sure. But you helped Mama in the kitchen more than I did. I was usually doing laundry and weeding flower beds and stuff, so you learned how recipes and how things like stoves work."

"Well, I guess there's a lot that we both don't know. Like when to keep your mouth shut." Quinn shot a cross look at her and Maggy's mouth dropped open.

"What?"

"You didn't have to go spewing my business in front of the whole church!" She waved her arm at the ladies conferring together, before dropping it with a soft plop.

Maggy glanced down at Quinn's clenched fists, and her comment about the gyms finally clicked. "Quinn, I'm sorry. I shouldn't have said anything. I didn't know—it wasn't my place."

Quinn just shook her head silently, cheeks coloring.

Before she could apologize further, Mrs. Greaves clapped them both on the back surprisingly hard, interrupting them. "It's decided. Quinn is one of the best cooks here, so she'll teach you. And, she has all your mama's old recipes. Between her and your mama, half of the church cookbook is comprised of Matins women alone."

Somehow, she had become one of them again, Maggy realized as she looked around the circle of buns, bobs, and blowouts all nodding in a matriarchal decree. With a glance at Quinn, she chuckled, trying to smooth things over.

"Well, I guess I'll have to see this legendary cookbook then."

Mrs. Greaves was already pulling a set of keys from her pocket. "There's a box of extras in the church office. We'll send Allie to fetch one from the administrative building."

"Where is Allie?" Quinn asked, looking around. Derek sprang up; his eagerness to be a part of things could be contained no longer, Maggy decided. He came over to the ladies. His hand rested reassuringly and unconsciously at the small of Maggy's back. She didn't mind, despite the pleased looks passed around the circle like a plate of divinity.

"Don't worry, Mrs. Quinn. I'm sure she's just in the restroom or outside with her dad. Mrs. Streisand, would you mind checking?" he asked.

Mrs. Streisand had just disappeared around the corner

towards the restrooms to check on her granddaughter, and Mrs. Greaves was explaining how Quinn and Catherine had headed the committee for assembling and designing the cookbook, to Maggy's growing discomfort, when the vestibule door slammed open.

"Collins! Will you stop doing that!" Derek bellowed. The ladies tittered, and he lowered his voice, embarrassed. "This is a church. Please treat it as such."

Collins stomped forward, undeterred by the Father's outburst. Maggy noticed his worried face and how he peered around the room hurriedly. He flapped a hand dismissively at Derek and grabbed Quinn's elbow.

"Is Harry in here? Did he come in to use the bathroom or something and decide to hide out?" His head continued to swivel so much Maggy thought he might begin scouring under seats next.

"No?" Quinn replied. "Is Allie with you?"

"Of course not!" He spun, surveying the room as if Harry would appear out of thin air. "She's with you, right? And that blasted boy has run off, probably to take a nap someplace, in the middle of a f… freaking windstorm. We've had to pause the dig to find him because Mullone has flipped his lid." Collins' eyes pinched with worry. Maggy and Quinn glanced at each other. A guilty blush rose to Quinn's cheeks; a millstone settled heavily in Maggy's stomach.

The sound of kitten heels beating a rapid approach interrupted them. Mrs. Streisand's voice reached them before she did.

"Allie isn't in the restroom. But the window was open!" She rounded the corner and spotted Collins. Candle wax popped and hissed in the silence that followed.

"Now, let's be calm about this…" Derek began.

Face mottling, Collins said, "I'm going to kill him. I swear to God, if we find them together, I'm going to kill him."

CHAPTER SIXTEEN

A horrendous screech echoed through the chapel, and the lights flickered. The candles guttered out from a gale of wind that blew in the open door. Maggy's skin crawled and involuntarily she took a small step towards Derek. Around the room, she saw the others jump and heard them titter nervously.

Mrs. Greaves took Maggy's elbow and said, "Steady, honey, it's just that confounded tree." The little battleship of a lady shot a sharp look at the Father in the sudden gloom. "We really should trim it back during our next congregational workday, like Alice suggested *last* quarter."

Derek looked down at his muddy sneakers, chastened. He rubbed at the back of his neck.

"I'll be sure it's added to the agenda, madam."

Maggy rubbed at her collarbone, trying to soothe the tightness in her chest that had returned. Mouth agape, Collins stared down the group.

"Are we going to stand around gabbing or are y'all going to help me find my daughter?" he asked, incredulous. Behind him, her mother's coffin had become an oppressive shadow.

"It's a windstorm in the middle of the night, for God's sake, man!" Mr. Mullone said, having slipped into the chapel—in time, Maggy guessed, to have heard Mrs. Streisand's announcement and Collins' outburst. He shoved closed the door Collins had left open. "No need to endanger more people looking for two foolish teenagers. The boys will find them soon enough."

He strode over to the corner and flipped some switches with a series of loud clicks. Light blazed on in the sconces overhead, alleviating the gloom and causing dark spots to float in Maggy's vision from the sudden change. Collins threw his hands up in frustration.

"Leave it to you, Mullone, to let someone else clean up your mess!"

The older man scowled at him then turned to study the heaving trees outside.

"We don't have anyone searching the west side of the grounds yet. There's not much over there but a few mausoleums and outbuildings, but I'd take some *volunteer*s to search them to be sure." Derek stepped over quickly to join him. "Collins, why don't you rejoin the men searching the rest of the graveyard and see how they're doing?" Mullone said evenly. Maggy hadn't thought it was possible, but Collins' face reddened further. Silently, he spun on his heel and headed out, letting the door fall to with a bang.

Quinn was already pacing back-and-forth anxiously, her steps echoing on the old floor. Maggy could feel the tension growing in her back from the insistent clacking, knotting under her shoulder blades like sharp stones. She could not stay cooped up here while others searched; that was a recipe for another panic attack.

"Mrs. Greaves, you wouldn't happen to have a flashlight in that purse of yours, would you?" Maggy asked.

Mrs. Greaves smiled, her dimpled cheeks incongruous in the tense scene. She rummaged briefly in her purse before coming up with a hefty, yellow-plastic monstrosity of a flashlight.

Maggy whistled. "Well, that looks tough enough to clobber a bear!" she said appreciatively as it was plunked into her hands. Mrs. Greaves winked.

"Careful with it. It has fresh batteries, so it can blind one too!"

Maggy waved down Mr. Mullone and Derek where they had withdrawn to talk over a game-plan for the search.

"I'm coming too!" she said with a curt lift of her chin. Mr. Mullone eyed her streaky mascara and muddy high heels skeptically, with a throaty "hmmm." Perturbed, she kicked the blasted things off and stood barefoot. One hand on her hip and the other resting the flashlight on her shoulder, she arched an eyebrow crossly at them.

Derek tried to stifle a laugh and ended up in a coughing fit. He turned away, red and embarrassed. Mr. Mullone chuckled and clapped her on the shoulder and pulled her in for a hug and a kiss on the temple.

"Ooh, it's good to have you home, Maggy."

She hugged him back tightly around the ribs.

"Same, Mr. Mullone, same."

A loud sniffle sounded behind them. A glance over her shoulder revealed Mrs. Streisand with clasped hands and teary eyes. She was not embarrassed at all.

"It's just… it's just… you look so much like your mother when she was being all sassy!" All the ladies doubled over in their chairs, laughing and agreeing. She even saw Quinn crack a tense smile before continuing her nervous march to-and-fro, avoiding her gaze.

"And on that note, let's go look for those hellions, shall we?" asked Maggy, blushing. The three of them hustled out of the door. Once outside, Mr. Mullone made them draw up short in the shelter of the awning. She turned quizzically towards him. Around the hall, the wind whistled and hooted eerily, lashing at their limbs and clothes, trying to drag them out into the night.

"Maggy, I know you know all about windstorms, but Father Fry isn't from around here." The thought of her father was sobering, and she nodded solemnly for him to continue. Mr. Mullone turned to Derek and pointed sternly to the trees that surrounded them.

"We're in a part of the countryside that's filled with some incredibly old trees. Their branches tend to snap halfway off and dangle or get caught in other branches, and then windstorms like this one will knock them down. If you're underneath, they can kill you. It's why we call them widow-makers. In the daylight, you can be on the lookout for them and go around. At night, all you can do is try to listen and run like hell if you hear a crash. Got it?"

"Got it. Listen. Run like hell."

Maggy chuckled at his summary.

Mr. Mullone patted his arm.

"Good. I'm going to send Maggy with you to check that half of the yard since she's got a flashlight, and I'm going to check this half. You two be careful. I don't want to dig a third Matins plot in my lifetime."

Derek's brow had gone from relaxed to knit at Mr. Mullone's last words, but Maggy was already tugging at his arm, drawing him across the darkened yard towards the shadowed buildings, anxious to find Allie and avoid the question that was all over his face.

Out in the gale, her hair tugged loose from its last pins and whipped viciously across her face, stinging her eyes and sticking to the remnants of her lipstick.

Her flashlight cast a strong beam, but it didn't do much to help her spot the gopher tunnels that crisscrossed the yard and she stumbled. Before she could face plant into the soft earth, a strong hand grasped her elbow and pulled her upright. She found herself in Derek's arms, uncomfortably aware of the rise and fall of his chest. They broke apart quickly.

Derek rubbed at the back of his neck as Maggy saw a blush creep into the tip of his ears. She glanced down at her bare feet and rubbed away a fire ant that had taken issue with her ankle. Dolefully, she thought that these kinds of scenes were much more romantic in books and made a mental note to toss hers in the trash when she got back to the house.

Before the silence could stretch out more awkwardly, she asked, "Shall we continue?" with a gesture of the flashlight to a nearby shed. She vaguely remembered this outbuilding housing lawnmowers and other yardwork paraphernalia. Its paint was a bit dingier now and the roof looked like it could use some new shingles.

"Lead the way," Derek said with a gallant wave of his hand. She walked over to the building and tried the front door, finding it locked securely. Wind shoved at her back, trying to knock her into the rough wood, and she scanned the nearby trees nervously. Their limbs lashed and whirled as if they had come alive and were now determined to pull themselves up from the roots and begin striding across the land, arms grasping at the sky. With the direction of their wild flailing impossible to guess, it would be best to skirt around as many of them as possible. She squinted into the dark, trying to decide on the best path forward. When she turned, she found Derek studying her face. She tried to wipe away the fearful puckering of her brow.

"I don't think we'll find much here," he said, "The vestry hasn't used this shed since I've been here. We really should tear it down." She stepped around him and headed around the corner. A memory had sprung up at his mention of the vestry.

"Never underestimate the ability of teenagers to get into trouble, Father," she replied, tossing the words over her shoulder into the wind. Spotting the double barn-style doors, she grinned. There was a large padlock rusted with age on them, of course—as it had been when she was sixteen. She grasped the ring the padlock was looped through, gave it a firm twist, and yanked hard. With a groan, the bar on the other side gave enough for the doors to swing free. She stepped into the darkness with a shiver.

With a flick of her flashlight, she could see at once that the shed was empty, haunted by nothing but dusty cobwebs and a few scattered leaves crumbling to dust on the floor that trembled and skittered in the sudden inrush of air. She was already turning to leave when she bumped into Derek.

"Sorry!" he stammered, "You move so quick."

"It's all right." She stepped back and looked up at him. He looked at the intact lock and back at her, his head swiveling between them comically.

"How did you do that?"

She smirked. "I was a bit of a hell-raiser myself back in the day. The stories I could tell you about this place. I know all the secrets."

He smiled warmly at her. "So, tell me."

She looked at him wondering if he were serious, and he held her gaze in a silent dare. She grinned back.

"Ok."

CHAPTER SEVENTEEN

Quinn could not stop pacing. She stalked from the vestibule to the far end of the room and back, hoping the repetitive motion would soothe her the same way it soothed her nightmare-addled children. Instead, her thoughts looped. With each pass, her mother's ebony coffin glimmered softly, and she resisted the urge to pause and rest her hands on the cool lid, to harangue her to rise up.

Outside the wind howled. Her heart seemed determined to match its frenetic shriek, stuttering and stumbling inside her chest. Every last living family member she loved was out in that hellish storm, while she was stuck here staring at her mother's sarcophagus, going insane. She so often felt unsettled these days, so far from that confident young girl who had everything before her: a career she adored, a brilliant little girl, and a husband who worshiped her.

Her thoughts snagged on Collins and how he'd hidden his messy breakup with Maggy. Such an old lie sent tremors through her; it struck at the bedrock of their relationship.

Would she have ever considered him, invited him in that first time knowing what she did now? She pushed the thought away, unwilling to face the implications. She crossed her arms, chafing at the goosebumps that rose under her fingertips like braille, trying to read the past in their pinpricks. It was silly to consider such impossible questions, to predict what she would have done. It was as foolish as wishing on a star. She dropped her hands and turned on her heel towards the Tree of Life sculpture twisting up the wall at the far end of the hall. Determinedly, she strode towards it, nervous energy driving her forward.

But Maggy's other words nagged her now: "No relationship is perfect. Stress happens. I'm sure you and Collins get that better than anyone with the gyms not doing so well right now." What did Maggy know that she didn't? Why had Collins confided something in Maggy instead of her? Her stomach flipped, and she fixed her eyes on the raging trees outside the window.

With a heart-stopping groan, she watched an oak lash its branches to the ground first on one side, then the other, leaves and twigs scattering in the mad wind. Fear clutched her throat. Unbidden, her father's blank face floated before her, the men swooping around their kitchen table in a vain attempt to save him. Mutely, she'd tugged tiny Maggy away from the doorway where she'd found her, standing wide-eyed and frozen. She'd pulled Maggy along ever since that day—right up until she'd left. The wind screamed through the eaves of the hall, shaking her from her memory.

The ladies buzzed and bumbled about relighting candles or hovered around the tables in the back in small clutches, eyeing her anxiously. Like any minute she would disintegrate into a puddle. Or whip into one of her teenage furies. The light caught on her wedding ring, dashing off the band in one dazzling flash. She paused in her pacing to study the worn gold and the clouded cubic zirconia. Collins had offered to replace it and she'd refused, holding onto it out of sentimentality.

Now she clenched her fist. The truth was, she had known what she had been doing, though she had pressed it far, far down. All the sneaking. All the lying over the phone, pretending she "was focused on her studies, not interested in dating right now," all the while Collins would be wrapped around her, nibbling her ear even. She knew she had been hurting Maggy. She had never admitted it out loud until tonight under the trees.

But still.

Outside, the wind whistled and shrieked, as angry as she had been since the day Maggy moved to New York with no warning, transforming from the sister who had forgiven and held her hand despite it all to the sister who abandoned her. For years, she had practiced being calm in the face of all the questions. Now... now, another storm and her child out in it. She spun on the balls of her feet towards the vestibule, just needing to keep moving. To be doing something. Her thoughts whirled on.

And Maggy was still Maggy. Selfish, impulsive Maggy. Not staying where she was supposed to, which was here, with her *sister* at their *mother's* wake. She had thought for a second, under the trees, maybe Maggy had changed. Instead, she was out there gallivanting in a dangerous storm with the pastor she had met seconds ago because he had a cute accent. No, she couldn't sit still for one night and do what needed to be done, like Quinn always had to do. Maggy had to be off somewhere, leaving Quinn behind to deal with it all again. Falling to pieces by herself, again.

Her mind drifted back to Maggy's words: "with the gyms not doing so well right now." The tips of her fingers tingled like she'd dipped them in mineral spirits. What did she mean? Besides, how would Maggy know something she didn't? They were fine. Collins' checks came in every week. If the gyms were in trouble, he would be the first to take a hit. Her stomach twisted, unsure.

Her head pounded as the stress-migraine that had threatened all evening finally sprang up in full force, a bolt of lightning stabbing behind her eyes. Quinn closed her eyes against the sparks. She rubbed at her temples and breathed deeply. Pivoting back from the door in the vestibule, she nearly collided with Mrs. Streisand. The older woman placed a hand to her pearls and clutched at Quinn's elbow in surprise.

"I'm so sorry, Mrs. Streisand!"

"Gracious, child..."

Mrs. Streisand did not release Quinn's elbow but stood studying her, the powdery corners of her eyes crinkled in amusement. Independently, her lips pressed together into a thin line of concern. Quinn realized it was the same look Mrs. Streisand had given her so many times during her piano lessons when she panicked over not being able to play arpeggios perfectly. With a decisive nod, her mother-in-law tucked Quinn's cold hand into the crook of her arm and began to stroll up and down the rows of chairs, a stark contrast to Quinn's harried trot a minute before. Her heartbeat slowed.

They took a pass or two on the hardwood in silence, Quinn's attempts at questioning firmly shushed and tutted away. Inwardly, Quinn groaned but held her tongue. The ache in her temples dulled from an ice pick to a vague throb.

"I've always loved storms." Quinn looked at Mrs. Streisand out of the side of her eye and waited for her to continue. Mrs. Streisand drew her along a row to look out one of the windows.

"They're nature's way of pruning things." She waved at the ancient trees which were old and full of dead limbs. "All gardeners know that sometimes the old has to go for the new to thrive."

Quinn was not in the mood for a lengthy, cryptic conversation about the vagaries of life. She had screwed herself over plenty already by being a doormat. She'd lost her sister, her career, her mother, and now possibly her husband. Her breath hitched and she blinked back angry tears, impatient to end this conversation. But as she looked at Mrs. Streisand, her eyes full of love and sympathy for Quinn, she softened. Quinn's fists clenched in the folds of her skirt as her mind searched for a reply that was honest but not harsh.

"My father died in a storm and my mother will be buried in one. I don't see the same appeal you do." She strung the words out, trying to lay them softly in the air, but they sliced nonetheless. She crossed her arms and looked back out the window, embarrassed.

She tried to explain, another burst of words bubbling up. "I mean, what good could come of this? It's great that you're optimistic, but I just don't see it." As she spoke, she gestured at the dark casket and the thrashing trees outside. She blinked, wanting everyone to leave so she could lay her head on the casket and wail. With a shake, she willed away the childish thought. Her heart throbbed, aching to talk to her mother, curled up on the porch swing with matching glasses of sweet tea.

Mrs. Streisand nodded, sympathetic. She patted Quinn's hand reassuringly. "It will always be easy to see the bad things. Sometimes, you have to teach yourself to look for the blessings in life." Quinn snorted.

"Mama had a cross-stitch hung in the kitchen that said the same thing."

"I know. I gave it to her after Truman died. I don't even embroider, but I knew she needed it."

Quinn looked down at her rough hands, the nails cut short and chewed. Her eyes burned and watered. The ice pick stabbed again. She put a hand to her pounding head.

Tilting her head to the side, Mrs. Streisand drew her down into a chair.

"What's on your mind, darling?"

Quinn thought for a moment, clasping and unclasping her hands, picking at her frayed cuticles. Mrs. Streisand bent her head forward to listen, her silver-gray hair curled and poofy in its perm.

"It's ok. You can tell me."

Quinn examined her mother's coffin for a second, the relit candles burning low and dim, then looked away. She cleared her throat, suddenly parched.

Quinn pressed her palms into the cushion of the chair. She thought of Maggy and New York, Collins' long hours at work, the old blouses in the back of her closet. Her barely contained anger against it all. Her knee jogged up and down. If she had secrets, as small and claustrophobic as her life had become, she knew the rest of her family did too. She lowered her voice, trying to be calm.

"I just… I don't want there to be any more secrets." Her voice steadied. "Maggy and I were starting to talk about it, and she mentioned Mama, but then…" She looked at Mrs. Streisand, her mother's lifelong friend and confidante, who stared fixedly at her hands clasped in her lap, and sighed, the sound trembling in the air. She shrugged.

A wavery smile answered her, and Mrs. Streisand lifted her palms. "So much has happened. But I do know that your mother wanted the best for you, both of you. Even if it meant blaming herself for so, so much."

Quinn's shoulders sagged, the knot behind her left shoulder blade stretching painfully. She kneaded at it. "What am I supposed to do with that?" Her voice trembled, raw and sore from crying.

Mrs. Streisand touched her knee. "I think it's time you finished talking to Maggy about what's really bothering you."

Two big tears worked themselves from the corners of her eyes, and Quinn rubbed at them. Before her, the candles shone dimly in the dark glass, their reflection wavering back and forth. If she didn't make things right with her sister, she would never feel truly settled; deep down she knew that. Finally, she nodded.

"I'll try to talk to her once we've gotten a little sleep." She paused, considering. "Maybe after the reception tomorrow."

Mrs. Streisand beamed.

"Sounds like a great plan." She touched Quinn's arm. "And to echo your mother, maybe it's time to talk to Collins too?" Unease at his name being mentioned a second time that evening twisted in her gut. Mrs. Streisand wasn't the meddling sort; his mother's hint confirmed Quinn's suspicion something was wrong. "I'm a little selfish of course, but I hate seeing how distant you two have become."

Quinn leaned forward and rubbed her shins, feeling off-balance. They hadn't had as much time to talk in the months since Clara's birth, but she hadn't felt particularly distant. Alarm coursed through her, but she forced a nod.

"I suppose I should talk to him as well since he's involved in…" she waved her hand in a vague circle "…all of this."

"I would advise it."

Mrs. Streisand suddenly grinned and elbowed her in the ribs.

"Maybe Roberta and I can treat you and Maggy to a spa day to make sure you do. Don't want you losing your resolve now, do we? And there's nothing like a relaxing day at the spa to get you feeling chatty."

Quinn winced, "Maybe not a day at the spa. I don't particularly enjoy being poked and prodded at. Or the smell of acetone. Pretty sure Mama just drug me there when she thought I was looking too mangy to be presentable any longer." Mrs. Streisand harrumphed in her throat and Quinn offered, "Maybe a massage? Those are nice enough."

Mrs. Streisand laughed, her hair quivering. "You've got a deal. If you need a bribe to talk to Maggy we'll take y'all for a massage."

Quinn chuckled and assured her she would take care of everything. But as her mother-in-law walked away a few minutes later, Quinn stared into the howling wind whipping the trees back-and-forth like ribbons and wondered what the hell was going on with her family. And how she could have been oblivious to it for so long.

CHAPTER EIGHTEEN

The old cedar next to them groaned and Maggy paused to listen to its branches crackle, lashing in mesmerizing swirls. Nothing sounded like it was about to come plummeting toward them though, so she waved Derek on with the flashlight, its beam skittering across the windswept grass.

"So, I think you agreed to a story," he prompted, grinning at her. She pointed the flashlight at his chest, and he grimaced at the brightness. He held up a hand in surrender.

"I'm trying to think which one is the best to start with. Don't get pushy."

"All right, all right!"

They continued, picking their way across the grass towards the next building, which looked like a newer storage shed. It was hard to tell in the dark, but the wooden boards didn't have that characteristic swell and sag to them that came from being out in decades of humid Mississippi summers.

Maggy's brain spun as she tried to pick one story and she didn't realize how long the silence had stretched until Derek cleared his throat quietly. She could barely hear him in the wind.

"I know I'm not supposed to be pushy, but can I ask a question?"

She shrugged since she was coming up blank. "Sure."

"How did an art scholar end up working as a fashion editor?" He added hastily, "Not that there's anything wrong with working outside your major. It just seems like an odd departure."

Maggy thought of all the links to job postings popping up in her email her senior year, and Mama worrying that she wouldn't be able to make a "decent" living. But Maggy shrugged. "It's what I fell into out of college and it's pretty hard to switch careers once you're that specialized. You have to start all over."

He shoved his hands into his pockets. "Ever thought about changing anyway?"

"Only every damn day." She glanced at him. "Sorry, that wasn't very polite."

He smiled. "But honest." They stumbled on in the dark and silence for a minute before he spoke again with a chuckle.

"I've heard Farmer Book tell this story a thousand times—how did you end up in his pasture riding a cow anyway?" One cheek dimpled in amusement at his own question.

A slow smile crept across Maggy's cheeks even as the wind plastered her hair into her face. She liked his curiosity. It made her feel interesting.

And the answer to that question was simple. All her stories started in the same place, or rather with the same person. She pushed the pesky strand back and began.

"Quinn and I were getting bored because Mama's ladies' meeting was running late. So, we snuck out. At the time, we were big on playing Truth or Dare except we already knew all of each other's secrets. So, it was mostly just dares."

"Ah yes, my brother and I had the same experience a few times as well."

Maggy nodded enthusiastically.

"Well, one thing led to another and we dared each other right out of the church, across the road, and into the field with the cows. I dared her to pet a cow which she was too scared to do. And of course, I teased her about it, and she got mad—she's got such a temper—so she bet me that I was too scared to ride one.

And I was stupid enough to ask if that was a dare. Which of course she said it was."

Derek put his face in his hand chuckling. "I know where this is going."

Maggy chuckled too. "The next thing I know, I find a great big cow standing next to a fencepost, paying no mind to me and chewing her cud. I think it will be a piece of cake and hop on." She made a flying motion with her hand. "And away we go! With me digging my heels in and clinging onto her ears for dear life. Fairly sure I would have died if Farmer Book hadn't seen the whole thing happen and come running. He stood in front of that raging, running cow and punched her straight in the nose. That poor thing was so stunned that she came to a dead halt for half a second and he was able to scoop me off, hysterically crying and screaming."

Derek whooped. "That is so much better than Farmer Book's version."

Maggy fanned at her face, laughing with him. "I'm sure his version is much kinder."

"He is a nice guy. He at least leaves out the hysterics. Makes it sound like you were halfway to having a tame cow."

Maggy shook her head. "Not in the least." As they walked up to the newer storage shed, Derek tripped over a downed branch, and she grabbed his arm, steadying him.

"Thank you." He looked down. "At least that limb was already on the ground."

"Hopefully, it's the only one we have problems with." She let go and turned, flashing her light across the building. He tugged at the door, finding it securely locked, then followed her as she made a quick circuit checking that there were no other windows or doors that teenagers could slip in through.

As she rounded the last corner it occurred to her to ask, "You said you have a brother. Are you two close?"

She looked back at Derek and found him with hands shoved in pockets staring at the ground. "Sorry. Didn't mean to pry if that's a sore subject." He looked at her, his eyes squinted.

"No. No, I know so much about your family—and I'm

practically a stranger to you—I think it only right that I share something of mine." His voice dropped low, easy to miss in the wind if she hadn't been straining to hear it.

"I'm sorry for being so awkward about this… your mother… was a bit of a mom to me as well. Which is odd for a pastor to say." Maggy cocked her head to the side and arched a brow. It was just like her Mama to "mother" someone lonely, but she had never mentioned the young pastor in their weekly phone calls which puzzled Maggy. Her thoughts trailed off as Derek sighed and rubbed at his hair, mussing it up more than the wind had.

"I'm making a mess of this. My family isn't religious, but we are… were… all close. My brother and I were only two years apart so growing up we did everything together. We often were mistaken for twins." He reached out and took the flashlight from Maggy gently.

"But I had the more even disposition. Gus… well, Gus was either off or he was on." He flicked the flashlight off and on to demonstrate, plunging them briefly into darkness. Maggy's stomach clenched. Derek continued. "He could be quite the life of the party, which made him my parents' favorite. And that intensified if he was drinking, which he got into early." He handed the flashlight back to Maggy.

"One night, I was visiting him at university so I could take him back for Mom and Dad's anniversary the next day. Anyway, we were at a friend's party, and Gus started drinking. And just didn't stop. And well, I ended up having to drive us back even though Gus was normally the better nighttime driver. It was dark and raining and I'd had a few drinks myself. We should have crashed for the night at our friend's. Anyway, we got into a wreck—I don't remember it. When I woke up in the hospital, Gus was gone, and my family wouldn't talk to me. They blamed me for everything." Her chest constricted like a rope had tightened around her ribcage. Her breathing hitched, but she refocused on Derek.

"That's awful. To be cut out like that. When you had just lost—"

Derek shrugged and cut her off. "I've made my peace with it."

She rubbed at her shoulder until the feeling eased a bit. "So, the military?"

"I guess I was looking for any place I could belong." Tears blurred Maggy's eyes and she reached out and grabbed his hand. She could feel a callus on the inside of his thumb, but his palm was smooth and warm as he squeezed her hand gently, the corner of his mouth tilting up but the lids of his eyes remaining low and sad. They paused together, wrapped in a wind-whipped silence.

After a moment, Maggy looked up at him. "You said Mama became like family to you?"

Derek shook himself and looked down at her, eyes squinched. "Yes, she kind of took me in when I got here. Invited me over for Sunday dinners, gave me notes on my sermons, tried to fix me up several times, fussed over me if I looked tired, things like that." A cobwebby feeling began at the tip of her nose and spread across her face as her heart sped up in an irregular tattoo.

"She has...had... a way of doing that," Maggy agreed, her pooling eyes finally overflowing. She released his hand and pulled the handkerchief from her pocket. "Sorry, here we are talking about you and your family and I'm the one crying." She fanned at her face.

Derek shook his head so hard his whole body wagged back and forth.

"It's ok to cry at your mother's wake—for whatever reason. You don't have to apologize." His voice was deep and earnest. Fatter, faster tears slid down her face despite her attempts to choke them back.

She fanned at her face harder. "I'm sorry! I'm sorry! It's just...I don't know what to do without her. With everything that's been happening, I kinda feel like my life is over." The world began to spin in a mad Tilt-A-Whirl. She bent over and grabbed her knees, gasping. She tried to focus on her breath, five counts in, seven counts out. Suddenly warm hands grabbed her shoulders, and the earth steadied a bit.

She could hear Derek saying, "Everything is ok. You're safe." It sounded as if he was on the far side of an echo-filled canyon, but it gave her something to latch onto. Slowly, the tension ebbed from her, her muscles releasing painfully one by one. Finally, she was able to meet his eyes and smile tiredly. He released her, hands out comically to make sure she could stand upright on her own, and a hollow opened in her stomach, lonely and hungry for more touch, for more comfort. She turned away and cleared her throat.

"Sorry. I have got to stop crying on you."

"It's not like you cried *on* me this time," he pointed out with a cheeky smile. "Besides, I've already told you, you don't have to apologize."

She glanced back at him. "You're the first person to tell me that." He blinked at her, his face going blank with disbelief.

"No!"

She nodded. "It's true. None of my boyfriends. None of my friends. Heck, not even Mama ever told me not to apologize."

"That's just…" he searched for words and she watched fascinated as he chewed on the inside of his cheek "…there's no need to apologize. You've done nothing wrong."

With a shrug, she flicked the light towards the next building ready to get moving again and put this awkward encounter behind her.

"Sometimes, I think it seems easier to apologize than to ask people to acknowledge our needs." She could see him shaking his head out of the corner of her eye at her words, but he followed her silently as she picked her way slowly across the invisible gopher holes.

Not wanting the silence to grow uncomfortable she offered, "Have you heard about the time my flying squirrel knocked Father James' toupee off?"

With a guffaw, Derek trotted up beside her and she began the story of how she smuggled her pet squirrel into the church.

CHAPTER NINETEEN

Collins swiped at the straggling grass angrily with his flashlight, sending a startled grasshopper leaping for safety in the bright beam. Checking this part of the yard was pointless. They were wasting time they couldn't afford.

He knew his daughter. If Allie had heard them calling for her, she would have come to meet them by now, head hung low but an impish grin on her lips she couldn't hide. Collins knew the look well. Another image flashed through his mind, of her lying pinned and bleeding under a heavy branch, unconscious and unable to call for help. He blinked the image away. No, she was off being a stupid teenager. He couldn't accept that she could be…

He arced his flashlight through the gloom over another crumbling headstone and stepped behind it to be thorough, despite his rising desperation to find his daughter. All that met his gaze was uncut grass, wildflowers growing through it. He scowled at the growth. Mullone needed to adjust their maintenance schedule; this was shameful.

He turned and looked at the flashes of light spread out, bobbing among the graves and off through the thrashing trees. He knew his daughter. Then again, he had never imagined he would be out in the middle of a windstorm after midnight searching for her because she'd run off with some idiot boy. He rubbed at his face, the stubble from the day sandpapery under his hands. Quinn always loved that feeling, luxuriating in running her hands over his face after a long day. He grimaced at the thought of her and all he was keeping from her. But there was no need to worry her right now. Not with everything she had to deal with taking care of the kids.

Rick grabbed his shoulder, jarring Collins from his thoughts. "C'mon man. Cheer up. We'll find 'em," he shouted into his ear. Wind hooted and whistled an eerie warning in the trees overhead, nearly drowning him out. Charlie hovered behind Rick, looking for everything like a spooked horse, eyes rolling and hair plastered back to his skull.

Collins swiped at his face, batting away the prickles of unease that thoughts of Quinn always stirred up these days. He looked at Rick, forcing his eyes to focus.

"You really shouldn't space out like that in a windstorm." Rick's words whipped away on the wind, barely reaching Collins. Nodding, Collins swung his flashlight beam around them as the trees shook and dipped angrily.

"We shouldn't even be out here." The unintended words burst out of Collins, but even as they hung in the air, he found that he meant them. Rick blinked. Charlie rolled his eyes towards him.

"We have to find the kids?"

"I mean we wouldn't be out here if it weren't for Mullone. He should have checked the site himself. He should have kept a closer eye on Harry. If it weren't for him, we wouldn't be here!"

Rick tilted his head to the side, studying Collins while he eyed the trees nervously. "Look, Collins, I know you're frustrated. But we're out here looking for your girl too."

Waving that away, Collins continued, "And where is this magical combined map he's always talking about? It's been at least five years that he's been talking about it and it has yet to appear." He swung the flashlight randomly as he stalked forward through the tall, damp grass towards the next set of monuments. Rick and Charlie hustled to keep up with him. "A lot of our problems with the openings have come from having to work from so many disjointed records."

He stomped behind one gravestone, tumbling awkwardly into a gopher hole with a burst of expletives. He righted himself and stomped to the next gravestone. He continued his rant undeterred. "If it's that hard for him to put together, I have landscaping experience."

Rick huffed, "We know. You've told us all many times." Collins shot him a glare and he held up his hands. "Don't look at me like that! It's true."

"I'm just saying I could help. I've offered. Or if he doesn't want my help there are plenty of firms that can do it." He leaned against a headstone and spread his arms wide in exasperation. "But if he can't even correctly run the opening of the grave for the woman he loved, well then, maybe he's not as good at this job as he says he is." He thumped the stone for emphasis. "Maybe it is time that we intervene." Charlie nodded emphatically before flinching away from a leaf skittering by.

Looking at the ground, Rick stood still for a minute, hands in his pockets. "Now see, that's the one opening I'd expect to go wrong." Collins crossed his arms and harrumphed. "Just listen for a minute! He's upset, he's flustered. This is *Alice* we're talking about; he's been carrying a torch for her for over twenty years. He's going to be distracted and not quite all here."

He stepped closer and put a hand on Collins' shoulder. "We can discuss your points about the maps and Harry and the last couple of openings at our next meeting. But this opening, however, let's give Roy a little grace, shall we?"

Collins rolled his eyes. The wind died down for a minute, creeping through the trees, sullen and surly. Knowing he couldn't win Rick over tonight, he finally muttered, "I suppose." The ingenuine words dropped heavily from his lips. Charlie huffed and rolled his eyes. Overhead the trees began churning, agitated.

"All right then. Good." Rick clapped him on the shoulder and stepped back. "Let's get going. We don't have too much more to cover over here, and I'd like to get out of this wind."

As they turned to continue, they heard a halloo behind them. The object of their discussion, Mr. Mullone, half-jogged up, panting and sweating.

The image of Allie lying unconscious and bleeding underneath a fallen limb flashed in Collins' mind, and he grabbed Mullone's arm. "Did you find them?" He gulped down his anxiety and released Mr. Mullone, kneading at the tension in his forearms.

With a knowing look and a shake of his head, Mr. Mullone leaned against the headstone Collins had been resting on and pulled out his bandana, now sweat-stained, to mop his face.

"No, but Maggy and Father Fry are starting to check the west side of the churchyard with all the outbuildings. So we have two extra sets of eyes." He grinned conspiratorially at Collins. "And Maggy knows all the good hiding spots so who better to send?"

Flushing, Collins remembered some of those spots himself. It would make more sense for Allie to head towards that side of the yard if she were out here and not necking in some car. He cracked the knuckles of his left fist and hefted the flashlight in his right, but he spoke calmly.

"Roy, Charlie, would you mind helping Rick finish up this section? I think I'll go help Maggy and Father Fry." The three men stared at him, alarm on their faces. Slowly, Mr. Mullone nodded.

"Of course, Collins." As Collins spun to head to the other side of the graveyard, Mr. Mullone called after him.

"Collins!"

He turned to look back at Mr. Mullone, whose eyes were full and pleading, an expression Collins had never seen before.

"Please, remember he's my nephew."

Collins paused. He nodded sharply before striding across the night-dark yard, long grass dragging at his sneakers.

CHAPTER TWENTY

The trees swayed overhead in a mad kaleidoscope of greens and greys and blacks. If Maggy stared too hard at their dark swirl, she was sure she would become sucked up into the dark void of the night and carried away on the wind. A click in her brain told her that was the fatigue talking, but she couldn't resist staring up at the trees as they bent and waved.

Two days cramped in a car and sleeping on hard motel beds had caught up with Maggy. As they trudged through the calf-high grass, her body hit new stages of exhaustion. First came the waves of prickles and shivers ebbing and flowing up and down her arms and legs. Those weren't so bad. At this moment, however, she was at the stage where wet sand filled her limbs, making her every move feel ridiculously sluggish and exaggerated. And itchy. Even on their worst deadlines at the magazine, it was usually at this stage that she'd find a quiet closet somewhere and grab a nap. Punchdrunk. But without any fun punch.

Still, she yawned and chuckled. Derek's presence was making this eerie, midnight search bearable, pleasant almost. To overcome their terror of the seemingly possessed trees whipping around them, they swapped tall tales of their childish escapades as cozily as if they were in a pub, competing to see who could make the other laugh harder. So far, he was winning with his story about mixing cayenne pepper into the actual punch at a town hall meeting. People drank more and more trying to quench the fire, only to increase their agony. Finally, one of the town aldermen spotted the rim of cayenne in the bowl and headed off the poor townspeople from drinking more. Derek had been forced to fess up and had spent the week going door to door, apologizing in person. Maggy was still clutching at her side, wind roaring overhead with her laughter when she spotted the light bobbing across the grass towards them.

Her shoulders pinched together painfully. She straightened up at seeing Collins' furrowed brow. He glanced between her and Derek, scanning her laughter-flushed cheeks and his sparkling eyes even though more than five feet stood between them.

"Joining the party?" Derek asked, oblivious. Maggy tried to shoot him a warning glance, but he was trying the knob of the playground shed. Not wanting to look like she was goofing off when she hadn't been anyway, Maggy eased into the gap of the bushes backing up to the shed and scooched around the side to check the window that could be jimmied open. Collins could be a jerk to the preacher all on his own if he were in that kind of mood.

"Looks like y'all are having a lot of fun. Did I miss anything—other than my kid?"

Maggy winced at his sharpness as she flicked her flashlight through the partially open window, not wanting to clamber through the dusty spider webs. Nothing but toys and some sandbox shovels. Not even leftover inflatables from last year's VBS. She wiped her cobwebby palms on her skirt and slid back around to the guys. Derek stood eyeing Collins with a flat expression on his face, clearly not put off by his sarcasm.

"Shed's clear."

Collins rolled his eyes at her. "Did you expect them to be making out next to the Tonka toys?"

"Tonka toys never stopped us."

Derek snorted. Collins glared at him while Maggy looked at him wide-eyed. He cleared his throat, "Oh. I'm sorry." Flatly, he said, "Shame on you. You shouldn't say such things in front of your pastor, you heathens." He looked between them. "That better?"

Collins turned to Maggy. "Well, you clearly have already corrupted our pastor."

The wind slapped her hair into her face and she impatiently pushed it away. "You give me way too much credit." She flicked her flashlight towards the last, and furthest, mausoleum left to check.

"Let's wrap this up, shall we?" She did not want Collins catching onto her way-too-fast crush on Derek. She'd never hear the end of it. His teasing, like his temper, was merciless. Hastily, she trotted towards the mausoleum.

Behind her, in the dark, she heard the two men chatting like old friends, and with a shock, it occurred to her they *were* friends. When she thought of Quinn and Collins, it was always in a bubble. It was never in the context of other people, outside of Mrs. Streisand and Mr. Mullone. Even people she knew that they knew, like Rick Seymour or Mrs. Vanderwahl—her brain simply didn't want to piece it together. She had dissociated Quinn and Collins entirely from everything besides Mama. Maybe that was why the thought of Quinn being friends with Catherine stung so much.

Her stomach flipped guiltily as she tuned back into what Derek was saying.

"So, should I bring anything to the reception tomorrow?"

Collins shot a wolfish grin at Maggy when he caught her glancing back over her shoulder at them. "Just a pair of boxing gloves."

"Ummmm…"

Collins called out to Maggy, "You going to pull any punches tomorrow, Maggy?"

"Don't be a jerk, Collins."

"I'm missing something here."

Maggy turned abruptly and Derek pulled up hastily, nearly

colliding with her again. She ignored him as he didn't back away from her nearly far enough, choosing instead to stare at Collins who crossed his arms and glared back at her.

"What *Collins* here means is that he thinks I'm going to make a scene tomorrow at *my mother's* funeral by dropping a bit of news on Quinn that he way overestimates the importance of. That's the punches he's talking about pulling." She refocused on Derek and softened her voice. "I found out yesterday that I'm the estate executor. Stopped and signed the papers on my way through town today. Haven't even had a chance to read the will, so I haven't told Quinn because there's nothing to tell."

She reached out and tapped Collins on the chest with her flashlight. "And for some reason, this hard head won't believe me. I'm not going to drop a bomb on my sister during one of the worst days of our lives. I know what I'm doing."

Collins harrumphed, clearing his throat of some phlegm and spitting it with a disgusting thwack into the grass. Maggy grimaced.

"I still think you should tell her. It concerns her. She has a right to know." He twisted the flashlight in his hands violently. A desperate look pinched the corners of his eyes and he began pacing, kicking at the ground, agitated.

She snapped, tired of his bluster. "It's not your decision!"

Collins recoiled from her as his eyes flickered into focus, pinpointing down to dark sparks. He spat, "I don't even see why Alice chose you to be the estate executor. It's not like you're ever here to do anything anyway." His face twisted, grotesque and spiteful in the low light as the clouds spat out a brief gust of vicious raindrops.

Maggy drew in a sharp breath. The wind stung her dry eyes, and she closed them, taking a deep breath, body shaking in anger. She pinched the bridge of her nose and laughed at the absurdity of this scene—fighting in front of the pastor in the middle of a midnight windstorm. The sound scratched her throat, raw and tender. Her bones ached with weariness.

"Collins, whatever issues you're having with Quinn, for the love of all that is good and holy, try not to take them out on me, would you?"

Collins took a step back, biting his lip and clenching his fist. She could see from the working of his throat that she'd hit the nail on the head. As he opened his mouth to retort, Derek cut in.

"Hey guys, I'm not sure what all...this... is about, but an estate executor just makes sure that someone's last wishes are carried out." Derek inhaled loudly through his nose as they focused on him. "As long as the will isn't too strange, it isn't that big of a deal."

Collins turned and stared at him, his face slack and his eyes owlish and gleaming in the flashlight. Maggy shivered. He blinked, his customary flush rising in his cheeks. Derek spread his hands and shrugged before letting them drop loosely to his sides.

"If Maggy just found out about it, as long as she tells Quinn in the next day or so it shouldn't make that big of a difference, right? You will still need to get with a lawyer to go over the particulars and that will take a little time to schedule." His Welsh brogue rumbled through Maggy's ears, like water over rocks, smoothing out her roughed-up emotions. She glanced at Collins and saw the pastor's words were having the same effect on him. His fists unclenched, the thick fingers unfurling like magnolia petals. Collins glanced back at Maggy then down at his feet.

"No, I don't suppose it does matter." He muttered, "Not in the long run anyways." He rolled his shoulders back and stared at the sky for a minute, at the fast clouds frothing like a cup of dark coffee. Maggy shifted nervously on her feet, not trusting either of their tempers.

"All right. Well. If that's decided, I'm going to go find my niece now." Maggy gestured with her flashlight towards the mausoleum, still several dozen yards away. Collins stomped past her sullenly, the grass rustling loudly under his feet. Derek shrugged at her and followed.

Maggy followed after them, dragging her feet and wondering how she was once again chasing after boys.

The Thompson's mausoleum was ink-dark and quiet. The

furthest of all the church's structures, Maggy eyed it skeptically as it loomed above her in the dark. A granite cherub returned her incredulous gaze from the doorway's peak. One arm lazed over a granite beam, and mildew whorled its way across his puckish brow. She dragged her eyes tiredly over the imposing structure, taking in the imp's shadowed companions along the eaves. There had been no way into the building in her hey-day and its distance from anything else made it a far tramp for a makeout session. Unless time had somehow managed to break a cast-iron lock, Maggy had her doubts about the likelihood of this hideout spot.

She yawned. "Has anyone thought to check the cars in the parking lot?"

Collins broke off staring up at the scowling cherub to glare at her.

"I'll take that as a no," she muttered. In silence, he stepped over the cracking blue and white tile on the first step that spelled out the Thompsons' name and straight up to the door. He twisted the handle viciously. She heard a grating squeak that produced a loose rattle and a shower of rust, but no click of a lock giving. Father Fry rolled his eyes and sighed as Collins shoved at and then pounded his fist on the door.

"Dammit!" Collins' shoulders slumped as; he turned, face stormy. "Let's head back." He gestured towards the parking lot with his light. "Guess we should check the cars after all." His flashlight glanced over a trampled bit of grass next to the door. Maggy grabbed his arm.

"Hold on!" She used his arm to point at the grass.

"Jesus, Maggy! What are you doing now?" He tried to wrench his arm back from her, but she simply pointed her light at it instead. Derek, catching on, placed a hand on Collins' shoulder and pointed.

"Did you stand there?"

Collins paused in his flailing.

"No... I didn't."

They all leaned forward and peered at the ground. They could see Collins' clunky sneakers tracking mud up onto the step, but to the side, another two pairs of footprints were pressed deeply into the soft earth: a pair of Vans and a pair of boots.

Maggy sprung forward first, beating Collins to the door and shoving him back. He held up his palms in defeat as Father Fry's jaw dropped.

"She was always better with the locks anyway."

First, she turned the knob and didn't feel any response in the tumbler. Jiggling it carefully, she realized a strike plate had never been installed for the bolt to go into. The slot of wood the latch inserted into within the jamb was completely dry rotted and worn away. She pushed down on the handle firmly and shoved.

The door swung open with an ear-splitting creak. Inside, she heard a squeak and some shuffling amongst muffled whisperings. Relieved, she stepped inside grinning, preparing to tease her niece ruthlessly as payback for this boneheaded escapade.

She was immediately bowled over by a roaring Collins. As she pushed herself off the cold granite wall of the mausoleum, Maggy turned to the strangest sight she had seen since the last backstage fashion show brawl. Allie stood, chin up, and an arm thrown across a cowering Harry, a snarl as fierce as her father's on her face. Father Fry had Collins in a wrestling clinch. The much slimmer man displayed surprising strength and picked Collins up bodily and hauled him back from the teenagers. Collins howled incoherently about not touching his baby girl. Maggy rubbed her eyes as Father Fry shoved him out the door.

Outside, a thunderous "Enough! Get it together man!" echoed from the pastor.

Inside, silence loomed as the teens and Maggy stared out the door as the wildly bobbing light receded. Maggy turned to Allie and Harry. Allie stood chewing her lip, just like her mother. Harry rubbed his shoulder and eyed the ground.

Maggy whistled silently. "Well, then." She eyed the teens and noted the spots of color in Allie's cheeks and the rapid rise and fall of her Adam's apple. She held out her arms. "Oh, come here. It's going to be all right!" The girl launched herself into Maggy's arms, sobbing.

She wrapped her arms around her niece, rubbing her back in slow, smooth circles, letting Allie cry herself out for a moment.

"I'm sorry," she hiccupped, "for causing all this mess. And now Dad… he hates me!"

"He doesn't hate you!"

"He hates me!" Allie repeated with conviction, snot, tears, and eyeliner running down her face. Maggy looked at the stony ceiling of the mausoleum. She remembered more than a few incidents like this with her own mom. She held Allie at arm's length and looked in her eyes. She took a deep breath, motioning for her niece to mimic her. Reluctantly, the girl followed suit, taking a big gulp of air and letting it out slowly. Harry shuffled his feet nervously in the corner but stayed silent, thankfully.

Seeing her calm down fractionally, Maggy patted her shoulder. "Your dad doesn't hate you. But he was *very* worried. You disappeared, Alice. In the middle of a windstorm. With a boy he didn't know you were seeing."

"It's just Harry," Allie muttered mutinously, her shoulders tensed up to her ears.

Maggy shook her head determinedly. "It doesn't matter. He's a boy. And you kept a secret from him. Not a harmless 'I like to write fan-fic' secret, but one that could get you hurt."

"I would never hurt her!" Harry interjected.

Maggy scowled at him. "Be quiet! I'll get to you in a minute." She turned back to Allie. "He was frantic trying to find you."

Allie's shoulders slumped. "He was?"

"Of course, he was. That's why he came in here all bluster and thunder. He came to save his little princess from the rogue who was trying to corrupt her. Or something like that."

"I wasn't trying to corrupt her!"

Maggy's glare made Harry back up a step. Allie chuckled. Then she crossed her arms and hugged herself, looking small and lost. "I guess I need to apologize to everyone. For being so thoughtless."

Maggy wrapped an arm around her and began to lead her out of the mausoleum. "That sounds like a very good place to start."

She looked at Harry and arched an eyebrow, nodding for him to follow.

With a grin, she said, "Now you. Collins might hate you."

"Me? What did I do?"

Allie's laugh rang out, clear as a bell. "Don't be dense, Harry." Her tone turned flirtatious. "You lured the poor, young maiden to a secluded den to woo away her innocence."

"Now that sounds creepy. Besides, it was as much your idea as mine. And I said we should just go to my car. You're the one who said you'd found a great new hiding spot."

Maggy snorted as they stepped out into the night, now calm with a few stars peeking through the clouds, and headed towards the warm glow of the church. Spotting the north star, she wished silently for this to be the end of the weekend's drama. Cheekily, the star winked at her before tucking itself behind a towering thunderhead.

CHAPTER TWENTY-ONE

Quinn eyed her nails woefully, chewed down to ragged crescents. Except for the occasional mandatory day at the spa with Mama, she'd stopped pretending to wear polish shortly after the twins were born. Mama had said something about all those chemicals being bad for the babies. With a long sigh at her decidedly unprofessional appearance, she turned back to her phone and studied the screen. Outside, the trees whipped around in a mad dance with the wind. Dark green leaves plastered themselves to the window before being stripped away. She turned her back to the sight and sank into a chair, a knot of anxiety hard in her stomach.

Now, trying to distract herself from the long search for her daughter, Quinn had decided to give the gyms' financials a real check-up for once, instead of the haphazard organization of paperwork and receipts that Ralph allowed her to do at tax time. Dredging up the old passwords for the gyms' bank accounts didn't take long. She had set them herself years ago and had been correct in her assumption that Ralph was too unoriginal or too lazy to change them since her abrupt banishment to the nursery.

Now her stomach sank for a different reason. The numbers on the screen weren't adding up even at a cursory glance. If what she was seeing was correct, the gyms were having a major cash crunch. Enrollment wasn't up nearly enough at the last two locations to justify the loan they took out to start the fancy new Lefleur gym, with its cutting-edge equipment and extra classroom spaces—that she knew weren't fully scheduled with instructors and classes yet. No self-respecting bank would accept the last two gyms as collateral with their current rate of membership unless Collins' dad co-signed the loan. And from the looks of things, she wasn't sure how they had financed the last two locations either.

The trees slowed then stilled outside, leaving only fitful bursts of rain, but caught up in the glow of her phone, Quinn didn't notice the quiet. With a swipe of her thumb, she opened the corporate account.

Her eyes goggled. Collins' salary was exactly what he had told her it was—she saw his checks in their bank account after all. But Ralph's... her cheeks heated to scalding. It was easily triple what she had expected. She had estimated a modest bump for each gym they had opened and a small cost of living increase, but this—this is what you paid the CFO of a much larger operation. It was more than what Collins was making. Rubbing her forehead, she wondered if Collins knew.

Her mind summoned Mrs. Streisand's words—had Mama had some inkling of all this trouble? Pressing a hand to her mouth, she fought against her twisting stomach. She sank further into the chair, weighed down by the immediacy of the problem. How were they affording all of this?

Glancing at her mom's glimmering casket, she watched as a single tear of wax ran down a taper and pooled on a doily below, slowly darkening the paper with its oily residue. Even as she thumbed open the Mortgages & Loans tab, hoping he'd convinced his father to co-sign multiple loans, she knew what she'd see. It only took a few swipes to confirm the worst. She pressed a trembling hand to her mouth as she swiped through page after page of documentation. They were in danger of losing everything—the children's college fund, the house, their retirement savings. It was more than that: they would lose everything if something wasn't done and done swiftly. She swiped the app closed, her eyes still smarting from the glow.

A buzzing grew inside her head. This was so much worse than her childish worry Collins would cheat on her with a cute instructor at the gym. Her entire family was in jeopardy.

And he hadn't said a word to her.

She let the phone drop to the velvet cushion of the chair and eased to her knees on the cold, pine floor, kneeling. Resting her head heavily on the chair in front of her, she closed her eyes and focused on the soft point of light in her mind that she had been angrily ignoring for months, giving over everything, her children, her husband, her sister, her feeling of safety and security, and her anger and grief for her mother, to the One who was always with her.

Salty tears ran into her mouth, coating her tongue and thickening her throat as she mouthed her prayers, but she didn't pause to wipe them away. Her shoulders heaved. Suddenly, gentle hands smoothed circles on her back and brushed her hair back from her face, warm and motherly. Quinn sobbed in earnest now, an ache pushing at her breastbone as she thought plaintively of her mother's hands, strong enough to wring a chicken's neck a few weeks before, folded like origami swans over her waist as the undertaker closed the coffin at her final inspection that morning. She had not told Maggy how pretty Mama had looked. How peaceful. Another sob welled up, hot and urgent.

A hush fell over the room as arms soft with age and hugs wrapped around her shoulders and waist, Mrs. Streisand on her right, Mrs. Greaves on her left. Catherine settled into the chair behind her and placed a hand gently on her shoulder. From the corners of her eyes, she could see the rest of the women gathering around her, kneeling as they could, sitting as they must, bowing their heads in prayer. Some lifted their hands. Many lifted their voices in a soft, supplicating keening. They rocked back and forth, holding each other up and wiping away each other's tears even as their own slid down their faces.

The sight of so many sisters surrounding her, entering her grief with her overwhelmed Quinn. The light in her chest bloomed into an all-encompassing glow that made her feel effervescently light yet comfortably earthbound. The ache did not subside—or the longing to see her mother's lively, infuriating face, but a small sense of this moment's harmony elbowed its way into her heart as well. As assuredly as her mother loved her, life was waiting for her on the other side of this. It was going to be up to her to form that life now. Not her wonderful, meddling mother; and not her lying husband.

Sitting back on her heels, she looked around and laughed weakly. A low chorus of laughs and smiles answered her. Hands stretched forward to grasp hers, pat her shoulders and knees, smooth her hair. Everywhere she looked she saw familiar faces, eyes watering, but shining with warmth and love.

The door flew open, a colossal bang that could only signal Collins. Quinn jumped, startled in the hush of the moment to see her husband stalk in, followed by a surprisingly angry-looking Father Fry. She stood, already more than a little pissed at his financial shenanigans—and irritated at the interruption.

Spotting her, he continued his ill-humored stomp, straight through the group of women, scattering them aside with squawks and harrumphs of protest. Father Fry trailed after him, his brow deepening into a scowl.

"Collins, this is inappropriate! Can't you see they were praying?" Father Fry's Welsh brogue turned his angry protest into a low rumble, similar to the thunder rolling outside. Quinn was impressed. He would have made a good fire-and-brimstone preacher if he went in for that sort of thing.

"I don't care! I will speak to my wife when I want to speak to my wife!" Collins' usual red mottling rose up his throat and into his cheeks. Quinn was not in the mood for his theatrics.

"And not a moment before, I see. Or do you prefer the company of Ralph?" She kept her face flat, impassive as stone. Her coldness drew him up short.

"Where is our daughter? Or have you failed to find her as well?" She regretted the words as they came out of her mouth, but she was too committed to this argument to back down now—and too angry. Collins' face paled. Around them the women stirred, nervous flecks eddying in a cup of tea. With a flick of her hand, Mrs. Greaves shooed them all away, taking Father Fry's arm to pull him safely out of the marital fray. Catherine lingered for a second, worry pinching her face, but Quinn sent her away with a decisive nod.

"Maggy's right behind me with the kids. We found them in the Thompsons' mausoleum." His voice was quiet. He eyed her and took a few tentative steps forward. Quinn had a temper, but she had never snapped at him like this before. At least not over something where he was so clearly in the wrong. He decided to take an offensive angle, his usual tactic in their arguments. "Did you know about Harry? Why didn't you tell me?"

Quinn batted his questions aside. She crossed her arms and pinned him to the wall with her stare. "Don't try to sidetrack me, Collins. I've seen the loan documents. How could you do that to your children? To me?" He fidgeted, mouth opening and shutting like a landed catfish.

"Your mother…" he began. What in God's name did her mother have to do with the loans? Her stomach flipped.

"Is not me. And does not speak for me." Her teeth clicked on the words. Quinn watched his jaw twitch and his throat work for a moment as he tried to comprehend the venom in her voice before he opened his mouth.

A clatter of footsteps in the portico saved him from whatever foolishness was about to come out. Quinn turned to see her daughter enter, Maggy's arm draped bannerlike around her shoulder, Harry trailing shame-facedly behind. Mr. Mullone hovered behind them.

Relief flooded through her, cooling her stomach. She ran to Allie, beaming. Feeling the weight of the day and the hour of the night, she sagged into a chair, pulling a very embarrassed Allie onto her lap like she was four again. Her happiness at seeing her daughter whole and well was almost enough to make her ignore Collins' hand clasped on her shoulder as he came to join them. She crushed her daughter into a hug, smelling the shampoo lingering in her hair and the faint crush of grass and sweat… and Harry's cloying cologne. She arched an eyebrow at him crossly.

"We will be having words, young man."

Harry shoved his hands into his pockets and nodded, resigned. "Yes, ma'am."

Collins stepped forward, ready to play hero, calm but eyes fiery. "I've got this." He clapped a hand on Harry's shoulder. "Let's talk while we rejoin the other men, shall we?" Harry stood still, petrified, eyes flitting back and forth between Collins and Allie. She stared at her dad pleadingly.

Quinn glared at Collins and growled in a low voice. "Coooolliiiins." She was not about to let him emotionally eviscerate a child. Her fingers twitched as she thought how her mother would disapprove of her reprimanding her husband in public like this.

He studied her and what the kids called her "soul-eating glare." She lowered her chin, so angry she was ready to do battle anyway. "All right. It will be a gentle, age-appropriate talking to. Happy?" His tone was sarcastic, but his eyes were sincere. Slowly, she nodded.

Collins steered Harry towards the door. Mr. Mullone eyed them anxiously, but Collins waved at him nonchalantly. As they clattered out the exit, Quinn could hear faintly, "Son, let me give you a math lesson. What do you get when you subtract 15 from 16?" Quinn saw Mr. Mullone's shoulders relax.

Allie buried her face in her hands and groaned. "Great, now I'm a life lesson for my boyfriend!" Behind her, the candles sputtered and popped. Mr. Mullone leaped to shut the door, yet the candles continued to crack and snap out in an unseen draft. Quinn rubbed her back, but before she could say anything, Allie bolted out of her lap, spinning in a frantic circle, staring wide-eyed at the ground. She pawed at her neck and dress.

"The necklace!" Allie waved wildly, her arms muscular and tan from days spent running cross country out in the sun and heat. Quinn's eyes finally registered her bare neck now that her hands weren't clenched around it and she sat forward to help look. Maggy took a step forward as well. "No! Don't move!" Allie whirled in a circle, oblivious to the rapid stomp of her own feet as her eyes searched the floor in panic.

Finally slowing, Allie blubbered, sounding more six than sixteen. "It's gone." Quinn pressed a hand to her gurgling stomach, eyes flitting to Maggy. Her sister's face paled then crumbled, mouth tightening and eyes blinking rapidly. At the back of the hall, the ladies scurried, relighting candles as they dimmed and died one by one, tapers still tall. "The clasp must have slipped and... I'm sorry, Mom. I don't know where... I've lost grandma's pearls!" With a twist of her mouth, Maggy's face lay smooth and calm, a magic trick of self-control. Quinn felt the corner of her eyes tighten.

Quinn looked back to her daughter, heart aching for the frantic grief she saw welling up. She reached out and stroked her hair. "It's ok. It's just a necklace. You're what's important."

Allie shook her head, dark hair frizzy from the humidity. "But it was grandma's and y'all trusted me to have it and I lost it and now we might never find it out in all that grass—" She looked out the dark window, as a few spatters of rain began to hit. Quinn rubbed Allie's back. She shook her head and took a deep breath, wondering how she would calm her this time.

Maggy spoke. "It's ok. What matters tonight is that you're safe." Allie looked up at her aunt, eyes wide, nodding. The frantic twisting of her hands stilled. "Your mom is right. It's just a necklace—and we'll look for it in the morning, ok? No need to worry over it tonight."

Quinn's vision narrowed to a point on Maggy's bleached white teeth. How long had brightening her teeth taken? She snapped. "Look for it in the morning? Are you so concerned about your stupid necklace that you'd have us search the whole church grounds? Or have you forgotten that we have *our mother's* funeral tomorrow?" Far behind Maggy, Mrs. Greaves shook her head agitatedly, having run out of matches with three more candles left to relight. Mr. Mullone offered her his trusty lighter.

"Quinn! That's not what I meant! I was just trying to help." Maggy pressed her lips together in the thin line that meant she thought Quinn was being unreasonable. Quinn hated that look. Mainly because she ended up agreeing with Maggy after all the fighting was over. But right now, she wanted her to butt the hell out and let her be the parent.

"Sure. Like all the other times you've helped. Oh, that's right. There are none because you're never here." Quinn wrapped an arm around Allie, who was crying in earnest at her muddy shoes now, and led her towards the door. With long faces, the ladies waved a solemn goodbye to her then looked towards Maggy pityingly. Behind them, the relit wicks of the candles burned straight and watchful, no sign of the pesky draft from a minute ago to set them aflutter. Her sister still stood where Quinn had left her, arms crossed and shoulders drooping. She followed Maggy's gaze to the ornate Tree of Life curling up the wall. The ice pick stabbed through her temple again.

Feeling guilty for how she'd snapped at Maggy, she snatched her sweater off the rack by the door and stuffed it into her already bulging purse. She placed a hand on Allie's arm. Her daughter didn't budge.

"Why did you do that?"

Quinn stared at Allie. She wasn't in the mood for a mouthy teenager, especially one pointing out her faults. Allie looked up from beneath the dark fringe of her bang.

"Why did you fuss at Aunt Maggy like that?" Eyes shimmering, Allie glanced down and rubbed at her elbow. "I'm the one who lost the necklace. She was trying to help. To make me feel better."

"Now is not the time to get into my history with your aunt, sweetie." Quinn massaged her temple, wishing Allie would move it.

"Ooook. Then why did you say it was 'her' necklace?" Allie bit her lip. "I thought you gave it to me."

With a long sigh, Quinn reached out and fiddled with a strand of Allie's hair. Gently, she said, "I was letting you borrow it for the evening. Your grandmother wanted Maggy to have the pearls." Eyes widening, Allie's mouth formed an O. She snapped her mouth shut and swallowed a couple of times, processing.

"Why isn't she mad at me then? For losing it?"

Inwardly, Quinn groaned. Why did children have to ask so many questions? "Because she loves you and it's just a necklace.

Now. Let's go home." She swept both hands towards the door in a pushing motion. After a long, conflicted look at her aunt, Allie nodded. They turned toward the door.

And immediately ran into Mr. Mullone. Quinn grumbled apologies and tried to step around him. He stretched out an arm to stop her, clearing his throat nervously. His eyes flitted back and forth, refusing to meet her own. She wasn't being that much of an angry troll right now, was she?

"Sorry to hold you up, Quinn, but I need to ask you and your sister a quick question." He waved his arm vigorously to draw Maggy over. Quinn rolled her eyes to the vaulted ceiling and prayed to whoever the patron saint of patience was that they would give her an extra portion of it that night.

Maggy trudged up, refusing to meet Quinn's eyes. Her bare feet slapped quietly against the wood floor. Quinn noticed with a small shock ant bites and scratches up and down her sister's legs. She hadn't noticed them when Maggy came in. She looked at Maggy's face, lined with exhaustion. Maggy kept her eyes on Mr. Mullone, arms crossed.

"I know you girls are tired, so I'll keep this quick. We've tried every spot we can think of in both the Matins and the Yellowley plots. We keep running into… previous occupants or roots." He clasped his hands over his belt buckle and took a deep breath. "Would you consider letting us put your mother in the same grave as your father?" He glanced up nervously and continued in a rush. "I know it's not something we often do here. Or ever. But there would still be space for two gravestones as planned."

Quinn watched the side of Maggy's mouth twitch up.

"Is that what all the fuss with the digging has been about?" Quinn asked.

Maggy chuckled. "Of course, it's all right! Mom would get a kick out of being cozied up to Dad for all eternity." Quinn caught Maggy's eye as she chuckled as well trying to show that she felt like a heel for how she'd acted a moment ago. Maggy fell silent, dropping her eyes.

Quinn answered Mr. Mullone, her voice soft and hesitant, "I think we both agree that as long as she's decently in the ground and we know where she is, it will be all right." Maggy nodded her agreement.

Mr. Mullone gathered all three of them up for a hug.

"Your mother would be so proud of you," he said huskily before releasing them and walking briskly into the cloudy night. Spinning on her heel, Maggy headed for the far side of the circled chairs without another glance at her. Catherine looked to Quinn who nodded towards her retreating back; wordlessly, Catherine followed Maggy. Outside, the angry spurts of rain eased into a soft patter. Anxious to be home, Quinn bundled Allie out the door before the drizzle could get any worse. She trusted her friend to smooth things over as best she could.

CHAPTER TWENTY-TWO

Far from the lights of the dig, Collins slammed the truck door and sat slumped in the pitch black, fists balled. He glared at the men's lanterns bobbing back and forth in the distance.

Dismissed. He'd been fucking dismissed. Not that Mullone saw it that way. He probably saw it as doing Collins a favor. He slammed the palm of his hand into the steering wheel and stabbed his keys into the ignition before peeling out of the gravel lot.

Collins had just finished talking to Harry, even managing to get a laugh out of the squirrely kid. As he sent the boy off to go help the guys finish closing the test plots, Collins' stomach coiled, unsettled from Quinn's piercing accusations. He had turned to see if he could catch her before she left and set things straight. Or at least tell her the long-due truth. However, he'd halted as Roy trotted out of the darkness with a satisfied grin on his face.

"Talked to the girls like we discussed," Roy had said. "And they are fine with having Alice all cozied up with Truman." Collins had clenched his fists as Roy clapped him on the shoulder, eyes twinkling, the bastard. "The boys are practically done refilling the holes in the Yellowley family plot and it won't take us any time at all to dig Alice's spot since we know Truman's is good. Why don't you go home and help Quinn get the kids settled and get to bed yourself? Y'all have a long day tomorrow."

Collins had stood silent for a moment, biting the inside of his cheek and resisting the urge to cold cock him. The old bastard had outmaneuvered him. Now he would get all the credit for Collins' idea. He narrowed his eyes. A few of the guys lingered, watching. Rick shrugged at him while Charlie stared, eyebrows raised and smirking.

"Are you sure you don't need a hand? I don't mind helping finish up," Collins had offered, choking down his resentment at being overshadowed.

"Nah. You go on and get some rest. You've got to be here before the rest of us tomorrow anyway. We'll see you then." Roy gave him one last friendly pat on the back, and Collins shrugged, acquiescing gracefully. Or as gracefully as he could muster while choking down expletives.

Now, he drove down the pitch-black highway towards home, hands shaking in rage.

Icy air blasted into his face, making the mist and humidity bead up and roll uncomfortably cool along his skin as Collins drummed his fingers restlessly on the wheel, mind spinning. He bashed the vents closed and swiped the chilled drops off his face. Hairs stood up on the backs of his arms as he squinted to see through the vapor rising in billows from the road, thick and eerie. A deer dashed across the glare of his headlights, a doe rolling her eyes back in their red sockets in alarm. He wrenched the truck to the side, careening across the road. The tires squealed as he hydroplaned before he managed to wrest it back under control, knuckles white on the steering wheel.

He exhaled a silent prayer of thanks, wondering if the doe was a warning. With a shaky laugh, he pressed the gas, ignoring his urge to pick up the phone and call Ralph, begin unraveling this whole thing right away. He was being overly superstitious; he had time. He would tell her everything, assure her he would figure it out. Quinn, well, Quinn would forgive him, wouldn't she?

CHAPTER TWENTY-THREE

For a moment after Quinn swept out of the church with Allie tucked under her arm, all Maggy could hear in the silence was the ticking of a grandfather clock, its hands counting down the hour, loud and rhythmic, as inexorable as death. How many times had she stood in the foyer of their house after Dad's death, looking up at the unwound clock forever stuck at high noon, and wishing he'd come bursting through the door like he always did after a work trip, smelling like sunshine and diesel? Her mind vaguely wondered what the equivalent ritual would be for Mama. She shook her head and realized there was no grandfather clock in the church, only Mrs. Greaves' watch ticking very loudly in the quiet as she stood sphinxlike beside her.

"How did you get there?" Maggy asked, perplexed. Her voice whispered out hoarsely.

"Same way you did. I walked!" Mrs. Greaves turned and began tapping her way back towards the circle of chairs in the glimmering candlelight. In the wavering light, her walk looked more unsteady than ever, and Maggy had to resist the urge to take her arm and guide her along. Mrs. Greaves turned and clicked her tongue. "Come on then. Father Fry wants to say a few words to finish us up for the evening." The urge passed.

With a chuckle, Maggy obeyed. Seeing a few pools of cooled wax on the coffin, she paused to gently scrape them off and reposition the doilies under the silver tapers. Mrs. Streisand leaned over.

"Don't worry, sweetie. I put a hairdryer and some furniture polish in my purse in case this happened. We'll make sure any drips are cleaned up before we leave."

Southern ladies' purses were magic! Maggy nodded gratefully before hurrying to settle into her chair. Catherine settled into the row behind her with a pat on her shoulder that made Maggy's whole body tense up painfully. Derek cleared his voice and said, "Let's take a few moments to finish this night peacefully, shall we?"

He smiled at her, the corners of his eyes crinkling. Underneath his hands the timeworn vestry Bible flipped itself open, his fingers gliding across the glowing pages.

As his voice rumbled through the familiar Psalm, Maggy caught Mrs. Greaves and Mrs. Streisand exchange glances with each other, eyebrows raised and foreheads puckered.

Praise the Lord!
Praise God in his sanctuary;
praise him in his mighty heavens!
Praise him for his mighty deeds;
praise him according to his excellent greatness…

Maggy simply let herself drift along with the rolling brogue, too tired to care what underlying message the preacher was opaquely hinting at this time. His voice eased some of the tension rippling through her from Quinn's reprimand— deserved or not.

…Let everything that has breath praise the Lord! Praise the Lord!

"Dear Friends: It was our Lord Jesus himself who said, "Come to me, all you who labor and are burdened, and I will give you rest…" Derek concluded. Too tired to risk closing her eyes, Maggy instead studied her companions, her attention drifting in and out as he continued with the usual "…Receive, O Lord, your servant, for she returns to you.'"

With a pang, she noted the deepening lines around Mrs. Greaves' eyes, the inflammation of her knuckles. Once more decoration than help, her cane was always with her now. Mrs. Streisand's thick hair had betrayed her and now revealed glimpses of her pale scalp through the carefully teased veil of her perm. Around and behind them bowed the heads of the other women, time's stamp clear on their bodies. Her peers wore the marks of exhaustion and motherhood. Her mother's friends had grown from a comfortable middle-age to the beginnings of seniority. With a shock, she noted that of those she thought of as true elders in the church, only one or two were present. She wondered how many she would see at the visitation tomorrow. How many she would see at all if she stayed longer than the weekend? A small part of her wanted to stay, to let down her hair and be Maggy instead of Margaret again. But what would staying even look like? Biting her lip, she refocused on Derek's prayer which had taken on a more earnest tone, straying from the formal cadences of the *Book of Common Prayer*.

"Lord, as we leave your sanctuary tonight, help us to rest in the hollow of your grace so that we may come together in unity, in one Spirit, to praise you tomorrow." Maggy pressed the acupressure point between the thumb and forefinger of her left hand. Unity? Quinn's words had made it clear there was little unity left between them, despite the promise of their earlier conversation.

Derek continued, "As we honor our sister Alice's life and grieve her passing, teach us to praise You in all things even as we miss our mother and friend. Be with us, tonight and always, drawing us together as one family knit together in peace and love. Amen."

Maggy slouched in her seat, kneading at her hand, then stood. As the women bustled around them, she strode up to Derek.

"I see what you did there, with the prayer."

He glanced at her as he tucked the Bible into the cabinet of the stand. "My agenda is always going to be to see families happy and together." A smile quirked up one side of his mouth. "I do fail at being subtle, however."

Maggy noted the dimple that appeared most disarmingly on his cheek, but even it wasn't enough to distract her from her anxiety.

"But you heard her! She hates me." She despised the tremble in her voice. How could her sister have this much effect on her after fifteen years and over a thousand miles of distance? Derek's eyes grew serious.

"Yes. I heard her. But she is still talking to you." He pursed his lips and tilted his head. "Angrily, perhaps. But talking. You couldn't make her so angry if she didn't still care about you."

Maggy froze, mouth agape. Quinn caring about her? Ever since her sister had announced she was pregnant, Maggy had tossed that thought out the door. She'd written her off as completely self-absorbed. She'd have to be, to not understand what she was doing to her, right? Blinking, she looked up at Derek, mind static with too many thoughts all at once.

Everything she'd done through the years, the cards, the visits at holidays, helping out with the babies, she'd told herself she was only doing it because Mama asked. But really it was because some small, buried part of her still hoped that Quinn loved her too, would be there for her too when her turn came. Maggy realized she'd been holding her breath.

"Do you really think she cares?" She gulped. Derek laughed. "Most definitely."

Her head pulsated with exhaustion. She needed a few minutes by herself to think. Spinning to gather her things, she swayed on her feet as she spotted her muddy stilettos across the room. With a groan, she took a step forward.

Derek tapped her arm. "Here, let me get your things and you sit for a minute. Do you have a purse somewhere or…?" His voice trailed as he glanced around helplessly. She waved him off, anxious to get out the door and to a place where she could be alone and hear herself.

"I'm all right. I just need to get on home." Sticking out her hand she smiled broadly at him, hoping he'd believe her. He looked at her skeptically, eyeing her scratched up legs and dark-circled eyes. Finally, he took her hand.

"If you don't feel like you can make it, pull over and give one of the ladies a call. They'll be more than happy to drive you home. No sense in being unsafe."

She nodded, but he held onto her hand firmly.

"I mean it. No sense in losing two Matins women this week." His words echoed Mr. Mullone's from earlier and she wondered how much time they spent together.

She gazed up at him. "I promise." With a squeeze, she added in a sudden burst of sincerity, "And thank you for all your help tonight. Everything, you said... I... I really appreciate it, Derek."

He smiled at her, cheek dimpling, before releasing her hand. As she turned, she caught the church ladies staring, pretending not to watch as they slowly tucked towel-wrapped Crock-Pots and casserole dishes into laundry baskets for easy carrying. Maggy made a low shooing motion with her hand and they whipped around, back to their work.

As she stooped to pick up her shoes on the way out the door, she found Catherine holding them out to her. The other lady nodded at Derek, or rather Father Fry, who now busied himself with a candle snuffer extinguishing the tapers one-by-one. "He's a hunky one, isn't he?"

Maggy goggled at her, "Aren't you married?"

Pursing her lips, completely serious, Catherine replied, "Married but not blind. And I meant for you. Sounds like you need a good guy for a change."

Snatching the shoes, Maggy shoved her aching feet into them. "What would you know of my needs?"

Catherine held up her hands. "Whoa! I was just trying to check on you after the way Quinn went in on you earlier." She sighed and brushed a strand of hair from her forehead. "That girl's my best friend and I love her, but bless it, when she's upset, she's got a tongue sharper than a serpent's tooth." She leaned against the doorframe. "And she knows it too. Probably why she asked me to check on you."

Maggy nodded grudgingly, confused at this turn of events, as she fiddled with the straps of the stilettos. As the hall grew a bit dimmer, divested of the candle's twinkling light, she watched Mrs. Greaves carefully lay the tapers and candlesticks in their appointed boxes. True to her word, Mrs. Streisand whipped a hairdryer and a tub of furniture polish out of her purse, along with some soft rags.

"I'd be willing to bet that she strikes below the belt with you too," Catherine spoke quietly, but her dark eyes stayed glued to Maggy's face.

"She always did know my sore spots," Maggy muttered. "Not that they're hard to find right now." She straightened up and rubbed her face, groaning. "What am I going to do with her?"

"Want me to beat her up for you? I know a little judo!" Catherine grinned at her, eyes twinkling. Maggy found herself smiling back, Catherine's infectious grin winning her over.

"Nah. No need for more casualties in this war."

Catherine shrugged. "All right. If you say so. But the offer for a mean judo chop stands."

Chuckling, Maggy patted her on the shoulder and paused at the door to wave to everyone. She slipped out into the night underneath their sweet smiles.

Catching a momentary reprieve from the fitful downpour, a gentle mist now rose in the parking lot, so lush it was almost an upward veil of rain. Maggy stood in its decadence for a minute, letting the humidity soothe the scraped skin of her legs. The mist quickly coated her, turning her clothes heavy and sticky, and she rushed for her car, punch-drunk and giggling at her own foolishness. Her hair plastered itself to her face in long strips.

In the cool of her air-conditioned cabin, windows fogging over, she leaned her head back, thinking. Maybe she should give Quinn some space tonight. When they were younger, giving her space after a fight was always the best way to handle things. Maggy could forget about her luggage, go to Mama's for tonight. There would be plenty of time to go to Quinn's and change clothes in the morning. She cranked the car and pulled down the church's drive, hesitating at the end. Turning left would take her to Mama's; right would take her to Quinn's.

Quinn's words rang in her head. *"You're never here!"*

The words were unfair, but there was a note of truth in them all the same. Maggy had been running away from Quinn for sixteen years, afraid of what it would mean if she had it out with her and things went... bad.

Staring out across Farmer Book's field, she drank in the night air, thick with the smell of honeysuckle, cut grass, and pine sap, a touch of hickory smoke from someone racking ribs in one of the far-off houses. It was the smell of home. The ladies' faces, pocked and etched by time and brimming with kindness and love, floated before her.

She spun the wheel and turned right.

CHAPTER TWENTY-FOUR

In the soft light of the lamp, the pile of clothes spilling from the closet looked comically large. Quinn imagined drifting down into them and pulling their soft folds over her in a gentle, Fresh Air-scented cocoon. Mama had always joked that one day they'd find Quinn smothered to death in them—followed of course with a "suggestion" to just fold things as they came out of the dryer.

Her eyes slid closed as she imagined Mama's mouth twisting into the pinched smile she wore when she was trying to be helpful, but knew she was stepping on Quinn's toes. A light nuzzling followed by an unpleasant pinch at her breast jolted her awake. Clara screwed up her face as if to wail and Quinn forced herself to relax. Her infant daughter's face smoothed to a slight scowl and she returned to suckling, making quiet slurping sounds. Quinn nestled back into the pillows on the bed, joints aching with exhaustion.

Somewhere along the road between the church and the house her fury at Collins had evaporated and with it the momentary burst of energy it had given her. Entering the kitchen with a quiet clattering of keys and Allie stepping on her heels, she'd been startled to see Mrs. Hernandez up at two in the morning and walking a soundly sleeping Clara back-and-forth in the living room. Mrs. Hernandez smiled wanly, pausing to sip from a cup of coffee sitting on the kitchen counter.

"It's the only way I've been able to get her to sleep."

Allie waved at Mrs. Hernandez then dragged herself up the stairs, leaning heavily on the banister. Quinn gently scooped Clara from her arms; Clara was already beginning to contort and whimper with the interruption.

"I am so sorry. She's been fussy but she hasn't done this in a while. Why don't I try feeding her while you sit down and rest a bit—finish your coffee?"

Now, in the dim light, each strand of Clara's downy hair glowed. Quinn brushed her fingers through it, and Clara nuzzled into her contentedly. The little sucker. Quinn was positive she was next in a long line of dramatic Matins women. She leaned her head back and listened to the nighttime stirrings of the house. First, the slam and whoosh of Allie's nightly ablutions, punctuated by the grinding of the garage door as Collins came in, murmuring greetings at Mrs. Hernandez. What would they do without her? With so many kids all over the place, she was constantly coming to their rescue. A soft click echoed through the kitchen as Maggy entered. Quinn opened her eyes.

Collins was saying something to Maggy, but even with the door ajar, Quinn couldn't catch it. Through the crack, she could barely make out Maggy standing behind the couch, arms crossed and head bowed thoughtfully, shoes dangling from one hand. She shrugged and turned away towards the stairs. She heard the squeak of springs as Collins collapsed on the couch. "*Soft words will get you farther than fussing,*" Mama had always said. Quinn plunked her head back with a sigh. She had blown that big-time tonight. A few seconds later, Quinn heard the complaint of pipes again as Maggy began her evening routine. As Quinn was about to drift off, Mrs. Hernandez shuffled in, nattering cheerfully.

"Let me get this little one from you." She rocked Clara carefully up to her shoulder. "And this!" With a deft lunge, she plucked the baby monitor off Quinn's side table. "Mama's going to get some sleep tonight!" She sing-songed over her shoulder on the way out the door. Quinn stared in amazement. Clara hadn't even stirred.

Bless that woman.

Just as she slid in between the sheets properly, Collins pushed the door open. Quinn looked up at him, an apology on her lips. He held Maggy's shoes towards her, eyes squinched. In his other hand, was the romance novel, the pages even more battered.

Gesturing with the shoes, he asked, "Do you have any clue how to clean these?"

Quinn let the apology die. Always freaking Maggy. Over a thousand miles of distance and she still couldn't have any peace from her sister. Now she was under her roof and wreaking more havoc. She took the shoes and turned them over, looking at the clay hardening around them. Despite the blood-red mud, they didn't look damaged. It would be a shame to waste something so expensive. She looked up.

"Where did you get these?"

He shrugged. "I went upstairs to check on the kids and turn out lights. Spotted them in the bathroom trash can. Pretty hard to miss."

"Ah. You can toss this then." She tapped the book in his hand. "No need to keep smut around."

Wordlessly, he went into their bathroom and chunked it into the trash can. She exhaled slowly, trying not to let her temper get the best of her again, and stood. She scrambled over the piles of clothes to Collins' closet and dug around the top shelf. Behind her, she heard Collins pause in the doorway of the bathroom. She spoke over her shoulder as if she didn't care much.

"What were y'all talking about when Maggy came in? I heard you say something to her but couldn't tell what." She turned, shoe cleaning kit in hand, and he clicked off the bathroom light and sat on the edge of the bed, taking off his grassy shoes, clippings littering the floor. She took a deep breath and then another.

"I said something kinda petty about Marcus buying all her stuff when she got to the church tonight. It was stupid." Quinn blinked. She hadn't expected *that* small of a confession. He stood and moved towards the closet as she grabbed a towel and sat cross-legged on the bed. "I was trying to apologize—but she brushed me off just now. I know how much her clothes and stuff mean to her, so I figured this might be a way to make it up?" The question in his voice caught her attention. Collins never asked for her opinion, not even about her sister.

She studied him as he stripped out of his wet clothes, letting them fall in a heap next to the shoes, much too close to the clean pile for her liking. She inhaled deeply and bit her lip. He glanced at her then away.

"She does love her... shoes," she murmured. Her brain hissed, white noise flipping up instead of the words she needed.

He looked up at her, swallowing.

"Do you want to talk?" He whispered the words, eyes large and fearful.

Shaking her head, Quinn looked down to the stilettos in her lap, gently brushing the crumbs of dirt onto the towel and working the worst of the stains away with the wax. Maggy preferred to have her confrontations as big and dramatic and *immediately* as possible. To "clear the air." She was not Maggy.

"Quinn. I'm so sorry, Quinn." His voice was ragged. She glanced up. His eyes were red-rimmed and his chest heaved with sincerity. Good. He could stew in it for a while longer.

She gripped the stiletto harder and took a deep breath, forcing down the heat in her chest. As she wiped the shoes, polishing the mud and grit away, she imagined brushing away her anger, until it was a barely noticeable tremor in her knees. Mama would have been proud of her control.

He grabbed her arm and she stilled. "Do you not believe me?"

"I believe you," she whispered. Some hair slipped from behind her ear and stuck stubbornly to her lip. Aggravated she swiped it away.

"Then why won't you look at me? Why won't you say you

forgive me?"

Her eyes snapped up to his and she snatched her arm away. "This isn't something you just say 'sorry' for and it all goes away!" she spat. "Did it seriously never occur to you to talk to your wife, the CPA, about the finances of *our businesses*?" She pressed her lips together.

"I just wanted—" he began, reaching towards her.

She laughed, the sound harsh and startling in the quiet. "I don't care what you wanted." She pressed her hands together to her mouth, thinking. "I have so many questions." She inhaled deeply, forcing calm. "And things I need to tell you too." She pressed a hand to her forehead, squeezing her eyes shut, as the cold sweep of fear replaced the angry flicker of rage. She wasn't ready for the truth—the why of it all. "But not now, not tonight. We're both too tired to go through all of this tonight."

He looked at her, frowning. "You know, you'll probably be getting some money from your mom. We could use that to get the gyms steady…"

Lightning crackled through her and she slapped the bed. "Enough!" She pressed her fist into the mattress and forced down the brushfire trying to claw its way up from her stomach. "We don't know anything about what Mama may or may not have left behind. If she left anything, we'll be setting straight the kids' college fund. Not bailing out your screw-up." She swallowed, thinking of the possibility of losing their home. "Beyond that, I can't even think of where to start. My mind is so fuzzy." She pressed her hands to her eyes. "Let's just get some sleep." In her mind she imagined them being held together by nothing more than fragile bands of ice, a little bit of frost melting in the fire licking along her limbs. So easy to fracture and fade.

He grabbed her hand. "Quinn, I've always tried to do right by you, to do what's best for you, for all of us. Please, try to understand, I've had all this weight on me for so long, carrying everything."

She leaned back and stared at him, her face heavy. "Honey, I'm right here. I've always been right here. You're the one who chose to go it alone." She shook her head and pulled her hand from his. "We have a lot of stuff to talk about. You lied to me about Maggy." His eyebrows swooped together. She held up a finger. "And you've kept so much from me about the gyms— stuff that puts us at risk… and somehow Mama is involved… and I don't know…" Her heart stuttered and she took a deep breath. "We have a lot to talk about, and tomorrow is already going to be a long day. Let's just get some sleep."

As they clicked off their respective lamps and scooched under the covers, Quinn stared into the darkness, shivering despite the comforter piled on top of her. A desperate heaviness pressed her into the mattress. She stared into the dark, trembling and pondering long after his familiar snores grew deep and steady.

DAY TWO: STORM BREAK

CHAPTER TWENTY-FIVE

The morning of Mrs. Matins' funeral, Father Derek Fry painstakingly searched the ground in a wide swath around the Thompson mausoleum. A flashlight aided him in the struggling dawn light as he carefully parted the tall grasses and kicked at last fall's leaves. Intermittently, petulant wind whipped the mist into rain and lashed at his long raincoat. His dark hair laid plastered against his forehead. He glanced at the racing clouds overhead, already an angry purple, and surveyed the yard around him. His footsteps had pressed deep into the saturated grass and were pooling with rainwater, clearly marking his fruitless search. He thought of his eulogy notes, waiting unfinished in his office; it would be impossible to search the grounds further until another day.

He turned and flashed his light on the mausoleum. Wryly, he realized that in the case of snogging, the place the snogging occurred would be the most likely spot to search. He chortled softly at his foolishness, shook the moisture from his face, and reached out to try the lock, the keys sitting on the same desk as his notes. Though he had not seen how Maggy had accomplished it the night before, a solid twisting shove revealed how the young love birds had entered the ancient mausoleum, and he stepped into the dark, *dry* interior quickly, swiveling his light around the tiny alcove.

While his attention to some parts of the grounds might lapse, Derek thought of the scraggly grass outside—Mr. Mullone's attention to the monuments themselves was unquestioned. Each urn stood dust-free in its niche and a lovely arrangement of red silk roses stood in its grotto. An equally impeccable stone bench was situated in the center of the small space. Derek quickly edged his way around the mausoleum, peering into all the corners and underneath the bench. He found nothing.

He sat down on the bench, sinking his head into his hands. The thought of Mrs. Matins' pearls, always glowing gently in the hollow of her neck, lost forever to the long wildness of grass and time, made him feel the lack of her presence acutely. Cold crept over him from fingertips to cheeks despite the clinging humidity.

It was then that he noticed the legs at either end of the bench were set imperfectly into grooves on the floor, with a gap of about an inch going all the way around their edge. The stone he sat on was a somewhat lighter hue than the rest of the surrounding architecture. At some point in time, the bench must have been replaced with one that didn't fit quite as snugly. Hastily, he dropped to his hands and knees and raked his fingers into the gap. His fingertips brushed something cool and smooth. With an exultant "aha!" he pulled out the long strand of pearls.

Holding his breath, he turned the pearls, radiant even in the dim light, this way and that, checking for damage. They were perfect, with no broken clasp or scratches to buff out. He pressed them to his lips with a whispered, "Thank you, Jesus!" He pulled out a handkerchief, wrapped them carefully, and stowed them away in his breast pocket before slipping out the door and back to his study through the spattering rain to prepare his final goodbyes for Mrs. Matins.

CHAPTER TWENTY-SIX

Wan light leaked through the blinds and limped across the floor, barely reaching the half-deflated air mattress where Maggy lay. As poorly as she'd slept, even its pale creep was offensive to her as she slapped at her phone's incessant beeping. Peering at the too-bright screen with one eye, she read another gentle reminder from Olivia that she needed some cash to bribe the landlord if Maggy was going to keep crashing with her. With a groan, she Venmoed Olivia the dregs of her account, and flopped her face back down into the pillow. Olivia had been such a trooper taking her in, it was the least she could do. She'd figure out gas money later she decided as she hugged the pillow to her.

But the smell of biscuits and bacon and the rumbling of her stomach were stronger than her desire for more sleep. Steeling herself to the chill of the A/C, Maggy slid out from under the warm comforter and peered outside, trying to think of a plan. Picking at a mosquito bite on her arm, all she saw was a smattering of rain blurring the window, turning the world into the grey-green smear of a Monet painting and promising a thoroughly bleak day.

As she had tumbled into bed last night, she'd resolved to tell Quinn first thing in the morning that she was estate executor.

Now, as she shoved her hair into some semblance of a ponytail, she wondered how that conversation would go.

"Hi, Sis! Guess what?" she muttered to herself, "Mom left me in charge of handling all her worldly possessions. Oh, by the way, I'll need you to spot me gas money so I can get back to being jobless and homeless in New York. Good talk!" She sighed, sputtering her lips, and hung her head.

Maybe Quinn would have gotten a good night's sleep and be happy to talk. Maybe. She did send Catherine to check on her last night, after all. Feeling defeated before the day had even begun, she headed for the door. And tripped over her useless briefcase, spilling paper and pens everywhere.

Kneeling, she scooped the materials back into the bag, shuffling sketches for photoshoots and notes for editorial pieces together. Her job had gotten to be such a cluster towards the end, she'd practically been working multiple positions. She turned the well-worn leather of the briefcase over in her hands lovingly. When Mama had first given her the bag, she'd thought it unnecessary and pretentious. Why would a lowly assistant need such an over-the-top designer piece? But she'd come to love the smooth leather and deep pockets always filled with pens and pencils, relying on it to hold all her essentials and give her an air of distinction the less-prepared staff had lacked. Looking back, the briefcase had lasted longer than any of her miserable jobs. She'd only ever wanted to make and sell art.

Spotting her sketchbook slid up under the nightstand, a half-formed thought sprung up. Maybe a change in career—and locale—was in order. She rolled back her shoulders, thinking of the possibility. The chance to come home and start over was appealing. She scooped the book into the bag and stood.

Stealing herself, Maggy flung open the door and strode out. And tripped again over something that scraped even more skin off the top of her feet. Stumbling over crap was not how she wanted to start her morning. Especially not *this* morning, while still half asleep and in her pajamas. She was about to holler at Davy again for leaving his things in the hall when she looked down and blinked. It was her Vuittons. The ones she had left in the trash as ruined.

A chaotic din echoed up the stairs from the kitchen from where the rest of the family was already up and starting this miserable day. Somewhere, the baby began fussing, and over her wails, Quinn fussed too. Maggy paused, her hopes of calmly talking to her sister already fading.

She picked up the stilettos and studied them. There was one small scratch on the left heel, but she couldn't see any other marks or stains from the red Yazoo clay that had encased them. A lump rose in her throat and she huffed, irritated with herself for getting emotional over a pair of shoes. Expensive shoes. But still just shoes. Her mind raced. None of the kids would have known how to clean a pair of shoes like this. Mrs. Hernandez would never take something out of the trash. And Quinn had been in bed. Collins had to have been the one to clean them. She bit her lip and thought of how rudely she'd brushed him off last night, embarrassed. Undoubtedly, she owed him an apology.

She patted at her eyes and set the Vuittons gently inside the room before padding downstairs in her bare feet to help with breakfast. As she stepped into the warmly lit kitchen, the sight of piping hot biscuits and eggs welcomed her in. Quinn's flushed and furious face, hovering over a sputtering skillet of bacon, told her to get out. Maggy hovered in the door, her instincts telling her to bolt back upstairs.

Collins stood bouncing and patting the back of an unhappy and equally flushed baby in one corner, a soiled spit rag over his shoulder, while Kylie ran laps around the table in a state of semi-nakedness. The boys were wheedling for cereal, sugary and forbidden, oblivious to their mother's impending explosion.

Maggy glanced at Quinn's flushed face, gauging the likelihood of getting her sister's attention as next to nil. Maybe if she could help get everyone fed, Quinn would calm down and they could talk. Deciding to suck it up, Maggy lined up four plates and portioned out eggs and biscuits with butter and jelly, hoping that getting food in front of the kids would be the quickest path to peace.

Liam, hanging over the back of his chair, dropped his full

cup of milk, spattering everyone and covering the yellow linoleum floor with a spreading white flood.

"Damn it, Liam!" Quinn shouted, slamming her spatula down on the counter and covering her face with shaking hands.

Maggy shot out an arm and arrested Kylie's pell-mell race as she reached the edge of the puddle. Scooping her into a nearby chair and patted her on the head, she whispered, "Stay put, chickadee." Liam's lower lip was protruding dangerously as he stared up at Quinn.

Hastily, Quinn wrapped her arms around her son, bacon forgotten on the stove. Maggy rummaged through a couple of drawers and, with a helpful point from Collins, grabbed a handful of kitchen towels and tossed them around the puddle of milk, halting its spread before it rolled beneath the fridge. With a little hop, she stepped over to the stove and managed to save the bacon before it charred to a crisp in the cast iron skillet, scooping it onto a paper towel-lined plate that sat ready nearby.

As she set the plate on the table, Maggy watched Quinn wipe at Liam's teary, snotty face, then her own with a towel that had missed the puddle.

"I'm sorry, baby. I'm just sad right now because of grandma and it's making me act weird. Can you forgive me?" Liam wrapped his arms around her neck.

"Because grandma died?" he asked, sobbing. Maggy turned away, the smoke from the scorching pan making her eyes burn and water.

"Yes," Quinn's voice wavered, then continued stronger, "Because grandma died. And I miss her very much. Do you forgive me?" The little boy nodded at her words.

"I forgive you, Mama," he said, still hiccupping. Quinn sighed and sat in the chair next to him, rubbing his back as he took deep breaths. Allie walked into the bright and bespattered kitchen, still rubbing at her eyes. She drew up abruptly at the mess.

"What happened here?" she asked, her voice thick with sleep.

"A dropped cup. Would you grab some more towels and help me clean up a bit?" Maggy replied, swiping at her eyes.

Quinn shot Maggy a sideways look as Allie shrugged and turned sluggishly to pull towels from the drawer. It was way too early to play "guess what was bothering Quinn now" Maggy decided and concentrated on mopping up the milk and wiping down the floor with Allie before it grew sticky. Satisfied with the quick clean, Allie plunked down into a chair with a groan, the legs sliding on the floor with an ear-grating *squeak*.

"Is there any coffee?" Allie asked. Maggy raised an eyebrow at Collins in silent question, but before he could respond Quinn sprang up and opened a cabinet. She nearly collided with Maggy as she was trying to maneuver bacon onto the plates in front of the twins and Kylie.

"I'll put a pot on," Quinn volunteered.

"I want coffee too!" Davy shrieked.

Collins shrugged at Maggy. Looking pointedly at Allie, he sternly said, "We'll make an exception this time since it's going to be a long day. You know the rule about caffeine though." He turned to Davy, "Just… no. No way." Davy pouted but was soon distracted by piling eggs on his biscuit.

With an impressive eye roll, Allie replied, "Yeah, yeah, I know the rule. Until I'm eighteen, I can only have caffeine when I'm cramming for exams."

Maggy grinned and winked at her. "Then you can chug Red Bulls all you want!" Allie giggled. Another glare from Quinn made her add on, "But try not to do it in the afternoon. I can tell you from experience that staying up all night with caffeine jitters is not fun." She demonstrated with a dramatic shuddering and shaking of her hands. Davy and Liam laughed as she pulled faces at them.

"Messing up your sleep with sugar and caffeine is not healthy," Quinn huffed, looking at Allie. It was something Mama had always said. Maggy glanced at Quinn, the coffee pot burbling behind her. Noticing her look, Quinn turned her back and pulled down a few coffee mugs, thunking them onto the counter. Catching her aunt's eye, Allie rolled her eyes with a cheeky grin as Quinn turned her back to pour the coffee. Collins reached over and lightly smacked the back of her head.

Suppressing a grin at the interaction, Maggy spooned eggs onto two more plates and set them out for Quinn and Collins.

A mug of black coffee appeared in front of her, sloshing onto the table slightly. Collins and Allie held mugs fixed the way they liked. Sighing, Maggy turned to find Quinn already slipping the sugar and cream back into the pantry and fridge. She stepped around her silently seething sister to retrieve them herself. Somehow, the small snubs stung the most.

As she stirred a healthy dose of cream and sugar into her coffee, she sat back down to finally serve up her plate. She glanced up at Collins. "Thank you. For the shoes. Cleaning them, I mean."

He nodded expressively at Quinn who was managing to eat bites of egg in between wiping smears of jelly off Kylie. Kylie wriggled in her seat, happily smashing a biscuit onto her face instead of into her mouth.

"You're welcome. I know how much you like your… stuff. And I wanted to make up for my comment about Marcus… and everything… yesterday." He bobbed his head towards Quinn, eyebrows arched meaningfully. "But really, Quinn was the one who did all the work. I just found them."

Slowly nodding, Maggy took a deep breath. "Well, thank you both. I know they must have been a pain to clean."

Allie had finally begun to perk up over her coffee. "I wanted to apologize about yesterday too. I know I caused a lot of fuss by sneaking off with Harry and I'm really sorry." She looked at Maggy. "And I'm sorry about losing the pearls." Maggy patted her hand as everyone assured her all was forgiven. Underneath the table, Quinn kicked her shin with a sharp jab, a clear sign to drop the subject. Widening her eyes at her, Maggy kicked back, hard. Quinn winced.

Collins flicked Allie on the shoulder, "Tonight though, you and I are going to have one long, awkward refresher about boys and why you shouldn't be sneaking off with them."

Allie flushed bright red down to her collarbone. "Daaad! Please. I promise to never do anything like that ever again."

Liam snickered. "He means the birds and the bees talk!"

Davy piped up, "What does that even mean?" Liam shrugged.

Maggy tapped them both on the back of the head. "Don't embarrass your sister."

Davy stared at Allie as he licked his butter knife thoughtfully. "She's already embarrassed. What does it matter?" Quinn shushed him.

Collins shook his head resolutely at Allie. "Nope, not getting out of this one. If you're old enough to sneak off with a boy, you're old enough to give your ole' man all the details." With a big grin, Collins sat forward and put his chin on his fist, resting his elbow on his knee and affected a coquettish accent. "Like, I need to know. Is Harry a good kisser? Does he stare deeply into your eyes?" His eyes glinted devilishly. Liam and Davy made gagging noises.

Allie slumped in her seat, groaning, "Oh my God, I can't believe this is happening."

"Worse things have happened," Maggy tried to cheer her up. "I had to have the talk from Mr. Mullone because Mama was too embarrassed. Quinn, didn't you get the talk from Mrs. Streisand?" Quinn ignored her, instead handing Kylie another biscuit to destroy.

Sourly, Allie stared at her, "That's not helping."

Maggy grinned at her, "Have another cup of coffee then. That will make you perk right back up!"

Collins turned to Maggy. "Speaking of perking up…" Maggy's stomach dropped.

"Did I spot you making googly eyes at a certain preacher man? Is there a romance afoot that we need to know about?" On Collins' other side, Allie wilted with relief at the attention turning from her; she buried her nose into her coffee mug as she grinned impishly at her aunt's discomfort.

Maggy crossed her arms. "I did not make googly eyes at Derek."

"So, you're on a first-name basis with the good Father already!"

Maggy rolled her eyes and opened her mouth to retort. With

a huff, Quinn stood up and began gathering plates amid protests.

"Someone got up on the wrong side of the bed," Allie drawled as her plate was snatched away.

Quinn pointed towards the stairs and said evenly, "It's time we all started getting ready! There'll be more things to snack on at the church. Shoo!" Sadly, Maggy watched her half-eaten breakfast be scraped into the trash. She did manage to save her coffee cup before it was dumped down the drain. As she was about to leave the kitchen, she turned back, trying one last time to have a quiet moment with her sister.

"Quinn, I'm happy to help clean up," she offered, wavering in the doorway.

She met Quinn's flat stare with a tentative smile as Quinn swept her hair up into a messy ponytail atop her head. Quinn turned to the full sink. Collins sat bouncing the baby on his knee, brow furrowed at his wife. Flicking on the tap, Quinn said over her shoulder, "You've helped enough." It was the first words she had spoken to Maggy all morning. Slowly, Maggy turned and climbed the stairs.

CHAPTER TWENTY-SEVEN

The water scalded Quinn's hands as it swirled over the dirty pans and rushed in a mad torrent down the drain. Through the window, she could see the dark, low clouds threatening a storm that looked as foul as she felt. She scoured the old cast iron harshly, not caring if she ruined the seasoning. Mama would have whipped her if she had seen how she was treating the pan she'd given her as a wedding gift, an heirloom from her great-grandmother. At the thought, she whirled to grab a dishtowel out of the drawer. Finding it empty, she slammed it shut, muttering to herself about unhelpful, know-it-all sisters.

A hand fell lightly on her shoulder and she jumped. Collins stood behind her, looking concerned. Behind him, the door to the laundry room stood ajar, and he handed her a clean bath towel.

"Here. This will do for now. It's old, so it doesn't matter if it gets messed up." She nodded and took it. But he didn't move away, still holding Clara, who lay contentedly on his shoulder, drool-covered fist shoved in her mouth.

"You don't have to be so hard on her, you know. She was just trying…" Collins began. Quinn cut him off, not exactly pleased with him either.

"You don't understand. She blows in here from doing God

knows what, gets the kids all riled up, playing parent to them like I'm not standing right here, and then blows on out whenever it suits her." She was getting worked up; she could feel the heat in her face and heard the tremor in her voice.

"I don't think she's trying to parent them. I think she's trying to help you."

"Help me? Helping me would have been to not run off to New York and never come back, with no explanation, when I was newly married with an infant. That would have been helping. Helping me would have been being here when Mama was sick and…" She took a deep breath, unable to finish the sentence. An image of the casket in the candlelight flashed in her mind, and she shut her eyes.

Things had been going so well with Maggy last night, and then she'd let her temper get the better of her. Quinn pinched the bridge of her nose, wondering how things had gone off the rails so fast. Why was she rehashing this again—and with Collins?

He raised his eyebrows. "It's not her fault she wasn't here when your mom was sick. We didn't think it would get that bad…" She watched him wince as his voice trailed off, remembering.

Quinn crossed her arms. "I know. But an irrational part of me says she should have been here anyway. I'm… I'm having a hard time getting over that." Understatement of the year. He cocked his head, waiting for her to continue. "She's my sister. She should have been here all along, and she wasn't. And that hurts. And I don't think she gets that it hurts."

Quinn could feel his stare as she studied her feet, avoiding his gaze. She hadn't had a chance to paint her toenails in ages. Ugly callouses covered her heels, thick and cracked. No matter where she looked, she couldn't find anything redeeming in her appearance.

He broke her thoughts, asking, "Have you ever said any of that to her?"

She crossed her arms over her chest. "I don't know if I can. It's been so long."

Collins looked down at her, face somber. "Maybe just say it. She's the only family you've got left. You two might fight like cats and dogs, but I know how much you love each other. Don't let things unsaid be the things that tear you apart." She twitched at the irony, and Collins pressed his lips together before adding, "Promise me you'll try?"

She nodded, brow furrowed. "I'll try. Can't promise it will go well, but I'll try."

Collins smiled, eyes pinched, and kissed her temple. "Good. That's all I ask." She tilted her head up and kissed him long and deep. Whatever else was happening between them, she was grateful for how grounding he could be sometimes. He smiled tenderly at her. "I'm going to go see if I can corral those kids into some somewhat presentable clothes." He pressed his forehead to hers. "I promise we'll talk about all of our stuff this afternoon. Ok?"

Fear fluttered in her stomach, beating against her ribs and clogging her throat. She so desperately wanted to believe they would make it through this. "Ok," she whispered.

Quinn watched him climb the stairs, cooing baby in tow. She turned back to the sink and flipped the water back on. As it ran over her hands, she watched the clouds swirl outside. Lowly at first, then louder, she began to sing.

"Can you hear it calling, riding on the wind? Place your hand in mine. Destiny is rising tonight."

CHAPTER TWENTY-EIGHT

Maggy eyed the van skeptically.

"It's more spacious than you think," Allie offered. Her flat tone and rolling eyes told Maggy she was regurgitating a line that she'd heard herself way too many times. At least the inside looked reasonably clean, only a few ground-in Cheerios. She counted the seats through the windows.

"Yeee-ah. It looks to me like it only fits seven, max." She glanced down at Kylie who was currently dancing a spastic jig around them in her rainbow tutu.

Allie shrugged, barely glancing up from her phone. "There are fold-down seats in the trun… I mean 'cargo area.'" She inserted air quotes sarcastically. "Haven't had to use 'em before, but I guess there's a first for everything." She returned to texting—Harry, Maggy assumed.

Davy and Liam, already feeling irritable and repressed in their dark Sunday suits, which they had loudly declared they never even wore on Sundays, were engaged in an enthusiastic pinching match that was quickly escalating to slaps and punches. She nodded towards them.

"Let me guess. I'm supposed to sit between them in the back seat and referee?"

The door to the van slid open with a soft beeping sound as Collins and Quinn finally exited the house, diaper bag and baby in tow. Allie scrambled in, claiming one of the two first-row bucket seats. She grinned at her aunt over her shoulder.

"It's that. Or the cargo area!"

Maggy sighed. The twins scrambled in with a flurry of shiny shoes and elbows.

Quinn smiled apologetically at Maggy. "I'm afraid it's cargo area, anyway. We had to put Kylie's booster seat on the back row to fit everyone."

"Aww, man!"

Maggy looked down at her niece, startled. She spoke! Collins looked at Maggy, grinning.

"She's been feeling a little shy since you got here. Looks like she's getting over it." He booped Kylie on the nose. "Aren't you, ladybug?"

An adorable pout crinkled her tiny brow. "Why do I have to sit in the back with the boys? Put Clara back there!" She added matter-of-factly, "She's a baby. She won't know the difference."

Quinn looked at Clara, snoozing peacefully on her shoulder, and shook her head. "Nope. No way am I risking the boys walloping this baby."

Maggy watched the parental negotiations with an increasing urge to throttle everyone. She cleared her throat, about to offer to strap in Kylie. Collins raised an eyebrow at her and shook his head. Quinn shot her a nasty look. Apparently, her black mood was not forgotten, just hidden.

Biting her lip, she stared at the ceiling of the garage and cursed her impatience. In the depths of her purse, the Imperial March began to play.

"Star Wars!" Liam screamed. He and Davy promptly began belting out the opening "Duh-duh-duh-da-duh-duh!" at full volume.

Mortified, Maggy mouthed, "I am so sorry," and slipped back inside to take the call. Marcus was so dead.

She opened full blast. "You'd better have a darn good reason to call me right now, Marcus. I'm trying to get my family out the door for my mother's visitation. Or did ya' forget the funeral is today?"

"Of course, I didn't forget!" Marcus snapped back. He sighed, the sound buzzing and crackling over the line. "Ok, I forgot it was this morning, but I didn't forget that's why you're in Mississippi."

She pursed her lips and waited silently.

"Maggy…"

"Marcus."

"Do we always have to talk like this? Sniping at each other?" She gritted her teeth. There had to be more of a reason than this stupid question for him to call. He was always conniving, hiding the real reason behind something else.

"Marcus, we are literally trying to get in the car. If this is going to take more than, like, thirty seconds, I need to know so I can take my car and not hold everyone up."

"I do need to talk to you about something important. I stopped by your work and picked up your things and talked to the HR people about your options."

She groaned. "Hold on." Sticking her head out the door, she waved at Collins who was buckling Clara into her car seat. "Y'all head on without me—" She paused, trying to figure out how best to phrase it so it wouldn't sound like she was trying to blow off the visitation for work. "This is something legal to do with my firing. It'll only take a few minutes, but I don't want to hold you up."

He nodded at her, looking unconcerned, and turned back to what he was doing. Behind the steering wheel, Quinn scowled. Maggy let the door fall to, resigned. She couldn't win everyone over.

Putting the phone back to her ear, she growled, "I thought you agreed to leave my job situation alone until I figured out what I wanted to do. Why'd you go sticking your nose in?"

"Hey! I wanted to be sure you didn't leave this situation hanging over us, Maggy. Now you have a couple of different options…"

Maggy's ears rang painfully, like someone had clanged a bell beside her head. She cut him off. "Us? Marcus, there is no us. You broke up with me, remember?" She took a deep, shuddering breath.

The line went silent. He exhaled, the sound tense and whispery over the bad connection. "I know. I messed up. I shouldn't have done it like that. But we can still work it out, right?" A few weeks ago, she'd have given anything to hear these words and feel like she mattered to him. Now, anger and resentment clawed through her belly, sharp-nailed.

He paused, and she heard the familiar sipping sound. She had not missed that sound, disgusting and loud, always preceding his wheedling and irresistibly large, begging eyes. Well, she wasn't there to see those eyes now. And Mama wasn't around to tell her to take it easy on him.

"Look, I know I messed up. Expected too much of you—things you weren't capable of." Weren't capable of? Did he think she wanted to be his maid and mother on top of working eighty hours a week?

He continued, voice smooth as the bourbon he was sipping, "But we were good together in other ways, right? And I... I miss you." Heat flared in her stomach, licking angrily along her ribs, but she remained silent, letting him set the trap for himself. An edge crept into his voice now, like the sharp bite of alcohol; the turn designed to make her woozy and confused. She sucked in her breath, knowing he was about to dangle the bait, but this time she would see the hook for what it was. "I can make all this trouble at your job disappear. You can have the career you've always wanted. Just come back to New York. Let's work this out."

She whispered into the phone, "And what happens the next time you get mad at me?"

"What?"

She spoke louder, vicious, as she had to be. "What happens the next time you get mad at me?" She leaned against the kitchen counter, the granite shockingly cold through her linen dress, and forced herself to speak evenly as she stared out the window and into the backyard. Bleached by the sun, the rocking horse tipped back-and-forth morosely on the swing set in the breeze that had picked up, droplets of last night's rain spattering to the ground.

"What was it this last time—a burnt lasagna—that made you so mad? And you practically threw me out because I wasn't 'carrying my weight' around the place. Because you don't like to do laundry or cook or clean. But somehow, that means I'm 'not carrying my weight.' But God forbid we hire a maid because they all steal. So, I couldn't hire a maid in the apartment that my trust fund mostly paid for."

Bitterly, she laughed, "God, I was so stupid to let you put only your name on the lease because you'd understand the contract the best. Because, when things turned, and they always turn nasty with you, you bullied me right into moving out of *my* apartment. And because you're the hotshot lawyer from the big firm and I'm a silly little fashion editor whose job doesn't matter according to you, I didn't want to spend years fighting you in court. So, I didn't fight it. And now? I'm practically homeless." Thank God, Mama wasn't alive to see the state she was in. A tiny bit of relief squeezed her throat.

She laughed, the sound crackling and raw. "So, no. We have nothing to work out. Because you're an asshole."

He sputtered. She could imagine his face ashen, hands shaking in rage. "Asshole? How am I an asshole? I'm here trying to help you get your job back! I want you to come home!"

"Only so you can get me back. Only because you're lonely and living in a garbage dump. But are you going to change anything that got us here in the first place?" She lowered her voice. "Are you going to magically start taking loads of laundry to the cleaners, or dusting, or taking out the trash, or any of the million other things it takes to live with another human being? Or is that going to default to me? Look around you, right now. What does it look like? Is it squeaky clean or full of your filth?"

Silence answered her.

"That's all on you. You're a slob. And you can't blame that on me."

"So, we'll hire a maid! Maggy, come back to New York."

"Do you still think my job's a joke?"

"I'm trying to help you get your job back!" Next to the horse, the swings began to career backward and forward in the wind, their bright red seats a maddening blur.

"Do you still think my job's a joke?"

"Jesus Christ, Maggy, it's fashion. It's hardly like it matters. Doesn't change that I want to help you. Just come home. Let's work through this."

An icy calm spread through Maggy. "Don't call me again, Marcus. And don't call my work. I don't need your help fixing this."

His voice pitched, "Maggy, don't do this. We can fix this. We can work this out."

She hung up with a satisfying punch. Immediately, she blocked his number and jammed her phone into her purse. Biting her lip, she pulled it back out and typed out a quick message to Olivia.

Hey doll! Be expecting to be harassed by Marcus. I just cut him off for good. #gladthatsover

Almost immediately, her phone lit up with a buzz.

Yaaaaaay! I've been telling you to stop talking to your exes. #finallylistened Anything I can do?

He's got my work files. Want to take one of your muscle-y friends and go retrieve them before he does anything stupid?

You've got it! <3 <3

After texting with Olivia, Maggy shot off a quick email to the head of HR, letting him know that Marcus in no way spoke for, represented, or in any way was affiliated with her and she did not approve him to have access to any information on the status of her employment or standing with the company. As the email fired off with a ping, she looked out the back window one more time.

Angry clouds the color of bruises scuttled overhead, and welts of rain struck the ground. Already on edge from the call, she zipped up her rain jacket, muttering as her hair caught in the zipper. Turning to go, she realized with a jolt the families' coats still hung by the door. She glanced out the window one more time. Would Quinn be peeved at her "interfering" again, or relieved with some backup bad weather gear? She bit her lip as she studied the clouds. Danged if she didn't think it was blowing up a good storm. Throwing caution and her sister's temper to the wind, she shoved the coats under her arm and dashed for the car, as the bottom fell out.

CHAPTER TWENTY-NINE

Quinn was avoiding starting this day and she knew it. However, the clock nailed to the oak paneling above the door was inevitably ticking down to ten a.m. She couldn't put off appearing in the fellowship hall forever, and she had to make sure everything was in place before the visitation started.

She slid the coffee pot back onto the burner with a click. Stirring in a massive amount of cream and sugar, she braced herself and downed half of the near-scalding cup, ignoring the throbbing of her tongue. The more caffeine she could get in her exhausted veins, the better right now. In the corner of the ladies' parlor, Mrs. Hernandez—dear, sweet Mrs. Hernandez—sat playing dolls with Kylie. Clara eyed them skeptically from her carrier. The boys slouched nearby on an overstuffed couch, playing on iPads and occasionally bumping each other in excitement. A tray of Mrs. Greaves' infamous chocolate chip muffins sat next to the coffeepot. Quinn cut one in half and, cradling it in her palm, slipped silently from the room with a small wave to Mrs. Hernandez so as not to draw the attention of the children. She needed them out from underfoot for the time being.

As she tiptoed down the dark hallway to the fellowship hall, nibbling on her muffin half, a blaring foghorn sounded. She jumped at her phone's emergency alert, nearly dropping her muffin. Swearing softly, she slipped the phone out of her pocket and glanced at the pop-up: flash flood. Great, now half the county would use this as an excuse to not show even though the roads would be perfectly fine. She groaned and crammed the phone back in her pocket and the rest of the muffin in her mouth. She stomped through the swinging doors into the hall and nearly crashed into Mrs. Greaves.

Poking her head out from behind a massive wreath of hideously pink peonies like an ancient tortoise, Mrs. Greaves squinted up at Quinn.

"Sugar, are you alright? You look very flushed." She plunked the wreath into Quinn's crumb-covered hands and pointed to the spot it needed to be set.

"'M fine," she mumbled around her half-chewed bite of muffin.

"Wha-aat?" Mrs. Greaves said, a bit too loudly in the near-deserted hall. Collins turned to see if everything was all right from where he stood—next to the windows with Father Fry, Mrs. Streisand, and Mr. Mullone. Quinn stared at Mrs. Greaves, knowing that she may have bad knees, but she did not have bad hearing. She choked down the muffin.

"I'm fine, Mrs. Greaves." She spoke clearly, being sure to not mutter. "I'm flustered about the weather, is all."

With a sympathetic smile, Mrs. Greaves patted her arm. "It will be alright, sweetie. With the number of arrangements that we've had delivered all morning…" She waved at an astounding number of baskets, wreaths, and vases surrounding and haloing out from the darkly shining casket. It was as if they had stepped into a hothouse filled with every shade of red, pink, and white in the stunning blossoms of roses, peonies, and lilies. "…No one has forgotten your mother. Or you. Even if the weather scares 'em off today."

Quinn clasped her hand with a dim smile, before turning to scowl at the flowers.

"Dear God. Who arranged them this way? It's like a weird,

modernist painting. It should be all according to height, no? Here, Mrs. Streisand!" She waved her mother-in-law over. With another wave, she ordered Allie over as well from where she sat giggling with Harry in one of the chairs, now arranged in orderly rows with an aisle down the middle of the hall. Her daughter dragged herself over with a pout.

"Let's rearrange these to look a little better. There's so many of them that if we don't do it strictly by height, it's going to look off-kilter." The two older ladies exchanged glances, and Allie rolled her eyes, but Quinn was already pulling arrangements aside, and handing them standing wreaths. She watched as they shrugged at each other and began ferrying flowers to-and-fro. She pointed out where she wanted each arrangement, feeling better to be in charge and doing something. Even if it was just moving flowers.

She found a beautiful wreath of lilies of the valley interspersed with baby's breath. Pulling it off the stand, she draped it on top of the coffin, letting the lilies hang gracefully down the side. Even in the wan morning light, the flowers shone bright and lovely against the dark wood, as if they had been plucked a moment ago.

"Oh, that's gorgeous, Quinn!" Mrs. Streisand stood beside her.

Mrs. Greaves cocked her head.

"It is rather pretty. But weren't your mother's favorite flowers peonies?"

Quinn huffed, exasperated. "Yes, but peonies are so... showy. Lilies are much more appropriate for a funeral, don't you think?"

Mrs. Greaves shrugged, noncommittal. Quinn turned, determined to be satisfied. Lilies were the more traditional choice, after all. She didn't have to bend to her mom's outlandish tastes in flowers now, did she?

With a light squeak, the inner door from the hallway swooshed open. Maggy strolled in, nursing a Styrofoam coffee cup. Even without eyeliner or high heels, her sister still screamed "fashionista" with her glossy hair and slate-colored peplum dress. She couldn't even be put upon to wear a proper black. Quinn sniffed and turned back to admire her handiwork with the flowers, trying to ignore her sister's blatant disrespect.

Maggy clacked over to them, the sound echoing loudly on the hardwood floor. Quinn glanced down to see why her footwear was so loud.

"Dear God, are those flip-flops?" she asked, horrified.

Maggy grimaced. "I was a little limited on footwear choices this morning. I tried to pack light but I didn't anticipate rain. Can't wear high heels out into the mud again. It was these or my UGG boots from college."

Quinn goggled at her. "You still have those?"

"Wear them as house shoes. They're pretty comfy to drive in too."

"Man, Mama hated those. Said they were one fashion trend that needed to die."

Maggy smirked at her, "I know. I wore them just to annoy her."

"You did not!"

With a shrug, Maggy turned to look at the flowers, brow furrowing. Quinn shook her head disbelievingly and studied the flip-flops a second longer. Admittedly, they were the nice kind with some decoration on the strap. And *they* were at least black.

"By the way, I brought raincoats for everybody." Maggy gestured towards the window where a storm was clearly brewing. Quinn scowled at the clouds, like that would help her forgetfulness. "Hung them in the parlor, just so you know where they're at."

"Thanks," she muttered, feeling called out. Maggy shrugged. "Not a big deal."

Mrs. Greaves bustled up with a picture frame tucked under one arm. As she propped up the watercolor portrait on the coffin amidst the lilies, Quinn recognized it as one that Maggy had painted a few years ago at Christmas.

Rubbing her thumb around the gilt frame, Mrs. Greaves said, "I've always loved how you captured the twinkle in her eyes, Maggy. So full of light and life." Quinn gazed into her mother's hazel eyes, at a loss for words. It looked just like Mama.

"I was just messing around when I painted that." Maggy took a sip of her coffee. "I should pull out my paints more often."

"Well, you're incredibly talented. She was always so proud of you, you know." Mrs. Greaves patted her arm. Maggy shook her head and remained silent.

Still eyeing the flowers, Maggy groaned and handed her coffee cup to Quinn. Startled, Quinn took the cup, staring at the slash of her sister's bright lipstick on the side.

"Hold this, would you? I've got to rearrange these flowers." Maggy began dragging the nearest wreath out of line. The ladies fluttered their hands nervously. "Looks like someone's messed with them. I had these all arranged the way Mama would have liked last night…" Quinn dug her nails into the cup, leaving moon-shaped indents, as she watched their work being undone. "…with the peonies next to the casket." Without looking at Quinn, she motioned towards the coffin with its cascading lilies. "And the lilies to the side." She looked at Quinn with a tentative smile that faded.

She offered quietly, "Because peonies were always her favorite?"

Quinn snapped, "And lilies were so waxy and morbid. Yes, I know." She slapped her sister's hand away from the wreath and shoved her cup back into her hands.

Dragging the wreath back into line, she glared at Maggy. "But Mama's not here now, and lilies are more traditional for a funeral. And it's going to look horrible to have everything so cattywampus if we don't do it strictly according to height." She crossed her arms and stared her sister down. "So why don't you stop meddling and leave things be?"

Maggy put her hands on her hips, jaw working. "Meddling?"

Quinn nodded, not wanting to give any ground.

"You're the one who is meddling here, Quinn. Or did you think the flowers magically arranged themselves that way?" Quinn looked down at her arms, heat flushing her cheeks. Of course, Maggy was the one who arranged the flowers; it looked like her style, and Quinn had instinctively known it. If she was honest, she had rearranged them partially out of spite. She shook her hair back, ignoring the guilt doing figure eights in her gut. Mrs. Streisand and Mrs. Greaves slid away a few feet and began fiddling with some of the arrangements, fixing flowers that hung too low or stuck out too far. They side-eyed Quinn and Maggy with deepening frowns.

"It doesn't matter. It still didn't look good. All haphazard and modern-ish." The words sounded lame even to Quinn.

"So what?" Maggy lifted her hands. "They're just flowers. Can't you let me do anything to be part of this without worrying about your random rules?" She scoffed. "God, I couldn't even help with breakfast this morning without somehow being the bad guy." She air-quoted. "Without 'meddling.'"

"This isn't about breakfast, Maggy! But while we're on the subject, yeah. I'd like you to stop stepping in and trying to parent my children as if you know better than I do what they need!"

Maggy flipped a piece of her shiny hair over her shoulder. Dear God, did she get keratin treatments done on it or something? "I'm their aunt. I think I sometimes know what they need."

"But if I tell you to stop, I want you to stop!" Quinn slapped one hand into another.

"Then you'll accuse me of doing nothing to help!"

Quinn guffawed. "Because you're never here to help!"

"You don't exactly act like you want me to be here! I hear more from Collins' Snapchats than I hear from you." Maggy jabbed a finger at her and then at Collins, who had stopped his conversation with Father Fry and Mr. Mullone to openly gawk at them. He held up his hands as if to say "don't bring me into this" and turned away.

Quinn hissed, pissed at the reference to Collins, who did have a better relationship at times with Maggy than she did. "That's because I don't want you around when you're acting like a spoiled little know-it-all!"

Maggy gritted her teeth, jaw spasming. Her voice was low and even, but her eyes snapped. "Fine! If you don't want me to be around, then I won't be around."

Maggy turned on her heel with a loud *clack* and strode out the side door. Quinn plunked her head into her hands. That had gotten out of hand. She inhaled deeply through her nose, trying to slow the thumping of her heart. How was she ever going to talk to Maggy if she couldn't even stop attacking her?

A shadow fell over her. She looked up, eyes stinging, to see Father Fry. The young pastor's gaze was kind as he stood next to her.

"I'm sorry for causing a scene, Father," she mumbled.

"No need to apologize." His words trilled, his Welsh brogue rich and rippling. "Grief often makes us say and do things we can never imagine at other times."

She exhaled heavily, the breath groaning out of her. "Why am I like this? Why, when all I want is for her to be here, do I keep running her off? Our mother…" She pressed her lips together, trembling. "Mama's dead. And I can't even keep it together long enough to tell my sister I'm glad to see her." She looked up at him. "You know, I never even said hello to her yesterday when she got here? I said something snippy about how loud she was." She pushed her hair back from her forehead and fanned at her face. He placed a hand gently on her shoulder.

"Could you do me a favor?" she asked. He nodded, eyes serious.

"I don't think it's a good idea for me to go after her right now. Would you… would you go check on her and see if you can get her to come back in here?" She nodded at the door. Outside, clouds gathered darkly. "I have a feeling she'll listen to you."

He nodded and turned for the door. "Of course."

Trying to release some nervous energy, Quinn pivoted back to the wreath and randomly fiddled with the flowers, realizing through a haze of tears that they were white roses. With a loud sniff, she looked at the card to see who sent them. Pressing a hand to her mouth, she looked up and caught Mr. Mullone's eye. He smiled sadly at her. Carefully, she pulled one from the back of the wreath and tucked it behind her ear.

CHAPTER THIRTY

Drops of rain splashed to the concrete, rebounding into a chilly spray that stung Maggy's legs where she stood, determinedly wiping tears from her face and trying to gather herself under the portico. She shuffled a few steps back to avoid a soaking and leaned against the frigid stone wall, watching the water gather and run into dark pools along the edges of the sidewalk. A lady should always be composed, Mama had said. Well, Maggy was doing a swell job of that right now, she thought, her mouth twisting bitterly.

In the summer heat, the chill of the downpour was unnerving. As a furious blast of wind sent a shiver up her arms, Maggy gave up on swiping at her face and hugged herself, her jacket abandoned inside. She studied the clouds. For now, they scurried straight on like men in grey coats down a busy street, but this morning's weather report of battling fronts had promised worse than a little wind and rain. Her heart sank with the plummeting temperature. She desperately wanted a hug from her mama, to lay her head on her soft shoulder and inhale the soothing scent of baby powder. She wanted it so badly she thought her chest was going to cave in on itself from the aching. More tears sprang to her eyes and rolled down her cheeks.

The door eased open behind her, revealing Derek's dark, damp hair. The good Father Fry slipped out quietly to stand beside her. She wiped at her face hopelessly, but he kept his eyes fixated on the water sheeting off the edge of the roof.

"Have you been sent to fetch me?" She couldn't keep the bitter edge from her voice. With a sniffle, she tucked her hair behind her ear and glanced up at him.

"Yes." He returned her look with a small smile. "But I wouldn't have come if I hadn't wanted to." He paused and turned back to the rain. "I wanted to be sure *you* were all right."

She tapped her toe into a rather large puddle that was beginning to form at the corner of the portico, pondering the emphasis of his words. Under his gentle look she found herself talking, babbling.

"As long as Mama was alive… I just always thought I could someday come home, and everything could go back to normal. We could all just *be* a family, finally. And I know that's foolish and naïve and all those other words. But…"

"You hoped."

She nodded and kicked the puddle hard, watching the droplets fly up and shatter in the light. "And now I don't know. My life is in shambles. And with the way Quinn is talking to me. Looking at me. It's like I'm something she wants to crush." She rubbed at her forehead and whispered, "I feel so lost."

Her voice cracked, and she wept. "I feel like I've lost my whole family. Not just my mother." She gasped. "My mother was bad enough. This. I can't take this." Pressure built in her chest and she gulped for air, sobbing.

Derek's eyes glistened, and he pulled her forward, gently hugging her. He held her until her sobs grew fainter and she began to hiccup. Holding her at arms-length, he looked at her seriously.

"Your sister is very complicated." Maggy waved a hand and shrugged. He shook her gently. "No, listen to me. I'm not excusing her. But I think a lot of her anger is really about herself and her own life and her own grief. It just gets pointed at you when you're around."

Maggy shook her head, bewildered. "That makes no sense. I haven't done anything."

He shrugged and let go. "It doesn't have to make sense. But sometimes it's easier to blame everyone else around us than to take responsibility for ourselves." He smiled sheepishly and pointed between her and him. "*We* can only examine ourselves to see where we're doing the same thing."

A dark Porsche pulled up, headlights slashing across them through the gloom, and parked neatly. Impervious to the rain in his sleek coat, Mr. Streisand strode past them into the church with a pleasant smile and hello to Father Fry and a friendly nod to Maggy. Behind him, a beat-up blue Honda sedan swung in crookedly next to the Porsche, one tire half in the grass that marked the curb. Ralph, whom Maggy vaguely remembered as some employee of Collins, hustled after Mr. Streisand, ignoring them both, water spots darkening his shirt as he slung on a cheap suit jacket.

Interruption past, she arched an eyebrow, curious. "And where are you not taking responsibility?"

He eyed her. "I'm afraid I'm better at preaching than practicing what I teach." He blew out a long sigh, lips buzzing. "It's taken me nearly twenty years to stop running from my past."

"Being rather cryptic, aren't we?" She nudged him.

He laughed nervously. "After Alice died, I was feeling rather morose. I called my own mother. To see how things were. See if my parents still weren't talking to me…" He trailed off, gazing at the rushing clouds sadly.

"I take it, it didn't go very well?"

He shook his head. "No one answered. I left a voicemail on the machine." He laughed, the sound catching in his throat. "They still have a machine." Shuffling his feet, he crossed his arms and turned to her. "Yesterday, right before the wake, my mother called me back. She… she told me everyone was fine. And she started crying, told me not to call ever again, and hung up." He shook his head. "Some doors are closed."

She placed a hand on his arm, and he covered it with his own.

"I'm so sorry."

"It's alright. I should have known after twenty years of silence." He chuckled darkly. "But still, the heart can't help but hope, right?"

She smiled at him, commiserating. "Everyone grieves in their own way. I remember after Daddy died. Mama couldn't stop grieving him." She leaned away and placed a hand on the cool stone. "The house became so quiet after that. Like a tomb itself. It had always been loud before, full. But after Dad died, the only time there was even a whisper of sound was when Mama sang while she washed dishes."

She looked up at him. "She even let the grandfather clock in the front hall die. I used to dream about it ticking sometimes." Staring out at the grey drizzle of the rain, she continued. "I think the only thing that saved her from becoming a shell of herself was Mrs. Greaves and Mrs. Streisand bodily dragging her from the house."

"Really?" He laughed.

"You laugh. But it happened. They'd show up. Haul her up from the couch or kitchen chair or wherever she was languishing that day and march her into her bedroom to get dressed. Then they'd drive into town for some 'socializing.' After a year of it, she gave up and started doing it on her own just to be rid of the nuisance." Maggy chuckled, but her face froze in a wince. "But she was still never the same. Mama was always religious, but after… she became more serious. Always up before dawn reading and praying. Lecturing us on loving each other and getting along." She smiled ruefully. "Guess that part didn't stick so good."

He shrugged. "To each their own."

She sucked on her teeth, looking for words. "It's just… Some people can't ever seem to stop… reliving… the grief. It's like they think if they stop hurting, it means they stop loving the one who's gone. Their love and their hurt are all tied up together and they can't separate them. If they stop hurting so much, that makes the love less real. I think maybe Mama was that way. Maybe that's how your folks are too."

Derek cleared his throat and stood up a bit straighter, drawing away. "Perhaps. Grief can be complicated like that." He placed a hand on her shoulder, face softening as he looked at her.

"But back to the original point I was making, I don't believe you've completely lost your chance with Quinn. You still have some means to communicate with your sister. The trick is going to be relearning how to understand each other."

She dipped her head to the side, acquiescing. Quinn wasn't the simple girl she'd left behind. The one she could slug it out with, and they'd be fine the next day. So much had been left unsaid for far too long. Her stomach sloshed nervously.

An alarm buzzed on Derek's phone.

"Oh! That's our cue. We've got fifteen minutes before people start arriving in earnest. We should get back inside so we can do the family prayer."

She nodded. "I need to wash my face as well." As she reached for the door, Derek grabbed her hand, stopping her. He withdrew quickly, flushing.

"I almost forgot." He reached into his jacket and drew out a handkerchief. Maggy watched, intrigued. A broad smile sprang to her face as he unwrapped her mother's pearls. He placed the cool strand in her outstretched palm.

"How?! Wha—Where in the world did you find them?"

He grinned, melting back into her boyish confidante from the night before. "In the Thompsons' mausoleum. Got up early this morning to look."

Tossing propriety aside, she threw her arms around his neck and squeezed him in a bear hug, rocking side to side delightedly.

Laughing, he hugged her back. "If I knew I'd be thanked this way every time, I'd go looking for lost treasure more often." A pleased blush crept up his neck.

Emboldened, Maggy turned and flounced into the church. "If you're the one looking, I'd lose my pearls more often." She winced at how risqué the words sounded but at his quiet snort of laughter, her heart fluttered, and she couldn't help but smile.

CHAPTER THIRTY-ONE

Maggy had been right about the peonies. Quinn bit her lip and tried not to huff at her foolishness as she swapped the arrangement on the casket. After all the commotion, she had turned around to see Mrs. Vanderwahl approaching timidly with the pall, pale as the blooms on top of the coffin. As the crisp white linen floated down over the casket, guided by the ladies' hands, a truant beam of sunlight slipped through the clouds and caught the golden threads of the delicately embroidered cross in a dazzling burst. As the cloth settled, so did the returning gloom.

Now here Quinn stood, annoyed with herself for causing a fight over flowers. Still, she eyed the outside door, wondering how long it was taking Father Fry to get Maggy back inside. For Christ's sake, she had sent the man to retrieve her sister, not to court her. She fluffed up the frilly peonies one last time and let her hands drop with an audible *kerplop.*

A familiar chuckle sounded behind her.

She didn't need to look to know who it was. "I know what you're thinking, Mr. Mullone. That I'm a silly girl who can't keep her mouth shut to save her life."

An arm slid around her shoulders and squeezed her once. Mr. Mullone kissed her temple. "Not quite." He let her go. "I was thinking about how much like your mother you are. She had the same temper. Maybe a bit more repressed. But it irked her all the same. You two are very much alike."

The corners of Quinn's mouth turned down in a skeptical sulk. "I don't feel very much like her. Mama was always so… poised, refined. She always knew what to say or not to say. I just blurt out the first thing I'm thinking."

He chuckled again. "In the right company, she would lose the veneer. She was much less polished than you think. In front of you two, she thought she had to have it all together." He pursed his lips and considered. "She controlled her 'lesser self,' as she called it, through sheer stubbornness. It's where your sister gets her charming personality quirks from as well."

"Ah. So, we're both dim reflections of our mother. That's great." Quinn forced a laugh, trying to sound lighthearted. Mr. Mullone smiled empathetically at her.

"Not at all. You're very much your own person." He cleared his own throat. "You have so much ahead of you, some great purpose. I think you can sense that." Quinn's heart leaped, and she balled her fists. A distant thrumming filled her ears. He shot her a knowing look. "You don't need someone else telling you where your place is. I told your mother as much for years."

"I wish she had listened to you," she whispered. She looked at him. "About everything." He nodded, eyes full, and remained silent, clutching her hand. Her chest ached for the man she had longed to have as a second father.

Under her fingers, she could feel the blisters from the night before riding atop calluses and scars from decades of burials. She looked up at his face, worn with years of working outside and lined with exhaustion. She noted dark bags beneath his eyes.

"Are you all right? You look like you're about to fall over."

He patted her shoulder. "I'm fine. I stayed up last night finishing my speech for the funeral today." He held up a hand when she opened her lips to protest. "I wouldn't have been able to sleep anyway."

She frowned at him and pointed demandingly towards the parlor, "Well, go get you a cup of coffee then." He harrumphed at her and she added, "I insist!"

"Aye! Aye! Captain!" He winked at her over his shoulder as he headed towards the swinging doors. She smiled at his retreating back and glanced at her watch. Ten minutes had passed, and the first few early arrivals had begun to straggle in from the direction of the parlor and its inviting smells of coffee and pastry. And still, Father Fry had not returned. She closed her eyes and took a deep breath, willing a calm she did not feel. Then she went to join Collins.

CHAPTER THIRTY-TWO

Collins and Rick stood by one of the arched windows studying the steady pour of rain. Smirking, Collins leaned over to Rick and elbowed him.

"Hey man, I'm sorry for your loss."

The other man looked at him, confused. "My loss?"

"Yeah, your loss of dignity when you have to shovel mud in that mess today," Collins teased, a lopsided grin sprawled across his face. His friend elbowed him back.

"Oh, screw you, dude."

"Hey, you know any other day I'd be right out there with you in it." Collins clapped him on the back. "We'll have plenty of towels and hot chocolate waiting for you at the house when you get there." He looked at Rick, concerned. "You did put a change of clothes in the car this morning, right?"

"Don't go into dad-mode on me! That's just weird. Yes, I put clothes in the car."

"What about clothes?" Quinn asked, as she took Collins' arm and leaned into him with a shiver. Her skin was cool to the touch and goosebumps crept up and down her arms. He wrapped an arm around her to warm her. She glanced at the clouds racing past outside with a worried frown and shook her head. Charlie strolled up behind her, shifty eyes taking in the scene.

"Change of clothes for after the burial," Rick explained.

Her eyes widened in understanding. "Ah yes. I dug out the Crock-Pot this morning. We'll have hot chocolate as well for all of y'all." Collins watched amusement dance in his friend's eyes.

"Collins mentioned something like that."

Quinn's eyes flicked to Collins' then out the window. Her hand clenched a little before releasing his. She was still upset with him, despite her calm expression. It would appear this storm was not going to bluster itself out.

Charlie inhaled, darting a look at Collins.

"Quinn, I'm so sorry about yesterday." Her eyes widened at Charlie's words, and she tilted her head in puzzlement. Collins wasn't sure where Charlie was going with this.

"Why are you sorry? We should have kept a closer eye on the kids." Her voice ticked up in a query. The back of Collins' neck prickled.

"Last night was poorly planned, and it reflected badly on the Guild. Your mother deserved better for her wake. It was irresponsible of us to let any of it happen, and I can assure you there won't be any more occurrences like it."

Quinn furrowed her brow at Charlie while behind her Collins shook his head emphatically at the younger man. Now was not an appropriate time to discuss Guild business, especially with his wife of all people. Whatever game Charlie was playing at, his wife did not need to be involved. Rick stood suspiciously still, hands shoved in pockets, staring at the floor. With a sinking feeling, Collins remembered his tirade of the night before.

Quinn's lips parted in question, but before she could speak the outside door to the fellowship hall swung open with a shuddering groan and in strode Mr. Jordan Streisand, Collins' dad and fitness mogul of the Southeast, looking tanned and self-satisfied. Collins practically wilted in relief at the interruption.

In Mr. Streisand's shadow trotted Ralph, a man of middling age and expanding girth. A poor copy of Mr. Streisand's luxurious look, his tan lotion had turned orange and streaky in the humidity. Today, he wore a suit that was meant to look expensive, but the fraying lapels and seams splitting in the armpit gave away its cheap construction.

Quinn dropped her hands from Collins' arm and clenched her fists. However, she remained immobile as a statue, her anger simmering dangerously beneath a calm façade. Rick glanced at her, mouth pursed up curiously. Mr. Streisand spotted his son and daughter-in-law and raised a hand, taking a step in their direction. Ralph immediately shadowed him. Quinn inhaled sharply, trembling. Trying to avert disaster, Collins leaped over to greet his father and employee.

"Hi, Dad!" He brushed by his father and gripped Ralph's arm, trying to steer him towards the back of the hall where a few other early arrivals clustered together, waiting for a signal to approach. In the echoing space, their murmurs rustled and slid against each other like layers of rubbed silk. Determined to stay close to Mr. Streisand, whom he followed like a creepy sycophant at every opportunity, Ralph refused to budge.

Irritated, Collins bent his head towards Ralph and hissed. "I'd keep your condolences to Quinn as short as possible." He darted a meaningful look at his wife. She stood glaring at them, arms crossed and hips jaunted in a silent challenge. "She knows."

Ralph blinked at him, face blank as a newborn baby. "Knows what?"

Exasperated, Collins sputtered, "About the loan! About the loan for the fourth gym, you nitwit. It was your blasted idea, remember?" His father was staring at them now, mouth pressed into a hard, thin line.

Ralph looked at him, eyes widening, "How'd she find out?!"

With a groan, Collins released his arm. "She has access to the gyms' books at any time. She is co-owner of them. Not that she's used her access in forever." He ran his hands through his hair. "And that account we used as collateral is her money—or the children's money or whatever. I can't very well hide it from her without raising a red flag, now can I?"

Through this exchange, Mr. Streisand had stood next to them, hands in pockets, studying the floor. At this point, he raised his head slowly and asked, his voice a thickly caramelized drawl, "Son, what the hell have you done?"

Collins raised his hands in protest but dropped them wordlessly, feeling ten years old and caught trying to forge his dad's signature on a bad progress report. He didn't know how to explain.

"It was all Alice's idea!" Ralph jumped in, all too eager. Startled, Collins stepped back and looked him up and down.

Mr. Streisand rolled his eyes. "Here we go again with one of Alice's hair-brained schemes," he muttered. "She can't stop plaguing us even in death." Ralph nodded, oblivious.

Overeager as always to please, Ralph launched into his story, head swiveling between Mr. Streisand and Collins.

"It was when memberships had stalled at the third gym and we couldn't get anywhere with the bank on financing for the fourth, although all the plans were done." He pointed at Collins. "You had me check the books for unnecessary or bloated expenses. And I wasn't finding anything helpful. Anyway, Alice came by one day to drop off the twins so you could take them... somewhere."

"Swim lessons," Collins murmured. Ralph stopped, looking at him expectantly.

Irritated, Collins urged him to continue, "Well go on; I wasn't in the room. I know she suggested it; she asked later if her finance 'tidbit' was helpful." He waved at his dad. "This story is for him anyway."

Ralph immediately swiveled, hands windmilling eagerly as he continued. "I was stressed, papers all over, and she asked me what the matter was. So, I told her. And she asked why don't we use the trust fund payout y'all had just gotten as collateral for the loan. If it all went well, we'd have it paid off in no time. So that's what I suggested." His dad tilted his head at Ralph like he was speaking in another language.

Collins blanched. "Wait... So, that's all that Alice said?"

Ralph bobbed his head. "Yep."

"So, she didn't know that we'd already put the trust fund money into an account for the kids' college fund? You didn't mention that to her?" He could feel his blood pressure rising.

Mr. Streisand rubbed at the back of his neck and groaned. Swiping at his forehead, Collins focused on Ralph's doughy face.

"I didn't mention it to her; I have no idea if she knew or not."

"And did she say anything about 'what Quinn doesn't know won't hurt her?'" He shoved his hands in his pockets and clenched his fists, feeling like an idiot. Worse than an idiot. He'd betrayed his wife at an idiot's suggestion.

"I… might have added that part myself." Ralph held up his hands with a broad grin, "I wanted you to think I had a good idea, something that could help."

"But the gym already wasn't doing well! I needed help the way I asked!"

Ralph's face fell. "But you seemed to like my idea. And for the last eight years, it's worked."

"No, Ralph! It hasn't. We haven't been able to make back our money on that gym, or the one after it, and now we're having the same problem at Lefleur. All three of those gyms should be doing as well or better than the first two. They have great locations, good programs, top-of-the-line equipment. We haven't been able to 'grow ourselves out of it' like you've been pushing me to." He tapped Ralph on the chest. "I needed you to identify the problem. Not come up with shady funding schemes that piss off my wife!"

Mr. Streisand looked at his son, then Ralph, contempt etched on his face. "You realize this is fraudulent embezzlement, right?" He tilted his head, thinking. "I take it, you forged her signature on multiple documents and, at some point, probably had a bank employee or two overlook the fact that she wasn't present. If she wants to, she can press charges against both of you." He looked at Collins, sorrow etching his face.

"I know I'm a hard businessman. Lord knows, I drive tough deals. But at the end of the day, they're above board and work for everyone. And I'd never dream of doing this to your mother or you. Quinn should divorce you for stealing her money and jeopardizing your children's future." He shook his head. "Even if she doesn't, if the bank finds out what you did, you could be looking at jail time." Collins' stomach twisted in his gut. He couldn't go to jail—the kids were still so little. And who would take care of Quinn?

His shoulders drooped. He looked over at Quinn, who stood talking with Mrs. Greaves and Mrs. Streisand. A wisp of silver was just starting to show in the hairline at her ear. He wanted to kiss it and plead with her to forgive him. To understand his desperation.

Beside him, Ralph sputtered.

"We did what we had to do! It was the only option!" He looked up at Collins, anger pinching his eyes. "Right? She'll understand. We'll make her understand!" He muttered, "It was the only way to keep our business going."

"My business."

"What?" Surprise smoothed Ralph's face. He inhaled and began sputtering incoherent syllables.

"It's my business, Ralph. Not ours." Collins looked back at Quinn. "And it wasn't the only option. It was an easy option. The first one that came to mind. We took a short-cut instead of doing the work." He shook his head and glanced at Ralph, who continued to sputter. "Now we've got to fix an even bigger mess."

Mr. Streisand stood, eyes narrowed, studying his son. He murmured, "I take it, I should have looked more closely at the loan I cosigned with you for Lefleur?"

Collins dropped his eyes. At the time he'd thought it was a sure thing, the way through all of this. His father sighed and rubbed both hands over his face. "We'll talk about it later."

Ralph finally managed to quit sputtering. "We're running on a shoestring! What do you want me to do?" Ralph's voice tinned and pinged. He shot a glance at Mr. Streisand, who shrugged, refusing to intercede. He wrung his hands together and folded them in petition, armpits blooming with sweat. "You can't expect me to take the blame for this, can you?"

Collins scoffed. "Of course not! I was an idiot too." He patted Ralph on the back. "But you scan in receipts and complain about the coffee more than anything else. I think you have some time to see what's going on." He patted him on the back again. "It's time to trim the fat."

CHAPTER THIRTY-THREE

A shiver ran down Quinn's back, all the way into her toes. She wrapped her arms around herself and glanced up as the outside door swung open, ushering in Maggy and Father Fry. Maggy had that sly smile on her face that meant she had a boy on the line, and she threw a glance over her shoulder at the pastor who returned her look. Quinn rolled her eyes at her sister's hasty and way too predictable crush. At least Father Fry had finally convinced her to come back inside. Even if he was in way over his head.

She turned back to Mrs. Streisand and Mrs. Greaves, with whom she had hurried to stand after excusing herself from the all too inquisitive remarks of Rick and Charlie. The sharp little biddies had, of course, caught Maggy and Father Fry's exchange. They grinned and leaned towards her. As Maggy strolled over to say hello to Mr. Streisand, Quinn braced herself for their volley.

"Well! It certainly looks like things are progressing on that front. Maybe we can expect a wedding this winter!" Mrs. Greaves waggled her eyebrows at Quinn.

"Do you think she's a Christmas kind of girl or more of a classic Winter Wonderland kind of girl?" Mrs. Streisand's eyes sparkled as she teased her daughter-in-law. She touched Quinn's arm affectionately and bobbed her head towards the altar. "Just imagine, an arch festooned with fir garlands, red and gold ribbons, and twinkle lights."

Imagining the lovely scene, and Maggy glowing and happy, Quinn suppressed the smile that crept to her face. She shook her head, and the ladies beamed at her. Mrs. Greaves crowed.

"Oh, picture how pretty their babies will be!"

Quinn threw up her hands, laughing.

"All right now, before you go marrying off my sister and our pastor, keep in mind she just got out of a pretty serious relationship. We don't want Father Fry to be her rebound, do we?"

Sniffing, Mrs. Greaves settled her shoulders and looked as satisfied as a milk-fed cat.

"Jordan was Judith's rebound, and I set that up. And that turned out, didn't it? I think it will work out be-yoo-tifully."

Mrs. Streisand winked at Quinn.

"Let us have our fun matchmaking, dear." She looked at Maggy and tilted her head speculatively. "Besides, we wouldn't do anything serious until we know whether or not she intends to stay." Her eyes glimmered, hopeful. "Have you asked her about that yet?"

Shaking her head, Quinn crossed her arms and rubbed at them. She needed to speak to Maggy soon, before things got even more out of hand. If she didn't, they might go from politely passing the potatoes to an all-out blood feud. Or worse, not speaking at all. Maybe she'd be able to pull Maggy aside this afternoon and apologize. Convince her to stay a little while. Her heart fluttered. Maybe even to come home for good.

Mrs. Streisand and Mrs. Greaves darted a look at each other. Mrs. Greaves pursed her mouth, her lips a brittle slash of mauve. Before she could reply, Mrs. Vanderwahl scuttled up to them.

"Father Fry asked me to gather the family for prayer so we can start the visitation." Her voice squeaked and she fluttered her hand towards the restless crowd beginning to gather in the back of the room. Several of them irritatedly flicked raindrops from hair and shoulders.

"Yes, of course." She waved the ladies on. "I just need a

second." Quinn smoothed her hair, a useless gesture in the humidity. With a nod and sympathetic pat on the shoulder, Mrs. Vanderwahl scuttled on to retrieve the rest of the family.

Taking a deep breath, Quinn turned towards the small group forming in front of the casket. Amber light filled the room, and struck the burnished threads of the shroud, dazzling her. Grief sliced through her as if she had stepped on broken glass, and time bubbled. Quinn froze, her breath caught in her throat like she always had been, and would always be standing there, staring at her mother's casket, alone. In the next second, she blinked, surprised to find that her feet had hurried her to Maggy's side.

Standing between Father Fry and Maggy with head bowed, Quinn couldn't stop her hands trembling. As the pastor asked for comfort and strength for their family, the tremors crept up her arms until she was shuddering. The room revolved around her slowly around, a mad parody of reality, the world tilting and bucking—trying to find its new balance without Mama in it.

The coffin, covered in its gold-threaded shroud, loomed behind Father Fry, a draft rippling the veiled cloth like a breath sighing in and out. Even in the weak light of the chandeliers, the peonies glowed blush pink, as bright and gorgeous as their mother had been in life. Tears burned in her nose and she resisted the sudden urge to sneeze. Instead, she sniffed, the sound loud and echoing and followed by a hiccup.

A soft palm slid into hers. Glancing over, she could see a tear trembling at the end of Maggy's nose, shimmering in the light. Her sister swiped at her nose and sniffled quietly. Maggy tilted her head back and inhaled deeply, flushed cheeks paling, before swallowing and dropping her chin forward. Quinn squeezed her fingers and Maggy shot her a small smile. Quinn's trembling stilled.

With a murmured "Amen," Father Fry looked around the circle at all of them, a sad smile weighing his eyes.

"All right, everybody. Deep breaths and we'll get through this day together, ok? Remember, you can always step out for a minute if you need to during the visitation." He laughed, the sound low and warm. "And if anyone misbehaves themselves,

I'm sure Mrs. Alice will have no problem rising right up and scolding them herself."

A nervous chuckle flitted amongst the group. Mrs. Greaves elbowed Mr. Mullone, who winked back at her.

Father Fry clasped his hands together. "Ok, grab some water and some tissues." He looked at Quinn and Collins. "Gather up any youngsters you want in here for this part and," he turned to the rest who had already begun to wander off and spoke a bit louder, "Make any stops at the loo that you might need to."

He tapped Quinn on the shoulder as she turned away. As she paused and looked back at him, she saw that he already held Maggy's elbow, cupped gently in his hand. He flushed and released them, clearing his throat. He was so easily embarrassed.

"I had a quick question for you two. I thought, since Maggy was here, that it might bring a nice bit of balance to the ceremony this morning to have you two sisters do the Scripture readings, as opposed to you and Allie?" He looked at Quinn questioningly. She twisted her hands together, annoyed. Quinn was almost positive that Father Fry was pandering to Maggy. Allie read beautifully, but hated being in front of people and had not been so keen on doing the reading. It had taken a lot of convincing to get her to agree. Maggy looked at Quinn, her face blank and calm.

"Your call, Quinn."

Quinn pulled at her thumb, feeling trapped and not wanting to look unreasonable. She forced a smile. "Sure! Why not? Allie will be thrilled to be off the hook."

Father Fry nodded, his eyes twinkling. "Excellent. You'll do the second reading as we had already planned and Maggy will do the first."

"Super." Quinn turned before the plastered-on smile could slip from her face and hurried down the hallway to round up the twins and Kylie. She told herself not to feel slighted and failed miserably. There had been something poetic to her about having Mama's namesake do a reading, but if she was outvoted—who was she to protest?

Leaving Clara with Mrs. Hernandez, she was re-entering the

fellowship hall from a tutu wrestling match in the bathroom with Kylie's outfit, and in an even stormier mood, when she spotted Maggy talking with Allie. The swinging door smacked into her back as the twins tumbled into the room with an exasperated Collins trailing behind them.

Somehow in going to the bathroom, they had managed to muss-up their perfectly combed hair, untie their shoes, and their shirttails were hanging out. Liam, spotting Aunt Maggy, tried to dart towards her, only to be roped back by Collins' quick arm. Davy sulked, already held firmly by the collar. Quinn knelt to tame the worst of the wildness, leaving Kylie to escape and run over to Maggy and Allie, where she firmly attached herself to her sister's leg. Collins shrugged apologetically at Quinn.

As she tucked in shirts and tied up the laces of her wriggling boys, she watched out of the corner of her eye as Maggy pulled something out of her pocket that was wrapped in a handkerchief. She slipped it into Allie's outstretched palms, her eyes wide and happy. Gingerly, Allie unwrapped the handkerchief, revealing a glowing strand of pearls.

Quinn blinked. Had Maggy gone searching for the pearls in the rain? Was that what had taken so long? Allie shrieked and threw her arms around Maggy's neck, flushed. She couldn't hear what her daughter was saying, but she could see her chattering excitedly.

Suddenly, Allie stopped and shook her head, thrusting the pearls back into Maggy's hands. Maggy's brow puckered, and she held the pearls back out to Allie, but Allie held up her hands, pointing between her and Quinn. She shook her head emphatically.

Maggy's mouth parted in a slight O, as her eyes flicked to Quinn. She held them out again, and again, Allie shook her head "no" and scuttled away. As her niece walked away dragging Kylie with her, Maggy dropped her hands to her waist and gazed down at the pearls, rubbing her thumbs over the strand reverently. Slowly, she wrapped them up and slipped them back into her pocket. Quinn watched, eyes narrowed, as her sister walked over to Father Fry and Mr. Mullone and folded her hands calmly.

Quinn straightened, knees crackling and aching from where she knelt. With a nod towards Maggy, she asked Collins,

"Did you see that?"

He muttered as he tried to finagle the last of Liam's cowlick into order, "What? Our daughter finally doing something sensible and *not* taking an heirloom she's already lost once?" He glanced at Quinn, the corners of his eyes crinkling in amusement.

She pursed her lips at him and dipped her chin, trying not to acknowledge his point.

"Not that." She squinted at Allie, who had swung Kylie onto her hip and was pointing out all the different flowers in the wreaths to her little sister. "I meant Maggy. Where did she get the pearls from?"

"Does it matter? She has them now. Seems like it all worked out." Collins shrugged. "They're Maggy's anyway, aren't they?"

Quinn rubbed at her lip, not wanting to concede. She tapped the boys on the head and pointed them towards Mrs. Streisand. They took off delightedly to attack their grandmother.

"Yes. I suppose it did work out." They slipped into line with Maggy and Quinn closest to the casket, and Collins and the children on Quinn's other side. Liam and Davy fidgeted, pulling at collars and cuffs and heaving Academy-worthy sighs. She shot Maggy another glance, suspicious about why Maggy hadn't told her about the pearls first.

Kylie decided she was exhausted with this affair already and fell to the floor in a poof of tulle.

"At least she's not wailing," observed Mrs. Greaves dryly as she drifted off to man the door to the hallway, should anyone need to be pointed towards the refreshments. "Maybe I'll join her if I get tired out." Her mouth quirked up as she spoke, and Maggy snickered. Quinn shushed them as the first wave of well-wishers washed over them, a wall of perfume and cologne and a buzzing of condolences rolling before them.

CHAPTER THIRTY-FOUR

Nodding to himself, Collins took in the sprays of flowers arranged artfully around the coffin. The girls had done a marvelous job getting everything together in the end, despite the tense moments. He squeezed Quinn's shoulder, and she shot him a tight smile as she gave some vaguely familiar lady with a bad perm an awkward side hug. Kylie star-fished her way underneath a nearby row of chairs, and he stepped over to slide her out by an ankle. She looked up at him with a pout as he stood her up and pointed back at the line. She plopped down on a chair in a huff of rainbow tulle and refused to move. Shrugging, he decided that was good enough as he sidled back over to Quinn.

The cloying smell of musk and ambergris coiled around the room, dank and heavy. Collins fidgeted with his tie, bored, before he stepped forward to shake another hand. If Alice were here, things would be much livelier. She'd stand at his shoulder and point out everyone worth knowing and their business too. He surveyed the room, fancying what she'd say. He spotted Mrs. Burrison scurrying towards the hall door.

"Ooh, now there's a woman whose family tree goes straight up!" He chuckled to himself as he imagined the comment, whispered with a sly smile. Sadly, he shook his head and brushed his hand over the pall, smoothing an invisible wrinkle. Tiredly, he turned back to the receiving line.

A dark spot caught his eye, and he swiveled his head. Several yards away huddled Rick Seymour with Charlie Plath and several others. If he strained, he could catch a low murmuring from their voices, but nothing distinct. Catching his eye, Rick waved him over, but Collins pointed at the receiving line. Rick shook his head and jogged over to him.

"I really think you should step out into the hall with us for a second, dude." Rick pointed at the group of men who stared at Collins expectantly. With a helpless shrug, Collins looked at his friend.

"This is kinda my mother-in-law's funeral. Not sure what you want me to do." He nodded at Quinn, who shook her head tightly at their whispering. He couldn't imagine what could be so important that it would take him away right this second.

Rick surprised him, stepping over to Quinn. "Quinn, could I borrow Collins for two seconds? We need to have a quick, impromptu meeting of some Guild members."

Quinn raised her eyebrows. She shrugged daintily. "Sure. If it's important enough to come up during *my mother's* funeral, it must be pretty big." She shot a look at Collins. "Go ahead." Collins shuddered at her sarcastic tone.

Collins leaned over to kiss her cheek. "Sorry, babe. It'll only take me a second to talk to the boys and see what this is about."

As Rick grabbed his arm and led him away, he knew he was going to pay for this one later.

One sickly fluorescent flickered in the dim hall where they had moved their little gathering. Underneath its wan glow, the men stood, arms crossed or hands shoved deep in pockets, grave looks etched into their faces. A pit opened in the center of Collins' stomach. Charlie Plath looked at him, a twinkle in his eye. The man lived on stirring shit up—as long as he didn't have to deal with the consequences. Notably missing was Mr. Mullone. Immediately, Collins didn't like the looks of things.

"All right, what's going on?" he demanded.

"We've been talking," Rick started, gesturing around the

circle. Heads nodded. "And we think it's time we do something about what's happening with the Guild."

Collins started shaking his head.

"Now's not the time..."

Rick held up his hands. "I know you're tight with Mr. Mullone. And we respect that. But hear us out, ok?" Collins gestured helplessly toward the fellowship hall door.

Charlie spoke up hastily, cutting off retreat. "The last couple of openings have gone terribly. We all know it. Roots and unmarked graves every single time. And where is this great map he keeps talking about?" A disgruntled murmuring ran around the circle. "Not to mention the state of the graveyard. Weeds everywhere. We should have hired an arborist ages ago for the trees. And I can't remember the last time we had a full workday coordinated with the vestry." Heads nodded. "And Harry." Even Collins scowled at his name. "Harry is a travesty. If Roy is trying to train that kid to take over for him like I think he is..."

Collins' head shot up. "Hold up! Roy's just teaching Harry responsibility. Not trying to turn over the Guild to him. He'd never put a teenager in charge."

Charlie frowned and wagged his hand. "What about after Harry goes to college?"

Shaking his head, Collins still disagreed. Roy didn't think Harry would ever be fit to lead the Guild. Of that he was sure. But looking around the group, he could see the doubt etched on their faces. The once rock-solid faith they had in Mr. Mullone was eroding—and fast. He couldn't believe he was arguing for him right now.

"Look, I'm with you that we've had some issues lately. Roy needs some help. Maybe it's time we elected a Vice President to help him out a bit. But Mullone has done right by us for decades. He deserves better than for us to be gossiping about him behind his back like a bunch of old women. If we're going to do this, we need to do it right and call a proper meeting. Let him speak his piece."

"Here! Here!" Rick called out, clapping. Nods of approval went around the circle as all the men clapped.

"I don't think we need just a Vice President. I think we need a new President. And I, for one, think it should be you." Charlie stared down Collins, a sly half-smile on his face. Never in his life had Collins wanted to strangle someone more. Done this way, it would look like Collins had stabbed Mr. Mullone in the back. And Charlie damn well knew it.

"I think Vice President would be fine," Collins said, drawing the words out. "I'd be able to help him without taking over his main duties. Take on some of the heavy lifting while he calls the shots. Works out for everyone."

Crossing his arms, Charlie countered. "Why don't we leave that up for debate in the meeting?"

A few soft "Ayes," echoed around the circle. With a sinking feeling, Collins realized most of this had been decided before he had ever been called back here. Rick grinned at him, oblivious.

"Dude, whether you're President or Vice President, I know you can get us back on track. No matter how much y'all argue, Roy listens to you." He grabbed his hand and pulled him into a hug, sealing his fate. Releasing him, he turned to the men and spoke, "All right, I say we don't waste any time on this. No sense in letting rumors float around about this. Let's hold the meeting this afternoon while we're all at Collins' house—we can step into the dining room or something for a few minutes."

As all the men filed past him, shaking his hand like he was some kind of statesman, Collins tried not to panic. He was going to pay for this. Quinn was going to nail him to the wall and dig his liver out with a spoon. If she didn't divorce him on the spot.

CHAPTER THIRTY-FIVE

The pearls thumped against Maggy's thigh, weighty and ponderous, as she shifted on her aching feet and leaned forward to kiss Mrs. Burrison's cheek. No dark circles or redness ringed her eyes. Instead, Mrs. Burrison looked well-rested, having opted to not attend the wake the night before.

Her teased hair quivered as she eyed the casket behind them. Face powder caked and cracked at the corners of her mouth. She wiggled her nose like a disgruntled hedgehog and looked back at Maggy haughtily.

"I should have loved to see her one last time." Maggy glanced at Quinn, who clenched her fists. "She was so lovely. I just can't believe I don't get to say a proper goodbye."

Maggy cleared her throat, thick and scratchy from lack of sleep and crying. Some people had no shame.

"Well, I would have loved to see her one more time too, but some things aren't meant to be." Mrs. Burrison blinked, eyes widening. Maggy gestured at the casket. "But the peonies are lovely. Exactly," Maggy paused for emphasis, holding her gaze, "what Mama wanted." Mrs. Burrison fiddled with the heavy knot-worked rings on her hands and muttered the appropriate dissemblance about how pretty the flowers were and how nice the turnout was. She hurried towards the back hall and the ladies' parlor to soothe herself with a muffin, her hair quivering with outrage.

Down the line, Mrs. Streisand leaned out behind the family and mimed a slow clap to Maggy while Mrs. Greaves faked a sobbing spell into her hanky to cover up her laughter. Even the ever-anxious Mrs. Vanderwahl ducked behind one of the wreaths to hide a smile.

Beside Maggy, Quinn made a soft gagging noise. Maggy patted her shoulder, smiling sympathetically.

"I know," she murmured before accepting the hand and hug of another person whose face looked familiar but whose name completely eluded her. She could barely remember her name right now, her brain was so sleep-deprived. She could only imagine how Quinn felt.

"Thank you for coming! It means so much that you're here."

"Of course, dear, your mother was one of the cornerstones of this church." The older gentleman was so bent over his cane that he could barely look up into her eyes as he patted her hand. "We wouldn't have been able to restore the parsonage without her haranguing half the county to come to our fundraisers." He patted her hand again, his skin papery and thin, cool to the touch. "Incredible woman, incredible. And you two, I can see, are going to be just like her."

Quinn touched his shoulder.

"Thank you, Mr. Daniels. We're so glad you could make it out today considering the weather."

"Weather is nothing. We honor our people rain or shine." He nodded at them with a jerk of his chin and tapped away towards the covered walkway to the sanctuary to claim his regular spot.

"The gall of some people," Quinn muttered. She was still upset over Mrs. Burrison.

Maggy hugged another body and nodded at Quinn, trying to calm her by agreeing with her. "Some people will always go sticking their nose where it doesn't belong."

"It still irks me."

Maggy shrugged. With the visitation stretching down the

aisle, now was not the time for Quinn's self-pity. "Most have been incredibly kind today."

"Still. Mama never wanted an open casket funeral. She couldn't stand looking at dead bodies."

Maggy was fairly sure that Mama's dislike of open caskets had more to do with Daddy than anything. He had been bludgeoned by a gigantic falling branch while going out to check on Mama's horses in a windstorm. The horrific scene rose in front of her eyes unbidden. A ghastly noise had pulled her from her bed, and she'd walked into the kitchen in time to see Mr. Streisand and Mr. Mullone lay Daddy on the dining room table. She'd frozen in the doorway, not daring to breathe as the adults scrambled around him, trying to stop the bleeding. He had moaned and turned his face towards her. She shuddered, remembering the shattered face, the missing eye, and the jagged white edge along with his caved-in skull...

The doors at the front of the fellowship hall flew open in a sudden gale of wind, whipping hair and skirts like particolored banners. Startled exclamations fluttered through the hall as everyone clutched at clothing and hats. Maggy and Quinn leaped towards the coffin, grabbing at the crazily fluttering pall and skidding arrangement. With a startled yelp, Mrs. Greaves sank to the floor beneath a tall spray of flowers. Father Fry rushed for the door.

In the sudden stillness, Maggy surveyed the room. The twins helped Mrs. Greaves to her feet, unharmed as her fall had been cushioned by another spray of flowers. Around the hall, their guests straightened hair and clothes with exasperated little yanks. Maggy felt a giggle bubbling up.

Everyone looked at her. "Leave it to Mama to start things off with a bang!" She doubled over laughing. A few nervous titters answered her. Then Mrs. Streisand let out a squeal of laughter and soon everyone was clutching the backs of chairs and each other, howling and snorting. Even Quinn let out a small, flat chuckle. As the sudden bubble of mirth died down, Maggy turned to right the overturned flower stands.

A short lull drifted over them, punctuated by snickers, and

the early comers drifted off to grab coffee or head to the sanctuary to wait for the service. Maggy set up the last overturned arrangement and gulped water from the bottle she'd stashed on a nearby chair. She pressed her hands to her knees for a small stretch before the next wave of well-wishers arrived. The flip-flops might be sparkly, but they were doing nothing for her arches. Next to her, Quinn huffed.

"It's just… Mama didn't want people patting and pawing at her! And Mrs. Burrison knew that perfectly well. She's the president of my PTA and served with Mama on the women's hospitality committee. She just wanted to nettle me, I'm sure." Maggy's shoulders hunched, tense and painful, at her sister's voice. They didn't need to add more misery to this day themselves, but apparently nothing would distract Quinn from trying.

"Oh my God! Are you still going on about Mrs. Burrison? Literally, no one else has said anything. Give it a break!" Maggy meant to laugh as she said it, but her voice cracked, and the words barked out sharp and flat. She opened her mouth to apologize but snapped it shut, teeth clacking. She had meant it. Quinn had been a massive brat the last two days, and she was tired of tiptoeing around her.

Her words set Quinn off, and she came at Maggy with a vengeance. "At least I care what Mama wanted! All you care about are those stupid pearls in your pocket!"

Maggy rubbed at her lips, anger coiling in her stomach and cold crackling into her fingertips. Her momentary silence seemed to give Quinn confirmation of her ridiculous accusation.

"What did you do? Go looking for them in the rain to spite me?"

Maggy stared at her, silent. She was so done with this. With the pettiness and the accusations over nothing every time Quinn was in a bad mood. The door creaked open, sweeping in a gust of their grumbling relatives. Aunt Hilda Matins surged forward several paces ahead of the crowd, shaking droplets from her coat and steel grey hair as she bellowed, "Darlings!"

Keeping her eyes locked on Quinn, Maggy hissed, "I have

had enough of you and your selfishness. You can't see past the end of your own nose you're such a self-centered bitch!"

Quinn's mouth gaped open.

Maggy sneered, throwing out Mama's old reprimand. "Careful dear, you'll catch flies like that." She turned and kissed Aunt Hilda's cheek with a broad smile, her eyes glistening.

Aunt Hilda kissed and patted Quinn's cold cheek, taking in the glassy, faraway look of her eyes. She clasped her hand, then reached over to grab Maggy's as well in her powder-soft grip. "Oh, you poor things. I can't even imagine what you're going through." She released them with one last squeeze and power-walked away, dabbing at her eyes. She had never been one to deal well with emotion.

Quinn blinked and her eyes pinpointed down to two furious black sparks trained on Maggy. "Selfish?" Maggy eyed second-cousin Howard, still several yards off and making slow progress with his walker. The rest of their extended relatives were bottle-necked behind him. She arched her brows and nodded, curious to hear how her sister was going to cast herself as a victim this time. "You're calling me selfish? I'm not the one who ran away and stayed gone for fifteen years!" Quinn leaned over the twins, whispering furiously. "You abandoned me. I needed you and you left me here! Family doesn't do that!"

"You never visited." She ground the words out, the words like sand between her teeth.

"What?" Quinn looked at her wide-eyed.

"Fifteen years. And you never visited me once. While I've been here for holidays, births, birthdays, and graduations."

Quinn shrugged, cutting her eyes away. "I can't leave my kids."

"Bullshit." Quinn covered Kylie's ears as Maggy continued. "Mama would have taken them. I know she offered." She snapped her fingers in Quinn's face. "Wake up and face it, you've been punishing me for needing to live my own life for the last fifteen years. Instead of sitting around here being your servant." She faced forward and cut her eyes at Quinn, who huffed.

Maggy snapped, her voice a furious hiss. "And may I remind you, again, family doesn't sleep with their sister's boyfriend and expect them to be all hunky-dory with it, do they?" She rolled back her shoulders and lifted her wobbling chin, "If being family means I have to do your bidding with no thanks and nothing in return, maybe I don't want to be your family."

Cousin Howard halted and began searching his pockets, causing the mass behind him to pile up comically. Maggy knew they were causing a scene but was beyond the point of caring. Out of the corner of her eye, she saw Father Fry watching them, hand over his mouth.

A tear slid down Quinn's cheek. "You don't mean that."

Maggy shook her head. She murmured, "No. But some family we've been. We used to be sisters. Now I'm lucky Collins sends me Snapchats of the kids."

"You're the one who left!"

"And you're the one who decided not to talk to me! About anything. Heck, Quinn, I didn't even know how sick Mama was until she was dying."

Maggy watched as Quinn swiped at her eyes. "Quinn, you never call. I'm lucky if I get a half-assed text." Quinn bit her lip; Maggy's voice wobbled, and she hated herself for it. "You stopped trying to understand me and how I feel the moment you decided to be with Collins. And you've never thought about it since."

"Understand you?" Quinn's voice growled out, mean and low. Kylie began crying and held out her arms for Allie to pick her up, where she buried her face into her sister's neck, wailing. "Have you even tried to understand me these last few days?" Planting her hands on her hips, she squared up facing Maggy. Exhaustion dragged at Maggy, curving her spine and rolling her shoulders; she'd known this would come up. "You stand there pretending like you didn't know what was going on. But she was in the hospital with pneumonia, *Sis!* So, don't stand there preaching at me like you're so shocked."

"Of course, I'm shocked! A healthy fifty-seven-year-old woman doesn't die of pneumonia. But one with a heart condition sure can. But did you think to mention to me that she was diagnosed with atrial fibrillation last year? And refused to have it treated? Noooo! So sorry if I wasn't exactly clued into the situation." Mrs. Streisand and Mr. Mullone pulled the children towards the side of the room and pointed out the windows at the swirling trees, trying to distract them with the tumultuous weather.

Quinn's voice grew hoarse. Maggy saw that the whites of her eyes were burned red from crying, but she rolled her shoulders back anyway as her sister spoke. "You talk about understanding, but you don't understand the horror of watching someone you love die! How empty and helpless it makes you feel!" Maggy flinched, crossing her arms. Her stomach churned, and she resisted the urge to cover her ears. "She wasn't… it wasn't… it wasn't even her at the end. Just her body mechanically breathing in and out; I still hear it in my dreams. I was shaking so bad, I swear if Mr. Mullone hadn't been there to grab me, I would have fainted. So yes, I needed you here."

Maggy stood silent, cheeks flushed. She could feel a slight tremor in her fingertips. Her body flashed white-hot. Quinn could have her anger and her guilt all to herself; Maggy had enough of her own to choke on. Her voice came out in a strangled whisper.

"You cannot hold that against me! You can't *not* communicate and withhold information, then be mad at me that I didn't magically show up. I called every day to ask how she was doing, and you told me, 'Everything's fine, we've got it handled here.'"

She laughed, the sound low and crackling, like stepping on a windowpane. "I'm not a mind reader, Quinn. I didn't know anything was wrong until I got the call to get on a plane right dammit now, she's dying."

The room blurred, and Maggy found herself gasping, sobbing for air. "Do you know how that made me feel? Like I'd let my mother die alone and that my sister lied to me about it. Do you hate me that much?"

She snatched a wad of tissues from a box and swiped at her

snotty face, trying to speak quietly. "By the time I got a suitcase packed and a ticket purchased, you called a second time crying, saying it was all over and you'd call with funeral details."

Pressing the tissues to the bottom of her eyes, Maggy forced in a deep breath. Trembling, she looked up at Quinn, whose face had whitened. "I would have been here all along if you had just said something. Instead, I had less than an hour heads up that my mother was dying. So, don't get all high and mighty and angry with me that you were alone. You chose to be!"

A tapping echoed in front of them. In unison, they pivoted to face the tsunami of well-wishers rolling towards them. Cousin Howard stood before them, hunched over his walker, his last dab of hair swaying back and forth gently in the breeze from the door as another round of aunts and uncles and cousins blew in on a gale. Tottering forward, he reached up to hug them both around the neck.

He studied them for a second, a sharp look in his eyes. Maggy knew despite the whispering their voices had carried, and an angry flush was still high in her cheeks. Behind him, the rest of her relatives fiddled with coats and purses, looking embarrassed for them. She glanced down at her shoes, feeling like a chastised child without him having spoken a word. Finally, he cleared his throat dustily.

"My two favorite cousins. This is a sad day. Your mother was truly a living legend." His voice was soft and warm as a purring kitten. He stretched out his arms for a hug. It seemed he was letting the incident pass. Behind him, the relatives wilted with relief.

As he patted their shoulders, the comforting aroma of mint and pipe tobacco permeated the air, chewing gum and smoking being Cousin Howard's two beloved vices. As Maggy wrapped her arms around him, she looked over at Quinn, who wore a woebegone expression. Their eyes met and Quinn glanced away, grimacing. So much for keeping this day drama-free.

Cousin Howard released them with a last squeeze and rolled away to go find a seat for his old bones in the sanctuary. As Maggy surveyed the line, each person blending into the next, and stretching out the door, she resigned herself, smoothing her face into the calm mask she used at fashion galas.

Collins slipped into line between her and Quinn, an unusual sheen of sweat on his brow that he wiped away hastily as he kissed her sister's cheek. Quinn continued to greet guests, giving Collins the most cursory of glances. Maggy startled, not having even realized how long he'd been away. With a hazy curiosity, she wondered what was causing Quinn to ice him out so blatantly; they liked to keep their fights private. Finding his wife not so welcoming, he leaned over to her.

"Looks like y'all have managed to keep things going ok while I've been gone!"

She looked at him numbly. "No black eyes yet."

He chuckled and hugged another warm body while Maggy studied the back of Quinn's head. With a clack of her flip-flop, she turned away from her, tired of the drama.

CHAPTER THIRTY-SIX

Air slowly trickled in and out of Maggy's lungs, cold and tingly. Everything else was numb. But at least there was air. Maggy forced herself to focus on her breathing, following her breath from the first cool inrush at her nostrils to the shuddering pull of her diaphragm to the overheated exhalation that gasped out through her lips.

From somewhere ahead of her, a voice rang out. Her mind registered the distantly familiar words of the Burial of the Dead rising melodiously from Derek's mouth as he led them in. She floated down the aisle, somehow following Mrs. Streisand, her feet carrying her to the front of the nave of their own accord. She could not feel her ankles or legs or knees or anything else. All was numb except for the hot and cold of her breath. If anyone had stopped in front of her, she would have kept going, blind to their presence. They arrived at the front pew and turned down its polished length.

Maggy wavered, wanting nothing more than to keep going, to walk out of the church and away from the hole in the ground behind it. Already she could feel it calling to her, threatening to pull her in and cover her in a darkness that would make the world go silent and still.

Behind her, she heard the wheels of the casket stand creak

and she wrapped her arms around her stomach as if she'd been stabbed. If she ran, then this day, this thing, grotesque and unreal, wouldn't happen. She wouldn't be a motherless daughter, an orphan. Two titles she never wanted and now would never be rid of.

She closed her eyes, squeezing the aching lids tight, and shuddered. Every muscle in her body pulled taut, poised to run. Mrs. Streisand wrapped an arm around her and held her close, rocking her slightly, and Maggy collapsed, huddling into the cool wood of the pew, utterly defeated. Allie slid close beside her and took her hand. A bell tolled. She opened her eyes.

The casket stood at the front, regal and glowing in an unexpected ray of noon light, sun catching the golden threads in a glorious halo. Laboriously, Maggy pushed herself up until she was sitting straight, then cast a feeble smile at Allie and patted her hand.

The opening prayer and hymns drifted by, Maggy watching as if she was peering through a pair of binoculars from a fire tower through a haze of smoky incense. As if she hadn't sat through a hundred of these services before. She pressed a hand to her chest, feeling her stuttering heart, and reminded herself perfunctorily that she had been through this before, just not from the front row. At least not since she was six years old. The weighted feeling crept over her again, but this time she didn't fight it, instead sinking into its blessed slough of turbidity, allowing it to drag her back down from whatever agitated state she was in.

As Maggy's heartbeat finally slowed, she wondered if she was simply exhausted or high from all the perfume and cologne trapped in the nave. A creak and a cough dragged her eyes to the chancel. In her delirious, detached state, she watched, slightly bemused, as Derek floated to the pulpit, swathed in his long, white vestiture.

He raised his hands and called them to order, his words washing over her in a roll thunderous enough to pull her out of her stupor. When he gestured towards her, she obeyed reflexively, her feet gliding to the lectern, her eyes landing on the page with her name written at the top in such a neat cursive—striking, slanted to the left. She read, her voice ringing out clear and strong from her hollow body:

"John 10, The Parable of the Good Shepherd:

So, Jesus said to them again, 'Truly, truly, I say to you, I am the door of the sheep. All who came before Me are thieves and robbers, but the sheep did not hear them. I am the door; if anyone enters through Me, he will be saved and will go in and out and find pasture. The thief comes only to steal and kill and destroy; I came that they may have life and have *it* abundantly. I am the good shepherd; the good shepherd lays down His life for the sheep.'"

She paused at the end, an unsettledness swirling around her in the rattling silence. Everyone looked at her expectantly. Finally, Quinn tilted her palms up, an impatient signal. Hastily, Maggy raised her hands.

"The Word of the Lord," she intoned. With a grateful sigh, she dropped her arms and hastened off the stage, Quinn brushing by her on the way up to do her reading.

As she sank into the pew, she heard Quinn's voice softly uttering her verses about the second coming of Christ. Maggy remembered them well from Sunday school, having loved to picture how glorious it would be to fly up in the clouds to meet her daddy and Jesus. She blinked back tears as she listened to Quinn read:

"First Thessalonians 4:13-18:

But we do not want you to be uninformed, brothers, about those who are asleep, that you may not grieve as others do who have no hope. For since we believe that Jesus died and rose again, even so, through Jesus, God will bring with him those who have fallen asleep…

As Quinn continued to read, Maggy pressed her hands over her eyes, feeling six years old again, except this time there was no warm lap to curl into on this horrible pew, not even her sister's hand to hold. The image of her father's battered and broken body on the kitchen table flashed before her and her breath hitched, pain stabbing through her ribs. She dropped her hands into her lap, forcing herself to walk through one of the grounding exercises her therapist had taught her, focusing on the coldness of the pew, the weave of her dress' fabric on her skin.

With a lurch, Maggy realized that Quinn was back in the pew and everyone was standing to sing. Allie clutched a hymnal and leaned over to Maggy, wrapping an arm around her waist to share the book, steady and warm. As the organ worked itself up to a full bellow, Maggy leaned lightly into Allie, grateful for small mercies and the simple love of children.

CHAPTER THIRTY-SEVEN

As the last notes echoed from the pipe organ, Quinn eased down into the pew gingerly, the wood cold and uncomfortable on the back of her arms, and counted heads to make sure everyone was present. Leave it to one of the twins to make a mad escape from their grandmother's funeral. Along her forearms, goosebumps prickled, and she chafed her arms, wishing she had brought a sweater even in the early summer heat. The readings hadn't been a total disaster, despite Maggy's flub-up.

Next to her, the kids fidgeted and fussed, dark and itchy little ducklings in their Sunday finery. Davy tugged at his sleeves before slouching down and eyeing grandma's coffin with a watery glare. Kylie buried her face in Quinn's lap and refused to look at all. Allie yanked on Liam's ear and tugged him back up to a half-sitting position from where he had slid over in a disgruntled heap out of Quinn's reach. Mrs. Hernandez sat next to her, cradling a blessedly sleeping Clara while Maggy sat at the far end with Mrs. Streisand, picking at her now-chipped nails. Quickly, Quinn looked away from her sister, her words, "Some family we've been," still reverberating in her head. Her eyes slid across the aisle and snagged on her husband. Collins shot Quinn an apologetic look from where he sat with the pallbearers.

A hush fell over the congregation as Mr. Mullone trod to the lectern, polishing his glasses. He pulled a single notecard from his pocket. Clearing his voice with a tremulous rasp, he set the card down and, taking off his glasses, wiped at his face. Quinn could see the tears sparkling in his eyes.

"As you know, we are here to honor and celebrate the life of Alice Matins today. Now I know it's unusual to have someone else speak before the pastor. We are Episcopalian, after all. We like our ceremonies traditional." A chuckle ran around the sanctuary. "But the family asked me to begin the service today, so I've prepared some words to share with you about Alice. Words about what a great woman she was. How she led our community in charity and service. How she'd always lend you a word of advice—whether you wanted it or not."

A few snickers bounced around the room and he smiled faintly. "But I think I'll speak from my heart to you, as I've always done." He inhaled deeply, holding the breath for a second.

"It's probably one of the worst-kept secrets in this congregation that I was in love with Alice Matins." A murmur rippled back over the assembled. Heads wagged back and forth as neighbors shot looks at one another. Maggy and Quinn stared wide-eyed at each other over the children's heads before turning back.

Mr. Mullone raised his hands, palms towards them. "Now, don't act so surprised. You know you've gossiped about it for years." Another round of chuckles answered him this time, and the murmuring quieted. "Yes, I was in love with her and," he emphasized by pointing with his forefinger, "Asked her many times to marry me. But Alice, Alice wouldn't, because she wanted to honor Truman's legacy. And because I suspect she never stopped desperately grieving him." Quinn studied Maggy out of the corner of her eye. Her sister sat frowning at her nails, listening intently.

"Unfortunately for me, this made me love her more. To act with integrity. Principle. Loyalty. Even though it cost her a lot."

Quinn bit her lip as her mind drifted, thinking about Collins, his betrayal and scheming that went back over a decade and a half ago. Seemingly before they were even married, all the way to Maggy. How she wished Mama were still here to help her through this.

She rubbed at her arms, still cold. Maybe if she'd taken Mama's advice and just talked to him years ago, when Ralph first showed up, as she had meant to. But no, it wasn't her fault Collins had hidden so much from her. She couldn't think like that or she'd come utterly undone. She blinked and crossed her arms, refocusing on Mr. Mullone.

"If you knew Alice before Truman's death, she was already an incredible woman. Charismatic and able to inspire the people around her. But soft and vulnerable to criticism. After his passing, she became a force of nature. Impervious to slights and stings and never stooping to their level. If you found yourself opposite her in a debate... let's say you better have done your homework. Because she certainly had done hers."

"But Alice was truly special. No matter how hotly she might debate you, she'd be the first to shake your hand, congratulate you on a big milestone, or encourage you through an illness or bad luck. She was always there with a pot of soup or a hearty casserole or to invite you over for supper. And somehow, she just knew, with one look, what you'd be good at, what your talent was and give you the nudge you needed to go after it." Heads bobbed in agreement all over and tissues pressed to noses. "She made everyone feel like family. Even this rough, ole' bachelor."

Sunlight glinted on his glasses as he coughed. "I am so incredibly thankful that I got to be a part of Alice's life and the girls' lives." He looked at Quinn and Maggy. "I might never have been an official part of the family, but I am glad I got to see you girls grow up and turn into the smart, talented, strong young women you are today. Your mama was so proud of you and I know that she is going to be looking down on you, with your father, and loving you just as fiercely from heaven." He swallowed.

"I don't have an elegant way to end this. Except to say that

Alice Matins was the most genuine person I knew. She walked in truth and kindness and integrity. Let's honor her legacy by doing the same."

Quinn pressed a tissue to her nose, trying not to sob, as Mr. Mullone returned to his seat. She thought she had gotten all the crying out in the shower this morning, but tears kept welling up. Right now, she wanted to run over and hug him as he pressed a crumpled tissue to his eyes.

He looked over at her, and she mouthed, "Thank you," to him, hand pressed to heart. He smiled at her, eyes watering, and glanced at Maggy, whose face was turned away, hand threaded with Allie's, sobbing silently.

CHAPTER THIRTY-EIGHT

As Derek stood and shook out his robe, Maggy swiped at her face, surprised she had enough water in her body to produce this many tears, not to mention snot. She reached for the box of tissue placed discreetly within arm's reach and tried to blow her nose as quietly as possible. In the stillness of the sanctuary, the honk resounded like a foghorn. She shrugged, figuring her very public fight with Quinn during the visitation this morning had already forfeited her dignity.

Derek shot her a sympathetic smile as he arranged his notes on the pulpit. She smiled back and settled her shoulders, hoping his eulogy would be the "few, simple words" Mama always wanted out of these affairs and not the gut-wrenching sob fest Mr. Mullone's address had been. Whatever had possessed Quinn to alter the ceremony for that emotional torture was beyond Maggy. Derek cleared his throat, and Maggy dragged her attention back to him, admiring the way the light struck his dark hair, now wavy in the humidity. Derek swallowed, Adam's apple bobbing nervously.

"For the last two years, it has been my pleasure to know Mrs. Alice Matins. She welcomed me not only into this church but into her family, with open arms and lots of food. In many ways, she became a second mother to me, and I have loved the kinship

I found at her table over many spirited debates, to the consternation of her children and grandchildren." Maggy chuckled, imagining Quinn's groans of dismay at another lengthy theological debate over the Sunday roast. Mama had described Quinn's dramatic attempts to distract the conversation with mundane gossip often on their weekly calls.

"One of the testaments of a woman is the love their children have for them. And Alice's children adored—do adore—her. Her attentive nature made her a wonderful listener and advisor—the best sort of confidante. Someone you could bring your deepest troubles and most vulnerable moments to and she would be ready with a glass of sweet tea and a word of wisdom." Maggy thought of the front porch swing swaying creakily as Alice drew someone down beside her with a look of empathy and a cold, tasty beverage. "I took advantage of this often, as I know many of you in this congregation did. I can only imagine what the loss of her solid counsel means to our congregation and her family." Maggy nodded and wiped at her cheeks as yet more tears slid down.

He continued, "I love the imagery we saw earlier in 'John 10 of the Good Shepherd.' Today, we're here, not because a life has ended, but because a life has been transformed, a life so much more abundant in the arms of the Good Shepherd. And how she will continue to live life abundantly beyond our imaginations in the glorious presence of our Father, forever reunited with her beloved husband Truman."

Father Fry paused, his eyes welling, and his throat working. "She never did stop loving Truman, did she? The love of a woman for her husband is a powerful testimony." He swallowed again, catching Maggy's eyes, and looked down, coughing.

"God has swallowed up death. And He has taken Alice's hand, like he took Truman's hand before, and He has led her to Himself. Which, if you knew Alice as I did, the gift of His presence was the only reward she ever asked. Today, we rejoice with exceeding joy that she is in the arms of our Lord."

Maggy clenched her fists as heat shot up and down her arms. The Lord had taken both her parents from her before she was even forty, before she was married—what did she have left to be joyful over? A congested sniff echoed through the nave.

Her eyes landed on Quinn, Kylie snuggled in her lap, and a tissue clenched in her own fist. Maggy unclenched her fists, her nails leaving white grooves in her palms. "This joy, however, does not make our grief less or out of place. As we saw in First Thessalonians, just because we do not grieve without hope doesn't mean that we don't grieve. Indeed, the love we have for each other in Christ makes our sorrow that much deeper and more keenly felt when we are parted by death, though the parting is temporary. Even Jesus himself wept at the grave of his friend."

He cleared his throat and took a sip of water, hands shaking. "So, while we rejoice that Alice has entered into God's presence, let us mourn and sorrow in sympathy with those who grieve her passing.

"Today is a day for weeping and for rejoicing. Let us remember this, beloved, even as you mourn. Let it comfort you. Today is a day of heavenly celebration, of a saint entering the presence of God and gaining her great reward! God has been faithful to His great promise and taken his beloved home. Hold on to this truth and trust in it. Trust in it. Amen."

As Father Fry led them in the communion prayer, Maggy closed her eyes, hoping that her emaciated, limping faith was enough to save what was left of her family.

Later, as they stood to file somberly out of the church after the pallbearers, Mrs. Greaves leaned precariously over the back of the pew to wrap her arms around Maggy's neck. She pressed another tissue into Maggy's palm.

"You had me boohooing like a baby, with all your waterworks. I'm a sympathy crier, ya' know." She wagged her finger in Maggy's face sternly. Mrs. Streisand wrapped an arm around her waist.

"Oof! Me too, dear. Tears! Just tears everywhere. I don't have a shred of mascara left." She pointed to her darkly ringed eyes as proof. Maggy chuckled through her stuffy nose and shrugged, dabbing at her eyes.

Mrs. Greaves smiled at her slyly. She patted Maggy on the back and pointed a careful forefinger at Father Fry, who busied himself putting away the sacraments at the altar.

"Now don't think for one second, that all this blubbering has earned you enough sympathy points to make us forget that your eyes were glued…" Maggy rolled her eyes already knowing what was coming and shrugged into her rain jacket, hoping the rustling would cover up some of their nattering.

"Glued!" crowed Mrs. Streisand.

"Glued," agreed Mrs. Greaves, "To our good Father Fry the entire service." She pursed her lips together mischievously and bobbed her head. "Keep up with that and we won't be able to keep ourselves from a bit of matchmaking." She tented her fingers together and grinned.

At her saucy statement, Maggy couldn't help but laugh, the unexpected sound scratching at her raw throat.

"Ladies!" She reached out and grasped their arms. "Thank you, truly, for thinking so highly of me. But your skills are wasted on me." At their crestfallen looks, she relented and leaned in conspiratorially. "Because I'm pretty sure I have my own matchmaking well underway when it comes to the good pastor."

Tittering like a bunch of schoolgirls, they slipped out the door and into a boisterous gale of wind.

CHAPTER THIRTY-NINE

The lighthearted mood was short-lived. Her father's, and now her mother's, grave yawned before Maggy's feet. At the bottom, she could see streaks and clods of clay, red as blood, and imagined the dark grey flash of her father's casket. She blinked.

The solid brick hue of Yazoo clay met her eyes. Of course, the men had left her father's casket respectfully covered with a thin layer of dirt. She inhaled deeply, the rusty musk of dirt and sharp slice of rain making her head spin.

With distant thunder constantly rumbling and the rain now coming down in a steady sheet, only immediate family and the pallbearers had accompanied them to the graveside. Mrs. Greaves had intrepidly led those who wanted to brave the weather to pay their respects to the family in a surprisingly long line out of the church parking lot and down the road, their headlights flashing out one by one through the gloom like the lamps of a lighthouse.

Mud squelched up into Maggy's flip-flops and squished, chilling and gooey, between her toes. The slick mess made even shifting her weight in the rain treacherous, much less walking. While navigating the churchyard, she had found herself clinging to Catherine's arm, who was in much the same state in her flimsy flats. They had exchanged a nervous, tittering smile before nearly sliding bottom first onto the slippery lawn.

Maybe the Ugg boots would have been a better choice. She thought of the hideous fluffy boots and shook her head, slinging cold droplets of rain everywhere. To her right huddled Quinn and Collins, bundled in jackets and sturdy overshoes and under the relative safety of a huge, black umbrella. Rain slashed in from the left, stinging Maggy's cheek, and running cold and unrelenting in a steady trickle down the neck of her rain jacket. She yanked at the cords, tightening the hood around her face. But the elastic and nylon were no match for merciless Mississippi rain. She shivered as a rivulet worked its way across her shoulder blade and down her spine.

Quinn shivered visibly and Collins wrapped an arm around her, shuffling to her left side to shield her from the rain. Immediately, his pants leg was drenched as the rain buffeted him and he angled the umbrella lower, obscuring their faces. The wind picked up speed and began to lash it up his side as well. Derek had left behind his robes and was now wrapped in a long, waterproof overcoat that looked much more substantial than anything else their group wore.

Maggy felt like a deflating marshmallow puff in her thin jacket, but she forced herself to stand up straight, imagining Mama's rap between her shoulder blades. Derek held up his hands for a quick prayer. As she bowed her head, she eyed Collins and Quinn. Despite whatever spat they were having, they held each other close, braving the weather together, united.

Shoving her hands deep into her pockets, she tried not to shiver in the rain. If she was honest, brutally honest, that was what she wanted. Not Collins. She hadn't thought of him in over a decade. But she wanted that kind of unwavering loyalty and commitment. Someone who didn't waver in their love for her just because the house wasn't perfect, or her job wasn't "wow-worthy." When she got right down to the heart of the matter, she envied Quinn having a happiness and a love she'd never been able to hold onto.

Belatedly, she realized her pockets were slowly filling with the water running down her sleeves. Grumbling, she pulled her hands out and zipped up. She brushed a sheet of frigid rainwater out of her face, frustrated at what was supposed to be a brief prayer. Derek sure was going on for a while. She kept her head bowed, her lips forming the responses automatically while growing numb in the cold rain. Finally, he said, "Amen," and the pallbearers stepped forward to lower the casket into the grave with a protesting shriek of levers and pulleys.

Thunder crashed overhead, scattering the graveside visitors without the usual pleasantries. Maggy found herself abandoned, Quinn and the kids already headed towards the dark line of cars, Collins and Allie shepherding them as best they could under upraised umbrellas. With a shivery exhale, she turned and took a step to follow.

Her foot slipped sideways in the flip-flop, popping the thong and continuing its mad career into the cold muck. A screech flew from her mouth as she plummeted to the churned-up ground. As she fell, Maggy glimpsed Quinn spinning towards her, her pale lips parted in shock.

CHAPTER FORTY

Quinn hadn't been able to see much from under the umbrella, walking blindly across the graveyard clinging to Collins' arm. The only reason she knew they had arrived at the graveside was that Collins halted, causing her to bump into him. She shoved the umbrella up out of her face, and he glanced at her, like a kicked puppy. Relenting, she squeezed his arm slightly, and he slid closer to her, though she found his looming presence a bit more cloying than sweet, given the circumstances. She wished he'd give her some space to calm down instead of this over-the-top Boy Scout act.

She exhaled through her stuffy nose, relieved at least that Ralph had taken off after the ceremony. She hoped he wasn't coming to the reception. It would be abominably tacky for that man to be sitting in her living room, drinking her sweet tea, and eating her finger foods. Trying to distract herself, she looked around to see who had accompanied them to the graveside.

Dark suits and jackets met her eyes, and she scanned the familiar faces, surprised at how few were out here, only yards from the church. A rumble of thunder boomed overhead, and she grimaced at herself, remembering Maggy's bitter accusation of selfishness. Well, maybe she shouldn't be that surprised. They were in the middle of a torrential downpour and a flash flood warning after all. And a pretty long line of people had headed towards their house too, she reminded herself.

She glanced over at Maggy, with streaks of mud covering her feet and ankles, standing a foot or so in front of Catherine. Even with her chapped nose and damp hair, and shrouded in a puffy white rain jacket, she looked stunning, impervious, and proud as the rain lashed at her—the pinnacle of independent womanhood. The umbrella dipped low again, blocking her view.

Quinn bowed her head dutifully as Father Fry intoned a blessing over the grave. What she wouldn't give to have a shred of Maggy's independence. Quinn didn't even have her own bank account. She'd put a paltry couple thousand saved from summer jobs into Collins' then closed out her own when they'd gotten married. The only job she'd ever had and ever wanted was the gyms. Since then, she'd done a few odd jobs for friends here and there, enough to keep up her hard-earned CPA license and put a few hundred dollars in the bank, but nothing steady. Nothing to call a career. She'd been thrilled with the trust fund payout, the biggest sum she'd ever received, thinking their children's college education was set. And her *darling* husband had probably gone and squandered that.

Maggy didn't know how good she had it, not having to rely on anyone else. The thought shocked her.

All these years, she'd been so grateful to have Collins' steadying presence, always there when she needed him, always there to fix the dishwasher or listen to her petty dramas surrounding the PTA ladies. Now, she found herself wondering if she knew her husband at all. She envied her sister's independence and career. Not having to worry about the man she loved and trusted most betraying her. She sniffed and Collins hastily handed her a tissue, speckled with rainwater. Looking at him, she burst into tears, pressing her lips together to keep from sobbing. Her heart pounded with the thunder and she wondered if she was losing her husband with her mother in the same week.

Sensing her distress, Catherine shot her a sympathetic glance, eyes pinched in commiseration. She rubbed at her forehead; it hadn't crossed her mind yet to tell Catherine. She'd be devastated for her. And what if they got divorced? The parade of horrors and pitying glances…

A distant part of Quinn's brain rattled the bars of consciousness, telling her she was tired and being melodramatic; she needed to stop with the theatrics and get down to the business of sorting things. She told her brain to shut it and let her cry it out. She had enough drama going on to justify being upset a while longer.

Blessedly, Father Fry finally said, "Amen," and Quinn whirled, hightailing her soggy self to the car, Collins trotting to keep up. Allie grunted in protest, hoisting a grumpy Kylie on her hip and poking the twins to hustle in front of her. Quinn eased her stride, reaching back to offer her hands to her little troopers.

Behind her, an unearthly banshee wail rang out. She looked over her shoulder and gasped, horrified to see Maggy falling as if in slow motion, flip-flops flying out from under her in the mud. She hit the ground and slid into a nearby monument, head slapping into it with a sickening crack.

CHAPTER FORTY-ONE

Lightning cracked outside, shattering the still of the room as everyone waited for Rick to make his pronouncement. From the doorway to the dining room, Mr. Mullone, having been forced to come to the house instead of the graveside by the indomitable Mrs. Greaves "on account of his arthritis," watched the rather strange tableau play out almost like a scene from one of his afternoon soap operas. Collins, toting a visibly pained and pissed off Maggy, ran into the crowded living room, shouting for everyone to clear off the sofa. Behind him trailed Rick and Catherine Seymour, Father Fry, Quinn, and the children.

After depositing the mud-soaked Maggy on the couch gently if gracelessly, Collins was immediately shooed away by Rick and Quinn. Quinn cradled Maggy's head, sobbing loudly how sorry she was, while Rick, who had brought in his physician's bag, proceeded to examine Maggy matter-of-factly while shooting irritated looks at Quinn. Father Fry stood anxiously behind the sofa, just out of arms' reach, on the fringe of the frantic activity. Catherine ran to the kitchen for a bag of frozen peas while Collins retreated to hover in the dining room door with Mr. Mullone.

Roy shot him a sympathetic look, and both men watched the

proceedings with bated breath while Collins filled him in on what happened. Roy chafed his hands, wanting desperately to do something. Mrs. Greaves, noticing his wavering steps forward and back, tapped him smartly on the shoulder and sent him to fetch towels and upholstery cleaner from the laundry room. When he returned, arms loaded, Maggy was sitting up, head in hands, Quinn still pressed far too close.

"Dear God, woman, give me some space to work!" Rick snapped. Quinn scooched back a tiny bit, hand on Maggy's shoulder as Rick urged her to sit up a little more. Frowning, Rick returned to shining a light in Maggy's eyes. Catherine laid the bag of frozen peas, wrapped in a tea towel, gingerly on the back of Maggy's soggy head. She winced but reached up and grasped the bag.

With a deep inhale, she finally spoke, "That helps a lot. Thank you, Catherine."

Sitting back on his heels, Rick nodded, announcing as much for the room's benefit as for the family's, "She's alright. You have a fair bit of bruising. Maybe a touch of a concussion, so try not to take a nap this afternoon. But all in all, it could have been a lot worse." He tapped Maggy on the knee. "Fortunately for you, you have quite a hard head."

Maggy smiled weakly. "That's what Mama always used to say."

Everyone chuckled and began murmuring. Roy sagged into the doorframe, heart hammering. Collins clapped him on the shoulder. Roy placed a hand on his chest, eyes misty.

"Oh, I couldn't take losing one of the girls right now, Collins."

Collins looked at the two women on the couch, Quinn's arm around Maggy as she helped her up and towards the stairs to get clean.

"Nor I," he murmured. The dark circles under Collins' eyes were much more pronounced, and Roy noted for the first time the touch of silver that echoed Quinn's beginning to show at the younger man's temples. The start of worry lines were already carving their way between his eyes. As much as Roy had longed for a family of his own, he couldn't imagine having to take on the responsibility at seventeen—while building up six businesses over the last sixteen years. Collins had done all that and more. Imperfect and hotheaded as he may be, Collins was made of tough stuff, and Roy didn't think he could have done the same in those circumstances. He swallowed.

"The salt and pepper look…" Roy said, nodding. Collins looked back at him, quizzical. "It looks good on you. Very distinguished." Collins nodded slowly. Turning to go clean the couch, Roy paused. "Collins, as much as you have going on, you've always taken care of you and your family first." He pointed decisively at Collins' chest. Making a circular motion with his finger, he said, "Keep it up and you'll be all right. Everything else can go to hell, but if you've got your family and your health, you'll be alright." Collins stared back at him, an inscrutably sad look on his face.

"Thank you, Roy. I'll keep that in mind."

As Roy headed back to the laundry room a few minutes later to replace the bottle of fabric cleaner, he passed Father Fry in the kitchen. The young pastor was decimating a pile of Mrs. Greaves' tea cakes, the plastic wrap shredded back from the edge of the platter.

He smiled at Roy ruefully, "I'm a bit of a stress eater."

Roy shrugged, amused. "Today has been enough to get to anyone."

"Amen to that."

Roy tucked the bottle away, then slid onto one of the plush bar stools across from Father Fry, folding his hands in a neat steeple on the counter. He examined the fragrant, buttery cookies piled smartly on the Blue Willow platter in front of him and, suddenly hungry, plucked one up and crammed a bite in his mouth.

"Believe I'll join ya'," he said, grinning.

Father Fry smiled faintly, face clouded. He took another big bite of tea cake, talking around the crumbly mouthful. He gestured at the stairs where Quinn and Maggy had disappeared moments before.

"What I don't get is why they can't stop fighting. They obviously love each other. Why can't they work it out?"

Mr. Mullone guffawed, and Father Fry scowled at him, looking like a grumpy hedgehog that's just been woken up.

"Oooh-wooh, sorry, sorry. Just, this is them working it out! If you'd known them when they were little, they'd show up with black eyes and scratches. Sure gave Alice a run for her money, keeping them in line. And they were thick as thieves then." Mr. Mullone wiped at his eyes, chuckling. "They've got sixteen years of nonsense to get out of their systems and haven't come to blows yet. They'll be fine."

Furrowing his brow, Father Fry asked the obvious question. "Why has it taken them sixteen years to talk? It's not like Maggy's been AWOL completely. I mean, this is my first time meeting her, but even I know she visits several times a year."

Roy chewed slowly, not sure how much he should say. "To sum up, their mother was afraid of their fighting. I think, at first, she was afraid if Maggy had it out with Quinn, that Quinn might not marry Collins. And then after that, I think she was afraid that if it got nasty enough, the family would splinter."

Father Fry stared out the window, nodding to himself speculatively. "I can see that," he murmured. He shook himself, "I never took Alice for a fearful woman."

Roy picked up another cookie and studied it, ruminating. He took a small bite, rolling the crunchy morsel around and around, savoring the nutmeg and vanilla as it melted on his tongue. "I warned her about her meddling so many times. I told her, 'The longer something sits, the longer it festers.' But she insisted she was doing what was best."

Shaking his head, Father Fry muttered, "When I was that young, not even my mother could have stopped me from having it out with my brother."

"You don't get how close, how dependent, these girls were on each other. Sure, they were best friends before, but after their father died… And they trusted their mother absolutely. They went to her with everything."

In unison, they both took another large bite of their tea

cakes. Mr. Mullone continued, grateful to have someone listen, "I was there one Thanksgiving before the big dinner. Allie couldn't have been more than three. Maggy and Collins had been arguing over something stupid like always and had gone into the living room. Suddenly, we hear Collins shouting, 'Why are you always such a b**** to me?' And she goes storming out of the house with him following her. Quinn was worried it was going to get out of hand for once and was about to follow and Alice goes and drops the whole dadgum turkey. It was a magnificent bird." He glumly remembered its roasted perfection; Alice was the best cook he knew. "And she goes and drops it, so Quinn had to help her clean it up. Just so she wouldn't go get up in the middle of it too and find out what was going on. Maggy and Collins were fine after that. I mean, they fuss at each other, but they haven't had a real fight in years."

Father Fry had stopped chewing at the turkey story. He busted out laughing, crumbs flying over the countertop. He brushed them up hastily. "Wow. I can see Alice doing that, causing drama to stop the drama. Wow. But why wouldn't she want it all out in the open?"

Roy rubbed at his face. "When it came to her family, she'd do anything to protect them. After Truman… well, she was so afraid of anything happening to them, she couldn't keep herself from meddling. I think that's why she encouraged the girls to maintain some distance, as it were. To keep that final fallout from happening." Roy shook his head, selecting another cookie. He broke it in half, enjoying the subtle smell of spices that wafted up to him.

"Still, the way she misses home, New York seems like an odd choice for Maggy."

Roy waved the half of his cookie he hadn't eaten. "Let me tell you! Everyone else was up in here, all gabbing about it and I'm just like, 'That's Maggy for you.' I sure wasn't surprised. That child took off across a muddy field in her Sunday best at her kindergarten graduation because she felt like going on an adventure." He bobbed his head to the side. "I'll grant you, I expected her back by now."

Roy popped the last half of the cookie in his mouth, eyeing the girls as they clattered back down the stairs, both in clean, dry clothes. Quinn ushered Maggy into a cozy corner of the couch, tucking a throw blanket around her and pressing the bag of peas back to her head. Father Fry's eyes lingered on Maggy, a worried frown tugging down the corners of his mouth. Recognition clicked in Roy's mind and he smiled broadly at Father Fry. "Yessir, Maggy's always up for an adventure."

CHAPTER FORTY-TWO

Quinn was fussing about and she knew it. Her clothes pulled at her, too tight and clingy, boggy. Worried, she checked for damp and found them perfectly dry. Not a drop of perspiration or rain to be seen. Pausing by the kitchen island, she fanned at herself, trying to get her frayed nerves to calm down. Perhaps it was the crowd of people crammed into her living room and kitchen, spilling onto the wide, covered back porch that was beginning to get to her. She hadn't had a moment's privacy in days.

She peeked at Maggy, still tucked securely into the corner of the couch. Mr. Mullone sat next to her and Catherine sat chummily on her other side, keeping her company. A full plate was already perched on her lap and as she watched, Mrs. Streisand glided by, pressing a punch cup into her hand, smooth as a swan on a lake. Knowing her sister was well looked after, she relaxed a little.

A distinct, raspy laugh reached her ears, causing her to cringe. Peering around the corner, she spotted Ralph through the big bay window to the porch, standing a few inches too close for comfort to her father-in-law. Half-shadowed, the man looked dumpier than ever.

Quinn couldn't believe she had ever allowed him to take her

job. She should have fired him on the spot, the day Collins brought him in without asking her. Glaring at his turned back, she wanted that son-of-a-bitch run out of town now.

As if she had summoned him by thinking too hard, Collins appeared at her elbow. His eyes followed her line of sight.

"I've made him promise to stay out there. He won't come in here and bother you."

"If he does, he's likely to have a plate cracked over his head." She stomped into the kitchen.

Collins rubbed at his jaw and followed her. "I'm not sure why you're on such a warpath about him right now." She shook her head, yanking open the fridge and snatching a tray of cucumber sandwiches out. Of course, Collins didn't understand. He'd never been fired from anything. Her throat closed at the thought, and she plunked the tray on the counter, picking futilely at the clingwrap. Gently, Collins slid it away from her and pulled the plastic off in one motion.

He took her shoulders. "Why don't you let my mom or Mrs. Vanderwahl get that? Just breathe for a minute."

She rubbed at her face. "If I pause right now, I'm going to fall to pieces. And I've got a house full of guests." With a brittle smile, she looked up at him. He nodded, rubbing her arms.

"What can I do to help?"

Her mind made a brittle clicking sound, wanting his hovering to end, as she rubbed at her chapped nose. Her eyes landed on the few bottles perched on the plate shelf, the amber liquid in them perilously low. "We're almost out of bourbon and whiskey. I forgot to check yesterday. And you know they're going to want to start the toasts in a minute. Could you run to the liquor store and grab a few bottles?"

He nodded and kissed her forehead, then grabbed his jacket as he dashed out the door, back into the rain. She crossed her arms thinking, relieved he was gone. Looking back at Maggy, she steadied herself. After a moment's hesitation, she reached up on tiptoe and groped around until her hand hit the distinct bottle of bourbon she'd hidden away. Selecting a couple of highball glasses, she headed for the living room. They needed to talk, and she needed a peace offering.

As she was about to pass into the stuffy living room, Mr. Mullone grabbed her elbow. She began to groan but stifled it when she spotted his flushed cheeks and knitted brow.

"Quinn, has Collins mentioned anything to you about the meeting this afternoon?" He pulled a napkin from his pocket and dabbed at his face, anxious beads of perspiration welling up. So she wasn't the only one feeling stifled.

Her mind flashed to the impromptu gathering at the church earlier.

"Another one?" she asked. He stared at her, eyes large and startled. "Several of the men had some sort of huddle this morning. I thought you were with them." He shook his head.

"Something's definitely going on," he murmured. "Collins has been pushing me to let him help me for a couple of years now. And Charlie's always stirring up trouble." He pressed his lips together.

Now concerned, she whispered to him, "Before the visitation this morning, Charlie mentioned something to me about last night not going well and how they weren't going to let it happen again."

Dabbing at his forehead, Mr. Mullone spoke low. "It sounds like they're planning some sort of coup." He looked at her dolefully. "I'm so sorry, Quinn. This kind of behavior is inappropriate from Guild members at any time, no less at a funeral reception for one of our own. I'll see what I can do to put it off to another day."

She squeezed his arm. "I'm sorry that it's happening to you at all." Her mind flashed to Collins and her nostrils flared. "And that my husband is somehow mixed up in it."

He patted her hand. "Collins would never push this kind of thing forward." He paused. "Not this way, at least. He'd talk to me about it." He smiled sadly at her. "Maybe it's time for me to step down anyway. I'm not what I used to be." Swinging his knee back and forth, she heard it crack. "These old bones aren't as sturdy as they used to be."

Quinn laughed and kissed his cheek. "You are still every bit as wonderful and an exceptional leader. They just need to be reminded of that."

"Thank you, dear." He exhaled heavily and stepped into the cheery light of the kitchen, no doubt in search of more of Mrs. Greaves' tea cakes she'd glimpsed him snacking on earlier.

Catherine glanced up at Quinn, and noting the bottle in her hand, beamed at her and patted Maggy's knee as she stood. As she slipped away, she squeezed Quinn's shoulder reassuringly. Quinn took a deep breath.

"We need to talk."

"We should talk."

Quinn and Maggy stared at each other then burst out giggling. Quinn flourished the bottle.

"To prove I come in peace," she said drily.

Maggy's mouth wobbled as she suppressed a grin. She gathered up the blanket as she stood and waved a hand, mock graciously.

"Proceed."

They slipped into the master bedroom away from the hubbub and settled cross-legged on the messy bed. Quinn's hand shook as she poured two big slugs of bourbon. She handed one of the elegantly cut crystal glasses to Maggy and took one for herself.

Maggy saluted her and took a dainty sip.

"Ah, you always do have the good stuff squirreled away somewhere, Sis," she said, smacking her lips. Quinn grinned.

"Learned that art from Mama. 'A good hostess is never without good booze,'" Quinn quoted. They both smiled reminiscently, then sniffled. Quinn frowned. "Should you be drinking..." she pointed to her head, "... you know, with your head and all."

Maggy shrugged. "Don't know. Don't care. Cheers!" She held her glass up with a lopsided grin.

Quinn toasted her and took a deep breath. "Look, I'm sorry. Seeing you today, how you fell..." She shuddered and Maggy reached out, gripping her hand. "It made me realize how stupid I've been for holding this grudge." Quinn pushed the hair back from her face. "I've been so focused on how I felt like you abandoned me, that I didn't care that I was giving you the silent treatment for *fifteen years* or how much of a jerk I was being to you when you were home. I had no right to stay on your case the way I did."

She heaved a big sigh, her eyes watering, "I know I have a lot of issues to work through and I need to pull myself together and work on my anger, but I want you to know that I'm sorry. I'm so sorry. Can you ever forgive me?"

Maggy swallowed, setting the glass down and twisting her other hand in the blanket. "I'm sorry too. I blamed you for everything and never owned up to my part in it all. I mean, fifteen years?! It only took our mother dying for us to talk." She laughed bitterly. "I should have picked up the phone. Or gotten on a plane. Or grabbed you by the face and made you listen like I used to." She swiped at her nose with the back of her hand. "I was just so afraid that you'd think I was still in love with Collins and you'd be furious with me." She whispered, "That you'd never want to talk to me again. Or worse, not marry Collins."

Quinn laid back on the bed hooting with laughter at the irony. Finally, she sat back up fanning her face.

"I know. I'm a genius!" Maggy laughed with her.

"We both are. Big, fat geniuses on opposite ends of the country. Not talking to each other." Quinn doubled over the other direction chuckling. She straightened up and took a sip of her bourbon.

Swirling her drink, she stared at the perfectly straight lines of the shiplap ceiling. At the time that they had redone the bedroom, she had picked shiplap because it was so precise, so orderly, nothing like her life now.

Quinn finally dropped her gaze from the ceiling. Maggy sat, waiting and staring into her drink, lips pursed. She tucked a strand of her golden hair behind her ear.

Rubbing her forehead, Quinn took another sip of her bourbon, rolling the sweet, biting liquor over her tongue.

"Man, we haven't really talked in years..." she murmured. Maggy sat forward and grabbed her hand again, eyes full and lips quivering. A tightness, as of a great metal band, snapped loose in Quinn's chest and an immense pressure she didn't know had been pent up all these years released. She looked at her glass of bourbon; it was hitting her pretty strong.

With a sniff, Maggy leaned back and patted the stack of books on Quinn's bedside table. A jumbled heap of parenting and marriage advice books with dog-eared pages and bookmarks in various places slumped under the lamp.

"I see you have a matching stack. Although mine is more of living your best life and dating for dummies than potty training and love languages."

Quinn giggled, "Yeah if Mama thought we wouldn't listen to her, a book was sure to show up as a 'little something' you might like." She ran her thumb fondly over the creased spines.

"That's Mama for you." They lapsed into silence again.

Finally, Maggy offered, "You're not the only one in this. Like I said, I should have tried harder."

Quinn burst into tears and threw her arms around Maggy's neck. "I should have tried at all."

Maggy rubbed her back, making shushing noises. "It's all right. It's all right." She pursed her lips. "Look, I know you have a lot on you. With the kids and the businesses. As much as I've wanted you to talk with me… I don't blame you for being busy."

Maggy pulled back and patted her on the knee, a solemn look on her face.

"There's just one thing I have to ask right now." She took a deep breath, brow furrowed. Quinn could see tears on her lashes. "And this might be a conversation for another day."

Quinn's stomach fluttered nervously, unsure of what Maggy was about to ask, but she nodded.

"Why didn't you tell me how sick Mom was—about her heart condition? I would have come immediately if I'd known…"

Quinn's face crumpled, the familiar guilt curling around her shoulders.

"Oh, sweetie! I thought she'd told you. Last year she'd been having palpitations and Dr. Mortimer told her she had AFib and they needed to treat it much more aggressively." Quinn remembered how Mama had paled, then settled her shoulders with a sniff and a "well, then" at the doctor's prognosis but had refused to say more. It had been left to Quinn to ask all the questions. In hindsight, she could see how foolish she'd been to assume that Mama would say anything; she'd always been so proud of her health and strength.

"I thought for sure she would have called and told you." Maggy shook her head and picked at her nails. Quinn continued quietly. "She didn't want to take all those medicines or undergo surgery for a pacemaker—you know how much all of that stuff eeked her out. She wasn't a sickly person in her mind." She clasped her hands together to stop their trembling. "So when the pneumonia hit, she was fine at first. Thought she could soldier through as she did with everything else. But the strain just got to be too much. Her heart gave out so quickly."

"You should have told me," Maggy whispered, eyes wide and pooling. Her mouth spasmed, and she turned her face away.

Quinn's heart lurched, and she reached out for her sister's hand. "You're right. I should have told you the whole of it from the start."

A tear ran down Maggy's cheek, and she wiped it away, clearing her throat. Calmly, she asked, "Why didn't you?"

Taking a deep breath, Quinn forced the words out, knowing they weren't right, weren't enough. "Mama insisted on not worrying you. Said you had a lot of pressure at work and didn't need more stress because of her." Maggy waved that away and Quinn replied, "I know! I know, but she insisted. And she was feeling all right if a bit tired and out of breath, right until the very end."

Trembling, Quinn finished, "I knew the risks and made the wrong call, downplayed it. I should have been honest with you. I'm sorry."

Maggy pressed her lips together and shut her eyes, not speaking for several minutes. Quinn knew Mama had been so keen on her getting that promotion. She could only imagine how it must feel now that it had all fallen apart. In less than a month, she'd lost her apartment, her boyfriend, her job. And now her mother.

But maybe it hadn't all been for nothing. Maybe there was still some hope for them. Quinn watched as her sister's throat worked up and down, praying for a miracle. If there was any way for her sister to let her back in, it would happen now. Finally, Maggy took a deep, shuddering breath.

Maggy gripped her hand harder. A spark flickered to life inside Quinn, the most unlikely hope. "It's… it's all right. You did the best you could. And I know… I know you took good care of Mama." She opened her eyes, ringed red from crying. "How was she, at the end?"

Quinn shook her head, wanting to be honest but the memory still too painful. "I don't know if I can talk about it now. It was so sudden and awful. Absolutely awful. I'll never get that image out of my head. I think I'm going to have nightmares about it for the rest of my life."

"Well, maybe one day it would help for you to talk about it. And maybe one day the person you talk with could be me?" Maggy offered.

Quinn smiled, her eyes watering. It was as if the sun had risen, warming every part of her and illuminating all the dusty, forgotten dreams she'd left abandoned in the corners. No bourbon could give her this feeling. Only her sister. She kissed the back of Maggy's hand then laughed, snot bubbling from her nose. She reached for a tissue, snorting like old times.

"I'd like that."

CHAPTER FORTY-THREE

The thawing bag of peas lay on the side table in a small puddle, forgotten while Maggy held Quinn's hand in both of her own. This was the first time in years she hadn't seen her brow pinched in its now-familiar furrow. A buoyancy had crept over her face that Maggy knew was mirrored in her own. A missing part of herself had snapped back into place and, while it couldn't ease the grief that was nagging at her, it did make her feel less alone.

Maggy leaned back and scanned the cozily cluttered room. "You've created such a beautiful life for your family, and if I'm honest, I'm jealous of that."

Quinn grimaced. "Believe me, it's nothing to be jealous of, at the moment. Between the sleepless nights, shouting matches with Allie, and never seeing my husband. Everything's gone to hell in a handbasket."

"Still. It's nice to be surrounded by a family of your own, and people who care about you. I haven't been able to build that in New York." Maggy frowned thinking of her work "friends"— not a single one of them had called to check on her.

Quinn touched her arm. "You could come home, you know."

Maggy looked up, stomach fluttering in surprise. "I didn't

know if you'd want me here. I... I've been thinking about it. Maybe starting my own studio."

Quinn's lips parted in surprise. "Are you kidding? I would love that!"

Before Maggy could tell her more of her idea, a bubble of conversation burst through the door with Kylie as the anxious toddler hurtled into the room and leaped onto Quinn's lap. She burrowed her face into Quinn's chest, tired tears cutting channels down her cheeks.

"Looks like it's someone's naptime," Quinn said, stroking Kylie's long, dark hair back from her face. She looked up at Maggy apologetically.

"We'll catch up more later?"

"Of course."

As Quinn bundled Kylie upstairs for her nap, Maggy picked up the quickly thawing peas, using the edge of the tea towel to sop up the worst of the mess, and made her way through the crowded living room. Tossing the peas back into the freezer, she surveyed the living area, crowded with familiar faces attached to forgotten names. She decided to play it safe and settled into the loveseat next to Mr. Mullone. He held a saucer filled with nothing but tea cakes.

He offered one to her with a wry grin.

"I have decided to pretend I am a schoolboy today and indulge myself."

"If there were any day for indulging, it would be today." She saluted him with the cookie before taking a big bite. The sinfully delicious treat melted in her mouth.

"Oooh, these have to be Mrs. Greaves' recipe," she mumbled around the buttery mouthful. Mr. Mullone nodded happily.

"'Best balm for a broken heart is good food,'" he quoted.

"Mama always did know best," Maggy agreed.

"That she did."

Maggy chuckled and shook her head, and they continued to munch in silence, Father Fry joining them with his own contemplative cookie. He stood next to the arm of the loveseat, looking out the back windows at the purple, swirling clouds, chewing slowly. Around them, conversation hummed, the familiar wisps of Mrs. Greaves and Mrs. Streisand's hushed conversation drifting to them from the settee under the stairs. Machine-gun bursts of laughter floated from the back porch where Maggy could see Mr. Streisand regaling a circle of men with one of his vivid stories, a glass of sweet tea in hand. Meanwhile, they sat in a bubble of companionable silence.

Derek finally broke the quiet with a question. "So Maggy, I believe we left off last night's little contest on your turn?"

"Contest?" Mr. Mullone queried. Quinn perched on the back of the loveseat and selected her own tea cake from Mr. Mullone's proffered plate.

"Yes, what contest?" Quinn asked with a devilish grin. Amused, Maggy caught her shooting Mr. Mullone a meaningful glance. It seemed even her sister was in on the matchmaking.

Derek quirked an eyebrow at his audience but answered gamely.

"Last night, to distract ourselves from the storm, we were regaling each other with amusing little anecdotes of our childhood pranks to see how hard we could make each other laugh. We left off on Maggy's turn." She noted he left out that Collins had interrupted them.

Cheeks flushing, Maggy explained, "It's not really a contest, there's no prize."

"Except for the prize of a story well-told," Derek rejoined.

"Shaving cream teddy bear," Quinn piped up, pointing at Maggy, smirking. Maggy groaned theatrically. Mr. Mullone snickered.

"You put shaving cream on your sister's teddy bear? How wicked!" Derek exclaimed.

Maggy crossed her legs primly. "I did not. I hid her teddy bear. I shaving-creamed a dummy made from toilet paper." She smacked Quinn's leg. "She chased me around the yard like a devil with a butcher knife until Mama spotted her and chased her down." Shooting a look at Quinn, "In all the excitement, I forgot where I hid her actual teddy bear, and it took us six months to find him. For that, if I recall, Mama couldn't get to you quite in time and you gave a black eye."

Mr. Mullone hooted. "Yep! You had to go to school looking like a one-eyed raccoon for a week."

Derek doubled over laughing and clapping. Quinn took a bite of her tea cake and looked out the window, shrugging abashedly.

"All right. Smart-aleck." Maggy poked Derek's stomach. He grunted in surprise. "Now that you've seen me in my finest hour. 'Fess up. What is one of the better pranks you pulled?"

Putting a hand on his chin, Derek mulled it over. "I don't know. I played a lot of pranks." He snapped his fingers. "I've got it! You know when Space Jam came out?" Everyone nodded. "I was working at a movie theatre at the time, and I was able to get one of the cardboard cut-outs of Michael Jordan they had to promote the movie."

Maggy pressed her lips together, already tittering. "It was my brother's first year at university, and he'd been saying how homesick he was, so I decided to cheer him up a bit, bring home *to* him if you will. Made the drive all the way to Cardiff, got his flatmate to let me in, and set up that cut-out in the loo, just inside the door with the light off." The group moaned; Quinn buried her head in her hands peeking between her fingers.

"I know my brother, so when he came in after a long night… out… I hid in the kitchen, and he headed to the bathroom. He screamed like a little girl and very well wet himself."

Dying laughing, Maggy asked, "Wait, are you metaphorically saying he wet himself, or did he actually wet himself?"

Derek looked down at his shoes. "Actually."

Another howl of laughter went up. Mr. Mullone reached out and patted Derek on the arm.

"I think Sunday dinners just got a lot more interesting." Derek blushed and stuttered, falling silent as he caught Maggy's eye. She smiled broadly and toasted him with her cookie.

"You win," she said, feeling more relaxed than she had in ages. She stood and slipped into the dining room to refresh her sweet tea glass. As she stood eyeing the table full of delectable looking treats, Quinn bustled in behind her.

"I really should be keeping a closer eye on things in here." She fiddled with a platter of pimento cheese sandwiches, restacking them into orderly piles.

"You know Mrs. Greaves will be in here in two seconds doing the same thing. I think you can take a break, today of all days." Maggy watched her sister fuss about.

Quinn laughed, the sound was brittle and hoarse. "Collins said the same thing." She pressed her mouth into a tight line as she tilted her head back. Her hands dropped limply to her side.

Maggy's stomach flipped. Something was definitely off. "Quinn, what's wrong? Something's been going on between you two since I got here."

Wiping at her nose with the back of her hand, Quinn cleared her throat. "It's just… I—" Behind Quinn, Maggy saw Mr. Leonard glide up, hands folded, waiting for someone to acknowledge him. Even if he was a bit quiet and strange, their mother's lawyer was an impeccably well-dressed and polite man, never one to interrupt. Quinn would be embarrassed if he heard whatever she was about to say. Maggy turned to greet him with a pleasant nod, signaling his presence. Startled, Quinn looked at him and straightened herself up from her defeated slouch.

He waved a hand languidly, "No need to be so formal on my account." He looked between Maggy and Quinn, his light grey eyes calm and inscrutable behind his glasses. "Sorry to interrupt. I was wondering if I might set up a time to speak with y'all about the details of your mother's will. It don't have to be today, but in the next couple of days."

Maggy nodded. "Of course."

"I don't know if you've had time to read the will yet, Maggy, but as the estate executor, you'll have a good deal to do executing your mother's holdings. And Quinn, your mother changed a good bit since the version that you witnessed, so I'd like you to be present, so you know all the particulars."

Maggy looked wide-eyed at Quinn. "You knew? About me being executor? Since when?"

Quinn glanced at her, amused. "Like five years ago. Like Mr.

Leonard said, I was the witness on the original paperwork." She shrugged. "It was a boilerplate will. I'm not surprised she changed it since then. It's not a big deal, Maggy."

Relief flooded Maggy. "Collins thought it would be."

Quinn rolled her eyes. "Of course he did. Even though he has no right." Maggy shot her a glance. She hoped Collins hadn't been stupid enough to cheat on Quinn. She gnawed at a nail, destroying what little was left of her manicure.

Mr. Leonard stood waiting patiently through their exchange. She turned back to him and they arranged for all of them to meet Monday afternoon at two. As he glided away, she turned back to Quinn who stood rubbing her neck, staring off into the distance.

Quinn blinked, her eyes finally focusing back on Maggy. Maggy opened her mouth to ask about Collins, but Quinn belted out, "That punch bowl is a travesty. I'm going to get some more sweet tea." Something was bothering Quinn, something she did not want to talk about right now. Quinn turned for the kitchen door, nodding back at the living room. "And you have a cute pastor out there to go flirt with." Maggy swatted at her. She winked and scooted away.

Maggy slipped back into the living room, head spinning with everything that had happened today. Despite everything going on, Maggy was glad to have her sister back. She looked over her shoulder towards the kitchen where Quinn had disappeared, and wondered if she should follow Quinn anyway, press her about what was bothering her. She looked again at the cozy little group clustered around the coffee table. As her eyes landed on Derek, beaming up at her, she decided it could wait. Outside, thunder rolled in the distance, long and low, like bowling pins crashing together over and over, matching the fluttering of her heart.

CHAPTER FORTY-FOUR

Humidity instantly clung to Quinn's body as she stepped into the sweltering garage. Thankfully, she had thought to stash extra sweet tea out here when she had made up the drinks the other day. The glow from the garage refrigerator's light bulb burned Quinn's tired eyes as she pulled a pitcher out and hurried back inside, clothes plastering to her like cling wrap.

Peeling the static wrap off the top of the overfilled jug, she had begun the perilous journey through the living room to the dining room when Collins dashed in the kitchen door, brown paper bag tucked in the crook of his arm. Through the door to the living room, she could see Mr. Mullone's eyes blink owlishly at Collins' reappearance. He frowned and hunched over his saucer. Oblivious, Collins shoved the hood of his jacket back and hoisted the sack like a trophy.

"I have returned triumphant!" he declared to the room. Glasses lifted to him and he was answered with huzzahs and cheers to break open the booze so they could toast Mrs. Alice. He caught Quinn's eye and grinned. She shook her head at him, lips pursed, and nodded at Mr. Mullone who had turned towards Maggy, his back to them. Collins' grin faded.

Passing the bag off to Rick, he hurried over to her, his damp loafers squeaking on the tile. He threw his jacket on the counter and swiped at his hair. She hefted the pitcher of sweet tea and began to wind her way towards the dining room, easing past the crush of legs and elbows. He trailed her, offering, "It's getting nasty out there. A couple of big limbs were down on the road."

Eyeing him, she whispered, "What is this I hear about an 'impromptu' meeting of the Guild?"

Collins rubbed at his neck and glanced at Rick, who was leaning against the kitchen counter with Charlie studying them. On catching their eyes, Rick looked away, flushing. Charlie popped another sausage roll in his mouth, smirking. Quinn thought of banishing him to the back porch with Ralph.

"It's nothing," he mumbled back. "Just straightening out a few things is all."

She stopped and faced him, the tea swirling dangerously. Talking in circles was getting them nowhere. It was time to do things a different way. Skidding to a halt so as not to tumble over her, Collins stepped on Mrs. Greaves' toes. She rapped him soundly on the shins with her cane, causing him to wince.

"So you are ambushing Mr. Mullone!"

"Don't you think, after all the chaos last night, that it's time someone stepped up and helped run the Guild?" Collins' eyes scanned her face, flicking back and forth nervously.

She planted her free hand on her hip. "And I suppose that someone should be you?" He groaned, but she continued. "Our daughter caused a good deal of that chaos too, or did you conveniently forget?" He rubbed her shoulders, speaking lowly, as if to an upset child. Behind him, through the window, the clouds swirled a sickly shade of green.

"There was a great deal happening you didn't see..." She hated when he used that tone with her like there was something she was incapable of understanding. Shifting her weight, she pinned him with a steely stare. He continued, "... with Harry and trying to find a good gravesite for your mother."

Quinn snapped at him, slapping his hand away from her shoulder, "Do whatever you want, Collins! You always do. Why should you start consulting me now? Why consider what I want at all?" She turned and stormed into the dining room, the pitcher of tea sloshing crazily. If she had to scrub the rug later, so be it. She was foggy from lack of sleep and everything that was going on, and she wanted a moment to breathe and be angry.

As she dumped the tea into the crystal punch bowl and stirred it way too vigorously with the ice and lemons, she sensed Collins walk up cautiously behind her. The rain began falling faster, weighty drops crashing into the roof angrily. A few people had drifted into the room to refill plates, and their banter died down at her enthusiastic pouring of the tea. She grabbed a cup and ladled the sticky sweet beverage into it, steadfastly ignoring him. She plunked the cup down at the end of a row already filled for people to grab as they passed. It spewed a rather large brown puddle over her hand and onto the table. That would leave a stain on the lace tablecloth.

With a grumble, she reached for some napkins only to find Collins already patting up the spill and Mrs. Greaves hurrying over to take charge. She patted Quinn's cheek with a "Let me, dearie" and a deft pluck of the ladle. Suddenly, the light from the sconces was sparkling harshly on the crystal bowls and platters of the table, making her eyes water. Frustrated tears bit at the edge of her lashes, and she blinked hard and struggled to clear her throat as she looked up at her husband.

Gently, Collins wrapped his arm around her and guided her to the corner of the room, the farthest they could get from prying eyes.

He pressed his forehead to hers, then planted a kiss between her eyes. She finally managed to lift her head. He gazed down at her, worry pinching his brow. Around them, their guests slid nervously from the room.

"I guess we need to go ahead and clear the air, don't we?"

Quinn shook her head, quickly. "I feel like I'm drowning right now."

He sighed.

"All right." With a weak smile, he asked, "So where do we begin?"

She clung to his arm, trembling. She was terrified of what was to come, but she was more terrified of feeling like this any longer. Despite everything Mama had ever told her, if she didn't get this out of her now, she knew she would break and there wouldn't be any fixing it. "No. That's just it. I feel like I'm drowning. I'm supposed to be happy with this house and this life and you and the kids. And I'm not. And I feel horrible."

He gazed down at her, cheeks colored, and took in a big gulp of air. He let it out slowly and gestured at their house, the overstuffed couch with the well-loved throw pillows that Mama had taught her how to cross-stitch in the weeks after Ralph had taken over at the gym, and her gallery wall filled with pieces she had found at flea markets and antique shops out of boredom, and the meticulously organized bins overflowing with toys.

"Isn't this what you always wanted? To have a life like this? To be here with the kids—what you've made for us here—it's home."

The words were an eerie echo of Mama's. She hadn't liked them ten years ago, and she despised them now. She gulped and looked down at her feet, scuffing one toe of her soft leather flats over the other. Her breastbone ached from all the words she'd held in for so long.

Shakily, she ran a hand through her hair—the hair she had cropped short again at Mama's urging after the baby was born because she didn't have time to style it every day. The curls frizzed and stood out at crazy angles while tangles snagged at her fingers, and she dropped her hand. The truth was the only way.

"Collins, I love you and our kids, and I don't regret *this*. But I do regret not getting to have my own… thing… outside of this." She crossed her arms. "And I guess I'm resentful that I never felt like I had a choice in it."

She took a deep breath, releasing it slowly. "We were supposed to be partners, but Ralph was just *there* all of a sudden, without asking me if that's what I wanted." She shrank into herself, her shoulders inching up towards her ears. "And then when I saw everything that you'd done with the gyms, with the kids' college fund and the lien on the house. Well, I'm feeling betrayed right now." Dropping his eyes, Collins rubbed at the back of his neck. "We could lose everything, and you didn't even ask me about it."

He reached for her, but she stepped back. "I just don't know if I can trust you—about anything. Do I even know you? I mean, we've been married for fifteen years, and you never mentioned to me once that you knew Maggy misunderstood what happened between you two?"

He muttered, teeth clenched, "I can't believe we're arguing over freaking Maggy right now."

"Maggy isn't the problem!" Quinn pressed a hand to her mouth and continued. "You going behind my back. Forging my name? Not talking to me. Acting like you're the only one involved in decisions around here. We're supposed to plan and take risks together. As a team. But you've been doing everything on your own and pushing me away." Her voice trembled as she admitted, "And I've let you because I was afraid to stand up for myself. That I'd lose control and hurt you. That's the problem." Chest heaving, she sobbed, "And now you've destroyed my trust. And I don't know if we can get it back." She turned to run, not wanting to have a full meltdown, but Collins grabbed her arm. On his face was a mirroring cascade of tears.

"Quinn, I've fucked up and I'm so sorry. I'm going to fix the mess with the gyms." He swallowed and released her. He stuttered, "I have no idea how to make the rest up to you." He wiped at his face.

Stomach sinking, Quinn whispered. "I don't know if you can." A weight settled onto her shoulders and she stared down at the carpet, wiping at tears and snot. Wind whistled eerily through the eaves.

"Please, just give me a chance. I want to make this right. *With* you." A gentle hand guided her chin upwards, and she stared into Collins' eyes, warm and sincere.

"Hey. The only way to get through this is together."

She nodded, hiccupping, and glanced into the living room where Mrs. Greaves and Mrs. Streisand had joined Maggy and Mr. Mullone in a cozy little circle. She knew the perfect place to start.

"You're not going to take over the Guild."

He sputtered, and she pointed at him, narrowing her eyes. She had to grow a backbone sometime.

She repeated, "You. Are. Not…"

"Jesus, woman. Stop giving me the murder stare. Fine. I promise. I'll figure it out." She gave him a tight smile as they turned back toward the living room together. There was so much more to repair, but if he could set aside his ego for this, maybe they could make it. It was such a big "maybe."

Slowly, Collins slid his palm into hers, and she let him squeeze her hand. He asked in a low, teasing voice, "Anything else you want to clear up, while we're at it?" Her rebellious stomach fluttered at his flirtatious tone. Sixteen years of history didn't just evaporate overnight, and he was trying so hard to diffuse the situation. Put her at ease again. Sucking on her lower lip, her thoughts slid to Ralph and what she knew. The butterflies disappeared at the memory of his smug look, sitting at her desk, waggling his fingers at her. Rage flashed through her at what Collins had allowed into their life. Shouldn't he pay for it, a little?

She squeezed Collins' hand and shook her head. The truth was the only way, but she wasn't ready for all of the truth. Not yet.

CHAPTER FORTY-FIVE

Maggy couldn't believe how long she had gone without stuffing herself like a pig. Mama would have been proud of this spread. In the dining room, she greedily heaped her plate high with broccoli salad, pimiento cheese and cucumber sandwiches, cheese balls, sausage wheels, and enough of Mrs. Greaves' tea cakes to give herself diabetes. She studied the leaning tower of food on her plate; she'd have to hit the rest of the dessert line later. The lights flickered overhead, and she paused, listening to voices murmur nervously in the next room, but the lights nodded back on with a buzz.

Maggy turned back to the table and added another pimiento cheese sandwich for good measure. At the New York parties Mama so heartily disapproved of, she'd have to suffer the whispered cautions about refined sugar and the danger to her arteries from jarred mayonnaise. Here, the only question worth debating was whether you were a Hellman's or a Blue-Plate kind of gal. Mama was decidedly a Blue-Plate person, while Mrs. Streisand was Hellman's. They liked to joke that it was the only disagreement that ever came between them. With a little burst of energy, Maggy realized she might be free from all those dreadful galas and cocktail parties, the endless droning on about the "it" designer of the week. She added another sandwich to her plate to celebrate.

As Maggy lovingly studied the next bite of her pimiento cheese, the rain drummed on the roof, its patter oddly reassuring compared to the emotional upheavals of the day. She gazed out of the window while she chewed, contemplating the soggy yard. The playset swing careened crazily in the wind. If you didn't like the weather in Mississippi, as Mama used to say, wait five minutes, just like the round-robin of drama always on parade. But this day seemed determined to stay nasty.

Mr. Streisand tapped her on the shoulder, and she turned to him, trying to hide the chipmunk-like wad of sandwich in her cheek with her hand. He smiled at her pleasantly, eyes crinkling in amusement at her stuffed cheek expression. She knew she'd always been his favorite. He'd told her as much over the eggnog one Christmas.

"Maggy, would you do me a favor?"

She nodded at him, dumbly.

"I've managed to shake that pest, Ralph, for a minute, so I'm going to go ahead and slip out while I can. Will you tell Quinn and Collins goodbye for me?"

She gave him a thumbs-up, mouth still full, and he saluted her with one last pimiento cheese sandwich he pilfered from the table before slipping into the kitchen and out through the side door.

As she crowned her glorious plate of gluttony a moment later with a punch cup of Quinn's sweet tea—sugary enough to cause a toothache, a hubbub broke out in the living room. She stuffed a crunchy cucumber sandwich in her mouth and trotted back in there, not wanting to miss the drama. As she dodged Cousin Howard's walker, she pulled up short at the sight of Mr. Mullone on his tiptoes, shouting in Collins' face, Quinn looking distressed and trying her best to push them apart. With a wistful look, Maggy abandoned her plate and cup on a side table.

"What the hell is this about, Collins?" Maggy had never seen Mr. Mullone's face so mottled.

"Roy, let's take this out onto the porch. We don't want to cause a scene."

"A scene! You're worried about causing a scene now? That's rich! You've never worried about that before."

"Really, Mr. Mullone, let's all calm down." Mr. Mullone shot a glare at Quinn, and she wilted.

Collins held up his hands, voice quiet. "I'm on your side, Roy. Really, I am."

Spotting the rest of the Guild members peering through the back windows from the porch, Maggy suddenly understood what was going on.

"Are you about to vote him out?" She crossed her arms. A murmur ran around the room as people exchanged horrified glances.

Flushing, Collins stammered. "No. I'm not, at least. Like I said. I'm on his side." He licked his lips, his eyes darting around. He opened his mouth, and Maggy hoped he had a darn good explanation ready. The unearthly wail of a tornado siren split the air.

Heads swiveled as people peered through the windows or hunkered down on the couches, uneasy. Around the room, the foggy horns of alerts blared as cell phone weather alarms sounded.

A worried frown pulled down the corners of his mouth as Collins studied his phone. Upstairs, Clara's thin howl drifted down to them. Quinn gripped Collins' shoulder, and he patted her hand, a tight smile on his face.

"All right everybody, this storm is right on top of us and the worst of it looks like it's headed straight for us. Seventy-mile-an-hour winds and one is already confirmed on the ground on the other side of Livingston." At his words, Quinn and Mrs. Streisand dashed upstairs. Above her, she could hear them hurrying back and forth, gathering up the kids with Mrs. Hernandez. "As many of you can, into the guest bathroom in the hall. The rest of you, into the bathroom in the master bedroom." He forced a chuckle and ran to kick clothes out of the way.

Maggy heard his vote floating down the hall. "Pardon the mess. Didn't know we'd have company in here." Nervous giggles answered him as people began filing towards the different rooms from the living room and back porch, Derek and Maggy gently guiding them along. Aunt Hilda guided Cousin Howard down the hall into the guest bathroom alongside the loudly protesting Mrs. Burrison.

"This is so inconvenient! Highly irregular!" Her voice floated above them down the hall. With a sharp jab of her elbow, Auntie edged past her and eased Cousin Howard into the crowded bathroom with a pointedly arched eyebrow at Mrs. Burrison's hair quivering with outrage.

"We can hardly help the weather now, can we? So we must all suffer together." Aunt Hilda's voice silenced her. Outside, the rain whipped angrily back and forth, and Maggy heard the first pings of hail strike the roof as she shepherded the stragglers into the bathrooms. The temperature dropped until her teeth chattered, and goosebumps rose along her arms.

Roy hustled to the front porch and began dragging in the flowerpots and chairs. Mrs. Greaves stood next to him, leaning on her cane and smiling placidly, watching the weather. She pointed towards a mass of clouds swirling an angry purple and green.

"Look at the triangle forming on that one!" Pausing beside her, Mr. Mullone placed his hands on his hips.

"That's a real humdinger. Wonder which way it will go?"

Horrified, Maggy ran towards them, Derek at her side. She shoved Mr. Mullone towards the door as a roaring sound began to grow. Behind her, Derek picked up Mrs. Greaves and dragged her unceremoniously inside, slamming the door behind him. Somewhere in the distance, a transformer blew, the sound reverberating like a bomb. With a grunt, Derek tripped and fell to the floor, dragging Mrs. Greaves with him. Clearly bewildered, he rolled to cover her with his arms even as she testily batted at him.

With a clatter, all the kids ran downstairs. Allie and Collins began frantically shoving the settee that was nestled under the stairs out of the way. Maggy's ears popped, and she turned to peer out the window as with a horrendous, wet, ripping sound, like flesh being torn, one of the pecan trees outside fell over, blocking the drive. Electricity surged through her body, and she sprang forward, shoving the settee the rest of the way out. Collins and the children hunkered behind it, his arms wrapped as far around them as he could get, with Mr. Mullone, Mrs. Streisand, and Mrs. Hernandez beside them.

Where the devil was Quinn? Frantic to find her, Maggy whirled towards the stairs.

Quinn stood frozen halfway up the stairs staring at the chaos swirling outside, Clara in her arms. Something dark and large flew past the window, like a witch taking flight. The roar grew louder, the sound of a train bearing down. The drum of the hail grew heavier, thumping off cars and breaking glass with maddening crashes and shatters. She had to move! Maggy dashed up to Quinn and slapped her, not knowing what else to do.

With a gasp, Quinn leaped down the stairs and crawled underneath. With a gulp, Maggy sprinted to Derek and Mrs. Greaves. She knelt beside them.

"Derek, get up." He peered up at her. A branch crashed down outside, way too close for comfort. "Derek, get up! It's not here yet." Finally comprehending her, he sprang up and helped her get Mrs. Greaves to her feet. "Let's get Mrs. Greaves under the stairs," she said as she took her other side.

"Closest I've been to a man in years," Mrs. Greaves quipped as Maggy helped her down the hall. Maggy smiled reflexively as she handed her to Mrs. Streisand and shoved Derek under the stairs as well. Behind her, the front door flew open with a bone-rattling smash, having not latched properly. Wind hurtled through, nearly pushing Maggy off her feet, picking up knick-knacks and hurling them through the room with deadly velocity. She grabbed the banister to steady herself and turned towards the door, knowing it had to be closed or the wind already howling angrily through the hall would form a vortex that could rip the house apart.

"Maggy, no!" Quinn grabbed her hand and tried to pull her down towards them. Above them the roof began to creak and groan, straining at the beams.

Yanking her hand away, Maggy turned, crying, "It's going to be all right." She ran back, and muscles screaming, forced the door closed and turned the deadbolt. Far over the fields, a dark funnel full of dust and debris screamed towards them. She threw herself to the floor, covering her head, and prayed.

CHAPTER FORTY-SIX

Quinn curled around Clara, cradling her shrieking infant, so scared she couldn't even cry herself. She pressed herself back into the wall, shuddering from the force of the winds tearing at the house. Reaching around the kids, she grasped Collins' hand, her eyes watering. He squeezed her fingers, wrapping his other arm around the twins and Kylie, Allie pressed to Quinn's side.

A sheet of plaster fell from the ceiling, shattering into white powder at their feet, and the lights flickered out. Quinn heard pictures falling in syncopated bangs and crashes around the house, years of memories shattering in a moment. Lightning flashed in bursts of blue and green, so continuously it was as if they were inside a fireworks display. Liam clapped his hands over his ears, tears leaking from the corners of his eyes.

"No! No! No!" he screamed. Waves of pressure rolled over them with the chugging whoosh of a steam engine. Eyes wide in fear, Davy wrapped his arms around his brother. Quinn's heart ripped in two, knowing she couldn't protect her children from what was coming. The darkness bearing down. She locked eyes helplessly with Collins and trembled as the front door shook in the frame, something worse than a burglar trying to break in. But the lock held.

On the roof, jackhammer thuds resounded and a heart-stuttering creak began, shuddering the house down to the foundation. Quinn stared up into the darkness, holding her breath in terror. Just then, a forgotten flowerpot flew through the front window, sending shards of glass hurtling down the hall like pieces of shrapnel. She heard Maggy scream and began to weep great heaving sobs as she rocked Clara back and forth.

Suddenly, Kylie lifted her little hands and hollered, "Jesus help!" her tiny voice barely audible over the crushing growl of the storm.

Silence settled over the house, sunlight flooding through the broken and cracked windows. The waves of pressure abated, then ceased as the rain slowed to a trickle. For several long moments, Quinn couldn't tear her eyes away from a stream of water spewing out of a jagged gutter, like a burst artery. The only audible sound in the sudden hush, the gurgling rush of water filled her bewildered ears until she tore her eyes away and pressed kisses to all of her children. They were alive by the grace of God.

Derek sprang up and rushed to the front hall. Quinn's heart leaped into her throat as she spotted Maggy lying there, completely still, blood trickling down her arms. Derek knelt next to her and gently brushed shards of glass from her hair. Slowly, Maggy raised her head, met Quinn's eyes, and grinned tiredly.

"Told you it was going to be all right."

Quinn sniffled. "Know-it-all."

Collins stared around them in astonishment. "It must have skipped over us." Derek just shook his head as he helped Maggy up.

Outside, a soft mist began to fall, barely dimming the sun's brightness. Halloos echoed through the house as people began to emerge, shaken, but unharmed. The tornado had disappeared as quickly as it had appeared.

In stunned silence, the group made its way to the driveway where they stood, taking it all in as the drizzle slowly let up. Faraway sirens wailed, making their way towards them through the wreckage. Quinn's shoulders slumped as she surveyed the damage to her beautiful home. Four of the huge pecan trees had fallen. Three lay crisscrossed over the drive, effectively blocking them and most of their guests in. One huge tree had been ripped up, roots and all, and been tossed into the middle of the yard, crushing her rose bed. The right corner of the roof lay peeled back like a tin can.

Around them, most of the cars were beat to hell, windshields caved in and gaping, hoods dented from the thrashing they had taken from the hail. Startled, Quinn realized the kids' swing set from the backyard was now upside down on the far side of the front lawn. Gratitude that they were all alive swept over her.

Her bones ached with fatigue. She wiped at her forehead in the humidity, and sat down on the front steps with Clara worn out and silent on her lap.

Rick swept off the hood of the nearest car, and Derek hovered as Maggy slowly eased down the steps past where Quinn sat. She watched as Rick ripped open the back of her shirt and drew shards of glass from her arms and back and carefully wrapped bandages around the deeper cuts. Allie hurried over with towels and a clean shirt. To one side of the yard, Davy, Liam, and Kylie had already climbed up onto the trunk of a fallen pine, its bark peeling back in long strips as red as a skinned knee, and were seeing how long they could balance on it while doing the most outlandish tricks. She shook her head. Leave it to kids to make a game out of disaster.

Several of the men stood in a circle nearby, gesturing at the house and fallen trees, already making plans for clean-up. A couple of them with trucks parked on the street began fishing for keys. Emptily, Quinn looked up at the sun, now blazing in the sky, and gazed at the wisps of mist rising off the lawn like steam from a boiling pot. One by one, birds began to sing.

Behind her on the porch, Mrs. Greaves thumped her cane, causing it to ring like a drum. Everyone turned, including Quinn. Spotting a familiar paper bag, she smirked despite her weariness. Leave it to Mrs. Greaves to save the booze.

"A day like this needs brightenin' up." Mrs. Greaves hoisted the bag. She waved everyone towards her with her cane. "Before we all get to work, let's not forget who we're here for…" She drew the bottles out, Mrs. Streisand darting back into the darkened house to grab plastic cups.

Quinn dragged herself over to sit by Maggy, who smiled at her through a grimace as Rick drew out a tiny shard of glass.

"That's the last one," he said, as he gently taped a band-aid over the small wound. He patted her on the knee and went to check on everybody else. Maggy rested her head on her knees, arms resting at awkward angles to avoid touching tender cuts.

Once all the adults had a red cup in hand, Mrs. Greaves raised her toast high. "To Alice." She looked at the blazingly bright sky. "Leave it to you, ole' girl, to see us off with a tornado so we'd never forget you, ya' piece of work."

"To Alice!" rang out with a cheer and laughter and shots of whiskey. "To Mama!" Quinn and Maggy called out. Around them, their friends and family hustled to sweep up broken glass. Engines revved as a few of the men left to retrieve more chainsaws and rope to cut away trees. Nearby, the buzz of a motor thrummed as Derek grimly cut into the pecan tree squashing her flowerbed. Quinn looked around and squeezed Maggy's hand.

"We have the best neighbors, don't we?" she asked, warmth filling her chest.

Maggy shook her head. "No." Quinn stared at her, confused. Maggy pointed around them, at all the people already working so hard to help them rebuild a shattered life. "We have the best family."

CHAPTER FORTY-SEVEN

As Quinn swept the porch clean of glass shards, languid notes from her battery-powered radio floating out over the lawn, a shadow fell over her. She looked up and met Mr. Leonard's gaze. He pushed a lock of tousled hair out of his eyes then tugged his cuffs down.

"I know the timing ain't ideal, but since you 'n Maggy are about to be preoccupied for quite some time, might we go over the details of your mother's will?"

She leaned the broom against the side of the house and followed him across the yard to where Maggy sat on the car, making calls to insurance adjusters. Around them, the buzzing of chainsaws filled the air, the din reassuringly normal after the whirlwind. Maggy ended her call and looked up at them expectantly, wiping at her forehead in the humidity.

"Adjuster will be out here first thing in the morning. In the meantime, the guys are going to get a tarp on the house and the driveway cleared as best they can." She pursed her lips. "Since we don't know how bad the roof is, I'm thinking we crash at Mama's tonight, if it hasn't been damaged?"

Quinn nodded, heart racing at the thought of Mama's house being ransacked or worse—gone, and pressed a hand to her chest. Maggy grabbed her elbow.

"I'm sure it's fine. Her house is in the opposite direction the storm was traveling." She nodded at Mr. Leonard. "What's up?"

"Oh, Mr. Leonard wanted to talk to us. About the will." She waved at the house, where Collins was currently scaling a ladder with a tarp under one arm. "Before we get too caught up in all of this."

Mr. Leonard stepped forward and clasped his hands. "Yes, ma'am. It's pretty straightforward." He touched Quinn's shoulder. "Quinn, you saw the original, which was a stock form—a pretty normal fifty-fifty division of all assets. But I don't believe you saw any details of what those assets were." Quinn nodded, wondering where he was going. Mama didn't have much; she'd been a widow for over twenty years, living off of her father's trust payouts. "And afterward, your mother redid her will in more detail, dividing her property in what she believed would be an agreeable way to you both." He held up his hands. "It's not my place to question my clients' desires."

Quinn tilted her head. "Exactly what are you trying to say, Mr. Leonard?"

"Your mother lived a modest life, but as you know your father did well in the oil and gas industry." A distant memory sparked in Quinn. She'd been so young when he passed, and he traveled a lot, that it hadn't occurred to her to ask exactly what he did. "So, with the payments she received—and invested— from his trust, by the time of her death, she was quite a wealthy woman."

Pressing her hands to the top of the car, Maggy laughed. "What do you mean 'wealthy'?"

"I mean this," he waved his hand at the mangled house and lawn, looking at Quinn, "shouldn't concern you. At all."

He turned to Maggy. "And she left her house to you. It's yours to do with as you will, apart from a few articles she had specified for Quinn and the children." Quinn pressed a hand to Maggy's shoulder as she bent over double, hands to her face. Her heart fluttered at the dream of Maggy living a few miles down the road. "You two can do anything you want. Start your own businesses. Travel. Open charities. It's up to you." With a gasp, Quinn's mouth fell open as her mind flew through the possibilities.

Maggy started laughing, the sound rising like bubbles popping, hysterical. "I overdrafted my account just this morning to pay my roommate rent and now you're telling me, we're rich? What is this—" Alarmed, Quinn tried shushing her, but she couldn't find a spot that wasn't covered in cuts. She settled for patting her hand.

Mr. Leonard wasn't fazed. He nodded seriously. "Yes. I know it's a lot to take in. And on a day like today." He tugged at his cuffs again. "But I thought it best to give you two some good news in the midst of all this." Looking at the busted-out windshield of the car Maggy was sitting on, he sniffed loudly, as if he disapproved of the disorder.

Quinn bobbed her head. "Thank you for letting us know. It's... it's a lot to process. But this is good. Right, Maggy?" Maggy stared at her with glazed-over eyes. "It's good, Mr. Leonard." She reached out and shook his hand. He gave her a thin smile and turned as if to leave.

"Oh." He drew an envelope from his coat pocket. "Normally, I'd handle this myself, but I seem to have lost track of 'em. Would you be so kind as to give this to Mr. Mullone when you see him next?" The envelope was the rich cream of Mama's stationery and Quinn ran her thumb delicately over "Dearest Roy" in her elegant, looping cursive. Mutely, she nodded. Mr. Leonard smiled tightly and strode away.

With a groan, Quinn plopped onto the hood of the car with Maggy. She snapped her fingers in front of her sister's face. Maggy blinked and leaned back, shaking her head.

"What do you suppose it is?" Maggy asked. She ran a forefinger reverently over the script as well.

"I have no idea." Quinn paused. "I hope it's something nice. Something that helps him understand..." she drifted off, and Maggy nodded.

Maggy held the envelope up to the light, squinting at it. Quinn snatched it.

"That's none of our business." At Maggy's miffed glance, she sniffed. "You know, she and Mr. Mullone had some sort of understanding. Infuriating as it was. They have a right to their little secret."

Unsatisfied, Maggy grumbled, "A secret the whole dang church knows." Quinn shook her head and tucked the letter carefully in her back pocket, being careful not to bend it. Maggy stared into space, chewing on her lower lip. They sat in silence for a few minutes. Trying to lighten the suddenly gloomy mood, Quinn jostled Maggy.

"You have a mean backhand, by the way," she cajoled. "My face still stings from where you slapped me."

Maggy smirked at her, "I'd say I'm sorry," she dropped her voice low, "But I'm not." They laughed together in the sunlight, watching the bustling work around them.

Quinn turned over what Mr. Leonard had just told them in her head. Being wealthy was a nice idea, but it was just an abstraction to her, a pretty bauble to play with, more than a reality. She hadn't a clue what to do with that kind of money.

The wind rustled through the trees. Maggy drew a lock of her hair through her lips absentmindedly, shaking her head. "Bless it. What a day it's been."

In the distance, the twins screeched in laughter as they tumbled off the tree. Quinn shook her head, the day tilting ever-so-slightly off its axis again. "Who knew Mama had that much cash squirreled away?" Quinn pulled her ponytail out and let the breeze play through her hair. "I mean, Mama never seemed like she needed anything, but still, she didn't live—lavishly."

Maggy nodded and remained quiet, thoughtful. She bit her lip, glancing over to where Father Fry wielded a chainsaw in the afternoon sun, and Quinn followed her gaze. Light caught on beads of sweat along his brow and Maggy looked away hastily. Quinn snickered, and Maggy looked at her abashed.

"Stop it!" Quinn laughed louder and Maggy smacked her arm. "Seriously! We hardly know each other. 'Sides, I've got to straighten some stuff out in New York before I can make anything here official."

"Fine. We'll let the studio or whatever you decide to do be a surprise." Quinn patted Maggy on the back and flinched when she winced. Her gaze drifted to Collins, tightening the ropes on the tarp, and she looked down, rubbing at her chapped hands. Maggy punched Quinn's arm, then leaned on her shoulder.

"Something's been botherin' you all day." She looked at Quinn expectantly, and Quinn's stomach flipped. "Come on, spill the tea. What's got you so on edge?"

Quinn studied a cloud floating peacefully overhead against a blue so stunning, she wondered if there was even a name for it.

"What am I going to tell Collins? About the inheritance?" she asked. Biting her lip, Quinn looked at Maggy. She whispered, "You were right about the cash crunch at the gyms. But it's worse than that—we might lose everything. And it's because of Collins. He's done some really stupid shit." Maggy reached for her hands.

"All of your money trouble can be over now if you want it to be. You can start with a clean slate." Maggy said it earnestly. Swallowing, Quinn looked down. "Isn't that what you want, Quinn?"

"I don't know." She admitted. "A part of me wants to make him pay. Another part of me wants to make it all go away." Quinn looked up at her, the end of her nose flushed. "But it really wouldn't be gone, would it?"

Sighing, Maggy shook her head and put an arm around her, cringing as she stretched against her cuts. "Not that I'm an expert in marriage, but I have a feeling you'd need a bit more than money to fix what ails you, if it's as bad as you say."

Pulling her knees up to her chest, Quinn perched awkwardly on the car. "He said something about working through this together, making this right. But I don't know. I'm just so hurt and angry." Her thoughts skittered guiltily to Ralph. She should have told Collins. Keeping this from him, well, it was no better than what he had done. She grimaced at the thought.

Maggy nodded, drumming the fingers of her other hand on the hood. "Would you give it a go—if you thought he was sincere?" Quinn shrugged.

"Maybe. We have been together sixteen years. There are the

kids to think about." She sniffed and wiped at her nose with the back of her wrist. "Did I ever tell you that I hated my wedding dress?"

"No! You have pictures of you in it all over the house!"

"Yes!" Quinn laughed, clutching at her chest. "I didn't even get to pick it. Mama just showed up with it, and it's this poofy, white monstrosity straight out of the eighties. But she was so dang proud of it, I didn't have the heart to tell her no."

"I thought you liked it!" Maggy wiped at her eyes, rocking back and forth, the car creaking underneath them, then quieted. "Would you have married Collins if it weren't for the baby?"

One perfect white cloud drifted by overhead, the shape of an ocean wave. Quinn rubbed her arms, thinking of how happy she'd been on her wedding day as Mama proudly walked her down the aisle. It hadn't been the big wedding with crushed rose petals lining the aisle like she'd dreamed of as a little girl. But all that mattered then was how Collins beamed at her adoringly from the end of that aisle, and how she knew they'd be together through thick and thin. Well, this was certainly a thin spot.

"Yes, I'd have married him even without Allie."

Maggy nodded and tilted her head. "What are your thoughts on some hard-core marriage counseling? Sky's the limit on what you could do?"

Quinn chuckled. "What? You going to throw us out of a plane together or something?"

Maggy slid off the car, grinning. "Or something."

Staring after her, Quinn called warningly, "Maggy…"

"Shush, dear! I've got some calls to make."

Quinn vaulted off the car, chasing her, their shrieks of laughter floating up into the clear sky.

CHAPTER FORTY-EIGHT

Gingerly, Maggy eased herself back down onto the hood of Rick's car. She watched her sister's retreating back as Quinn disappeared into the darkened house in search of bottled water. She peered over her shoulder at the bandages on her upper back and winced at the spots of blood peeking through. The reopened cuts from the jaunt around the yard chasing Quinn stung, but not as much as Rick's tongue lashing would when he found out.

A gentle breeze teased her hair, pulling a loose strand out of her ponytail. She tucked it behind her ear. As the sun eased its way down the sky, a murmuration of blackbirds swirled and settled into the rocking trees up and down the drive, their raucous calls echoing through the honeyed light like a hundred popping bottles. Mesmerized, she watched the fluttering of their wings rush and flick amidst the branches.

A thumping sounded on the stairs behind her, startling her from her reverie. The familiar wheeze of Aunt Hilda floated to Maggy as she made her way laboriously down the steps, Cousin Howard clinging to her arm. Maggy leaped to her feet, wincing against her bandages, and reached for his other arm to help steady him.

"Oh, aren't you just a darling! And all stitched up yourself!"

She gestured down the drive to where Harry waved at them. "Allie's young man is just about to drive us home since our car has been towed." Aunt Hilda's earrings quivered in the late afternoon sun. As she blinked, her glasses made her large eyes seem as if they covered half her face like a bushbaby. Cousin Howard deposited safely on firm ground with his walker, Aunt Hilda turned to Maggy and grasped her arm. "Darling, I meant to speak to you about something before we go."

Aunt Hilda had a habit of pressing the most esoteric bits of advice onto her nieces. She and Quinn had spent countless hours pondering her strange bits of advice like "never catch the same fish twice" and "beware free gifts" as teens. Intrigued by what today's tidbit might be, Maggy leaned in.

"Of course, Auntie. What is it?"

The earrings were quivering again as Aunt Hilda released her and began digging in her purse. She withdrew her wallet and pulled several bills from it. Pressing them into Maggy's hands, she smiled, the adorable gap in her front teeth whistling as she said, "I need a portrait!"

Maggy blinked down at the bills. They were hundreds, several of them. Eyes wide, she looked up at Aunt Hilda.

"A portrait?" Her mouth hung open slightly.

With a decisive nod that sent the earrings swinging, Aunt Hilda pulled a photo of a smiling Corgi from the other side of her wallet. "I just adored the portrait of your mother I saw at the funeral, and I know you did it. It's just your style." Without pausing to hear a yes or no from Maggy, she pressed the photo into Maggy's palm atop the bills. "Now, this is Puddles, my baby. And I want you to do a portrait of him—take any creative liberties you want! I trust you completely! You're the only one I would trust with my baby. Will you do it?"

Maggy chewed her lip. "I haven't painted anything serious in years."

"I know how talented you are, child. Your mother positively cooed over that portrait of her you did for Roberta. Say you will!"

A portrait of a dog—it was comic, lighthearted, and most

importantly got her painting. Tightening her fingers gently around the photo, Maggy took a deep breath and nodded. "All right. But Aunt Hilda, you know I'd do a picture for free for you."

"Nonsense, child! You're an artist." She said the word with a drawling French flair that elicited a chuckle from Maggy. "I'm paying you for the portrait, and that's the last I want to hear of it." She squeezed Maggy in an anaconda hug so fierce it made the cuts on her back scream, then scurried off down the drive.

Cousin Howard smirked up at her, a greying wisp of hair on the top of his head bending back and forth in the wind, graceful as a dancer.

"Looks like you're in business, Coz." He leaned over the walker and kissed her on the cheek. He whispered in her ear, "Let the people who love you help you." With a wink and a squeeze of her other hand, he trundled off after Aunt Hilda.

She looked down to find two hard butterscotch candies and the card of a business coach. Her laughter startled the blackbirds from the trees.

CHAPTER FORTY-NINE

Collins brushed his hands against his pants to get rid of the yellow paint flakes coating his palms, wincing as the rope burns covering his fingers scratched roughly over the denim. He gazed up at the blue tarp covering the corner of his battered house. A gust of wind made it ripple, but it stayed in place. Next to him, Mr. Mullone polished his glasses, then studied his handiwork as well.

"Well, it ain't pretty, but it should hold any rain out until we can get a structural engineer and a team of roofers out here next week." The older man clapped him on the shoulder. "Course, you didn't have much to work with the way that thing was peeled back like the film on a TV dinner."

Shaking his head, Collins stretched a knot out of his shoulder, then reached to pull the ladder down. The last thing he needed was for one of the twins to get it into their heads to try to climb to the roof right now.

Rick strained at a branch the size of a small tree behind them and Collins called out, "Oi! Leave it. We need to cut that one up to move it." He didn't want anyone else getting hurt today.

Rick threw his hands up with a scowl but left the massive branch to join them in surveying the house. The three men gazed up at it tiredly, surveying the work done and still to do.

The tarp fluttered in a stray breeze, like a limp flag of truce. Siding lay peeled back in several places and cracks crazed across every window.

Quinn had made it clear that any money from her mother was to go to the kids' future to fix what he had screwed up; Collins had no idea how he was going to fix all this if the insurance didn't come through generously. And there was still the matter of possible jail time. As he wiped the sweat from his face, he groaned. Mr. Mullone darted a glance towards him but remained silent. Collins couldn't believe he'd been such a fool, putting them in this situation with no savings to speak of and a lien on the house. It would take a small miracle to save them. Mr. Mullone pointed out a few windows with missing panes that still needed to be boarded up before they could leave off for the evening.

"Isn't Charlie in charge of that? Where is he?" asked Rick. A burst of profanity from around the corner met their ears. Charlie appeared, red-faced and muttering. He snapped one hand limply in the air while a hammer dangled from the other one.

"Dang thing ain't balanced properly," he said when he noticed them staring at him.

"That so?" asked Collins. "Where's Mike and Sam? They left for the day?"

"Nah. I told them to go help with tree clean-up. They were slowing me down." Charlie studied his insulted hand. Collins exchanged a significant glance with Mr. Mullone and Rick. He'd had enough of Charlie's bluster.

Charlie looked up, cradling his offended hand in the opposite elbow. "Say, weren't we in the middle of a meeting earlier? Why don't we finish up real quick before everyone heads out?" He began looking around for the others, head swiveling like a radar dish. Collins clenched his fists so tightly he could feel the knuckles pop.

"Charlie?"

"Yeah?"

"Shut. Up."

Charlie looked at him, stunned. A flush rose slowly up his

neck and he swallowed once. Dropping the hammer, he turned on his heel and strode off. Down the driveway, they heard a car door slam and engine rev, gravel spinning out. Across the lawn, men shot them curious glances and Collins shrugged. Rick grinned at him.

"That was marvelous!"

"Gonna be heck to pay for it." Mr. Mullone added quietly. "That man's made of trouble."

He looked over to where Quinn sat laughing with Maggy on the hood of Rick's car. She looked happier than she had in years. He was determined to keep it that way. Even if it took the shirt off his back.

"Less than what I'd have to deal with from Quinn if I let him keep going any longer," Collins rejoined as he ran his hands through his hair. He'd make peace with Charlie another day. Today, he needed to make peace with Quinn.

A few minutes later, with Mr. Mullone's help, the windows were tightly boarded. Setting the hammer down on the top step of the porch, Collins turned around to find Quinn so close he almost bumped into her. She stared up at him. The corners of her mouth tugged down, and in the humidity, her hair frizzed out in the adorable halo she hated. Self-conscious, she smoothed it down.

"I wasn't completely honest with you earlier."

He blinked at her. Quinn was the most honest person he knew. She continued, fidgeting with her hands. "You see, there's something about the gyms you need to know. And I wasn't sure how to tell you. And I was kinda angry and thought you deserved to be suckered anyway. And... well, I was wrong."

He crossed his arms, not sure where she was going. "A little angry?" he teased.

"Just a bit." She held up her forefinger and thumb just a hair's width apart, then dropped them. "Still am, to be honest." There was the Quinn he knew. She took a deep breath. "I think Ralph is stealing from you."

"What?" Besides Quinn, he'd entrusted Ralph with more control over his life than anyone else. A crushing weight settled onto his shoulders. He'd given him complete charge of all the gyms' financials.

"His paycheck is enormous. And some of the vendor payments look odd. I think he might be getting kickbacks. Or something. It's worth looking into. And not from statements that he prepares."

Collins rubbed at his neck. On a shoestring. No budget to spare. If what Quinn was saying was true, that bastard could have been stealing from him since the day he brought him on. He squeezed his eyes shut, overwhelmed. What would he do without his accountant to help him dig out from under all this? They would lose everything. Then an idea occurred to him. He peeked at Quinn.

"Would you help me?"

She brightened, a smile creeping across her face until the corners of her eyes crinkled. He hadn't seen her smile like that in years. "You want me to?"

He took her hand and kissed it. "What do you say, partner?"

She nodded, choked up, "Yes."

EPILOGUE: LIGHT DAWNS

Outside, the oak trees swayed gently in the breeze above Alice's grave, their leaves drenched in sunlight and the whistling trill of plovers. Inside, the pews gleamed, the polished wood warm under Mr. Mullone's hand, filling him with a serenity that had been hard to grasp these last few months.

Around him, a gentle rustling filled the nave as the congregation settled in before the sermon. Even with the heat of September shimmering in the air, saturated with cicada song and the green smell of cut grass, the sanctuary felt emptier and dimmer without Alice in it.

Harry clattered down the pew aisle to him before his thoughts could drift too far. "Uncle, do you mind if I sit with Alice today?" The name startled Mr. Mullone, and he blinked up at his nephew for a second, mind static.

"Uncle?" Harry peered down at him, annoyed. The impatience of youth would not be denied, he mused to himself.

"Of course. Go ahead. Just remember we have the Guild meeting at the Seymour's after church so don't be wandering off," he finally murmured and watched as Harry clunked away across the nave to cuddle up next to Allie. At a pointed stare from Collins, his nephew slid away from her the appropriate few inches. Quinn frowned at Collins but relaxed when he leaned

303

over Kylie's head and kissed her cheek. Roy chuckled to himself as he studied the day's bulletin.

Mrs. Greaves plopped down next to him.

"Interesting sermon series we've been going through, isn't it?" she asked with a sly glimmer.

"It's not every day you see a church go through *Song of Solomon*," he admitted. "It's quite… vivid."

"Well, Maggy certainly seems to be enjoying it," Mrs. Streisand leaned forward to whisper loudly from behind them. Mr. Streisand sat beside her, rolling his eyes to commiserate with Roy at his wife's gossiping.

"Good Lord, woman, where did you come from?" Mr. Mullone asked. She sniffed, nose turned up, pretending to be offended.

"I've been here, Roy, like I am every week."

"You snuck up on me again, is what you did."

She smirked at him and they all turned to study Maggy as she glided down the aisle, radiant in her ivory sundress and mules, pearls clasped around her neck. Tucked carefully under her arm was Alice's old Bible. She paused to kiss Mr. Mullone on the cheek and squeeze Mrs. Greaves' hand before moving on to sit next to Quinn.

As she moved away, Mrs. Greaves sighed, jealousy etching her face, "That girl should have been a model. Look at those calves."

"And waste all that talent? Hardly!" exclaimed Mr. Mullone. He crossed his arms stubbornly, "She and Quinn have been doing marvelously with the new art studio."

Batting his arm, Mrs. Streisand whispered back as Father Fry walked to the pulpit, "Well, I'd say her talent isn't going to go to waste in any area if Father Fry has a say in the matter."

Tittering, Mrs. Greaves pressed a hand to her mouth. "You're so bad."

Father Fry lifted his hands, beaming, and they stood. "Blessed be God: the Father, the Son, and the Holy Spirit."

Their voices chorused out joyfully, "And blessed be his kingdom, now and forever. Amen!" Mr. Mullone studied Maggy as she and Father Fry gazed at each other. His heart lifted at the soft look on her face, dreamy happiness and hope he had known the feeling of a long time ago.

Alice's words drifted through his mind, *You will always have my heart. You have been my lighthouse, saving me from the dark again and again with your constant light. It is you I am thinking of when I wake up and when I go to sleep. I will love you until the day I die...* The rest of the letter faded beside those shining words. His Alice would always be with him.

A beam of sun played in Maggy's hair, shimmering in her golden strands, illuminating her in a soft halo. Next to her stood Quinn, with her short, light curls, and her face wreathed in an irresistible smile as she glanced at her sister. Wedding bells would ring here soon, and while they might not ring for him, he smiled at the thought that Alice would still have cried at this particular wedding.

HUNGRY FOR MORE?

Sign up for Susan Farris' newsletter to receive bonus content, special offers, and info on new releases and other great reads at www.susanfarris.me.

Want to see what other books Susan has available? Check them out at www.susanfarris.me.

ACKNOWLEDGMENTS

I want to thank all the family, friends, classmates, and colleagues who have cheered me on in the creation of this book. When I think over the great number of people who have supported me as this idea first took shape as a short story in grad school, eventually became my thesis, then bloomed into something more, the list becomes awe-inspiring. My heart swells to think how loved I am.

I want to thank in particular my beta readers: Pete, Josh, Morgan, Kim, Brenda, Abbie, and Kimber. They spent many hours poring over early drafts of *The Gravedigger's Guild* and helping to make it so much better by pointing out plot holes, suspiciously acting characters, and just plain, weird wording.

There are two other people who I want to especially thank. Without them, this book would be a much dimmer, less-informed version of itself. First, I would like to thank Becky Herren of the Chapel of the Cross. Without her helpful instruction and the thorough information she provided on the church and the Gravedigger's Guild, this book would not have been possible. I am most indebted to her. Second, a hearty thanks to Cecile Wardlaw of the Greenwood Cemetery Association and her masterful knowledge of Jackson's historic graveyard and its practices, as well as her patient answering of my questions.

And last on the page, but first in my heart. My wonderful husband, Pete Farris. You supplied me with endless cups of coffee, kept me sane through grad school, but more than that, you have made it possible for me to run after my dreams. Words of thanks aren't enough. I love you, always and forever.

OLD-FASHIONED TEA CAKES

makes 2 dozen

- 1 c. butter, room temperature
- 1 ¾ c. sugar
- 2 eggs
- 3 c. all-purpose flour
- ½ tsp. baking powder
- ½ tsp. salt
- ¼ tsp. ground nutmeg
- 1 tsp. vanilla extract, high-quality
- 1 tbsp. milk

1. In a medium bowl, cream together butter and sugar until smooth. Beat eggs in one at a time, then stir in vanilla and milk. In another bowl, combine flour, baking powder, salt, and nutmeg, then stir into the wet mixture until just combined. Turn out onto a floured surface and knead until smooth. Cover and refrigerate until firm.

2. Preheat oven to 325 degrees F. Roll out dough to ¼" on a floured surface and cut into desired shapes. Place 1 ½" apart onto parchment paper-lined cookie sheets.

3. Bake for 8-10 minutes then allow to cool for 5 minutes on sheet before moving to a wire rack to completely cool. Best 1-2 days old (and served with black tea!)

ABOUT THE AUTHOR

Susan E. Farris is a Mississippi author who lives in Jackson with her husband and menagerie of pets. She has an MFA in Creative Writing from Lindenwood University. An insomniac since childhood, she developed a habit early on of telling herself stories in order to fall asleep and it slowly bled over into her waking hours. *The Gravedigger's Guild* is her first novel.

CPSIA information can be obtained
at www.ICGtesting.com
Printed in the USA
FSHW010730150321
79458FS